OVERBITE

By Meg Cabot

Insatiable
Ransom My Heart (with Mia Thermopolis)
Queen of Babble series
Heather Wells series
The Boy series
She Went All the Way
The Princess Diaries series
The Mediator series
The 1-800-WHERE-R-YOU series
All-American Girl series
Nicola and the Viscount
Victoria and the Rogue
Jinx
How to Be Popular
Pants on Fire
Avalon High series
The Airhead series
Allie Finkle's Rules for Girls series

OVER

BITE

MEG CABOT

WM
WILLIAM MORROW
An Imprint of HarperCollinsPublishers

OVERBITE. Copyright © 2011 by Meg Cabot, LLC. Excerpt from *Size 12 and
Ready to Rock* copyright © 2012 by Meg Cabot, LLC. All rights reserved.
Printed in the United States of America. No part of this book may be used
or reproduced in any manner whatsoever without written permission except
in the case of brief quotations embodied in critical articles and reviews. For
information address HarperCollins Publishers, 10 East 53rd Street, New
York, NY 10022.

HarperCollins books may be purchased for educational, business, or sales
promotional use. For information please write: Special Markets Department, HarperCollins Publishers, 10 East 53rd Street, New York, NY
10022.

A hardcover edition of this book was published in 2011 by William Morrow,
an imprint of HarperCollins Publishers.

FIRST WILLIAM MORROW PAPERBACK EDITION PUBLISHED 2012.

Library of Congress Cataloging-in-Publication Data has been applied for.

ISBN 978-0-06-173511-0

12 13 14 15 16   OV/RRD   10 9 8 7 6 5 4 3 2 1

OVERBITE

Part One

Friday, September 17

Chapter One

Meena Harper knew things, things no one else knew . . . things no one *could* know.

One of those things was that the man sitting in the car beside her was going to die.

There were also many things Meena Harper did not know.

One of those was how she was going to break the news of this man's impending death to him.

"Meena," he said, gazing at her profile. "You have no idea how happy I am to see you. It's funny that you called. I was just thinking of you."

"It's great to see you, too," she said.

This was a lie. It wasn't great seeing him. How was she going to tell him? Especially when he looked so terrible. He *smelled* terrible. Or maybe it was the inside of his car. She couldn't figure out what the smell was.

"I was thinking of you, too," she lied some more. "Thanks for meeting me."

She looked around the dark, narrow street. She felt guilty for telling him all these lies, including that this was the street where she lived, then saying he couldn't come up because her roommate's parents were visiting.

"Are you sure you don't want to get a cup of coffee?" she asked. "There's a place right around the corner. It would be much nicer than sitting in your car."

Especially considering the smell. And what she had to tell him.

"I'm sure," he said, smiling. "You have no idea how much I've missed you."

This was news to Meena. She hadn't heard from him in more than a year. Their split had been relatively amicable—though at the time, she'd been convinced that her heart was broken. She was a dialogue-writer who'd been trying to make a living scratching out scripts for a now-canceled soap opera. He was a dentist specializing in veneers who'd wanted to move out to the suburbs and start a family.

Naturally, things hadn't worked out.

"I thought you and Brianna were really happy," she said. "What with the new practice and the baby and all."

Which made it even worse. How was she going to break the news about his impending death when he had so much to live for?

He let out a bitter laugh. "Brianna," he said. "She means nothing to me."

"Of course she does," Meena said, surprised. "What are you talking about?"

Now Meena was really worried about him. David had dumped her for Brianna. Brianna meant the world to him.

It had to be a brain tumor. That's what had almost killed him the first time. But she'd sensed it and warned him, and the doctors had been able to find it in time to save his life.

Too bad the fact that she'd known about it had freaked him out so much that he'd run from her, straight into the arms of his radiology nurse.

But it was all right. Meena had built a new life for herself now. Sure, that life had been destroyed by Lucien Antonescu, the man who'd taught her what a broken heart *really* felt like.

But she managed never to think about him anymore.

Almost never.

It was only that lately, she'd been having such horrible dreams about David. In them, he was dead. It wasn't that she could see his corpse. In the dream, she could see David's future.

And he didn't have one. Just darkness.

When she'd woken from the dream for a third morning in a row, breathless from feeling as if the darkness was closing in on her, she knew she had no choice but to call him.

But she also knew she couldn't deliver news like this over the phone. They had to meet in person.

David had been surprisingly eager, offering to stop by on his way back to New Jersey after lunch and some dental meeting he had in the city.

But since Meena knew better than to give out her new address to anyone—even old boyfriends with whom she'd once lived—she'd automatically rattled off a fake one, and then met his car as he pulled up in front of the building.

Now, however, she was starting to regret this arrangement. Because David was acting so peculiarly. And what was that *smell*?

"You," he said. "You were always the one, Meena."

"David." Meena was confused. "You dumped me for Brianna. You said you wanted to be with someone who *gave* people life, not someone who predicted their death. Remember?"

"I should've stayed with you," David said. "I should've. We were so much better together, you and me, than me 'n Brianna. Why didn't I stay with you, Meena? Why didn't I? You were magical, with your . . . *magic*."

Finally, comprehension dawned. At least now she knew what was causing the funny smell. It made her job a lot simpler.

"Okay," she said, looking around on the floor of the car for the bottle. Or maybe he was just still soused from his lunch? How many martinis did dentists drink when they got together in the city for lunch meetings, anyway?

"Remember when you used your magic on me before," he said, "and made me all better? Do it again. I'm begging you."

"That's not really how it works," Meena said, still looking for the bottle. "I'm not saying I can't help you. Because I think I can. You're just going to have to meet me halfway and tell me where the bottle is."

That's when he lunged across the seat to kiss her. And she found the bottle. It was actually a flask, and it was pressing aggressively against her thigh through his pants pocket.

Oh, well, Meena thought. *That's what I get, I guess, for trying to play the rescuer. Why do I always do that, again?*

Oh, right. Because it was her job.

Which was a good thing, since she didn't think she could live with the guilt of another soul dying on her watch. It had happened more than once, especially since she'd hooked up with Lucien Antonescu, who'd unfortunately turned out to be one of the demons the Palatine—the organization by whom she'd been hired, after her unceremonious firing from the soap opera (before its cancellation)—was hunting.

Not just any demon either. The ruler of all demons on earth, the prince of darkness.

Meena had never really had much luck in the boyfriend department.

And since most people didn't believe her when she told them they were about to die, she'd never really had much luck in that area either.

She wasn't entirely sure what had ever made her think her ex, David Delmonico, was worth saving. As far as she could tell, the earth wouldn't be that much worse off if he simply disappeared from it.

But there was his new baby, she supposed. The baby deserved a father.

"Meena," David kept groaning. Mercifully, his lips had moved away from hers, and were now clamped to her neck. Thank God, because his breath smelled even worse than the inside of his car.

Except that now he was trying to slip his hands down the front of the sweetheart neckline of her dress . . . the dress she'd hemmed herself—well, with a little help from Yalena at the thrift shop. Because though Meena's new job paid well, she'd had to replace her entire wardrobe, thanks to her last one having been destroyed by a bunch of Lucien Antonescu's relatives, the Dracul. So thrifting had become a new hobby.

"David," she said, using an elbow to jab him in the shoulder. Although not too hard, because she felt a little sorry for him. He was a dying man, after all. "This isn't why I called you."

"Yes," he said with another groan. "Oh yes, it is. Beautiful Meena. What a fool I was . . ."

"*David.*" She yanked up his head by his hair and looked into his eyes. They were drunken slits.

"Wha . . . ?" he asked blearily.

"I'm sorry that you are having problems in your personal life right now," she said. "But you chose Brianna over me, remember? And I moved on."

"But . . ." His eyes started to focus a little more. "You said on the phone you weren't seeing anyone."

She continued to hold up his head by his hair. "I'm not." Nice of him to rub in the fact that she was single. Like it was her fault her last boyfriend had tried to burn down half of the Upper East Side. "But why would you think that means I'm up for a fling with you?"

He wagged a finger at her. "Face it, Meena," he said. "The fact that you're still single means that you've never really gotten over me."

"Or maybe," Meena said, "it means that there's a guy who I dated *after* you that I've never really gotten over. Or did that possibility never occur to you? No, I didn't think so." She let go of his head to lean over and pluck the car keys from his ignition. "David, go home and sober up."

She wasn't going to tell him. Not this way. Not while he was so drunk, and behaving so badly. For one thing, he might not remember it once he sobered up.

And for another, he might not handle the information well. Who knows what he could do? Jump off the George Washington Bridge, maybe.

And there was always a chance, Meena had learned, that things could get better. Our destinies weren't set in stone. Look at David. She'd warned him once that he was dying, and he'd taken a proactive approach to his health, and now he was . . .

Well, maybe David wasn't a good example. But she could think of lots of others. Alaric Wulf, for instance, one of the Palatine Guards with whom she worked. She warned him every day, practically, of some new threat he was walking into somewhere, and because he listened, he didn't die.

It was just too bad he wouldn't listen to her about anything else.

"Appreciate what you have, David," Meena said, instead of warning him that his number was up. Again. "Because it's a lot, and the truth is . . . you might not have it for long."

"But," he said, looking confused, "I want *you*."

"No," Meena said firmly. "Dumping me for Brianna was actually the smartest move you ever made. Trust me. You and I were not meant to be. You can grab a cab to Penn Station and take the train back to your nice, safe house in New Jersey. I'll mail these to you." She jingled the keys in front of him. "You'll thank me for this one day, I promise."

Just probably not until after he'd sobered up and she'd called him to deliver the bad news, and he'd had a chance to make an appointment for a complete physical.

She started to open the door so she could get out of the car and head back to her new apartment, back to her new life, the one she was so sure that David, if he knew anything about it, would flee from in a nanosecond.

Because there were many things Meena Harper knew that her ex-boyfriend didn't. Not only how people were going to die, or that demons and demon hunters weren't just the stuff of fiction, but that there was, in every creature on earth, demon or not, a capacity for good and evil.

And that all it took to send any one of them over the edge was the tiniest of pushes.

It was just too bad her precognition didn't tell her when one of those pushes might be necessary, or in which direction . . . or when someone other than herself was going to die.

That information might have been useful for her now, as she eased out of David's car, and his hand shot out and wrapped around her wrist, entrapping it in a grip of iron.

The worst part of it was that he didn't say anything. He just kept one hand clamped around her wrist, his gaze a dead-eyed stare.

Then he opened his mouth wide to reveal a set of pointed fangs.

Chapter Two

Meena's reaction was purely instinctual. She sent the tips of his car keys, which she still had clutched in her free hand, plunging into his face.

But—with reflexes surprisingly sharp for someone so inebriated—he caught her hand in his, well before the keys could come anywhere near his skin.

Then he calmly lifted her arm up over her head, until he was pressing both her wrists against the headrest of the seat with one hand.

A second later, he'd pulled a lever so that her seat collapsed backward, and she was lying almost fully supine in his car.

The next thing she knew, her ex-boyfriend was on top of her.

She stared up at him with mingled feelings of fear, outrage, humiliation, and surprise. How had this happened? And how could she have been so stupid? How could she not have seen that all those dreams about David had been a *warning,* not a prophecy? His brain tumor hadn't come back.

He'd been turned into a vampire.

Only how? And by whom? The Palatine, the organization by which Meena was currently employed, had spent the past six months hunting down and destroying every demonic life-form in the tristate area that it could find, with a systematic brutality that had caused even Meena, who had every reason in the world to detest them, to feel a little bit sorry for the poor things. It wasn't their fault, after all, they'd been infected.

This could *not* be happening.

Especially to her. She'd been trained to defend herself against exactly this kind of thing.

"David." She grunted as she tried to wrestle her hands free from his grip. If she could just grab her purse, she'd pull out the sharpened stake she always carried with her, and plunge it into his heart.

Then she remembered she hadn't bothered to bring a purse with her. She'd dashed out of her apartment with nothing more than her cell phone and keys tucked inside the pocket of the light wool cardigan she'd thrown on as she was leaving. She hadn't expected their meeting to take that long. She was, after all, only going to tell him that he was dying.

He wasn't, though. He was already dead.

Which was why she couldn't pull her hands from his grip. Because he had inhuman strength.

"Who did this to you?" she demanded. "How did this happen? And what do you want?"

"What do you *think* I want?" he said, slurring his words. His dead eyes still weren't even open all the way. He outweighed her significantly. His torso was practically dead weight on top of her. And he was so, so strong. And his breath still reeked.

"Do you know who I work for now?" she asked from between gritted teeth. "You had better let go, or you have no idea of the world of trouble that you're going to be in."

"No," he said simply, and dipped his face back toward her neck.

Her dress was full-skirted and a little on the short side. She should easily have been able to lift a knee to get him where it mattered.

But it was difficult with the dashboard in the way, not to mention the weight of David's body pressing down on her. It was also hard to breathe, and he was holding her wrists so tightly, cutting off the circulation to her hands.

Meena's panic grew. Not just because of the fangs she hadn't yet felt pierce her skin, but because she realized the hard thing pressing against her through his pants wasn't just a flask. Not anymore.

When David started fumbling with his zipper with his free hand, Meena's desire to escape crowded out all rational thought.

Filling her lungs with the foul-smelling, fetid air, she let out an ear-splitting shriek that caused David, whose ear was beside her mouth, to lift his lips from her neck and curse.

That was when the door to the driver's side of David's Volvo was not so much flung open as torn off its hinges.

And a second later, David disappeared entirely.

He seemed simply to vanish. One minute he was there on top of her. And the next, he was gone.

Disoriented from shock, Meena lay there, panting as she attempted to catch her breath and get the blood circulating back in her hands, then trying to figure out what had just happened. Had she dreamed it? The part where she'd been trying to do the right thing, and rescue David Delmonico—who quite clearly had never deserved rescuing in the first place—and he'd turned out to be a vampire?

But no. Because when she turned her head, she saw that the door to the driver's side of David's car was gone.

It was quiet on the deserted street, except for the usual sounds of the city . . . somewhere off in the distance, a siren wailed. She could hear traffic on the avenue. Not so far away, music played from someone's open window.

Then, from out of nowhere, a body slammed onto the hood of David's car, causing the entire vehicle to bounce like a children's amusement-park ride. The windshield caved in, splintering.

Meena screamed again, her voice echoing up and down the deserted street.

David lay there completely still—not unlike one dead.

She didn't realize what had happened to David—that he hadn't been seized by flying monkeys, then dropped lifeless to the hood of his own car, where he now lay sprawled, unseeing and unmoving—until the man who'd done all this tapped politely on the still-closed window of her own car door.

She screamed again before she recognized who was looking at her through the glass.

"Meena?" His dark eyes were filled with concern. "Are you all right?"

It was Lucien Antonescu.

Chapter Three

I'm fine," she said automatically.

She unlocked and opened the door, then climbed—a little shakily, but with all the dignity she could muster—from the car. Lucien held the door open for her, because he was the kind of man who always remembered to hold the door open for women.

He was also the kind of man who had, before Meena's eyes, once destroyed a church and nearly killed her, along with a number of her friends. So, there was that to be considered.

"You're sure you're all right?" he asked her again.

Truthfully, she felt as if she were going to pass out, but she lied and repeated, "I'm fine." It wasn't quite a lie. Now that she was out of the car, the night air—delightfully fresh smelling after the inside of David's Volvo, despite the garbage piled in the cans along the street nearby—had revived her a little.

"Is he . . . ?" She looked over at David, who was still sprawled across his own car's hood with his head tilted in a most unnatural position. She looked quickly away. "Is he . . . ?"

Lucien was frowning. "Technically, he was dead before I arrived. But no, he's merely recovering from a broken neck at the moment. Here. You're bleeding."

He handed her a handkerchief. Meena, startled, looked down at herself. There were drops of blood splashed across the front of her dress.

"Oh my God," she said. "Where . . . ?"

Lucien gestured in the general vicinity of his throat.

"He *bit* me?" Too late, she remembered how David had pressed his lips to her neck, and how relieved she'd been that she hadn't had to taste his rank-smelling breath anymore. "But I didn't feel anything—"

She broke off. She hadn't felt anything the other times she'd been bitten in the past either.

By the man standing beside her.

"No. You aren't meant to feel it." It was apparent Lucien was remembering those times, as well. But he looked discreetly away from her and toward David. "Who is he? A friend of yours?"

He said the word *friend* with distaste, though he was tactfully trying not to show it.

"He's just someone I used to go out with," she said. She pressed the handkerchief to her throat, staring at Lucien, thinking the exact same thing could be said about him.

He, however, appeared to be in considerably better shape than David was at the moment. Intimidatingly tall and broad-shouldered, his dark hair thick and lustrous, Lucien appeared as handsome and put together in his dark Brioni suit and crisp white shirt as always. It was as if no time at all had passed since she'd last seen him.

But it had actually been six months.

Six months during which the people with whom she worked—Alaric Wulf in particular—had combed every inch of the city as well as its outer boroughs, looking for him, without success.

And yet here he was, standing right in front of her as if he'd never left.

"I've been having bad dreams about him," Meena went on slowly. She still felt a little bit dazed. "I wanted to let him know he was in danger . . ."

"Of course you did," Lucien said. The corners of his mouth curled up a little, as if he found something amusing. "I assume he's the one who chose the location for your rendezvous?"

"No. I did. But . . ." She stood there, her wrists still throbbing from where David had gripped them with such fierce violence. "How could this have happened?"

"Apparently he's been keeping different company since you knew him," Lucien said. He'd stopped smiling. "Very few people can resist immortality when offered, you know. Vampirism is an extremely tempting and exciting lifestyle choice."

Meena looked at the ground. She was one of the "very few people" who'd resisted the lifestyle "choice" of vampirism when offered. It was why she and Lucien were no longer together.

Well, one of the reasons.

"I just can't believe he'd be one of those people," she said. "He had a wife. And a *baby.*"

"Well, he hasn't got anything now," Lucien said. "Except a ravenous appetite for blood. Oh, and alcohol, apparently. He smells like a distillery."

"I took his keys away," Meena said, holding them up. "I thought I'd be protecting him from drinking and driving. I didn't think it was safe for him to be out on the roads in his condition."

"It *isn't* safe for him to be out on the roads in his condition," Lucien agreed. "But not because of his driving."

Meena felt depressed, and not just because of David. This wasn't how she'd pictured running into Lucien again.

And she *had* pictured running into him again, more times than she'd like to admit.

But she knew this was wrong, and not just because he was the most wanted man in the entire demon-fighting world—black-and-white photos of him papered nearly every wall of Palatine headquarters. She had to pass them every day in the hallways at work—but because of the *other* dreams she'd been having. The ones that she'd been having ever since she and Lucien had parted—long before the ones she'd started having lately about David.

These were the dreams that had driven her to make an unorthodox request from a highly restricted area—to the public, anyway—belonging to her employer.

Meena wasn't even a hundred percent certain what she wanted was there. But if it was, it could hold the key to everything.

The answer, so far, had been a resounding No Response.

"How could I have not noticed right away that he was *already* dead?" she asked bleakly, staring at David's body. If this was how things were going to go from now on, she might as well just quit. It was possible she'd be better off working back in scriptwriting.

Then again, no one she knew in that field could find jobs anymore, thanks to the success of reality shows, like the one about the housewives of New York City.

"I wouldn't be too hard on yourself," Lucien said, smiling again. "He's very freshly turned, no more than a day or two at the most. And not handling it well, judging by the alcohol intake. And of course, had he gone home, he'd have killed the baby and its mother. So you did save two lives tonight."

"*You* saved two lives tonight," she said, glancing at him. This was definitely something she was going to tell Alaric Wulf, who often swore that Lucien Antonescu was evil incarnate. But why would someone evil be interested in *saving* lives? And, of course, she couldn't tell Alaric, because he'd just hunt Lucien down and decapitate him. "Three, if you include mine."

"I don't think so," Lucien said coolly. "He didn't want to kill you." He waved a hand, indicating her throat. "Would you mind? I'm finding that a bit . . . distracting."

"Oh." Flushing, she pressed his handkerchief against the wound in her neck. "Sorry."

This, she thought grimly, didn't exactly help bolster her theory that Lucien wasn't like other vampires. He obviously wasn't immune to the sight of blood.

Not even her blood.

"Might I ask," Lucien was saying as he abruptly crossed the street toward some old furniture piled by the garbage cans near a front stoop, "why you agreed to meet with him in his vehicle? I would have thought you'd know by now to be more cautious than that."

Meena tied the handkerchief around her neck. She watched as he tipped over an abandoned armchair and gave a vicious kick to one of its legs.

"Especially"—he took the jagged piece of chair and handed it to her, then approached David, who was starting to come around, despite his hideously contorted neck—"considering your new place of employment. Or haven't they trained you better?"

She stuck out her chin indignantly.

"Certainly," she said. "They have. But this was different. I *know* him."

"*Knew* him," Lucien corrected her.

"I meant that we're old friends," Meena said. "We used to live together. Even so, I was careful. It wasn't like I told him where I live, or anything."

He looked wry. "No. You do a good job of keeping that information private."

She glanced at him sharply. What did he mean by that? Had he been looking for her, the same way the Palatine had been looking for him?

Well, he'd obviously found her. Probably some time ago, too. She wondered why he'd waited until someone was attacking her before attempting to speak to her.

"I guess it just never occurred to me," she said dejectedly as David began to rub his neck and moan, "that someone I once loved might actually want to kill me."

Although Lucien had once tried to do precisely the same thing . . . for slightly different reasons.

"But he didn't want to kill you, did he?" Lucien asked. "I thought you understood that. What was it you once told me about the daughter of the Trojan king?"

Meena's eyes suddenly filled with tears . . . not at the reproach, but at the fact that he remembered. It had been a conversation during a happier time. She was fairly certain now that she'd never know such happiness again. Not unless she was able somehow to prove to everyone—including Lucien himself—that he was not the monster he seemed.

"That she was given the gift of prophecy," she said, keeping her gaze on the ground in the hope that Lucien wouldn't notice her brimming eyelids. "And because she did not return a god's love, that gift was turned by that god into a curse, so that her prophecies, though true, would never be believed."

"Well," Lucien said, "your prophecies *are* believed. By *them*." His tone was bitter as he thrust his chin in David's direction. "As you know, any demon who drinks your blood temporarily possesses your gift of prophecy. That's an irresistible temptation to most of them. And they're apparently not above resorting to turning your friends and family members into one of themselves in order to lure you out into the open to get it. I once offered you protection from this, but you turned it down."

Meena lifted a wrist to swipe at her moist eyes.

"You're right," she said, looking at David as he twisted on the hood of the car, trying to get his head back into a normal position. "I did turn down your offer of protection, because it came with a price that was too high for me. And I should never have agreed to meet him. I should never have come out of my apartment, except to go to work. Why should I expect to have a normal life, considering what I am?"

Lucien looked at her, his expression remorseful.

"Meena," he said, apparently regretting his harsh words. "I didn't mean—"

"No." She cut him off with a shrug. "It's true. Except for one thing." There were no tears in her eyes as she lifted her gaze to look back at him. "You're not a god, Lucien."

"No." His mouth twisted painfully. "I know I'm not. If I were, I'd—"

But he didn't have a chance to finish, because it was at this point that David, his head pushed back into something like its normal position, sat up and looked at them. "Who are you?" he demanded of Lucien.

The sky, which had been cloudless, grew dark. The moon disappeared behind a bank of storm clouds. The music playing in the nearby window had long since gone dead. A cool wind stirred, whipping up dead leaves and abandoned plastic bags, and ruffling Meena's hair and the hem of her skirt.

"You should know me." Lucien's voice was so deep and commanding, it seemed to reverberate through her chest. It also held an undercurrent of ice that caused goose bumps to rise on the back of her arms. "I am the unholy one, ruler of all demon life on the mortal side of hell, evil in human form. I am, in fact, the dark prince, son of Vlad the Impaler, also known as Dracula."

As he said the name *Dracula,* another wind swept the street, this time from a different direction, sending all the leaves and plastic bags that had been stirred up before whipping the other way. Meena shivered and held her cardigan closed with one hand. David seemed to notice her for the first time since waking up.

"Oh," he said, in a slightly less truculent voice. He began to lean away from Lucien and toward her. "I remember now. I think someone did mention you. But they said you were dead—"

"As you can see," Lucien said, reaching out to grab the front of David's shirt and pull him closer, "they were misinformed. Now who is *they*?"

David's gaze darted back toward Meena. "Hey," he said to her. "Aren't you going to help me out here?"

She used the piece of wood Lucien had handed her to point at the handkerchief wrapped around her neck.

"Excuse me," she said. "Remember this? You did this. Among other things I could mention but won't."

David, to her surprise, burst into tears.

"I'm sorry," he cried. "I didn't want to. I swear I didn't. I couldn't stop myself. I don't know what's come over me lately. I think I'm sick or something. Meena, could you feel my head? I think I'm running a fever."

Meena raised her eyebrows. "Uh," she said. "I'm pretty sure it's not a fever."

Lucien wasn't tolerating any of David's theatrics. He lifted the smaller man by his shirtfront from the hood of his car.

"Tell me who turned you," he said, "and who sent you to this girl, or this time, I'll rip your head off."

"I don't know," David insisted with a sob. "I don't know what you're talking about. Please put me down. I'm sorry for what I did to Meena. I told you I couldn't help it—"

Lucien squeezed David's throat, choking off the rest of his words. Though of course vampires couldn't breathe, the noises David began to make were unbearable to Meena. He was obviously suffering terribly.

"Lucien," she said, her heart aching. "Stop it. You're hurting him. He said he doesn't know anything."

"He's lying," Lucien said emotionlessly. He didn't even glance in her direction. "He's a vicious, evil fiend."

"There are people I know who'd say the same thing about you," she said. "How am I going to convince them they're mistaken, and to give you a second chance, when you won't do the slightest thing to prove them wrong?"

Lucien hurled a startled glance at her over his shoulder. "What are you talking about?"

"I *know* there's good in you, Lucien," she said. "And I'm trying to persuade the people I work with that I'm right. But you make it really hard when you go around torturing people. Even people who might deserve it."

He stared at her as if she were insane.

"How can you, of all people, ask me to show him mercy?" he asked. "Especially after what he tried to do to you? How can you possibly pity him? There is no vestige of humanity left in him."

"That might be true of David," Meena said. "But I refuse to believe it about you. How can I, after what we've been through together? But if that's what *you* really believe," she went on, reaching into her pocket, "fine."

"What are you doing?" he asked, looking astonished as she pulled out her cell phone.

"My job," she said. She didn't know any other way to make him understand. "You're a vicious, evil fiend. So is he. I'm calling the Palatine to report having spotted you both."

Their gazes met as she brought the phone to her ear.

And for a moment, it all seemed to disappear . . . the dark, deserted street; the whimpering vampire; the shattered windshield; the broken car. Everything. It was just the two of them, the way it had been before—before she'd discovered he was a vampire, before he had discovered she was cursed with her horrible gift—when they had been so in love, and filled with so much hope for the future.

A future that had been dashed when Alaric Wulf had arrived at Meena's door with the news of Lucien's true identity.

It was at that exact moment—when she and Lucien were distracted, lost in each other's dark-eyed gaze—that David proved he really was without any vestige of humanity, and the demon inside him had completely taken over. He lashed out at Lucien, striking him so forcefully that Lucien staggered back a few steps in surprise, releasing his hold on him entirely.

Which gave David just enough time . . . not to get away, as any other demon might have, but to lunge directly toward Meena, his face contorted in a mask of rage and hate, his mouth spread wide open, razor-sharp fangs ready to sink into her throat.

Lucien sprang after him, but it was too late. Unfortunately for David.

Because Meena was more than ready for him this time. She merely held out the jagged piece of chair leg Lucien had given to her. It was David's own momentum—and her steady hold—that drove it into the center of his chest.

He looked down at it in wonder.

"Meena," he said, in a slightly wounded voice.

A second later, he was gone, in a cloud of exploding bone and dust.

Chapter Four

Meena stared at the space where, a second before, David had stood. Then she looked down at the wooden stake she held in one hand, and the cell phone she held in the other. She hadn't actually pressed send.

She glanced at Lucien. He was standing just a few feet away from her, an expression she didn't recognize on his face . . . or at least wasn't sure she remembered ever having seen him wear before, anyway. What was it? Alarm, certainly. Concern for her, yes.

But there was something else there, too. What was it? Was it . . . pain?

But it couldn't possibly be. Because he was the prince of darkness. He wasn't capable of feeling pain.

That's what everyone back at the Palatine, especially Alaric Wulf, kept telling her, anyway.

"Are you all right?" he asked her. "I'm sorry, he surprised me. I'm not . . . I shouldn't have allowed that to happen."

She opened her mouth to reply . . .

But before she had a chance, she became aware of sounds—footsteps, approaching rapidly—behind them.

People were coming. But who? She hadn't dialed.

And David hadn't made a sound as he'd imploded.

She squinted into the darkness, trying to see. But some of the bulbs in the streetlights overhead were burned out, leaving large sections of the block in darkness. She hadn't known this when she'd chosen this address as a meeting spot, or noticed it when she arrived.

Now she wondered if someone—or something—had broken the bulbs on purpose, knowing she was coming.

"Meena," Lucien said, his tone anxious. He'd heard the foot-steps, too.

Meena wasn't normally called upon to make lightning-fast deci-sions in her new position at the Palatine. This was her first time in the field, since she was considered too valuable an asset to be allowed anywhere near actual demon activity. She'd always been confined to Palatine headquarters during working hours, where she stuck to de-termining who among her colleagues was most likely to run into fatal danger while on assignment.

And when demon activity was slow in North America, Meena spent her days Skyping with units overseas . . . or researching the online sections of the incredibly large Biblioteca Apostolica Vaticana, to which she had unlimited access as an employee of the Palatine, the military branch of the Vatican. This meant she was allowed to enter the Vatican Library's secret archives, as well, which were restricted to members of the public. She was supposed to be looking for anything that might help in the Palatine's battle against paranormal beings.

But of course what she was actually looking for was much more per-sonal. Recently, she thought she'd found it.

Now, her heart hammering against the back of her ribs, she realized she had to act fast, or everything for which she'd been working so hard these past six months—especially the last two—would be ruined.

So she dropped her cell phone back into the pocket of her cardi-gan, where earlier, she'd slipped David's car keys. Then instinctively, she dropped the stake . . .

But before it could strike the pavement, Lucien snatched it in midair. He slipped it into the pocket of his suit jacket.

"Let's go," he said, putting an arm around her shoulders and spin-ning her toward the closest busy street.

"Why—" Then comprehension dawned. "Oh, of course," she said. She'd killed vampires before, but never quite like that. "Evidence. My fingerprints are all over it." But there was no body. She would never get used to any of this.

She kept walking, panic mounting as the footsteps behind them seemed to increase in speed. Who could it be? Surely not the Palatine, since she hadn't called them . . . although her cell phone had a built-in GPS tracker. But who could have alerted them? Surely not the police, or there'd be sirens . . .

"It's all right," Lucien was saying. He, too, seemed concerned about the footsteps. She saw him glance behind them several times.

He possessed strength and powers considered by the Palatine to be superior to those of any other paranormal entity. She herself had witnessed him do things that no living being ought to have been able to do, including transform himself into a creature twelve times the size of a normal man. That breathed fire. Just a quarter of an hour earlier, he'd ripped the locked door off a Volvo station wagon and hurled a man so far into the air, he hadn't fallen back to earth until many seconds later.

But maybe these things, coupled with David's sucker punch, had taken more out of him than he'd realized, since for some reason Lucien didn't snatch her up and fly off, or dissipate into thin air, both of which she knew he was perfectly capable of doing. He didn't even pick up the pace, really, though she could tell he was as anxious as she was to get out of there.

What was wrong with him? she wondered He almost seemed . . .

"Are you all right?" she asked, putting an arm around him. "Here, lean on me."

"Meena," he growled. "I'm *fine*."

"Of course you are," she said. "We both are."

She didn't sound convincing even to herself.

They turned onto a better-lighted, much more highly trafficked street. There were couples out walking their dogs, and families standing at every corner, waiting for the light to turn so they could cross, eager to get to the Feast of San Gennaro, which had recently started in Little Italy, a few blocks away. Everyone was laughing, enjoying the late-summer air.

No one paid the slightest bit of attention to the man with his arm around the shoulders of the girl with the white kerchief encircling her neck. No one seemed to notice that her arm was around his waist beneath the jacket of his suit, or that they were possibly being pursued.

"Are they still behind us?" he asked her tersely.

She peeked over her shoulder.

"I can't tell," she said. "I didn't get a good look at them. Did you?"

He shook his head. "It was probably whoever turned your friend, then sent him after you."

"Then . . ." she said, looking around at all the smiling people, enjoying the first night of their weekend, "Vampires."

It seemed hard to believe that on such a warm, pretty evening, something so evil could exist.

But she had just killed one. And she had her arm around the waist of another.

"It isn't anyone from my clan, I can tell you that much," he said. "Your friends at your new *job* have done excellent work annihilating almost every single one of them."

"You told David you rule over all demon life on this side of hell," Meena said, ignoring his sarcasm. "So how can any of them do something like this without your knowing about it?"

Lucien's dark eyes flashed menacingly.

"I haven't been very . . . available lately," he replied.

She wasn't sure if his curtness was due to her having touched upon a sensitive subject, or to their having reached an intersection, and the light was warning them to wait. A bus roared by, followed by a dozen taxis, making it impossible to cross.

She could feel the tension in Lucien's body, and saw the way he was scanning the crowds of weekend revelers around them.

She also saw, for the first time, the faint purple shadows beneath those dark eyes of his, now easily visible in the much brighter lights along this street.

Meena wasn't quite sure what it meant for a vampire to have shadows beneath his eyes. At no time during her training with the Palatine had this subject ever come up.

But she was beginning to suspect that despite the impeccable suit and lustrous hair, Lucien had not spent the months since she'd last seen him in some kind of vampire resort, relaxing in a lounge chair in the shade. He had obviously been suffering in some way.

"Lucien, *are* you all right?" she asked him. "I mean . . . are you sick, or something?"

He looked down at her, clearly offended by the question. "I told you," he said. "I'm fine."

"Well," she said, "it's just that you don't seem like your old self . . . not in a bad way," she hastened to add.

"How unfortunate," he said. "I try so hard to be bad."

He smiled down at her then. She instantly wished he hadn't.

Because Lucien Antonescu's smile did things to her, things that the smile of a vampire had no business doing to a girl who had joined an organization dedicated to eradicating his kind.

But there was still a part of him that was human. Or maybe—as she'd recently begun trying to prove—even better than human.

"You shouldn't joke about that," she said, nervously pushing some of her hair from her eyes. "I was serious when I said before that I think—"

That's when someone—a kid, walking shoulder to shoulder with a group of his college friends down the sidewalk—slammed right into Meena, as if he hadn't seen her at all.

"Oof," she said as Lucien pulled her protectively against him.

The kid spun, then landed on the sidewalk. "What the hell?" he complained good-naturedly as his friends laughed at him. He obviously wasn't hurt, just a little buzzed on beer, and confused.

"I'm so sorry," Meena said to him, even though technically, he'd been the one who'd walked into her.

The kid said nothing, just continued to laugh as his friends pulled him back to his feet, calling him rude names. Lucien, meanwhile, had already steered Meena away from the group, navigating her quickly back down the crowded sidewalk.

"That was weird," Meena said. "It was like he didn't even see me."

"He couldn't see you," Lucien said.

"Couldn't see me?" Meena looked up at him in shock. "What do you mean? How could he not see me?"

"No one can see us right now," Lucien said, his face devoid of expression. "It's called a glamour. I'm afraid I can't keep it up for long. But it should last us until I can get you back to your apartment. You should be safe there, providing you've taken the usual precautions against unwanted demon entry."

She stared up at him, feeling a sudden mix of emotions. Especially when she realized they were turning onto her street.

"Lucien," she said, freezing suddenly in her tracks. "How do you know where I live?"

She had been so careful, leaving the rectory at the Shrine of St. Clare's—where she'd moved after his minions had gutted her last apartment—as soon as she'd realized he knew she was there. She'd had all her mail forwarded to a post office box, canceled her old cell phone, her gym membership, even her library card. She'd sold her old apartment and now shared a sublet with her brother in which even the cable bill was under the original owner's name.

How could he possibly have known?

Then again . . . how could he not have?

She wasn't afraid, necessarily. Not as afraid as she'd been just minutes before. And she certainly wasn't afraid for her life. All she had to do was press a button on her phone, and the entire Manhattan unit of the Palatine would be there within a few minutes.

Of course, by that time, she could easily be dead.

But dying wasn't what she was most afraid of. Not anymore.

"Meena," he said. The smile was long gone. "What you were saying, about my not seeming like my old self . . ."

The effort it was causing him to form the words was obvious. And now she recognized what it was she hadn't been able to identify in his face before. It *was* pain. It was deeply etched in the hollows beneath his eyes.

"I suppose," he said, "that's part of my problem."

She cocked her head, confused.

"What is?" she asked.

He took another step, but this time it was more of a stumble. Only not a drunken one, like the boy they'd seen down the block. His body weight began to sag against hers.

"That in spite of your choice last spring," he said, his voice a ragged whisper, "my feelings for you are unchanged. I'm still as in love with you as ever."

Chapter Five

E verything was a disaster.

Now, in one night, Meena had not only slain one ex-boyfriend who'd turned out to be a vampire, but she had another one in her bed.

She couldn't imagine how things could possibly get worse, unless her brother walked into the apartment, found Lucien Antonescu there, and called Alaric Wulf, who would undoubtedly launch an all-out military assault on the place that would include smoke grenades and possibly tear gas.

But she'd already phoned Jon and learned that he was working his normal Friday-night shift at the Beanery, where he'd found employment as a barista. He wasn't planning to be home until after eleven.

This gave Meena exactly one hour to get Lucien out of the apartment.

The question was, how was she going to do this?

She had no idea what was wrong with Lucien. But his announcing that he was still in love with her certainly hadn't made things any better. The admission had, in fact, only seemed to cause him to grow weaker. She'd had to half support him as she staggered the rest of the way to her building.

She hadn't wanted to bring him inside. But he seemed so ill, she didn't know what else to do. She couldn't leave him outside, even though this was what he asked of her.

But that was ludicrous. He'd already admitted he was so weak, he couldn't maintain his glamour, or whatever it was, much longer. She certainly wasn't going to abandon him in this condition, defenseless. She wasn't just concerned about whoever—or whatever—had been following them, but about *anyone* who might happen to stumble across him. Alaric Wulf, for instance. True, Alaric lived in a completely different neighborhood, but she wasn't taking any chances.

Fortunately, her building had an elevator, even though it was ancient, barely had room for two people and a laundry basket, and was so slow it was usually simpler to take the stairs. She was able to prop Lucien up inside, though, and get him safely to her floor.

From there things got more complicated. She'd grown so used to them, she'd forgotten the radical lengths to which she and the Palatine had gone to vampire-proof the apartment. There was a crucifix hanging over every window and doorway. Strands of garlic hung across her bed. Father Bernard, who led the parish of the Shrine of St. Clare's, had blessed the place when she'd moved in, sprinkling every corner of it with holy water. Sister Gertrude had lately taken to dropping by with patron-saint devotional candles.

Lucien had groaned upon entering.

"It's not *that* bad," Meena had said defensively.

"That's your opinion," he replied.

But then there was her dog. Even before she'd known they existed, Meena had had a secret weapon in the fight against vampires. Because somehow she'd managed to pick the one Pomeranian mix in the entire Manhattan animal-shelter system that was particularly sensitive to—and infuriated by—the scent of the undead. Or perhaps the dog had picked her. One of them, in any case, had picked the other, maybe with some idea of what the future held in store.

Jack Bauer—so named because his anxiety level was exceeded only by his determination to save the world from all evil—leaped from his basket the minute Lucien entered the apartment, curled back his lips, and began to snarl as if the Apocalypse were occurring in the living room right in front of him.

Which was why Meena had had to pick him up and lock him in the bathroom, with a bowl of water and his favorite chew toy. He immediately began to whimper, sad to be missing out on all the fun.

When she returned to her bedroom, where Lucien had retreated to escape the vicious mini-assault, she saw that he had collapsed onto her light blue duvet. He had one arm over his eyes to shield them from the garlic overhead. The rest of her walls—also light blue—were bare, because Meena had been so busy, she still had not gotten around to decorating, beyond what Sister Gertrude had dropped by and the apartment's owner had chosen, which was the minimum of furnishings.

She took a deep breath and sank down onto the bed beside him. The flouncy red skirt of her dress, now looking a little worse for wear after her battle with David, swirled out around them both.

"Lucien, you've *got* to tell me. What's wrong?" she asked. "Are you hurt? Is there anything I can bring you?"

It was a stupid question. She didn't have any spare pints of blood lying around the apartment. And she wasn't about to offer up her own neck.

But she didn't have the slightest idea what else to say.

"I don't believe so," he said. He lowered his arm. His dark-eyed gaze latched onto hers, and he managed another one of those heart-wrenching smiles. "Being this close to you again is enough. For now. Although I'll admit in my weaker moments I question the wisdom of being in love with a woman who chooses to work for an organization intent on exterminating my people. Believe me, if I could, I would prefer not to be."

She felt as if she couldn't breathe. She'd forgotten what it was like to have a man say that he loved her.

Oh, sure, guys occasionally indicated that they wanted to sleep with her. And sometimes—like with David—it even seemed like the relationship might actually go somewhere.

But it never did. Take her relationship with Alaric Wulf. He had kissed her—quite passionately—once.

But he had been semiconscious from blood loss at the time. Since then, he had not tried to kiss her again. He had, in fact, been seriously standoffish, except for asking her to dinner once, *in his apartment.*

Which had so obviously been an invitation for casual sex, Meena had been insulted. She'd thought she'd meant a little more to him than *that.* He could get *that* from any silly girl he met at any nightclub in Manhattan. If he wasn't going to do anything to indicate that she meant something more to him than that, she wasn't going to bother with him.

On the other hand, it *was* Alaric Wulf who'd more or less raised himself. So it was possible he hadn't known any better. Instead of telling him to go to hell, she'd just politely refused the invitation.

But with Lucien, everything was different. Because Lucien had always gotten the love thing down perfectly.

True, he had no soul. True, he was the five-hundred-year-old son of one of the most prolific serial killers in history, who had made an unholy pact with Satan in order to achieve immortality, and so needed to consume human blood to survive.

And true, their relationship had gone from amazing to unmitigated disaster in record time because he'd kept biting her. And then the members of his family kept trying to do the same. And now vampires all over the world seemed to think of Meena's blood as a refreshing pick-me-up, like Dr Pepper.

Still. He'd never stopped loving her.

"I really don't think," Meena said, aware that the lighting in the room was far too low—it could almost have been called romantic—because she had no overhead light, just a small bedside lamp, "this is the time or place to be talking about this." Even though, truthfully, she never wanted to stop talking about it. "There's obviously something really wrong with you. I think you should tell me what it is so I can try to help you."

But Lucien just shook his head.

"I told you I would love you until the end of time," he said, the corners of that irresistible mouth of his turned up. But not like he actually thought the situation was funny. More like he was sad . . . but in an amused way. "Coming from someone who, in all likelihood, will live until then, those aren't words to be spoken lightly. I've been in love with you ever since that horrible dinner party at my cousin's apartment, and we went to the Metropolitan Museum afterward, and you showed me the painting you love, the one of Joan of Arc. You look even more like her now, with your hair like that. Although I'm not entirely sure what color that's supposed to be . . ."

She reached up instinctively to tug on a lock of her hair. Her best friend, Leisha, the highest-paid stylist at the B.A.O. (By Appointment

Only) Salon, had given her permission to grow out her pixie cut, on the condition that Leisha be allowed to experiment with color. Meena now had different-colored hair each month.

But underneath it, she was still the exact same person she'd been the day she'd met Lucien.

She knew that no one else believed he could possibly have changed his colors as easily.

No one but her. Because she'd always been able to see his true colors.

"You're not like any other woman I've ever met," he was saying, his gaze intent on hers. "I didn't think you did, but you seemed really to mean it when you said you were going to save mankind from creatures like myself. Nothing was going to stand in your way. And nothing has. You're amazing. You know that, don't you?"

Amazing? *She* was amazing? No one had ever called her amazing before. Weird, yes. A flake, often. Crazy, lots of times.

But never amazing. She couldn't believe Lucien even remembered that conversation at the museum in front of the Joan of Arc painting . . . her favorite painting, because Joan of Arc, like her, made predictions that at first no one believed. But soon she convinced enough people that she was telling the truth that she was given an audience with the king, and eventually her own army to command.

Still, this was hardly the kind of discussion you'd expect someone who'd been around for half a millennium to remember.

But he had.

Lucien seemed to realize she'd been rendered speechless by his revelation, and laid a hand over hers.

"You have every reason to despise me," he said. He was still smiling ruefully to himself. "As you've so aptly pointed out, I didn't just endanger your life—and the lives of all the people you love—when I came into it, I ruined it. Not a moment goes by that I'm not still fully aware of this fact. More than anything in this world, I wish I could take that back—even more than I wish I could bring back the lives my father and half brother took before they were eventually stopped. But I can't. And the last thing I want to do now is put you in jeopardy again. But I feel like I already have. So all I can do instead is take this opportunity to make sure you know how I feel . . ." The strong hand tightened over hers. "How I'll always feel. Not that I expect you to feel the same way, or that I have any hope at all that it will make a difference."

"Lucien . . ."

If she could have thrown herself into his arms and started kissing him wildly then and there, she would have.

If she could have said, "I love you, too," forgotten all about the vampire thing—the fact that he was dead and she was alive and she had family and friends and, oh yes, an entire species who was depending on her—she would have.

But she couldn't.

Because considering his weakness—and what she'd been dreaming lately—it seemed more vital than ever that one of them, at least, keep their head.

"Lucien," she said again. "Remember that night we were in the museum, and you showed me the woodcut of the castle where you grew up, and told me about your mother?"

His grip on her hand loosened slightly.

"I remember," he said, flinching a little. "But it's hardly a good idea to bring up a man's mother at moments like this, Meena . . ."

"I'm sorry," she said. "But it can't be helped. You told me she was your father's first wife, and that she was very beautiful and innocent, and that he loved her very much. You said after her death, people used to whisper that she might have been an angel . . ."

Now he pulled his hand from hers entirely.

"And now *definitely*," he said, sitting up, "isn't the time to be bringing up angels." He threw a speculative glance at the window, which was nailed shut, and had the largest crucifix of all hanging over it. "Although I could see how it might be difficult for you not to around here."

"Lucien, you have to listen to this," Meena said urgently. "I keep having this dream. It's been the same one every night. And I think it's about you and your mother. I don't know who else it could be. It takes place in that castle in the woodcut. I went online to research where you grew up—Poenari Castle—and it looks like the same place. In the dream, this woman is sitting on a seat by a window, reading a book with a little boy. The little boy looks exactly like you, and so does the woman. She has long black hair and big dark eyes and is wearing a blue dress—"

"I don't understand why you're telling me this." Lucien's voice was curt. "So you keep having this dream. So what? I thought your gift was that you could see into the future, not the past."

"It is," Meena said, a little hurt by his harsh tone. "I mean, it was. It always has been. But lately, I don't know. I think it's been changing. Getting stronger, or something. Because, Lucien, in this dream, the part from this book that the woman is reading to this little boy—who I think is you—is about good and evil. I don't know how I can understand what she's saying, because she's speaking in a language I've never heard before. But somehow I can. She's talking about how none of us is completely good or completely evil, and *all* of God's creatures—she stresses this part, *all* of them—have the ability to choose. How evil can't exist without good, and how even some of God's angels—"

Lucien started to get up from the bed, clearly eager to get away from her.

Only he couldn't, because whatever was wrong with him, it seemed to knock him back, and off his feet. He sank down again onto the mattress, kneading his forehead and muttering a curse.

"Lucien." Meena crawled toward him and laid her hands upon his shoulders. "What? What is it? What is the matter with you?"

"Nothing." He barked the word with such surprising savagery, she dropped her hands.

Now, finally, she felt afraid.

Of him.

What had she done? What had she said? She'd thought he'd be glad to hear about her dream. It wasn't a sad dream. To her, it was a hopeful dream . . . even if no one else in the Palatine agreed with her that it meant demons had within them the capacity to be good.

At the very least, she'd argued—particularly with Alaric Wulf, who disliked her mentioning the dream so much, he almost always left the room in a rage whenever she brought it up—it meant that whatever his father might have done, Lucien Antonescu had had a mother who'd loved him, and taught him right from wrong . . . at least until she'd killed herself by throwing herself into the river that ran beneath Poenari Castle . . . the river that came to be known, forever after, as the Princess River.

Maybe it was this painful memory of his mother that caused Lucien to swing suddenly in her direction, seize her by both shoulders, and bring her roughly toward him.

There was no sign of weakness in him now. Whatever it was Meena had said to upset him, it seemed to have rid him of that, at least.

"What?" she cried, her heart jackhammering. "What is it?"

He didn't say a word. He just looked down at her, his dark-eyed gaze seeming to rake her with a need she couldn't understand. For a moment, she could see in the lamplight that there was a muscle or a nerve twitching in his cheekbone, just above his jaw. It was almost as if he was trying to keep something contained, and not quite mastering it. She stared at that muscle fearfully, watching it jump, asking herself what it was he so badly wanted to do or say that he couldn't quite seem to bring himself to. She wondered if she needed to run for her cell phone, which she'd left in the next room. . .

But before she had a chance, he'd lowered his mouth to hers.

And then nothing else seemed to matter. All that mattered was the roughness of his slight five o'clock shadow as it grazed her and the way his arms slid around her, cradling her as gently as if he were afraid she might break if he held her as tightly as he wished to . . .

. . . then the growing urgency with which he deepened the kiss, the fierceness with which he grasped her to his long-dead heart when he realized she wasn't going to crumble beneath his touch.

She lifted her arms to wrap them around his neck, even as he was crushing her against him, making her feel things just with his lips and tongue that she hadn't felt since . . . well, since the last time he'd held her in his arms this way.

It couldn't last, of course.

Because a second later he broke the kiss—literally tore his face from hers just as certain parts of herself had started to turn to liquid—and let go of her, so suddenly that her eyelids fluttered open and she actually had to put a hand out to catch herself from falling back against the mattress without his arms to support her anymore. Because, suddenly, he'd disappeared.

She was so taken aback by the abrupt end to their kiss, she wanted to ask him what he thought he was doing, and drag his mouth back down to hers again.

But then she saw that he'd flung himself a few feet away, and was in a darkened corner of her room, just looking at her from the shadows, his eyes no longer deep pools of ebony, but twin spots of red . . .

The same red his eyes had always turned when he was at his angriest.

Or hungriest.

Oh God.

She stared back at him. It had never occurred to her to ask what he was living on these days.

Now, as she looked into those bloodred eyes, it was all she could think about.

"The Palatine have frozen all your financial assets," she said quietly.

"The ones they could trace back to the name I used to use," he replied, his voice like liquid smoke, drifting from the shadows and curling around her in burning tendrils.

"Still," Meena said, shivering. She felt as if she were sitting in a cool, dense fog. "It must be difficult to find human blood to purchase on such restricted resources." She gripped her duvet, white-knuckled, as she waited for his reply.

"Are you worried I'm not eating enough, Meena?" She heard a hint of mockery in his tone. "Or worried I'm resorting to murder for my meals? Let me put your mind at rest on both counts." She heard a rustle of cloth. He was reaching into his coat pocket. "Here." He tossed something onto the bed. She reached instinctively to catch it.

It was the impromptu stake he'd given her, and that she'd used to kill David.

"You have my permission to kill me if I ever try to bite you again," he said. "Against your will, anyway. I should hope there's still enough man in me to keep me from ever hurting you. But should an occasion ever arise to prove otherwise . . . well, you've more than amply proved this evening that you know what to do with one of those."

Meena stared down at the chair leg. She had to swallow before she felt able to speak.

"Lucien," she said. "I told you six months ago: I don't ever want to hurt you. I'll always do everything in my power to try to help you . . . even help you despite yourself. That's why I told you about the dream. I think I can prove—"

He stepped from the shadows then. His eyes had gone back to their normal color, but a million different emotions played upon his face.

"You know what I want from you, Meena," he said, in a rasping voice. "As soon as you're ready to give it—and admit that's what you want, as well—come find me. You won't have to look far. I'll be close. I always have been."

Then he opened the bedroom door and walked out. A second later, she heard the apartment door slam.

Chapter Six

Alaric Wulf was not having a good day. Technically, he wasn't having a good week.

This streak of misfortune had started when his supervisor, Abraham Holtzman, called him into his office, saying he had something he wished to discuss in private.

"I already know," Alaric announced the minute he arrived.

"You do?" Holtzman looked up from his computer screen, surprised. "How?"

Alaric shrugged. "You're kidding, right? She told me. She's been telling anyone who'll listen. You should hear her in the commissary at lunch. 'What if there is good in Lucien Antonescu, and in all demons? And our job isn't to destroy them, but to restore the good in them?'"

He felt like his imitation of Meena Harper was dead-on. Sometimes he found himself mimicking her when he was alone. Not on purpose, which was faintly disheartening. He couldn't seem to get her voice out of his head.

"Oh." Holtzman lowered his scraggly gray eyebrows. "*That.*"

"Yes, that," Alaric said, annoyed. "What else? I certainly hope you put a freeze on that request she made to the Secret Archives."

Now Holtzman's eyebrows went up. "I did no such thing," he said, looking offended. "If any of my staff members wants to request material the Vatican Library might have on file—even material from the Secret Archives—that might in any way help us in our efforts to better understand our enemies, why on earth would I stand in their way?"

"You must be joking." Alaric could hardly believe what he was hearing. "You don't believe this dream she's been having has any sort of merit, do you?"

"I don't know that it doesn't," Holtzman said. "And I don't see why you feel it doesn't. In any case, Meena Harper is not why I asked you in here today."

Alaric's frown deepened. "Are you saying you actually believe that there's a chance that Lucien Antonescu—the anointed one, listed in the *Palatine Guide to Otherworldly Creatures* as he who performs the devil's work on earth—may have a *choice* in whether or not he commits good or evil?"

"I'm saying," Holtzman said, "I like to keep myself open to all possibilities." When Alaric openly balked at this, Holtzman lifted a hand and said, "I understand that certain prejudices exist about Antonescu, and rightly so. Sometimes old memories die hard, and the fact that so many of us, including yourself, are still recovering from injuries sustained fighting him and the Dracul last spring certainly hasn't exactly fostered a spirit of goodwill toward Meena's theory. I, however, am willing to give it a chance . . . if she can prove it, which is a big if. Now, if I may get to the reason I asked you to step in here this evening, which, as I said, has nothing to do with Meena Harper . . . I know you aren't going to like this, but there's no getting around it. I'm sure you're aware of the Church's efforts to . . ."

Alaric instantly switched off his attention and turned to stare out of one of Holtzman's office—formerly a principal's office—windows facing Mulberry Street. The moment he heard the words *church* and *efforts to,* he knew that whatever was being discussed was going to bore him. It might possibly have something to do with his being in trouble for killing something in too public or violent a manner.

But that, too, was boring.

He reflected, instead, on Meena Harper, and her theory.

"Saint Thomas said it," she insisted almost daily in the commissary. "Not me. He believed there is no positive source of evil, or even evil beings, but rather an absence of good in some beings."

"Which," Alaric had pointed out, "is why we are employed, and will continue to be so for many years to come."

This always provoked a great deal of laughter from his fellow guards.

But then Meena would come in with some quote from Saint Thomas like, "'Fire could not exist without the corruption of what it consumes; the lion must slay the ass in order to live. And if there were no wrongdoing, there would be no sphere for patience and justice.' True," she'd go on, "without evil we'd be out of a job. But maybe our job is to provide better fireproofing and protection for the asses, rather than kill all the lions."

None of this made Alaric feel any better about this book Meena had requested from the Vatican Secret Archives, which she swore—if it was the book from her dream, and what were the chances of that?— was going to prove her theory correct. The still-healing scars that he and many of his fellow guards bore from their battle last spring with Lucien Antonescu and his clan was all the proof Alaric needed of just how wrong she was . . .

. . . as was the feeling he and so many of them had in their guts since the fire that had ripped through and destroyed St. George's Cathedral, the site of that battle.

It was a belief every guard—but especially one who had put in as many years as Alaric had on the force—shared, honed from sheer experience:

True evil did indeed exist, and it was out there, waiting.

Like the quiet just before a storm, they could feel it. It had the hairs on the back of all their necks standing up. Maybe they couldn't see the clouds rolling in, and maybe they couldn't hear the thunder . . .

But that didn't mean there wasn't something on its way.

Maybe that something wasn't Lucien Antonescu. Meena swore up and down that he hadn't been in contact with her in months.

And there was no reason not to believe her. While they'd had plenty of reports of other paranormal phenomena—succubi, werewolves, and more ghosts than he could count—there'd been no reports from anywhere in the tristate area of attacks by members of Antonescu's clan, the Dracul. In fact, there'd been no reports of any attacks at all that could be attributed to vampires.

This was frustrating, because the entire reason the Manhattan unit had been created was to root out and destroy the prince of darkness.

If they killed him, it was theorized, the demonic beings over which he ruled would be weakened. Demoralized and disorganized without their leader, they'd be that much easier to slay.

Alaric wasn't certain how much credence he put into this theory. But he did know Antonescu *had* to be close by. Because what kind of man—even a half man, half beast like that bloodsucking son of all that was evil, Antonescu—would simply fade into the night with a girl like Meena around? Every time Alaric glanced at her, *he* felt an almost magnetic pull in her direction.

And he hadn't risked half a millennium of anonymity to be with her, the way Antonescu had.

It didn't make sense to believe that the vampire would give up now, even if she'd rejected him. He was only biding his time, Alaric knew. Biding it a little too well, unfortunately.

Because everything between Alaric and Meena had gone wrong as well. Not as spectacularly wrong as it had between her and the vampire because, well, for one thing, he wasn't a vampire. And for another, he and Meena had never actually gone out.

But he'd at least considered them friends. Now he wasn't sure they were even that anymore.

It seemed to have started not long after he'd been released from the hospital for the wound he'd sustained protecting her from what undoubtedly would have been certain death at St. George's Cathedral, when he'd asked Meena if she'd like to have dinner with him.

When she'd looked up at him with those big dark eyes and asked, "Where would you like to eat?" he'd replied, "Well, my apartment, of course. I'll cook for you." His culinary skills were excellent.

And why should they go to a stuck-up Manhattan restaurant where some customer was bound to do something to annoy him—such as talk too loudly on a cell phone, Alaric's number one pet peeve—causing him to have to get into a fight, when he could make something just as good in his own apartment, where no one would annoy him?

She'd instantly looked wary. He had no idea why.

"Do you really think that's such a good idea?" she'd asked.

"Why would that be a problem?" he'd inquired, genuinely confused.

"Maybe we should just keep it professional," she'd said, giving him what he supposed she considered a "professional" pat on the shoulder.

That had been weeks and weeks ago, and she was still treating him like he had the plague and leprosy combined. He couldn't understand it. What had he done that was so wrong? He'd asked Carolina de Silva, a fellow guard with whom Meena had become friendly, and she'd only smiled and told him he should have gone for the restaurant after all.

This information only made him more confused.

Now she wouldn't shut up about her damned dream.

Why did *he* get "Maybe we should just keep it professional" when that soulless creature of the night got to be in her dreams?

"Wulf!" Holtzman barked the name. It echoed throughout the high-ceilinged room. The new headquarters for the Manhattan unit of the Palatine Guard had, just six months earlier, been a Catholic elementary school.

A cataclysmic decline in enrollment—no one who could afford to live in such a trendy neighborhood of Manhattan had children . . . or if they did, they were certainly not choosing to send them to Catholic school—and the building's general state of disrepair had caused the Church to shut down St. Bernadette's, with zero protest from the community, at exactly the same time as the Palatine had put in their request for a similar-size space in New York City.

Abraham Holtzman had been pleased . . . until he'd stepped inside and seen its dismal state, and the tiny desks still littering its hallways. It had taken weeks to clear them all out. The fountain in the courtyard—of Saint Bernadette kneeling before the Virgin Mary at Lourdes—still didn't work. Apparently, it had been dry for almost a hundred years.

"What?" Alaric blurted, startled from his private thoughts.

"I was *saying,*" Holtzman snapped, "since I'm aware of your previous, er, *dealings* with Father Henrique Mauricio from the archdiocese of São Sebastio do Rio de Janeiro in Brazil, that I thought I ought to mention to you privately, *before* you heard it from anyone else, that the Vatican has been very impressed with him, and the way he handled himself during the outbreaks of the Lamir in the favelas, and he's being transferred to America . . ."

Alaric sank backward into the seat closest to Holtzman's desk. Unfortunately, it turned out to be some kind of secretarial chair dating from World War II. It squeaked in what sounded like terror and protest as Alaric's muscular weight hit it. Apparently it was used to the significantly softer backsides of nuns.

"Tell me you're joking." Alaric tried to keep his tone neutral and failed.

"Honestly, Alaric, I've never understood what your problem is with the man. He's had, after all, close to a hundred kills. And considering his age—he's just a bit younger than you, barely thirty-three or -four, I believe—and profession—he's a priest, after all, *not* a Vatican-trained demon hunter—that's thoroughly impressive."

Alaric stared at his boss. "Is it?" he asked impassively.

"Yes," Holtzman cried. "It is! You know the Lamir are the most mysterious vampire clan in the entire world. We know very little about them because they're relatively new, and they come from the heart of the Amazon. Really, Alaric, I know he may not be your favorite person in the world—I'll never understand what happened between the two of you during that exorcism in Vidigal a few years back—but can't you give Father Henrique a second chance?"

"No," Alaric said, leaning precariously back in the office chair. As he did so, he casually lifted some files that were lying on top of a still-unpacked box near his boss's desk. The files were marked *Missing Persons*. "I don't think I can, actually."

"Well," Holtzman said drily, "you'd better try. There's a gala at the Metropolitan Museum of Art tomorrow night for the opening of the new exhibit of Vatican treasures, and all the high-ups from the archdiocese are expected to attend, which means we'll be pulling security. Since he's been appointed the new pastor at St. George's Cathedral, Father Henrique will be a guest of honor, so I don't want you—"

Alaric was so startled he would have fallen out of the chair if he hadn't dropped his feet with a crash to the wood floor in order to regain his balance. The stack of files toppled over.

"*What?*" he cried. "*Padre Caliente? Here?*"

"I've asked you before," Holtzman said exasperatedly, "not to call him that. He is a man of the cloth who has taken a lifelong vow of chastity. It's both inappropriate and disrespectful to refer to him as Padre Caliente. Which isn't even Portuguese, by the way. I asked Carolina, who you might recall is from São Paulo. So it only shows your ignorance. And pick those up."

"We don't need him here," Alaric said. "What's he coming *here* for?"

"If you'd listened to a word I'd said, you'd have heard that Father Henrique hasn't been assigned to work *here,* for our unit. He's the new pastor at St. George's, now that the reconstruction is nearing completion—"

"Right," Alaric said sarcastically. "You honestly think I'm that stupid?" He was doing a poor job of restacking the files. "Hasn't this city got any of its own priests? What's wrong with the old priest from St. George's?"

"Considering he had a massive coronary after he heard his parish was nearly burned to the ground by the prince of darkness, and died, quite a lot." Holtzman regarded Alaric impatiently. "You were in the hospital at the time, so I suppose it's only natural you might not have heard, but *must* you be so insensitive? Is it the leg that's bothering you so much? My understanding is that you came through your physical therapy with flying colors and are as good as new. It's the sessions with your Palatine-assigned psychiatrist that you haven't quite completed, because you keep walking out of them—"

Alaric straightened up and glared at him. "Fiske is giving me a discharge due to my not passing my psych eval?"

"Don't be ridiculous, Alaric," Holtzman said. "Dr. Fiske seems to be impressed with your progress . . . when you show up. You just need to show up more often." He held out his hand for the files Alaric was holding. "One thing you might want to consider discussing with him is the hostility you feel toward Father Henrique. Have you ever considered that it might be rooted in jealousy?"

Alaric rolled his eyes, surrendering the files. "Yes, Abraham. That's exactly it. I'm jealous of a pretentious blowhard who's so in love with himself that it doesn't bother him at all that one of the requirements for his job is that he's not allowed to have sex."

"The Church is expecting to get quite a lot of press—and some sizable donations—out of this show at the museum," Holtzman said, ignoring Alaric's crudeness as he neatly restacked the files. "That's why they worked so hard to time it to coincide with the Feast of San Gennaro, which is one of the largest, longest-running, and most revered outdoor festivals in the United States. This opening tomorrow night at the Met is expected to be one of the premier social events in the city. Transferring Padre Cali—I mean, Father Henrique—here in time for it was a deliberate move on the part of our superiors—"

"I'm certain it was," Alaric muttered. "The padre definitely isn't camera shy."

"*You* may consider him a preening prima donna," Holtzman continued, "but I assure you, the rest of us have the utmost admiration and respect for him. And I'm going to expect you to treat him accordingly. I will no longer tolerate your complete lack of respect for proper procedure. If you have a problem with him, you're to go through established channels. You will *not* mock or humiliate him. And that includes pranks and physical displays of aggression. Do you understand?"

Alaric ignored him. "Why do we have so many missing-persons files? No one's mentioned them to me."

"Oh." Holtzman shrugged and set the files aside. "There's always an uptick in missing people—especially in the Manhattan area—in the fall, I'm told."

When Alaric continued to stare at him, Holtzman elaborated. "The fall is the beginning of the new school year and often students starting college in the city drop out and don't tell their parents because they're embarrassed over their poor grades or experimentation with drugs or their sexuality and whatnot. So there's nothing nefarious behind it. Our contact with the NYPD sent the files over anyway because this year there's a larger than usual number of reports, but I couldn't find anything unusual, so I'm sending them back—"

Alaric leaned forward to take the stack away from his boss again, then began to shuffle through them.

"I *said*," Holtzman repeated irritably, "I didn't notice anything out of the ordinary."

Alaric only grunted as he opened first one, then another file from the stack, then tossed them onto Holtzman's desk.

"There's nothing there, Wulf," his supervisor said tiredly. "You know, Dr. Fiske's quite positive about many areas of your recovery. You're one of our finest guards—impressive number of kills, splendid record at interrogation, and all of that. But there's one area in which the doctor says he's yet to see any difference at all, and I must say, I've got to agree. Your interpersonal communication skills have always been sadly lacking." Another file hit the top of Holtzman's desk. "You still haven't gotten over what happened to your partner in Berlin, even though he's perfectly fine now—"

"Except for missing his face," Alaric said, with a grunt. Another file hit Holtzman's desk.

"This resentment you feel toward Father Henrique is another example," Holtzman said. "What did the man ever do to you? Nothing. So he botched that exorcism. It was his first one. He was young. Do you know what I did at my first exorcism?"

"Ran," Alaric said, at the same time as his boss.

"That's exactly right," Holtzman went on. "It's extremely frightening to look into the face of evil for the first time."

"Not," Alaric said, "as frightening as looking into the face of a man who has willingly taken a vow of chastity."

"That is a bad habit of yours," Holtzman commented. "Expecting everyone to conform to your standards of behavior."

Alaric stared at him. The man was clearly growing senile . . . or had he been hit over the head so many times by escaping yeti that he didn't know what he was saying.

"I do not expect Henrique Mauricio to conform to my standards of behavior," Alaric said. "I expect him not to do things that make me want to pound his face into a bloody pulp. Sadly, every time I meet him, he fails to live up to this expectation."

"I understand," Holtzman said kindly. "And given the circumstances of your upbringing, it sometimes surprises me that you don't beat more people that you don't like into bloody pulps. It took me quite some time to dissuade you from indulging in such behavior after I plucked you from the streets as a teenager, if you'll recall. But there's still a part of you that becomes quite angry when others don't conform to your beliefs. I believe that's why you're so angry with Meena Harper."

Alaric's head came up with a snap. "I am not angry with Meena Harper."

"That is a lie," Holtzman said. "Why else are you so outraged about a theory she has that, for all we know, could be completely valid? Do you know what I was thinking the other day?"

"That this building still smells like vomit and school paste? Because it's true."

"If you like Meena so much, you should ask her out on a date."

Alaric ducked his head back into the files. "I do not date. And besides, I did ask her over to dinner once. She said no, that it wouldn't be pro—"

"What do you mean, you don't date?" Holtzman looked annoyed. "All single people date. And of course she said no to dinner at your apartment. *I* wouldn't come to dinner at your apartment if I was a woman. That's like the spider asking the fly to step into his web. You truly are an imbe—" Another file landed on the older man's desk. He snatched it up and said, "Would you stop? I told you, I've been through these. There's nothing there. No commonality whatsoever."

"There is," Alaric said, laying down two more files. "All of them are from out of town."

"What do you mean?" Holtzman looked more annoyed than ever.

"Each of the people in those files was a tourist on vacation in this city when he or she disappeared," Alaric said. "All of those reports were filed in the missing person's home state, though the victim actually disappeared here in Manhattan within the last few months. You said you were looking for a commonality. I found it for you."

"I beg your pardon," Holtzman said, his gaze dipping to all the files spread across his desk. "But are you seriously suggesting to me that there is someone out there killing *tourists*?"

"It looks like it," Alaric said. He thumbed through one file. "Here's an entire family. The O'Brians from Illinois, a family of five. Last seen by the concierge at their midtown hotel when they asked directions to

M&M World. They never checked out. No one seems to have thought anything about it until Mr. O'Brian never showed back up at his job and the kids never returned to school. That's when Grandma contacted the police in Illinois, and they, in turn, contacted the hotel, who assumed the family had simply flaked out—"

"Give me that." Holtzman snatched the file away from him. "This can't be possible. It would have been all over the local media. Someone snatching tourists from Manhattan? Just as the Feast of San Gennaro is starting up?"

"Not someone," Alaric said. "Some*thing*." He laid the rest of the files down with a *thump*. "Because where are all the bodies? You'd think by now they'd have started to turn a little ripe."

Holtzman looked slightly sick to his stomach, but Alaric only looked thoughtful. Then he brightened. "I know. Let's ask Padre Caliente tomorrow night at the Vatican treasures show. He'll know what to do. He knows everything."

Holtzman had already picked up the phone. He pointed at the door. "Out. Get out of my office. Now."

Alaric was no more than a few steps out of the building and down the block before he began to reflect on the news his supervisor had imparted about Henrique Mauricio, and its implications for him personally and the unit as a whole. None of them, he concluded, was good.

His Palatine-appointed therapist, Dr. Fiske, was always encouraging Alaric to picture the worst-case scenario. It was healthy, the doctor said. Pessimists apparently lived longer than optimists.

"Because reality," the doctor liked to say, "is never anywhere near as bad as what we *imagine* might happen."

"I don't know, Doc," Alaric had said the last time they'd met. "Can you *imagine* anything worse than demons turning out to have a choice between being good and being evil?"

"Oh yes," Dr. Fiske had replied cheerfully. "There are lots of things worse than that. After all, they could choose to be good."

It was at this point during the session that Alaric had stood up and walked out. If he hadn't, he imagined he probably would have stuck his fist through the doctor's drywall. Or through the doctor's face.

Alaric spent the evening after his meeting with Abraham Holtzman trying to imagine every worst-case scenario that Father Henrique's being transferred to Manhattan could entail.

This was how he found himself working over the punching bag in his apartment until after midnight. Exhausted, he eventually showered and went to bed, only to be tortured by dreams in which Lucien Antonescu had chosen to be good. In one dream, he was lying in the bright sunshine in the grass in Central Park, with his head in Meena Harper's lap . . . which was impossible, of course, because the prince of darkness would turn to ash if he stepped into sunlight.

Meena was laughing. Lucien Antonescu kept kissing her hair, which was long and dark and, for some reason, was continually falling into Lucien's face.

It was a great relief when Alaric's cell phone woke him early the next morning.

At least until he answered it and heard his boss's voice saying, "Meena Harper is in some kind of trouble."

Then something seemed to tighten in his chest. He knew it was not a pulled muscle from overworking the bag.

It was hard to think things could possibly get worse than that until he heard the words *New Jersey* and *I'll drive* from Holtzman's mouth.

But when he actually saw Meena Harper emerge from a taxi in front of the Freewell, New Jersey, Police Department, wearing one of those too-tight-in-the-chest dresses—this one black with little pink roses on it—she seemed to favor, the morning sun glinting on her newly auburn hair, he realized that all the worst-case scenarios he'd been imagining came nowhere close to the horror of this one:

There was a pink scarf tied around her throat.

Part Two

Saturday, September 18

Chapter Seven

M eena woke to the shrill vibration of her cell phone and glanced at the digital clock by the side of her bed. It was only six o'clock in the morning, two hours before she usually had to wake, because she lived so close to work. No one would call this early unless something was wrong.

Something, it turned out, *was* very wrong. She knew it the minute she picked up her phone and saw the New Jersey area code.

Meena didn't know anyone who lived in New Jersey anymore. Not since her parents had retired to Florida.

Her pulse slowed almost to a standstill.

"Who the hell is that?" her brother demanded, stumbling shirtless from his room to stand in her doorway, blinking down at her sleepily. Jack Bauer had also scrambled from his basket in the corner and was now eagerly bouncing around beside her bed, thinking it was time to get up.

"Work," she lied. "Can you take Jack out?"

"What the hell," Jonathan said, but without rancor. "Come on, Jack," he said to the dog, and went to go find his shoes and the dog's leash.

Meena answered the phone.

"Hello," said a woman's voice, familiar, but older and more quavering than Meena had been expecting. "This is Olivia Delmonico. To whom am I speaking?"

Meena had thought she might eventually hear from the woman in David's life.

But not this one.

"Um," she said. She wasn't ready. She—

"Hello?" Mrs. Delmonico said. "Is anyone there?"

"Yes," Meena said. "Yes, Mrs. Delmonico. It's me, Meena Harper."

"Meena Harper?"

Mrs. Delmonico formed the words with obvious distaste. David's parents had never liked Meena. Though neither they nor David had ever come right out and said so, Meena had always gotten the feeling they hadn't approved of their son moving in with her after college, and not just because they didn't believe in couples living together without the benefit of marriage, but because . . .

Well, they just hadn't liked Meena. Maybe they'd felt like an aspiring writer wasn't good enough for their ambitious son . . .

Or maybe it had had something to do with Meena mentioning, during her first dinner out with them, a celebration of David's graduation from dental school, that Mr. Delmonico didn't have to order any wine on her account, especially considering his "health concerns."

Mr. Delmonico's ongoing struggle with alcoholism had turned out to be a secret his parents had managed to keep from David his whole life. Up until that night, that is, when she'd blown it.

Oops.

"Well," Mrs. Delmonico said. "This is . . . I don't know what to say. I just found your number on a notepad by the side of David's kitchen phone. I wasn't aware the two of you were still . . . in touch."

"Oh," Meena said. She thought fast. "That. Well, you know I moved out of our old apartment recently, and I found I still had some boxes of his, so I got in touch with him about picking them up—"

"Oh yes," Mrs. Delmonico said coldly. "Of course. Well, I apologize for calling so early. But I'm actually at David and Brianna's right now. I'm going through every number I can find, trying to see if I can track down anyone who might have heard from David. He didn't come home last night, you see."

"He didn't?" Meena tried to sound genuinely surprised. "That's strange."

"It's very strange," Mrs. Delmonico said. "Not like him at all." Then, her voice dripping with ill-disguised dislike, she asked, "I don't suppose *you* know where he is, do you, Meena?"

A picture of Mrs. Delmonico sitting in her pearls and Chanel suit in David and Brianna's contemporary four-bedroom home—with its open kitchen and great room, three-car garage, and heated pool—flashed through Meena's mind. Meena had never actually *been* to David's home in Freewell, a fancy suburb about an hour's drive from the city.

But somehow she could picture Mrs. Delmonico in it, all the same.

She could tell from the woman's tone that she suspected that her son was right there in bed next to Meena, and that Meena was covering up for him.

Maybe in an alternate universe—one in which vampires, and therefore Lucien Antonescu, did not exist—this might have been true. Because then David would never have gotten bitten, and then Meena might actually have had the low self-esteem to have brought him home with her. Because she wouldn't have known that something better existed out there.

But in this universe?

Never.

"No," Meena said. "I do not know where David is."

It wasn't a lie. She didn't know where David was. She hoped he was in heaven, but she wasn't going to bet on it.

"Oh. Well, then." Mrs. Delmonico's voice sounded suddenly defeated. "I just don't know what to do. I've called every number in his address book, and no one else has heard from him either. This number . . . well, it was my last hope. His cell phone goes straight to voice mail, just like Brianna's. David Junior was up all night crying. He's never spent a night before without his mother *and* his father, and he's just hysterical—"

Meena sat bolt upright in bed. Her pulse, which had been racing before, now felt as if it had stopped.

"Wait," she said. "Are you saying that you don't know where David's *wife* is either?"

"Yes," Mrs. Delmonico said. She was sobbing openly now. The picture of her sitting in her pearls and Chanel suit vanished from Meena's head. Now she heard only the voice of a frantic grandmother. "No one's heard from her since she went to pick up some formula. And that was at six o'clock last night. I've called all the hospitals, but no one fitting David or Brianna's description was brought in—"

Meena swung her legs from her bed. This wasn't possible. Because she'd killed David. *She'd killed him.* There was no way Brianna could be gone, too. Meena had saved Brianna. Last night, *she'd saved her.*

"I just don't know what to do," Mrs. Delmonico was babbling, in a shaking voice. "Just now a New York City policeman called. David's car has been found—its registration was still inside—near Little Italy. Why would David have been there? He never goes into the city. Maybe he and Brianna decided at the last minute to go to the Feast of San Gennaro? But why wouldn't they have called?"

"Mrs. Delmonico," Meena said, her throat very dry. "I want you to listen to me. This is very important. Are you in David's house right now?"

"Of course," Mrs. Delmonico said. "Someone has to stay with David Junior. My husband is here, too. He's on the other line with the impound people, trying to figure out how we can get David's car back—"

"Mrs. Delmonico," Meena said. "Is there anywhere else you can take the baby? Just for a little while?"

"Well, I suppose we could take him to my daughter's house." Mrs. Delmonico sounded confused. "David's sister lives a few miles away. But what does Naomi have to do with any of this? I already spoke to her and she hasn't heard from David or Brianna—"

"I just think it would be best if you and your husband packed up some of the baby's things and took him over to Naomi's. Right away."

"But when we spoke to that police officer from New York, he said the best thing to do was sit by the phone and wait for David to call. Or if we wanted to formally report that David and Brianna were missing, we could go over to the police station here in Freewell, which I thought was rude since I had him right on the phone, and you would have thought he could have taken the information. But he said we've got to do it in the jurisdiction in which they live."

Meena took a deep, steadying breath. She realized now that just like Cassandra, she really was cursed.

Because Cassandra—poor, clairvoyant Cassandra, who'd denied the love of a god—had taken up with Agamemnon, only to end up murdered by his vengeful wife, Clytemnestra.

"Mrs. Delmonico," she said, her mouth gone dry as sand, "*have* you reported them missing yet?"

"Well," Mrs. Delmonico said, "no. The officer said we'd have to do it in person, and we can't just leave the baby here by himself—"

"Exactly," Meena said. "Drop the baby off at David's sister's, and then go to the Freewell Police Department *as soon as you can*. Do you hear me, Mrs. Delmonico? It's very important that you report David and Brianna missing *right away*."

Mrs. Delmonico sounded even more surprised. "Oh," she said. "Well, the police officer didn't say that. I don't know how Naomi is going to feel about us leaving David Junior with her. She's got the triplets now, you know. But I suppose under these circumstances, it would be all right. I just don't know what we're going to do about David's car. Apparently, the impound people are being difficult. The police are searching it, or something—"

"Look," Meena said, finally, in desperation. "Why don't I just meet you? At the police station in Freewell. I might be able to help."

Now Mrs. Delmonico sounded more than just surprised. She sounded stunned. "Help? How?"

"I might have some information," Meena said. "About David. Information that the police may find useful. It'll take me a little while to get there, because I'll have to shower, then take the train. But I'll be there no later than nine o'clock. You'll meet me there, right? You and Mr. Delmonico? And you'll leave the baby at David's sister's house?"

"Well," Mrs. Delmonico said, clearly flabbergasted, "I . . . yes. Thank you, Meena. That's very . . . kind."

Meena said it was no problem and hung up, feeling guilty.

Because she wasn't being kind. She had no other choice. She was the last person to have seen David Delmonico alive.

She was also the person who'd tried to save his wife's life.

And apparently, she'd failed. She couldn't understand how . . . except for the part where she'd made out with the guy who'd provided her with the weapon with which she'd murdered Brianna's husband.

Now she had the lives of David's parents, and his baby, to worry about. Who knew where Brianna Delmonico was?

But Meena wasn't taking any chances that Brianna might be looking for breakfast in her own house. She had to make sure the Delmonicos got out of there, just in case.

She could see she had a lot of work to do if she was going to rectify all the wrongs she'd committed the night before.

But when she got to the station house where she'd promised to meet Mrs. Delmonico, she could see that her karmic punishment was going to be even worse than she'd anticipated.

That's because the last person in the world she wanted to see was waiting for her on the station-house steps:

Alaric Wulf.

Chapter Eight

"Why are *you* here?" she demanded.

He thrust a cup of coffee at her. "I thought you might need this."

The truth, however, was that *he* needed it. Especially now that he'd seen the scarf.

"I called Abraham, not *you*," she said rudely.

"I noticed," he said. "Do you want the coffee or not?"

She looked down at the cup. "Light?"

She had on sunglasses, so he couldn't see her eyes. But he guessed from the throatiness in her voice that she'd been crying.

"I think I know by now how you take your coffee," he said stiffly.

She took it from him. "Thanks," she grumbled.

They stood outside the station house in silence, drinking coffee and watching the good people of Freewell drive by on their way to work . . . or wherever they were going so early on a Saturday morning.

The police department was a fairly new building, on a grassy embankment attractively landscaped with new trees. Birds sang prettily in the treetops, oblivious to the impending doom. Alaric reflected that, if they had been in front of a station house in the city, police officers would have been hauling transvestite hookers past them. Instead, a squirrel, foraging for nuts for the winter, hopped nearby.

"Are you going to tell me what's going on," Alaric asked, "or am I supposed to guess?"

"It's not what you think," Meena said.

"I thought you could only tell how people are going to die, not what they're thinking."

"You're not exactly hard to read, Alaric," she said.

This stung. He said, "Well, as it happens, neither are you. The last time you wore a scarf like that around your neck, it nearly cost me a leg. So I'd appreciate a little heads-up this time, since I happen to enjoy being able to walk."

Her cheeks went almost the same color pink of the scarf.

"All right," she said, reaching up to remove the sunglasses. Beneath them her dark eyes, which she'd carefully made up, were nevertheless red-rimmed from crying. "Yes. I did get bitten last night. But it wasn't by Lucien, Alaric. Not this time, I swear."

He felt the sidewalk sway beneath him. He didn't understand this, because despite his protests that they should get to Freewell as quickly as possible, Abraham had pulled into a fast-food drive-through in the Prius (Alaric would never get over the indignity of having been forced to ride in such a vehicle) along the way, insisting that breakfast was the most important meal of the day, and they'd need the protein.

Now Alaric was glad, even if the alleged "McMuffin" he had eaten was sitting like a rock in his stomach.

"Impossible," he said to her. "We haven't had a vampire sighting in the city—in North *America*—in six months. We killed all the Dracul. You know that. You were there."

"This wasn't a Dracul," she said.

Alaric shook his head, confused. "But there's never been another clan reported in—"

"Well," Meena said, "then someone needs to alert Homeland Security. Because last night I had a close encounter with an illegal immigrant of the very fanged kind."

"Why didn't you call it in until this morning?" Alaric demanded. "What's going on, exactly, Meena? Abraham wouldn't tell me anything. He said you'd tell me. *If* you chose to." He didn't mention how angry this information had made him. What had Holtzman meant, *if* Meena chose to tell him?

And why had Meena chosen to tell Holtzman anything instead of him? He was the one who'd saved her life at St. George's, not Holtzman. Was this all because he refused to believe her theory about Antonescu?

But who could? It was crazy. Demons were inherently evil. They were not capable of free will. He didn't care what Saint Thomas Aquinas had written eight hundred years ago.

"Look, I appreciate the coffee, but can we just go inside?" Meena said, suddenly looking less mulish, and more tired. "It took me forever to get a cab from the train station, and now I'm late, and I'm sure everyone is wondering where I am."

"Abraham's already inside," Alaric said. "He's told everyone he's your lawyer."

Meena rolled her eyes and tossed her coffee cup into a nearby trash can. "Great. My lawyer. Now it looks like I did something wrong."

Alaric caught her by the wrist as she started to walk past him and into the building. Her bones felt as small and fine as a bird's.

"*Did* you do something wrong?" he asked, his gaze burning down into hers. He didn't want to ask it. He knew it was wrong of him, and he probably shouldn't have.

But he couldn't help it.

She reached up with her free hand to push some bright copper hair from her eyes. Eyes that, he saw, were suddenly brimming with tears. "I guess that depends from whose point of view you're looking at it. Yours? No. My own? Yeah. Yeah, I definitely did."

He felt a sudden wave of tenderness toward her that, had it been anyone else, he'd have ignored. He *tried* to ignore it. She'd violated every rule in the book.

Then again, so had he, at one time or another.

But this was different. She'd also put herself in danger. And then she hadn't called him. It hurt his feelings . . . even though he'd go to his grave before he'd admit it.

But now she was shaken and upset about something. And she'd called *Holtzman*. *He* wanted to be the person she turned to when she was shaken and upset. Not *Holtzman*.

How could he have let everything go so wrong? And how could he possibly fix it?

She looked pointedly down at the wrist he was holding. Instantly, he released it. She turned away and started to walk past him, into the building.

He should have let it end there. But he couldn't.

So instead, he reached out and wrapped an arm around her shoulders, pulling her toward him in an embrace that was awkward as much because she wasn't expecting it as because Alaric Wulf was not used to hugging people, and wasn't very good at it.

"It's all right," he said, in what he hoped was a soothing voice. He stroked her hair. The fine threads, a little coarse from all the dye her friend Leisha had been using on them lately, were hot from the sun. "Whatever it is. It's going to be fine."

She finally seemed to realize what he was doing and stopped trying to pull away. To his surprise, he actually felt her relax in his arms. Something warm and wet touched his neck, and he realized, with a shock, that it was her tears.

"I don't think so, Alaric," she whispered. "I really don't. Not this time."

He didn't know what to do. He'd gotten so accustomed to her giving him the cold shoulder that for her to completely drop all her defenses and melt against him like this was a little unnerving. He almost preferred the hostile glances and sarcasm. It was certainly better than tears. Hundreds of women had cried in front of him before, and it had never bothered him.

But this was awful.

He tightened his grip and said, lamely, "It can't be that bad." Then he wanted to kick himself. Actually, it really could be that bad. What did he know?

A squad car pulled up beside them. A Freewell police officer got out from behind the wheel, then walked around to haul a surprisingly tall and colorfully dressed—for suburban New Jersey—drag queen from the backseat.

"Honey," the drag queen said to Meena as the officer escorted her into the building, "you save me a piece of that boy's ass. I will be right out to get it."

Alaric looked skyward, thankful he had taken Holtzman's advice not to bring his sword.

"I think we should go inside and find Abraham," Meena said in a small voice, stepping away from him.

"I think that's an excellent idea," Alaric said, and hurried to open the door for her. He didn't understand the look Meena gave him when he did this, one that seemed to be of mingled shock, gratitude, and something else that he could not identify.

But it did not make him feel any better.

Chapter Nine

M eena, followed closely by Alaric, walked into the impeccably clean, high-tech Freewell Police Department. She wondered why every head in the room did not swivel toward her as she came in. That's how loudly her heartbeat was slamming inside her ears. She felt as if everyone in the whole world must be able to hear it.

But apparently, she was the only one who could.

She could see Abraham Holtzman sitting in the conference room the polite receptionist led them to, speaking to a sleepy-looking woman in a beige suit, and to David's parents, who appeared decades older than they had the last time Meena had seen them.

Of course they did. Because their son was dead. Although they didn't know it yet.

Meena swallowed and tried to plaster a warm smile of greeting on her face.

It was difficult to do so, however, when she was so hyperaware of Alaric Wulf behind her. She'd never forget the look in his eyes when he'd seen the scarf she'd tied around her neck to hide the ugly bruise David's bite mark had left behind. She'd thought he was going to throw the coffee he was holding right into her face.

That he was only half wrong about how the bite had been acquired—since she *had* seen Lucien last night—caused her cheeks to burn. She wondered if he noticed.

"Ah, here's Ms. Harper now, along with one of my associates, Mr. Wulf." That gaze of Abraham's was like a pair of lasers beneath the overhang of those shaggy eyebrows, so unkempt that they gave the appearance of a disordered mind.

And yet Meena knew better than anyone that Dr. Holtzman's mind was very ordered indeed.

And that meant she was in big trouble. Because though she'd finally done her duty and reported last night's "vampire-related incident," she'd only reported *one* of them. She was determined to keep Lucien's name out of it for as long as she could.

But between Abraham Holtzman and Alaric Wulf, both of whom were the most stubborn men—in their different ways—she'd ever encountered, she wasn't certain how long she was going to be able to.

"Sorry I'm late," Meena said, nervously, looking around. This was just like a scene from a TV crime show where they interviewed murder suspects.

But there were no two-way mirrors in the Freewell Police Department's conference room, just a bank of windows looking out over the pleasantly landscaped lawn in front of the station house, and some photos scattered across the table . . . photos of David and Brianna that Meena presumed the Delmonicos had brought along with them.

They were recent studio portraits in which the baby was only a few months old. The attractive couple looked blissfully happy, beaming into the camera without a hair—or tooth—out of place.

David's specialty was veneers. He'd always wanted to put some over Meena's slightly crooked front teeth, but when he'd explained that to do so, he'd actually have to cut into her gums, she'd declined the offer.

"I'm still not sure," Mrs. Delmonico was saying in a querulous voice, "why she had to bring so many lawyers along when all she said was that she just wanted to meet us here to—"

"We're all just here to help, Mrs. Delmonico," Abraham interrupted, in a soothing voice. "Ms. Harper, meet Detective Rogerson—" Abraham gestured to the tired-looking woman, who gave the impression of wishing she'd rather be anywhere but sitting with all of them. Meena didn't blame her. "And of course you remember the Delmonicos."

As David's parents' gazes landed on her, bruised and bewildered, Meena lost all ability to control her mouth. Her smile vanished, and she could only mutter, "Hello," softly as she lowered herself onto the hard plastic chair Abraham offered her. She barely managed to keep herself from murmuring *Sorry for your loss.*

Because of course the Delmonicos didn't yet know they'd had a loss . . . perhaps two.

And *she* certainly wasn't going to be the one to tell them.

"So, Ms. Harper," the detective said in a businesslike tone. She flicked a glance at Alaric, who, rather than taking a seat at the conference table, perched himself on the windowsill, where he could best take in the view. He then whipped out his cell phone to check his text messages, appearing not in the least interested in the proceedings.

The detective looked away, then flipped open a notepad in front of her. "Mrs. Delmonico here says you might have some information about her son, who didn't come home last night. What can you tell us about that?"

Meena glanced quickly at Abraham.

"Um," she said. "I thought . . . on TV, they always interview the suspects in separate rooms."

Detective Rogerson stared at her unsmilingly, her pen poised over her notepad. "This isn't TV, and you aren't suspected of anything, Ms. Harper, because at this time, no crime has been committed. Unless you're the one who vandalized Mr. Delmonico's car in the city last night."

"Well, that is hardly likely," Abraham said, "given my client's small stature and the extreme strength it would have taken to do the sort of damage—"

Detective Rogerson shot Abraham a look. He smiled at her pleasantly.

"Well," Meena said hastily, "that's true. I had nothing to do with what happened to David's car."

Realizing she'd already made a strategic mistake, Meena was careful to look Detective Rogerson in the eye the whole time she was speaking so that she could not be accused of lying. She'd read this was one way the police could detect if you were telling the truth.

Then she explained how she and David had arranged to meet the night before so that she could give him the "belongings" of his that she'd found, and that afterward she had sat in David's parked car for a few moments, just to "talk." It was then, she said, that she'd noticed David was a little intoxicated. She'd felt it best that David not drive home, and he'd agreed.

Mrs. Delmonico inhaled sharply at this, even though Meena avoided mentioning the rest of it—what David had done to her in his car. No way was she bringing *that* up . . . not ever. Especially not in front of Mrs. Delmonico, who really was wearing her pearls, exactly the way Meena had pictured. She was twisting them so tightly as she listened to Meena that her fingertips had turned purple. Meena half expected the strand to break at any moment.

Then there was David's dad, who looked close to tears, his nose redder with broken capillaries (from drinking, Meena suspected) than ever. The couple looked upset enough at her mentioning David's drinking—even though she'd significantly downplayed it.

There was *no way* she was going to make things worse by saying he'd attacked her, too. They'd never have believed it, for one thing.

And for another, now that she was employed by the Palatine—a *secret* demon-hunting branch of the Vatican—she couldn't. She was forbidden by her employers from ever admitting in front of civilians the existence of vampires.

So even if she'd wanted to, she could not say that David had not only been drunk, but had apparently been turned into a member of the undead, and that he had attacked her.

But of course she didn't want to.

Because what Meena wanted, above all, was to keep from dragging Lucien into any of this. Not only was none of it his fault—it was *her* screwup, after all—but he'd risked his own neck by coming out of hiding after so many months just to rescue her from David, when he apparently—for reasons he would not reveal to her, but it seemed obvious enough—was not even well.

And now Alaric Wulf was involved. Alaric was one of the Palatine's best guards, and as such, had heard a lot of stories from a lot of victims, many of whom were as deeply in love with the vampires who were using them as human feed bags as she was with Lucien, and wouldn't hesitate to lie to protect them.

But this was different. Lucien hadn't been the one who'd attacked her last night. And he didn't want to eat her. He loved her.

That's why she had to keep his name out of this. Even though he'd been the one who'd saved her, no one at the Palatine—particularly Alaric—would understand that. None of what had happened had been Lucien's fault.

But they'd end up blaming Lucien, just the same. The Palatine, just like any bureaucracy, had its blind spots.

Meena had hoped that by phoning Abraham directly after receiving Mrs. Delmonico's call, and not the Palatine's main emergency line, she could keep things under some semblance of control. She was just, she'd explained, filling him in about an unfortunate incident that had occurred the night before that she had, perhaps, not handled as well as she could, though there was probably nothing to worry about. Nothing at all.

Well, maybe a *little* something . . .

She should have known from the concern in Abraham's voice as he'd questioned her so urgently on the phone that he would bring Alaric in on it. Alaric, who, when she'd been unable to hold back her tears outside, had seemed so uncertain what to do, but had nevertheless stood there with his arms held tightly around her, sturdy and tall and strong as a tree, which nothing could ever sway or knock over or bend.

He'd even smelled fresh and cool and leafy, in a way. Oh God. Why had she ever called the Palatine in the first place? She didn't know.

But they'd have found out anyway. They always did.

When Meena finished her halting narrative, she glanced nervously down at Detective Rogerson's notepad. She happened to be sitting at an angle from which she could see exactly what it contained, though she was certain the detective didn't know this.

That's how she was able to discern, with some surprise, that the detective had been drawing a very detailed portrait of a ladybug. The ladybug was dressed in a top hat, complete with a tuxedo and tails.

"So the last time you saw David," Detective Rogerson said, in a bored voice, "he was slightly intoxicated, and walking toward Houston Street to get a cab to Penn Station?"

"Yes," Meena said. She tried to sound urgent, but not too urgent. "I have to say, I'm a little worried about Brianna. My best friend, Leisha, had a baby six months ago, and she would never, ever spend a night away from home, especially without calling. I'll admit I don't know Brianna well, but I think it's really odd—"

Detective Rogerson, however, had already dropped her gaze. She was beginning to draw a second ladybug.

"And you don't know anything about how his vehicle ended up getting vandalized?"

"Vandalized?" Mr. Delmonico sounded indignant. "The police officer on the phone said the driver's-side door was literally *ripped off its hinges* and tossed onto the sidewalk, and the windshield smashed. I'd hardly call that vandalized. That was a brand-new Volvo V50. That's more like assault, is what that is."

Detective Rogerson flicked a glance at him. "Yes," she said. "But the car's stereo and registration and even the baby seat were still inside. According to your conversation with the New York police this morning, nothing appeared to be missing."

"Except the owner," Mrs. Delmonico cried. Her husband leaned over to squeeze her hand. "And his wife! She's missing, too." She reached out for one of the photos and held it up. "What about her? Doesn't anyone care about her?"

"We care, Mrs. Delmonico," Detective Rogerson said. Meena saw that the detective was adding a bridal veil to the second ladybug. "That's why we're all here. In the meantime, the best thing you can do is stay by the phone."

"Their own phone," Meena said.

Detective Rogerson glanced at her. "I beg your pardon?"

"Well," Meena said, "they're sitting by their son's phone, at his house."

"Precisely," Abraham said quickly. "David isn't likely to call himself, is he? So Mr. and Mrs. Delmonico should go home to their own house and sit by their own phone."

Detective Rogerson looked from Meena to Abraham and then back again. Meena was aware that Alaric had finally glanced up from his cell phone and was staring at her. Had he figured it out? She supposed he had. Well, he was going to eventually.

Detective Rogerson shrugged and returned to her ladybug wedding scene. "Yes," she said in a bored voice. "Absolutely. Nobody missing ever called themselves."

Mrs. Delmonico looked scandalized. "But all of David Junior's things are at *his* house!"

"We'd be happy to go with you to David's house now," Meena said, "and help you move the baby's things to your home. Just for the time being."

The Delmonicos looked completely stunned at this suggestion. So did Alaric, who had not returned his gaze to his cell-phone screen.

"Er," Mr. Delmonico said. "There's no need for that. I'm sure we can manage on our own—"

"No, no," Abraham said firmly. "We'd be delighted."

"Well," Mr. Delmonico said, looking impressed. "Your firm certainly appears to be very full service."

"Oh, don't you see what they're doing?" Mrs. Delmonico's voice lashed out like a whip. "They're trying to get us to forget the fact that Meena left our son, drunk and defenseless, alone in the middle of New York City, to be set upon by hooligans!"

Mr. Delmonico flung a startled looked over at Meena.

"I wouldn't say *that's* what we're doing," Meena murmured. "I want to help—"

"He's probably lying in an alley somewhere," Mrs. Delmonico cried, "bleeding, because she got him drunk and left him there for thieves to rob blind. And it's all her fault."

"Considering that your son is the one who showed up drunk to the meeting Ms. Harper had scheduled with him," Abraham said, in a matter-of-fact voice, "and then made unwanted sexual advances toward her, I think you might want to reconsider that charge, madam."

Mr. and Mrs. Delmonico instantly began sputtering in outrage. Detective Rogerson's pen stilled on her notepad, while Alaric raised his eyebrows. Abraham Holtzman, however, only looked at the ceiling.

Meena wanted to drop her head into her hands and disappear, but unfortunately, she could not. This was a piece of information she'd shared with Abraham in confidence. She hadn't expected him to blurt it out in front of David's parents like that.

But she supposed, as her "lawyer," he'd had no choice.

"That . . . that is outrageous!" Mrs. Delmonico cried, looking close to tears. "My son would never in his life do such a—"

"Meena," Abraham interrupted. "I know you don't want to say anything negative about David in front of his parents, for fear of upsetting them. But it's important you tell the truth so the detective here can get the whole picture."

"I did," Meena said quickly. "I *did* tell the truth." She gave him an arctic stare.

"Did something happen between you and David that you aren't telling us, Ms. Harper?" Detective Rogerson asked curiously.

"No," Meena said. "There's nothing that I'm not telling you."

"Well, there must be *something*," the detective said. "Because you're turning bright red."

Meena realized she'd completely misjudged Detective Rogerson. Sketching those ladybugs had not been a sign that she wasn't concentrating on the interview.

She'd been sketching them because doodling helped her concentrate better.

"Well, I wouldn't call it *something*." Meena kept her gaze on one of the photos of Brianna's bright, smiling face in the center of the table. "David was a little drunk, like I said, and yes, all right, he tried to kiss me, but . . . adjusting to life after a new baby can be hard on some couples." She said this last bit very quickly. "My friend Leisha, the one I was telling you about, who had the baby, says things haven't exactly been the same between her and her husband, Adam, you know, since their baby Jeanie came, even though he's a great guy, a truly devoted stay-at-home dad. I mean, she says they haven't been out to dinner *once* since the baby came . . ."

As she realized that everyone was staring at her, Meena's voice trailed off. She could actually feel herself blushing again.

"Not," she added, "that David said anything like this about Brianna."

"So," Detective Rogerson said, "I take it you do not want to file any sort of sexual assault charges against David Delmonico at this time?"

"Oh my God." Mrs. Delmonico flung a hand over her mouth. Her husband put a comforting arm around her, then pulled her toward him.

Though all anyone could talk about on the local news were the unseasonably high temperatures outside, the air-conditioning in the Freewell, New Jersey, PD had apparently been turned off. It was warm in the conference room. Everyone had a thin sheen of perspiration across their foreheads.

Still, Meena felt chilled, despite the cardigan she'd pulled over her sleeveless dress.

"N-no," she stammered. "Not at all. And I'm so sorry, but I don't know anything more that might help you find him other than what I've told you."

"Of course she doesn't," Abraham said, in his stern attorney's voice. He actually did have a law degree. Now he was packing the many legal pads he'd brought with him back into his briefcase. "This is clearly a personal matter between the Delmonicos' son and his wife. It's unfortunate, of course, but I'm sure the two of them will be home as soon as they work it out. In the meantime, like Ms. Harper said, we would be happy to help you move the baby's things from—"

"No!" Mrs. Delmonico cried. "You've done enough!"

Her husband said, in a calmer voice, "Thank you, but I think what my wife means is that we have enough family in the area to help us right now."

"Right," Abraham said. "Well, Detective Rogerson, if there's anything more my client can do to be of assistance in your investigation, be sure to contact me, and she'll be happy to . . ."

His voice faded away as David's mother turned to face Meena, her blue eyes snapping like Venus flytraps.

"If you know what's happened to my son, Meena Harper," she hissed, "you have to tell. I know you know things. David told me after his brain tumor was removed that you knew it was there before they'd ever even diagnosed it. And we all know you knew about his father. So you tell me. *Tell me what's happened to my son.*"

Meena froze. She didn't blame this woman for hating her. She hadn't done anything except try to help David . . . who hadn't really deserved her help in the end, it was true.

But he hadn't deserved to die. Not the way he had. And his poor wife . . .

Meena couldn't help glancing at the enlarged, eight-by-ten glossy studio portraits lying on the middle of the table. Brianna looked so pretty, and happy, and hopeful.

"I'm sorry," she said, lifting her gaze toward Mrs. Delmonico. Tears sprang into her eyes. "I'm so, so sorry . . ."

Suddenly a strong pair of hands gripped her shoulders. Someone was forcing her to stand up. Alaric.

"I hope your son turns up soon," Alaric was saying in his deep voice to the Delmonicos as he steered Meena from the conference room. "Your daughter-in-law, too. Good-bye."

Meena realized she was shaking.

She tried to hide it. She kept her arms folded as she, Alaric, and Abraham left the building.

But she couldn't hide her suddenly shallow, ragged breathing.

David wasn't going to turn up soon, or ever again.

But Brianna. Where was Brianna? She *might* turn up soon . . .

And when she did, she was going to be hungry.

Chapter Ten

"Well, that didn't go as badly as I feared it would," Abraham Holtzman said as he slid behind the wheel and started the engine.

"I wouldn't know." Alaric put down the window of the front passenger-side door so that he could stick his elbow out of it. He had never liked being cooped up in a small space, Meena had noticed, a characteristic that had only gotten worse since the two of them had been trapped together beneath a collapsed wall inside St. George's Cathedral. "Considering no one will tell me what is going on."

"Wulf." Abraham shot Alaric a frustrated look. "Remember that conversation we had yesterday in my office about your interpersonal skills? There's a good reason you are kept out of the loop regarding certain matters."

"Then why bring me along at all?" Alaric demanded.

"I would think that would be obvious," Abraham said. "I need you to escort Meena back to the city. She's evidently become popular with our fanged friends once again." He smiled at Meena in the rearview mirror. "Don't worry, my dear. Alaric will take very good care of you. I'm sure you'll recall what an excellent job he did last time."

Meena, hiding her shaking hands between her knees, felt her heart sink. She was going to have *Alaric* around, 24/7? Oh, this was just perfect.

"Yes," she said, with feigned enthusiasm. "Great. And I'm sorry that I didn't handle this by the book. But I don't think it's necessary to reassign Alaric from his normal duties. I'm sure David coming after me like that was an isolated, freak incident—"

"*David?*" Alaric spun around as much as his seat belt and the confined seat would allow, in order to stare, wide-eyed, at Meena. "*David's* the one who bit you?"

"Yes," Meena said. "Of course *David* is the one who bit me. What did you think?" Even though she knew perfectly well.

"Just that it's a bit coincidental," Alaric said, "for anyone to have had *two* boyfriends who've turned out to be vampires."

"You're one to talk," she said, sticking out her chin. "Don't think Carolina didn't tell about the time you got tricked into getting it on with that succubus in Prague. I heard they practically had to peel you off her—"

"That situation," Alaric said, scowling, "has been grossly exaggerated."

"Uh," Meena said, "I don't think so. Carolina showed me the video—"

Alaric looked furious. "That was nearly a decade ago," he said. "And that succubus didn't happen to be evil incarnate, the ruler of all that is—"

"Don't you dare," Meena snapped, "bring Lucien into this."

"Children," Abraham scolded them as he drove, "please. Alaric, you mustn't be so hard on Meena. Yes, it would have spared us a great deal of trouble if she'd simply called headquarters last night when all of this actually occurred. I would hope by now she'd consider the Palatine her family, and as such, people she can turn to in times of duress. But I also understand why she might have been feeling vulnerable and even traumatized, considering the . . . er, personal nature of the incident, as you did, Alaric, when it happened to you. To have to kill someone with whom you were once close . . . well, that's a nightmare few of us have ever had to endure, and to which all of us might react differently—"

Alaric had turned back toward Meena. His blue-eyed gaze was as penetrating as an X-ray.

"You *staked* him?" he asked, looking astonished.

Meena narrowed her eyes at him. "Yes," she said, waiting for him to ask what had happened to her theory about the lion having to slay the ass in order to live, and how that didn't mean one had the right to kill all the lions.

But he didn't. Instead, he only raised his eyebrows and said, "Nice," sounding impressed. Then he turned back around in his seat to stare out the window.

But she noticed that he was smiling.

And her heart sank even more.

"I'm certain it must have been absolutely terrifying for you, Meena," Abraham was saying comfortingly. "You mustn't blame yourself for what happened, or for your failure to abide by standard Palatine protocol afterward. I'm sure you weren't even thinking straight. I presume you locked yourself inside the car to get away from him? And he tore the door off in order to get at you? That's how it occurred?"

Meena, who had never considered how she was going to explain what had happened with the car door, bowed her head so he could not see her expression in the rearview mirror and said, "Yes." She was quite certain she could not lie to Abraham Holtzman's face.

"It's a wonder to me you were even able to make it out of bed this morning," Abraham said admiringly. "We'll be sure to schedule some post-traumatic stress counseling for you with Dr. Fiske."

Alaric let out a sound that seemed suspiciously like a snort from where Meena sat. She knew Dr. Fiske was his therapist, and that he didn't like him. But she wasn't certain why. Alaric never talked about his therapy sessions.

Her voice catching, she said, "I didn't even realize he was dead until he was on top of me. And after I staked him, I just thought . . . well, that it was over. I always meant to report it. I just thought it could wait. I didn't find out until this morning that David's wife was missing, when his mother called me to ask where he was. Now I know it must have been his wife's death I was sensing, not David's . . ."

"No worries," Abraham said lightly. "Most newly infected vampires do return to their homes within the first twenty-four to forty-eight hours of awakening in their transformed bodies, if they aren't immediately provided with food. I ordered an extermination team to be assembled and dispatched from headquarters to David's home the moment you phoned, Meena. We're meeting them there now, while the Delmonicos are occupied at the police station. With any luck, we should have the wife taken care of by this afternoon."

Taken care of. She knew what that meant. Tears prickled Meena's nose. She didn't know what was wrong with her. All this crying was so pointless. She lifted her wrist to dab at her eyes.

"We're going to David's house?" she asked.

Abraham glanced at her questioningly in the rearview mirror. "That's all right, isn't it?"

"Oh," she said quickly, "it's fine."

It wasn't fine. She did not want to see Brianna Delmonico *taken care of.* And she definitely did not want to see where David Delmonico had lived—and had presumably once been happy, before she'd staked him. She just wanted to go home, get back into bed, and go to sleep.

Only she couldn't even do that, because then she'd dream of Lucien.

"Good," Abraham said with a smile. "The two of you know what this means, don't you?"

"It means that the Dracul are back, and still want Meena's blood," Alaric said darkly.

Meena inhaled to protest that this was not what it meant it all, but Abraham beat her to it.

"On the contrary," he said. "This whole attack smacks of an amateurism that I would think the Dracul—if they were still around, which I do not believe—would consider beneath them."

"Exactly," Meena said. "And though I know you've never believed me about this, the Dracul were forbidden to murder their prey, unless they intended to turn them into one of their own kind. And David definitely wanted to kill me."

"I don't know," Alaric said skeptically. "Tricking the victim into a false sense of security by turning a former lover into one of them seems exactly like something a Dracul would do, if you ask me."

"But attacking Meena?" Abraham shook his head. "No, no. Think of the anger—the retribution—the prince rained down upon his own clan for hurting Meena the last time. That was truly a fearsome display of aggression. Only a clan that didn't witness—or hear about—it would dare risk Lucien Antonescu's wrath in such a way again . . . not after what he did to his own minions."

"True," Alaric said. Meena noticed that Alaric, who still had his elbow out the window, as usual, had turned the side-view mirror to point at her. She saw that he was staring at her neck. She looked away.

"But the prince doesn't seem to be around," Alaric went on. "So he's hardly likely to be raining down much of anything on anyone these days."

"Which makes this an exciting development," Abraham said. Then, with a nervous glance at Meena, he added, "Er, apart from the tragedy that a young mother is missing and could be a demon, and the death of Meena's friend. But it means a completely new and different clan may be moving into the Dracul's former North American territory. We've theorized, of course, that this was likely to happen, because the eradication of the Dracul here and in Europe has left ample feeding grounds ripe for the taking . . . particularly since Lucien Antonescu seems truly to be gone. It was really just a matter of time—and which clan. Personally, I felt the Aswang from the Philippines would be most likely to take hold—"

Alaric shook his head. "Not likely. You know they don't like the cold."

"But," Abraham said, "it's still summer. And we can't rule out the allure of the Pine Barrens . . . The Pine Barrens of southern New Jersey," he explained, looking at Meena in the rearview mirror, "has long been considered a hellmouth, due to the fact that they are where the New Jersey Devil fled soon after its birth."

"Wait." Meena, who'd been born in New Jersey, couldn't believe what she was hearing. "The New Jersey Devil isn't just the mascot of a hockey team? It's *real*?"

"Unfortunately," Alaric muttered.

"Quite real," Abraham said. "Malevolent beings, you see, expend enormous energy every time they perform one of their nefarious deeds, and then they need to draw more of it—energy, that is—from certain places thought to be linked directly to Satan. The New Jersey Devil is one of those creatures, a cryptid, bipedal, with wings that, according to the most popular legend—though of course we've never been able to prove it—was the thirteenth child of a Mrs. Leeds, who was understandably put out with Mr. Leeds for having already impregnated her a dozen times before. Upon its birth in 1735, she was said to have shouted to the midwife that this particular child could 'go to the devil.' Well, it didn't. It became one instead, and flew up the chimney and off to the Pine Barrens, where it's lived ever since, making those woods, and New Jersey in general, quite an attractive gathering place for the forces of evil—"

"I think we should change the subject," Alaric interrupted, having caught a glimpse of Meena's face.

"Oh," Abraham said. "Yes. I apologize . . ."

But it was too late. Meena's mind was spinning. Malevolent beings drew energy from places thought to be linked directly to the devil? In all her reading about demons, Meena had never encountered anything about this.

But she supposed it made sense. Why else did the Palatine ask Father Bernard—or the rabbis and other religious leaders with whom they worked—to perform blessings on the homes in which they'd found paranormal entities?

But if places of pure evil—hellmouths, such as the home of the New Jersey Devil—existed, wouldn't that mean, logically, that their opposite existed, as well? Places of pure good?

She opened her mouth to ask, then became aware that Abraham had continued speaking.

"Once Brianna Delmonico's been detained and quarantined," he was saying, "we'll extract any information she holds about who might have infected David, and, of course, collect whatever DNA we can, since finding the host parasite is always key in stopping any spread of a new vampiric outbreak—"

Detained? Quarantined? That's what was going to happen to David's wife?

Meena had never exactly liked Brianna—she was the woman David had dumped her for, after all. How was Meena *supposed* to like her?

But she wouldn't wish such horrible things on anyone, much less the owner of the heart-shaped face she'd seen beaming up at her from the center of all that curly blond hair in the studio portrait.

So when the car stopped, and a sultry woman's voice announced from the dashboard, "You have arrived at your destination," and Meena looked up and saw the home in which David Delmonico had lived . . .

. . . for a moment, she couldn't breathe.

With its sweeping green lawn, three-car garage, and grand-looking steps leading toward the double front door, David and Brianna's house looked like an estate. Or a country club. All that was missing was a parking valet.

But even if the two-bedroom apartment she shared with her brother—the second bedroom was actually little more than an alcove—was slightly cramped, and the only thing they had that remotely resembled a lawn was the building's roof, she was glad to live there, and not here.

"How lovely," Abraham said, from the front seat. "I do enjoy getting out of the city from time to time. You forget what grass looks like, don't you?"

Meena swallowed. How could they not see it? Was she really the only one?

Because there was no life inside this house. There hadn't been for a long time.

There was no good either.

Only evil.

Chapter Eleven

We are *not* going in there," Meena said firmly.

"No," Alaric said. "*We* aren't. You and I are going back to the city. We're just dropping Abraham off."

"What?" Meena grasped the back of Abraham's headrest as he unbuckled his seat belt. "You're not going in there. Are you?"

"Of course I am," Abraham said, chuckling a little. "Alaric's temperament, as we all know, isn't particularly suited to missions that require the subject to be taken alive. Why?" Abraham smiled at Meena. "Is that a problem?"

"Yes," Meena said. Only she couldn't say which was causing her heart to pound more: the idea of leaving an old man to hunt a vampire in such a sinister-looking house, or having to spend time alone in a car with Alaric Wulf. "Sort of. I just think it would make more sense, since Alaric has so much experience in the field, for him to—"

"Ms. Harper," Abraham interrupted gently. "I've been doing this a great many more years than Alaric. Despite outward appearances, I do know my way around a demon infestation. But I'm touched by your concern. Now, tell the truth. Is this a roundabout way of telling me you've had one of your visions?"

Meena, flushing, said, "Something like that. It's just that ... well, I know Brianna looked very sweet in the photos. But you just said New Jersey is a hellmouth. And last night, David was like someone I'd never met—"

"Of course he was," Abraham said to her consolingly. "He'd lost his humanity. He was a creature of darkness, without a soul, incapable of compassion or pity. You did well to put him out of his misery. When we discover what clan he was from—after we interrogate his wife—it will help explain a little about his behavior, I hope."

Meena nibbled worriedly on a thumbnail. She knew the Palatine considered all vampires exactly that—soulless creatures.

And David *had* been like that. No doubt about it.

Of course, she'd never gotten that feeling from Lucien, who was also—allegedly—without a soul. Her old neighbors, his cousins, the Antonescus, hadn't been that way either. They'd once saved her dog from being murdered by the same group of rampaging Dracul that had destroyed her apartment.

Alaric knew it, too.

But he didn't say anything in their defense. Instead, he unbuckled his seat belt and got out of the car. Now that he was going to have a chance behind the wheel, he looked relaxed and happy, despite the fact that the car was a hybrid and not the kind of gas-guzzling sports vehicle he preferred.

"I do appreciate your anxiety on my behalf, Meena," Abraham went on. He had reached into the back of the car, pulled his briefcase up from the floor, and opened it to reveal a secret compartment, from which he removed a pistol, several extremely lethal-looking stakes, a vial of holy water, and a large crucifix, all of which he began tucking into various pockets of his suit.

"But while I may seem to you like an old man who has spent too much time behind a desk, I assure you I can handle myself in the face of evil," he said. "You might recall I took out a good many of your previous ex-boyfriend's clan that night at St. George's. This little outing is not going to be much of a challenge in comparison."

"I don't know," Meena murmured. She looked anxiously at the house. "I have a bad feeling about this."

"I do, too," Alaric leaned in the window to say. "Abraham's about to do battle with a housewife from New Jersey, and there's no reality television crew here to film it."

"It's not funny," Meena said. "I think we should stay here to help. What if the Delmonicos show up? I could—"

Abraham opened his car door. "Alaric is attending the opening of the Vatican Treasures show at the Metropolitan Museum of Art, a show I know he's anxious not to miss." Alaric rolled his eyes as Abraham stepped from the car. "And in light of recent events, it would make sense for you to attend with him, Meena, since I must say, I'm uneasy at the idea at your being left alone after what happened last evening . . ."

Meena said quickly, "I think I've already proved I'm more than capable of taking care of myself, Dr. Holtzman."

"Yes," Abraham said. "You certainly did. But let's not press our luck. And there's been a request—" Abraham broke off as his phone chirped. He looked down at the screen, then said, "Oh. They got a late start, apparently, then ran into some traffic. But they should be here in a few minutes."

"I think I'll wait here," Meena began to say. She started to open the back door of the car. "I don't think it's a good idea for you to—"

But Alaric was already behind the wheel and pulling away from the curb.

"When you're finally ready to admit there's a paranormal connection to all those missing tourists," he yelled to Abraham, "call me."

"I won't," Abraham said, waving. "Because there's no proof that there is."

"Right," Alaric muttered sarcastically under his breath, and pressed more heavily on the gas. "We'll see."

"Wait," Meena said. She'd barely managed to pull her foot back into the car and close the door before Alaric took off. "What's the matter with you? We can't just leave him there. He could be killed. What missing tourists?" She clambered from the backseat into the front. "Alaric, what is going on? What are you not telling me?"

"A hell of a lot less than you're not telling me," he snapped.

"I've told you everything." Meena twisted around in the seat and watched as Abraham trudged up David Delmonico's impeccably groomed front lawn, then disappeared around the corner of the house. The bad feeling she'd had about all of this—not just getting attacked by David, or picking up the phone and hearing Mrs. Delmonico's voice, or getting out of the cab and seeing Alaric Wulf—was definitely getting worse, not better. "When something horrible happens to Abraham because we just abandoned him at a hellmouth, I'm telling everyone it was your fault."

"My fault." He laughed, but there was no humor in the sound. "I like that."

"It certainly wasn't *my* fault," she said. "I tried to warn you—"

"Oh yes," Alaric said. "Let's talk about that. Let's talk about how open and communicative you've been about all of this, shall we?"

"Well, I have been," Meena said, although she did feel a flash of guilt. Though only a slight one. She couldn't tell Alaric the whole truth, for obvious reasons. But Lucien's part in the story didn't matter. She'd been up front about all the important things. "What tourists were you talking about?"

"Oh no," he said. "If you won't do me the courtesy, after everything we've been through together, of telling me what's really going on, why should I tell you?"

Meena stared out the windshield with a dumbfounded expression that wasn't entirely feigned. "What are you talking about? I *did* tell you what's really going on. Maybe Abraham was right and I should have called last night, but—"

"You were not sitting alone inside that vehicle when its door got ripped off," Alaric said. He pulled his arm inside the car and pushed the power button to close the window. This revealed to Meena how deeply serious he was. He hated driving with the windows closed. "You couldn't have been, because there's no conceivable way a vampire would have gotten out of a car while his prey was still inside it."

Meena kept her gaze straight ahead, stubbornly saying nothing.

But the feeling of dread that had been growing inside her seemed to wrap around her heart like roots from a particularly fast-growing and poisonous plant.

"Therefore, I'm thinking there was a third person at the scene," Alaric went on. "Someone whose name you've conspicuously left out of your little tale, someone who, as Abraham so aptly put it, rained down some pretty serious retribution upon all those minions of his who last dared to hurt you. Someone who has gone by a number of names over the five hundred years he's been active, but lately has been going by Lucien Antones—"

"Stop it!" Meena whirled in her seat to face him. "Just stop it. If you knew all along he was there, why didn't you just say so? And that's still no reason to have left Abraham. Can we *please* go back? I really do have a horrible feeling about him, and that place—"

"For God's sake, Meena," Alaric said. "Abraham can take care of himself. It's *you* I'm worried about. And you know as well as I do that I am not letting you out of this car until you tell me the truth. All of it, this time. So start at the beginning. Because I have all day."

Something in his voice—the seriousness of his expression—the fact that she knew he meant every word . . . he really *wouldn't* let her out of the car until she told him what he wanted to know—caused her to give up. It was pointless. He would wear her down, one way or another.

"Fine," she said. "David was trying to kill me. Lucien showed up out of nowhere . . . and I'm lucky he did, because he saved my life. But I swear last night is the first time I've seen him since last spring—"

Alaric's knuckles went white on the steering wheel. "God*dammit,* Meena," he said, refusing even to look at her.

"That's the truth, Alaric," she said, desperate to make him understand. "I swear. And Lucien didn't bite me, and he didn't turn David, and whatever is going on back in Freewell, I'm positive Lucien doesn't know anything about it—"

"How can that be?" Alaric demanded. "He's the *prince of darkness,* Meena. He has to know. He knows everything every demonic entity is doing. That's his *job.* That's why he exists."

"It isn't like that, Alaric," she said. "I know that's how it's supposed to be, but it isn't. He didn't know last time, when his own brother—"

"Is that what he told you?" Alaric asked. "What else did he tell you last night? That his love for you still burns like a flame that will never be extinguished and that every moment apart is like an open stabbing flesh wound? Lines, by the way, he's given scores of women just like you. Just because they're all dead now and there's no one left to remember them and he thinks your love has redeemed him doesn't mean he can be allowed to get away with their murders."

Meena glared at him. "Actually, that wasn't what he said at all." Not in so many words, anyway. "And you don't need to give me 'the speech,' Alaric. I'm not one of those silly teenage girls you're always having to perform interventions on in order to convince them to stop being passive feed bags to their user vampire boyfriends and go home to their parents. I actually work for the organization that does that, remember? I helped write the latest round of speeches."

"Then why are you so quick to believe everything he says?" he asked. "You're aware there's no such thing as a vegetarian vampire, right? He has to drink human blood in order to stay alive."

"Lucien gave up human blood a long time ago. Well, I mean, he drinks it, but not from live humans. Only from blood banks."

"Is that what he told you?" Alaric asked again, this time with cynical laughter in his voice. "That's a very cute story. And just where do you think he is getting that blood now, Meena? The accounting department has found and frozen all of his assets. He doesn't have a cent to his name. Black-market human blood isn't cheap, you know. Use your head instead of your heart. *Where is he getting the blood?*"

Meena had lain awake all night, worrying about this very problem. How was Lucien—penniless now that the Palatine, with brutal ruthlessness, had stripped him not just of his latest identity, but of his substantial fortune as well—purchasing the blood he needed to survive? How could Lucien go on without money, and still remain true to his promise never to take a human life?

She'd felt the cloth of his suit beneath her fingers the night before. It had been as soft as Jack Bauer's underbelly.

Lucien seemed to be living well.

Then she remembered the red heat that had flamed up in his eyes after he'd kissed her, and how weak and ill he seemed.

Maybe he wasn't living quite that well after all.

She tried to push this thought from her head.

"Someone must be helping him," she said. It was more a hope than a real conviction. "He must have friends . . ." She thought of her former neighbors, Mary Lou and Emil Antonescu. They had gotten away in the fight at St. George's. The Palatine had yet to trace their current whereabouts—or financial accounts. Surely they wouldn't have left their prince bereft . . .

"Doubtful," Alaric said. "Demons don't have friends. And have you met those pencil pushers in accounting? They leave no stone unturned when it comes to finding funds that might be flowing toward the undead. More likely he's stealing. That would be typical of his kind."

She sucked in her breath.

"Why do you hate him so much?" she asked. "You're always calling him a soulless monster. And yet that night at St. George's, he didn't kill you when he had the chance. In fact, he protected you. And Father Bernard, and Sister Gertrude, and me, and even those firefighters who came to dig us out. Instead, he killed his own kind. Was that the act of a soulless monster? When are you going to admit that not every demon is one hundred percent evil, just like not every human is one hundred percent good? When, Alaric? *When?*"

He tore his gaze from the road to look at her. The bright blue of his eyes never failed to startle her. Occasionally, while they were attending boring staff meetings, their gazes met across the room. Sometimes he raised one of those blond eyebrows—particularly if it was Abraham speaking, delivering one of his sometime pedantic speeches—and she had to stifle a laugh, because he looked exactly like a mischievous schoolboy.

It was always hard to believe on those occasions that he'd ruthlessly whacked off the heads of as many of Lucien's relatives as he actually had.

But she'd seen him do it, and knew that his boyish expression could turn deadly serious in a split second.

It did so as she stared at him in the car on their way back from Freewell.

"I think I know how your boyfriend has been keeping himself alive since the last time we saw him," he said.

"Oh, really?" she asked. It was warm inside the car, because the air-conditioning wasn't on. There was just the warm rush of air from his window, which he'd finally lowered, causing her hair and the ends of her pink scarf to whip around. "Enlighten me."

"I will," he said. "But I'm going to warn you right now, when I'm done, you're going to wish I hadn't told you. And it's going to be because deep down, you know it's true."

"I highly doubt that," she said. "But go ahead and tell me anyway."

Except it turned out that he was right. When he was through telling her, she really did wish he hadn't.

Chapter Twelve

In the four centuries since Europeans first set foot on the island that had come to be known as Manhattan, Lucien Antonescu had watched them try to tame the stream that flowed down the center of Fifth Avenue.

The stream—known to the island's original inhabitants, the Lenape Indians, as Mannette, misspelled and mispronounced by later Dutch settlers as Minetta—was considered an abomination to city planners . . . but not because they, unlike those Dutch settlers, understood what the word *Mannette* actually meant:

Devil's Water.

Though the stream was filled with trout, the Lenape gave it a wide berth. It didn't take long for those early settlers to discover why . . . and how the brook came to earn its curious name. Soon they, too, were avoiding it. Because though the fish were plentiful, the cost of catching them was too high . . . as the bodies of children who'd fallen into the seemingly shallow water, then inexplicably drowned, attested.

Over the course of several centuries, Lucien watched as city engineers attempted to wall up the Minetta Stream, then pave over it, and finally, construct buildings on top of it.

Bubbling up from an underground spring located on East Twentieth Street, the brook originally ran through the center of Washington Square Park, meandered through the West Village, then let out via Spring Street into the Hudson River, which separates Manhattan from New Jersey . . . a distance of roughly twenty-seven blocks, or two and a half miles.

None of the efforts to force the Minetta Stream underground

worked. All it took for it to rise once again was a good strong downpour. And then . . .

Chaos. Basements flooded. Subway tracks submerged. The stream gushed down the middle of city streets like something unleashed after years of captivity.

When neither rock nor pavement succeeded in damming the stream, a young engineer insisted he'd found a way to convert the water's flow into pipes that would force it out through a fountain that graced the courtyard of a Catholic school from which his fiancée had graduated, and to which her parents were proud donors.

On the day of the fountain's dedication ceremony, however, there was an unexpected storm.

And when the engineer's fiancée bent to turn on the fountain, the stream, instead of trickling gently from the feet of the statue of the Virgin Mary—symbolizing the miracle Saint Bernadette experienced at Lourdes—exploded from them, causing a chunk of the bronze sculpture to lodge itself in the girl's skull, killing her instantly.

The horrified engineer fled the city, and the pipes leading to the stream were filled with cement to prevent their ever being switched on again. The statue of the Virgin Mary, now footless, continued to sit in the school's courtyard, its fountain dry, a testament to man's folly in thinking he could ever triumph over nature.

In the century that followed, the spring—and the reason for the Virgin Mary's lack of feet—was all but forgotten . . .

. . . except to home and business owners in the area who wondered why, every time it rained, their basements flooded. And to exterminators who saw—but tactfully kept to themselves—a marked increase in requests for rat traps in restaurants along the route of the underground stream.

And to Lucien Antonescu.

Because though the stream once known as the Devil's Water now only rose to its former glory when it rained, it still very much existed beneath the ground, its constant ebb and flow carving out over time underground caverns large enough for a grown man to move about in freely.

These secret caverns beneath the Greenwich Village streets provided excellent housing for many creatures . . . especially those that preferred the darkness to the light.

But that wasn't all it provided.

What hardly anyone—not even the exterminators—realized was that
it wasn't just rats that made their home in these dark tunnels. All manner
of beings dwelled there . . . including some that weren't, technically, alive.

Because so few remembered the existence of the Minetta Stream,
or the stories about it, no one human ventured into the caverns its
waters had carved. These caves were unconnected in any way to the
vast, underground, but well-documented maze of used and abandoned
subway, steam, water, gas, and electrical tunnels that existed beneath
Manhattan. The only hint they ever gave of their existence was during
times of particularly dark and violent weather . . .

Lucien Antonescu—during his many visits to the city, from its days
as a bustling Dutch settlement until the turn of the early twentieth century, just before the disaster involving the fountain at St. Bernadette's—
had always felt a strangely magnetic pull toward the Minetta Stream . . .

. . . and not only because, as a creature of darkness himself, he drew
strength from its demonic source, but because he'd admired the way it
had stubbornly refused to succumb to man's plans for it.

It had never occurred to him that one day he, just like that young
engineer, might have to pay for his own arrogance. Because hadn't he,
too, thought that he could control nature? Only in Lucien's case, nature
had been a woman, not a stream.

But the woman he'd chosen was just as volatile a force, it turned
out, as any spring that welled up from under the ground.

And though she hadn't erupted and killed anyone—the opposite,
in fact, since her gift was foretelling when death was imminent, and attempting to prevent it—Meena had, in the end, turned from him.

And the effect on Lucien had been just as devastating.

It was why he was currently living in the caverns carved by the Minetta Stream, hoping the spring would provide him with the thing he
needed most . . . if he couldn't have *her*. If he was truly destined to be the
prince of all evil, it would help actually to *be* truly evil.

He'd always seemed to have problems in that area.

But an ancient spring called the Devil's Water, which had taken the lives of children and a man's beautiful fiancée, would surely solve that.

And since the stream happened to flow beneath the streets along which Meena now lived and worked, where he could watch over and protect her without her actually seeing him, that made it a perfect solution to his problem.

Though she had made it clear at their meeting last spring—that horrible night in her apartment—that his protection was the last thing she wanted, it had always been just as clear to him that it was something she badly needed.

And so he'd watched. And waited.

And last night, when she'd finally needed him, he'd been there for her, exactly the way he'd promised . . .

Although it hadn't gone as well as he might have hoped. He was furious at himself for having shown so much weakness in front of her. The spring didn't appear to be working.

Still, she hadn't rebuffed him the way he'd been sure she would.

She had, however, done *something* to him. He wasn't entirely sure what—mentioning that dream about his mother certainly hadn't helped—but something that had only made things worse.

And now, just when he ought to have had hope—because he'd held her in his arms at last, and felt her heart beating against the place where his own had been half a millennium before, and glimpsed happiness once again—he felt nothing but bone-crushing dread.

Why did she have to mention that dream? And the thing about the angels? *Why?* Especially when he was so close—he knew it. He was sure of it. The stream was going to work. It *had* to.

They wouldn't have called it the Devil's Water for nothing.

When it did work, he'd go back to her. He'd be strong again. He'd explain the reality of the situation. He was the prince of darkness. That was simply how it was, how it always had been, and how it was always going to be.

And she was going to have to deal with it. She wasn't going to have any choice.

Because he wasn't going to give her one.

Chapter Thirteen

At first he thought he was dreaming.

Except that vampires don't dream.

But that was the only possible way he could be hearing his cousin Emil and Emil's wife, Mary Lou, having the following exchange about him, apparently unaware that Lucien was perfectly able to hear them . . . he just couldn't see them, for some reason.

"But what's wrong with him?" Mary Lou wanted to know. "Why won't he open his eyes?"

"It's nothing, Mary Lou," Emil was saying. "He's perfectly all right. He's just resting."

"But why won't he wake up? He looks terrible, frankly. I think there's something wrong with him. Do you think he's been eating? And why is he living *here,* when he could be living in the W Hotel, where they've got over five hundred channels *and* room service. If it's that nonsense about protecting Meena Harper, he could protect her just as well from the W. It makes no earthly sense."

"Mary Lou." Emil sounded frustrated. "I'm hungry, hungover from all those martinis I had during the flight, and really not in the mood to have to explain this again. The prince, like us, is wanted by the Palatine. There's no Palatine unit in Singapore, where we live. But there *is* one here in Manhattan. Even with his new name and identity, his lordship runs a high risk of discover—"

"Emil. I'm not stupid." Lucien could tell from the way that Mary Lou's southern twang was growing more pronounced that she was running out of patience. "None of that explains why he's living in a *cave.*"

With what seemed like a tremendous effort, Lucien lifted his eyelids. He wasn't surprised to see his cousin and his cousin's wife bending over him as he lay on the dark leather chesterfield he had managed to have smuggled, along with other essentials, into the tunnel carved by the Mannette, thanks to a few weak-willed (and therefore easily misguided) deliverymen.

While he'd made sure the men were amply rewarded for their efforts, he'd made equally sure they'd been unable to remember later where the money had come from—or where the furniture they'd delivered had disappeared to.

Failing to murder them for their blood had probably been his first mistake.

Letting himself be seen about the tunnel by other creatures of the night had evidently been his second.

"Hello," Lucien said, sitting up. "I wasn't expecting you."

Mary Lou—who was wearing spike-heeled purple suede thigh-high boots and some kind of fur-trimmed poncho—let out a smothered scream. Emil jumped back as if someone had doused him with holy water.

"We're so very sorry to have disturbed your rest, my lord," he cried. He looked it, too. Sorry, and also fearful for his life. "You . . . you seemed—"

"We thought you were dead," Mary Lou said bluntly. "Except, of course, you already are. So we didn't know what was wrong. You look terrible. Why are you living in a cave?"

Lucien looked from Mary Lou to her husband, whose face, in the light thrown from the wall sconces, looked apoplectic with embarrassment. It occurred to him that his cousin Emil would always be spared one marital worry, at least: he would never have to worry about what his wife was saying about him behind his back. Mary Lou could always be counted on to say exactly what she was thinking directly to his face.

"Never mind that now, Mary Lou," Emil said quickly, darting a furious look at his wife. To Lucien he said, "Sire, you know I would never have intruded on your privacy had not an urgent matter arisen, something I felt could not wait until our weekly call. I hope you don't mind—"

"Not at all," Lucien lied graciously. Though inwardly, his temper boiled. "I'm delighted to see you both. May I get you something to drink? The good thing about living in a cave," he said to Mary Lou as he rose from the couch and went to his wine rack, "is that it's the perfect temperature for storing my collection."

"I beg your pardon, my lord," her husband said apologetically. The look he sent Mary Lou might have skewered her on the spot had she been paying attention to him. But she only had eyes for Lucien. "I don't know what you may have overheard, but Mary Lou was only . . . well, she's simply concerned about you. We both are. And, of course, she's still so young. There are some things about our way of life that she doesn't quite understand—"

"I'm over a hundred and fifty years old," Mary Lou interrupted. "I realize that might be chump change to y'all, but it's not like I haven't been around—"

"I believe," Emil said nervously, "what she means, sire, is that—"

"Don't put words in my mouth, Emil," Mary Lou said. "I'm just going to come out and say it. Because someone needs to. Prince, I completely get it. Sometimes I will admit I sit around and blame myself for everything that happened. If it weren't for me inviting Meena Harper over for dinner that night, the two of you would never have met, and this whole horrible mess would never have happened . . ."

She paused dramatically, as if waiting for someone to jump in and say, *Oh no, Mary Lou. None of this was your fault.*

But Lucien only raised an eyebrow, while Emil stared at her, looking as if he longed to wrap his hands around her neck and choke the life from her.

Unfortunately this effort would have been fruitless, as Mary Lou had died shortly after the Civil War, when she'd met and—unlikely as it seemed—fallen in love with Emil, who Lucien had always suspected of hastening her demise. She seemed never to have harbored any ill feelings toward him for it, however.

"But," Mary Lou went on, a little less self-confidently, "if I hadn't, then you, Lucien, would just have gone on through eternity never knowing what true love is. And then how would you have felt?"

"Considerably better than I've felt over the course of the past six months, I imagine," he replied.

"Oh." Mary Lou looked crestfallen.

"Mary Lou," Emil said, looking angrier than ever. "There's something of vital importance his lordship and I need to discuss, and I don't think you're going to find it at all interesting. Didn't you say you had some shopping to do?" He glanced at Lucien. "I apologize, my lord. I really did beg her not to come with me."

Mary Lou's jaw dropped. "That isn't true," she said. "You begged me *to* come. You know how you hate caves." She looked back at Lucien. "Anyway, regardless, I *am* sorry. I could kill that Meena, I really could. I know I got it all wrong, and now you're the one paying the price. I cannot understand why she would choose working for the *Palatine* instead of immortality—and of course, being with the man she loves."

"*Mary Lou,*" Emil said from between gritted teeth. He tilted his head meaningfully toward the way they'd come in.

"Well, I'm sorry," she said. She shot her husband a look. "Emil says I talk too much. But I just wanted to let you know I'll do whatever I can to help. Because it certainly looks as if you need it." She leaned down to lift her Birkin, then stood up. "I suppose I'd better go shopping now."

"I think that would be for the best," her husband said.

Mary Lou walked stiffly from the cavern, her stilettos—once they'd left the antique carpets Lucien had thrown across the parts of the floor through which water wasn't trickling—clicking on the stone surface. Eventually, the clicking faded into the distance. Lucien pulled the cork on the bottle of wine he held.

"So what did you have to travel halfway around the world to discuss with me, Emil?" he asked as he poured.

"Well . . ." Emil said. Suddenly he seemed to grow reticent, but carried on just the same, compelled by duty, as he had for so many centuries. "*This,* obviously, my lord." He swept a hand to indicate the cavern.

One corner of Lucien's mouth rose. "You agree with your wife, then, that it isn't suitable for a man of my noble birth to make his home in an underground riverbed?"

"It's not just that it isn't suitable, Lucien," Emil said. "It's madness."

"Is it?" Now both corners of Lucien's mouth rose. "But I'm the prince of darkness. And you know as well as I do, Emil, I've never been very good at my profession. Under my rule, I've done nothing but issue such edicts as the one permitting my clan to drink all the human blood they like, but forbidding them from ever killing their victims. I never even knew what any of the other clans out there were doing, because I was always too busy teaching Eastern European history to undergraduates at night school in Bucharest to care. What sort of son of Satan does that make me? Everything that your wife was talking about earlier—'the horrible mess' from last spring, in which all of us, and so many innocents, nearly perished—none of that was her fault. It was my fault, Emil. *Mine*. And none of it would have happened if I'd accepted the destiny my father left me when he died, instead of fighting it, as I have been for so long."

Emil's eyes widened. He looked more surprised than horrified. "You mean—"

"Absolutely," Lucien said. "That's why I'm here. The spring is my only hope. I don't have the willpower to do it on my own. But with Mannette . . ."

"But it's obviously killing you," Emil burst out. "I celebrate your decision finally to embrace your true destiny, since I know your unwillingness to do so before has made you many enemies—enemies who have striven to hurt us, and you. This will make you a stronger leader. But this spring . . . I don't know. Just because you are Satan's son on earth, and this spring is a direct source to his power, I cannot say with any certainty that you're drawing any benefit from it. My wife may have been too blunt in her way of putting it, but you do indeed look very ill, my lord. *Have* you been eating?"

Lucien pointed to a stainless-steel refrigerator in the shadows. "Of course."

"I cannot understand it, then," Emil said. "Perhaps because it's just a few blocks from the Palatine headquarters? And Meena Harper? If you'll pardon me saying so, sire, she seems to have a debilitating effect on you . . ."

"I have a plan for that, too," Lucien said darkly, pouring some wine into a glass. "Don't worry. May I ask how you discovered me?"

"Oh." Emil looked miserable as he took the glass of rich dark red wine the prince offered him. "I suppose no one's told you. Of course not. Who would?"

"Told me what?" Lucien sat back down on the couch. "Why do you look so frightened? I'm angry with you, but I'm not going to kill you. Not today. You happen to have caught me at a good time. Though I am slightly disturbed about something."

Emil gulped the wine. "What?"

"Someone turned one of Meena's friends. And the friend attacked her last night. Then we were followed. We need to find out who it was."

Emil choked. "It wasn't one of us. I can assure you," he said, after he'd recovered. "There *are* no us left."

"Yes, I know." Lucien handed him a napkin. "Which leaves who?"

Emil shook his head as he dabbed at the corners of his mouth. "I don't know. There's plenty of riffraff about. That's how I heard about this." He waved to indicate the cavern. "Someone saw you in the tunnels. At least, that's the rumor. I didn't believe it could possibly be true. I knew you were in the city, of course—where, you will recall, I advised you against staying. But then I remembered how you used to like to go and stand by this stream, to see how they were progressing with damming it up—and I thought, 'No, he couldn't possibly.' But you did. My lord." He shook his head. "I understand your motivations. I do. And I respect them. But there must be another way. Another place, not as close to the Palatine, to *her,* for you to—"

Lucien shook his head. "No. This is the place. I feel it, Emil. I will admit, I've had a slight setback. Last night when Meena was attacked, I had an . . . altercation. It took more out of me than I'd have expected. I haven't been as strong as I was since the incident at St. George's. But I'm recovering steadily, and soon, I hope, I'll—"

"No." Emil reached into the pocket of his coat and produced a pamphlet, which he handed Lucien. "You need to leave this place. Now."

Lucien looked down at the purple-and-gold pamphlet, which was advertising a new exhibit at the Metropolitan Museum of Art. "*Vatican Treasures: A Journey Through Faith and Art.* What could this possibly have to do with me?"

"The exhibit features rare art objects and historical documents relating to the evolution of the Church and the papacy," Emil explained. "It's one of the largest collections the Vatican has ever released to tour the world. It includes more than five hundred objects, *many of which have never before been on public view*. Its first stop is the Metropolitan."

"This isn't a show I'm particularly eager to rush out to see," Lucien said wryly. "But I still fail to see how it endangers me."

"Lucien, I've looked at the catalog. One of the objects on display dates back to the days of your father, before his death. His *original* death. It's a *certain illuminated manuscript*."

Lucien looked puzzled. "So?"

"It's a book of hours dating from the fifteenth century. It's said to have come from the region near Poenari Castle . . . and from the description, to have been a gift to a young princess upon her betrothal from her doting husband-to-be."

Lucien stared at him for a full minute. He wasn't certain he'd heard him correctly. He had spent a lot of time underground lately, living in darkness . . . absorbing the darkness, trying to become one with the darkness.

The darkness, however, had a way of playing with a man's mind.

"My *mother's* book of hours?" he finally croaked. "How is that even possible? That was lost when I was captured by the Ottomans, before my father . . ." His voice trailed off. The memory of what his father had done—not just to him, but to Emil—was too painful for either of them ever to mention. Lucien's father had made them what they were.

He'd then gone on to kill what scholars estimated were tens of thousands of human beings. But anyone who'd been around at the time knew the number was actually much higher than that.

Lucien had spent five hundred years swearing he would never be anything like his father.

But recently he'd come to realize that the only way he was ever going to get what he desired was to become a little more like his father.

Emil coughed. "Yes," he said. "Well, I only mention it because it seems to me that—"

"The *Vatican* has had it?" Lucien was still stunned. "All this time?"

"Those were confusing times," Emil said soothingly. "Especially after your father . . . well." He fell tactfully silent.

Lucien leaped to his feet and began to pace the length of the carpets.

"That book," he said. "Last night, Meena spoke of it."

"But that means . . ." Emil looked appalled. "My lord, you *know* what that means. If it's in the collection, it can only mean she had something to do with it being placed there."

"No," Lucien said. "I'm certain she didn't. She said she saw it in a dream."

Lucien closed, then opened, his fists, hardly aware of the gesture. Practically the only happy memories he had from his childhood were about that book. His mother had taught him to read from it.

That was why he'd found Meena's dream so disturbing. The scene she'd described—of the dark-haired woman sitting by a window, turning the pages of an illuminated manuscript with a young boy—seemed almost to have been plucked from his mind.

It was one of the images he'd been hoping so desperately that the Mannette would rob him of forever, because he found that it—like the knowledge that Meena Harper existed, but would not be with him—did nothing but torment him.

How could this be happening *now*, when he was so close? And *why*? Was this some kind of last temptation, a test, to see if he was finally worthy of the dark crown?

Or was it something else? An unprecedented release from the Vatican of historical documents and works of art? An exhibit of those objects at a museum in the city where he was rumored to be dwelling? And then . . .

"Last night," he murmured, stunned. "It was all a setup. It had to be. To make sure I'd come crawling out of my lair, if I was still in the vicinity. And she was the bait."

"I'm not sure I quite follow you, sir," Emil said. "Are you speaking of Ms. Harper?"

Lucien ignored him. "She just didn't know it. I'd swear she didn't know it. Those damned, soulless bastards."

"Sire," Emil said. "I don't know who you're talking about. *Who's* a damned, soulless bastard?"

"Not us this time, Emil." Lucien shook his head. "Believe it or not. Not one of us."

"Well," Emil replied. "We always knew they were, sire. That's why I came as soon as I heard. I knew you would be in need of me. I suggest you let me take you from here as soon as possible. It's obvious that however strong the powers of this place might once have been, they aren't strong enough now to match the powers of whatever is happening within the Palatine. Mary Lou and I will find another place for you to—"

"No," Lucien said, shaking his head. "No need. I'll go. I always planned on going eventually. But not until I'm ready." He threw Emil a steely glance. "And I won't leave without that which rightfully belongs to me."

Emil set down his wineglass with a sigh.

"My lord, retrieving the book is exactly what they'll be *expecting* you to do. It's undoubtedly why they put it in the collection in the first place. It's the Vatican. Tonight is the gala to celebrate the exhibit's grand opening in the U.S. Everyone from the archdiocese is going to be there. And, I suspect, everyone from the Palatine. They'll be lying in wait."

"That," Lucien said, a red glow growing in his eyes, "is what I am counting on."

"So," Emil said, looking uncomfortable, "when you said you won't leave without that which rightfully belongs to you, you weren't referring strictly to your mother's book."

"I was not," Lucien said.

Emil picked his wineglass back up and drained it.

"I was afraid of that," he said.

Chapter Fourteen

J on lifted up his sunglasses, squinting at the object perched on the edge of the roof.

"Can you see any difference?" he asked.

"I think he's leering at you," his best friend, Adam, said.

"I don't care about his expression," Jon said. "Is he dead?"

"Well," Adam said. "Considering he was never alive to begin with, it's kind of hard to tell."

Jon scowled. Adam was right. The garden gnome balanced between the roof of his building and the one next door not only showed no sign of having been shot, it did appear to be wearing a slightly mocking expression.

Jon ran his hand over the stubble where his muttonchops were growing in, just not as quickly as he might have hoped. He had a lot of time to think during his shift behind the counter at the Beanery—except when Yalena came in, before her shift at the thrift shop next door, which always distracted him—and he'd decided that he might stand a better chance of getting hired by the Palatine Guard if he looked the part. Alaric Wulf, for example, had that kind of blond Captain America thing going on.

Jon knew he was never going to achieve that level of awesomeness, but he could probably get away with a little more Wolverine in his personal style.

He glanced at Adam. Adam, on the other hand, was never going to be anything more than the nerdy sidekick. It wasn't his fault, really. It was simply the role he'd been born to. Jon was actually a little relieved it wasn't the role he'd been relegated to. That would fully suck.

"Maybe it works and gnomes are immune to UV rays," Adam offered.

Definitely nerdy sidekick.

"Gnomes are immune to UV rays," Jon said. "Especially ones made out of plaster. I already explained that this was just a hypothetical."

"Then I guess I don't really get why you're shooting at one." Adam sank into the closest folding deck chair, then reached down to lift his baby, Joanie, from her car seat and pull her onto his lap.

Joanie, unfortunately, didn't like that. She let out a wail loud enough to startle the pigeons roosting on a nearby cable wire. They took off into the air with a flutter.

Adam hastily removed his hands, saying, "Sorry, I forgot."

Jack Bauer, who was sprawled in the shade of the baby seat, lifted his head to shoot both men an annoyed look. As soon as Adam leaned back in his chair, the dog lay back down and relaxed. Joanie stopped crying and began to coo contentedly.

"What was *that* all about?" Jon asked.

"Dogs," Adam said with a sigh. "The kid is nuts about them. Especially *that* one. I don't know why."

"Oh," Jon said. "Probably because she feels safe and secure around him, seeing as how he's a demon-scenting dog. I bet she picked up a little bit of her mother's unease about vampires from the womb."

Adam sighed again. "Great. Like I don't have enough problems. Now I've got a baby who loves vampire-hunting dogs, a wife who's so terrified of demons that she's repressed all memory that they exist, and a best friend who won't talk about anything else. Can we please change the subject?"

"No problem," Jon said.

He folded himself into the deck chair beside Adam's, then reached for a cold one from the cooler between them. It actually didn't get much better than this, he thought. His dog, his best bud, an actual Bud, and his best bud's baby, chilling out on the roof, with the sounds of the city moving below them. He could hear the not-so-distant roar of the San Gennaro Festival farther on down the street, the carnival music of the Ferris wheel, the guys at the food booths hawking their wares. When the breeze blew just right, he could smell fried mozzarella sticks and roast pork.

Life was good.

He patted the object in his lap, which looked like a hair dryer, only bulkier, and much less streamlined. "I'm telling you, dude, if I can get this thing to work, Leisha doesn't have to worry anymore. And neither do you, since you helped with the design. That little girl's future is going to be made."

"I told you. Leisha doesn't remember what happened that night at St. George's," Adam pointed out, "and I actually prefer it that way. And do you honestly think that you're going to be able to get hired by the most elite demon-fighting force on the planet just by inventing a gun that uses UV rays to kill vampires?"

"Why not?" Jon asked. "Wouldn't *you* rather shoot a vampire from a hundred feet away, as opposed to staking him in the heart from a foot away, and get so close to those fangs?"

"I guess," Adam said, with a shrug.

"Exactly," Jon said. "Police forces already use spectroscopy technology to detect trace evidence, like blood and residue left by chemicals used in meth-making labs. I'm just applying it in a new way. And I've doubled the amount of UV filaments in the mirrored chamber, to intensify and focus the ray. It *should* work." He looked down at the gun in his lap. "It's got to."

"That's ultraviolet light," Adam said. "It isn't sunlight. How do you know UV light does anything to vampires?"

"It's what grows plants, doesn't it?" Jon demanded. "Where do you think I got the filaments?"

"Oh," Adam said. The baby had leaned over and was grabbing handfuls of Jack Bauer's fur. The dog looked up inquiringly, saw that it was just Joanie, yawned, and went back to sleep. "Sorry. I forgot. Those pothead friends of yours?"

"They're horticulturists, Adam," Jon said. "Not potheads. They're providing a service to people in need. Such as cancer patients."

"Got it," Adam said.

"And don't forget Meena's next-door neighbors. Remember?"

"Oh, right," he said. "The ones who turned out to be vampires."

"Right. They were fine as long as they didn't walk into any direct sunlight. They had UV-ray coating on all their windows. I'm telling you, the SuperStaker is going to sell itself."

"I suppose," Adam said noncommittally.

"I guess we should talk to Meena about finding a real vampire to test it out on first, before we schedule a meeting with the Wulf Man. You know. To make sure it really dusts vamps before we go bragging that it works. Wouldn't want to make fools of ourselves."

"Wouldn't be the first time," Adam said.

"True. There are these guys who come into the Beanery every Sunday . . . I swear they could be blood junkies. They get Americanos and sit there nursing them for, like, hours, staring at their laptops. They don't even look at Yalena when she comes in. What's up with that? It's not normal. I mean, even gay dudes look at Yalena."

Adam glanced at his watch. "Is this the part where you start talking about Yalena? Because Joanie and I have to go pick up Leisha from work, and we could actually leave early if that's what this is going to descend into."

Jon, offended, said, "I don't do that. Talk about Yalena too much? Do I do that?"

"You do that," Adam said.

Jon sighed. "If I can get the Palatine to seriously consider this gun, and then get a real job and make some real money, I could get my own place to live, so I'm not mooching off my sister. Then Yalena might go out with me."

"Jonathan," Adam said. "Do you want my advice?"

"I should shoot those guys, right? The next time they come into the Beanery? If they really are vamps, they'll blow up. And if they aren't, it won't do anything to them, like the gnome. No harm, no foul."

"No," Adam said. "I think you should ask Yalena out now. I don't think she cares about you not having a real job or living with your sister. She's a nice girl. I don't know what you've been waiting around for. Life is short. I mean, look at me and Leisha. I've been out of work what . . . almost two years?"

Jon thought about it. "Yeah. That sounds about right."

"And in that time, we were both nearly killed by murderous vampires, thanks to your sister."

"True," Jon said.

"But we've got this beautiful baby." Adam nodded at Joanie, who was beaming as she thrust her bottle at Jack Bauer to lick, which he was doing enthusiastically.

"And I'm not saying we don't have problems," Adam said. "We do. Like the fact that our baby prefers the company of your dog to human beings. But this isn't the worst problem to have. And to reach it, I had to take the first step of asking Leisha out. So stop being such a douche, and just do it."

Jon looked dubious. "I don't know, man," he said.

Adam put down his own beer bottle and stood up. "Well, think about it. In the meantime, Joanie and I are headed for the salon to pick up Leisha. We'll see you in a bit. Oh, you might want to plug your ears."

He lifted the baby seat. This had the swift and immediate effect of causing Joanie to begin shrieking, so loudly that the pigeons who'd resettled on the cable wires flew off. Jack Bauer flattened back his ears and let out a whimper.

"Later," Adam called, waving, his voice mostly inaudible due to his daughter's protests at being taken away from the dog she adored.

"Later," Jon said, standing up to wave back.

Adam and Joanie disappeared through the door to the rooftop. Jon could still hear the baby's cries for several minutes more until finally, they faded away.

"Stop being such a douche, and just do it," he repeated. Then he spun around, the SuperStaker in hand, and assumed a gunslinger's stance.

"*Hasta la vista,* vampire," he said to the gnome.

He pulled the trigger.

Chapter Fifteen

M eena took a deep breath, then undid all three locks to the sublet she shared with her brother and opened the door. She was met by the enthusiastic barking of Jack Bauer and the smell of pizza.

"Where have you been?" Jonathan asked. He was sprawled across the couch in front of the television and a laptop computer, which was open on the coffee table next to a plate containing a half-eaten slice of pizza.

"New Jersey," Meena said, closing and locking the door behind her. She took another deep breath before turning around to bend and greet the dog, giving his ears plenty of affectionate scratches.

"Oh God," Jon groaned. He took a slurp from the can of soda he was holding, his gaze never straying from the TV in front of him. There was some kind of football game on. "New Jersey? *Why?*"

"Because," Meena said, straightening up. She tried to keep her voice steady. "I killed David Delmonico last night."

Jonathan choked on the mouthful of soda he'd just taken. Droplets sprayed onto his computer screen and even reached the wide-screen TV. But he didn't appear to notice. He just stared at Meena in horror.

"You *what?*"

"Somebody turned him into a vampire," Meena said. She walked over to the couch to lift up the remote, then turned down the volume of the television. "He attacked me. I staked him. That was his mother who called this morning. I had to go out to New Jersey to talk to a police detective. Is there any of that pizza left? I'm starving."

Jonathan continued to stare at her. She hoped it wasn't because he could see that she'd been crying. She'd tried to wipe away all the evidence of her tears in the sun-visor mirror in the car, just before Alaric dropped her off.

It wasn't that she didn't want her brother to know how upset the events of the past twenty-four hours had made her. It was that she wanted to protect him, and keep him from becoming upset as well. The two of them were close . . . they'd survived being raised by their parents, after all, a couple who had turned out to be uniquely unqualified to have children.

Displeased and embarrassed by a daughter who told everyone she met how they were going to die, Mr. and Mrs. Harper chose to believe a psychiatrist who counseled that the problem would go away if they didn't encourage it.

But because Meena was informing her friends and loved ones of their imminent deaths out of a genuine desire to prevent their perishing, not in an effort to get attention, her parents' withdrawal produced a neurotic, isolated teenager, who then became—as so often happened—a neurotic, isolated writer.

The Harpers' heaping all of their positive attention instead onto their athletic, popular son, Jonathan, made him a well-adjusted, outgoing young man . . .

. . . until he lost his job as a successful financial analyst.

Mr. and Mrs. Harper decided that this, too, was attention-seeking behavior, that could be solved with a little lesson in tough love, and turned their backs, thinking that their son would get back on his feet sooner if he knew he didn't have his parents to lean on.

This might have been the correct course of action if Jonathan had lost his job as the result of a drug or performance issue.

But he had been laid off, like so many millions of others, during the recession.

So it was Meena who ended up taking her older brother, Jonathan, in when he was evicted from his apartment, and Jonathan who'd tried to rescue Meena from the Dracul when they attempted to drain her of every last ounce of her blood so that they, too, could predict the future.

Meena loved her brother and would do anything for him, and knew he felt the same way about her. They didn't have anyone else but each other.

But she also knew there were some things he just couldn't handle. This was why the Palatine had chosen to employ her, and not him, even though he'd been the one who'd so badly wanted to get a job with them. Precisely because he said things like he did when she walked through the door that afternoon after returning from New Jersey:

"You know, I'm not surprised David Delmonico got vamped and tried to kill you." Jonathan reached down onto the floor and scooped up a pizza box, which he handed to Meena without once taking his gaze from the television screen. "That guy was such an asshole. I don't know what you ever saw in him. What was that thing he had with wanting to put veneers on everyone?"

Meena reached inside the box and pulled out a slice. She hoped Jonathan didn't notice how much her hands were trembling. When was she going to calm down?

Probably not anytime soon, after the things Alaric had told her in the car about all those missing tourists.

"I don't know," she said. "He was sweet when I first met him, you know."

"If by sweet you mean he had a great big expiration date stamped on his forehead," Jonathan said. "I can't believe *you're* the one who ended up offing him. Didn't he marry a nurse, or something?"

Meena winced halfway into a bite of pizza. "Yeah," she said. "Brianna. She's missing."

"Missing?" Jonathan looked excited. "No shit! Did David kill her?"

She dropped the pizza crust back into the box.

"You know what," she said. It was hard to keep her voice steady. "It's been a long day, and I don't really feel like talking right now. All I want to do is take a hot bath before I have to change to go out again—"

"Look," Jonathan said, taking the pizza box off her lap. "If you want me to call Adam and Leisha and ask them to come over a little later, I can. No problem. They're going to flip out when they hear David's dead, though—"

Meena stared at him.

"Adam and Leisha are coming over? What are you talking about?"

"The Feast of San Gennaro," he said, staring back. "Remember? Leisha and Adam are on their way over here with the baby so we can go. Adam's picking her up from work right now and bringing her back here. We've only been planning to go today for about eight weeks. Don't tell me you forgot."

Meena reached a shaking hand to rub Jack Bauer's belly, since the dog had leaped into her lap.

"I forgot," she said faintly.

"Meena. If you're about to say you want to cancel, let me just tell you one thing," Jonathan warned. "Adam was here all day, talking about how much he's been looking forward to this. They haven't had a day out of the apartment together in, like, months. Literally. Months."

Meena flinched. She knew this was true. She also knew, however, that now was the worst time in the world for her friends to decide to start socializing again.

"Jonathan," Meena said. "You have to call Adam and tell him there's been a change of plans. Tell them to go home and order Chinese and watch a movie on pay-per-view."

"What the hell, Meena," Jonathan said, springing up from the couch. "I'm supposed to call them and say you can't go because . . . why? You're so upset that you killed your ex-boyfriend?"

"That isn't why," Meena said, glaring at him. "I can't go because someone's turning people I know into *vampires* and setting them loose in the city, and last night one of them tried to *kill* me. Currently, his wife is missing. You think I'm going to put Adam and Leisha's lives at risk by inviting them over to hang out with me at some street fair? Especially one that's supposed to have over a million people attending it this weekend? While they've got the *baby* with them? That's just crazy. Anything could happen. They shouldn't even be on the streets right now."

Jonathan looked sheepish.

"Oh," he said. "Well, I guess if you put it *that* way . . . yeah, they're probably safer staying home. What's with you and all the undead guys wanting to kill you, anyway?"

"I don't know," Meena said glumly as she stroked Jack Bauer's fur. "I have a special gift."

"Seriously." Then Jonathan brightened. "Hey, does this mean they're sending someone over to guard you? From the Palatine? Alaric, maybe?"

Meena sighed. It seemed like only a few weeks ago that she and her brother had first been informed—at sword point, practically—that dark, paranormal forces existed, and that Meena's new boyfriend, Lucien Antonescu, was behind them all. Alaric Wulf—the individual sent to inform them—had declared he wasn't budging from her apartment until she revealed Lucien's location.

That's when Jonathan had developed his fascination with the Palatine . . . *and* his man-crush on Alaric Wulf. Meena wished her brother would find a girlfriend already so he'd get over it, and have a distraction.

But she knew it was hard to find a girlfriend when you were working as a barista and sleeping in an alcove-sized second bedroom of your sister's sublet in Little Italy. Even when the object of your affections was an aspiring actress from Eastern Europe who, just half a year earlier, had been a slave in a vampire sex ring, and was now working as a seamstress in the church thrift shop.

But Meena couldn't entirely blame her brother for his man-crush on Alaric. As frustrating as Alaric could be at times, at others—like outside the Freewell police station that morning, for instance, when he'd held her in his arms and been so sweet and strong and reassuring, and made her feel so safe—he could be . . . well, amazing.

Although *this,* she knew, was not why Jonathan eagerly awaited his arrival.

"Do you think he'll look at my SuperStaker?" Jonathan asked.

Meena saw that her brother was holding a curious item in his hand. It was her hair dryer.

And yet it wasn't. Her hair dryer was yellow. This was black.

"I've nearly got it working, you know," Jonathan was saying. He squeezed the trigger. Only when he did, no sound came out of it. No air either. "Well, almost. It's still got a few kinks. And I haven't actually been able to test it. Too bad you weren't carrying it when David came around. He'd have been a perfect test subject."

Meena didn't have the slightest idea what he was talking about. But she loved her brother.

"I'm sure," she said hesitantly, "Alaric will check it when he comes over. He just stopped by his place for a few things. Then he'll be over to drop them off and pick me up. We have to go to some function tonight. So, listen, while we're gone, it's important you don't go out or invite anyone over. *Anyone.* You have your stakes, right? And holy water? Keep all the windows closed, and don't open the door until we get home."

Jonathan looked shocked. "You're going out? But if the city is under some kind of vampire attack, wouldn't it be safer for you to—"

"For *work*," Meena said, emphasizing the word strongly. "It's a *work* function. Palatine business."

She had agreed to attend the opening not because Alaric had browbeaten her into it (though of course he'd tried), but because Abraham had stressed the importance of her attendance.

And after hearing Alaric's theory on what he thought was happening to all those missing tourists, she felt it would probably be prudent to put in an appearance, if only to make sure he didn't mention it to anyone else.

Lucien might be part monster. But that didn't make him a beast.

Of course, there was a very small part of her that couldn't help remembering Lucien's eyes the night before, when he'd kissed her in her bedroom. They hadn't looked particularly human.

But didn't that only prove her point that Lucien *couldn't* be the person responsible, if those tourists really were being devoured by some demonic creature? Otherwise, he wouldn't have looked so famished.

And *if* someone—or some*thing*—really was going around Manhattan, feasting on the city's tourist population, surely the prince of darkness would know about it. He was the ruler of fiends.

But Meena wasn't certain, considering the condition Lucien had been in last night, how much ruling he was doing these days. Would he know—or even care—who or what was responsible for the fact that human beings were disappearing at a fairly alarming rate from Manhattan? He hadn't known who'd turned David.

Meena was more worried than ever about Lucien, especially because he refused to listen to her theory about her dream. It had seemed almost to cause him physical pain when she'd brought it up.

And now that she'd invited him into her bedroom, she couldn't *un*-invite him. Something told her he was going to show up there tonight, looking for her.

And not to talk about her dream either.

This wasn't the only reason, of course, why, when Alaric had declared in the car that he'd be staying over at her place for the foreseeable future, she'd just shrugged and said, "There's no need, but fine. Whatever."

She didn't want him to suspect the truth . . . that Lucien not only already knew where she lived, but that last night she'd invited him inside. Evil spirits could not enter a home unless they were invited. Now Lucien had free rein in the place, and could come in anytime he wanted, just so long as he avoided the crosses and garlic.

But what frightened her even more than this was that after the way Lucien had behaved—the way his eyes had glowed, like there'd been some kind of fire burning inside him—the thought of Alaric being within calling distance in case Lucien did show up again actually seemed a little comforting . . .

What was happening to her? She'd always trusted Lucien, and believed he would never do anything to hurt her. Last night, he'd sworn he still loved her, and there'd been a desperation in his kisses that convinced her he was telling the truth.

So why would she find the thought of having Alaric around—who'd only ever wanted one thing: Lucien's demise—comforting?

She didn't know. There was a part of her that was pretty sure she didn't *want* to know.

Which might have been why, a few hours later, when she recognized the knock on her door that she and Alaric had arranged, Meena's heart gave a little lurch. She'd begun to feel almost human again, having bathed and changed into a body-hugging black dress and heels she'd purchased new (though they'd been on sale).

She didn't understand the lurch. She certainly wasn't looking forward to seeing Alaric.

"I'll get it," she said.

The minute she unlocked the door and saw his face, she knew.

It wasn't what Alaric was wearing. He looked handsome in the tuxedo he'd changed into, his dark blond hair still damp from the shower. Alaric was fastidious about his wardrobe and grooming.

No. It was his eyes. There was no hint of that boyish mischievousness she was used to seeing in them. For once, they weren't gleaming with deadly determination either. She didn't recognize the look in them.

"What is it?" she asked, feeling the lurch again, much more strongly this time. What had happened? Lucien. Had something happened to Lucien? Already? But Alaric had only just arrived. Had Lucien been in the hallway . . . ? Meena tried to peer past one of Alaric's broad shoulders.

"Turn on the news," he said grimly.

It was only then that she recognized the look in his eyes. She'd seen it only once before: that night at St. George's, when Lucien Antonescu had almost killed them.

It was fear.

Chapter Sixteen

Alaric came inside, dropping the duffel bag he'd slung over one shoulder onto the floor, then closed and locked the door behind him. Meena had already lifted the remote from the coffee table.

"Oh, hey, Alaric." Jonathan emerged from his bedroom alcove, trying to look as if Alaric's visit were a big surprise.

Except that Meena saw he'd changed from the sweats he'd been wearing to the pressed shirts and khakis he reserved for work. But he had no shift that night, because they'd been supposed to go out with Leisha and Adam.

And he just *happened* to be carrying that thing he'd invented.

"I didn't know you were stopping by," he said. "Sharp-looking tux there, dude. Very Daniel Craig in *Casino Royale.*"

Alaric ignored him. He sank onto the couch, his gaze glued to the television screen. He didn't seem to be aware that Jack Bauer—who counted Alaric among his favorite humans, ever since he'd risked his life for the dog's, knowing how much Meena adored him—had leaped up onto the arm of the couch and was panting happily into his ear.

Meena had turned it to the twenty-four-hour local news station.

"And starting tomorrow tristate residents will have a chance to see one of the world's rarest and most valuable art collections," an amiable-looking anchorman was saying into the camera. "The new exhibit—*Vatican Treasures: A Journey Through Faith and Art*—will be on display through the end of December at the Metropolitan Museum of Art. New York City is the first stop on the exhibit's American tour. Our own Genevieve Fox is at tonight's star-studded grand opening. Genevieve?"

Meena, who'd sat down on the couch beside Alaric, looked up at him questioningly.

"Isn't this what we're going to in, like, five minutes?" she asked.

He shushed her sharply, taking the remote from Meena's hand and turning up the volume.

"Hello, Pat," Genevieve said. She was standing on a red carpet in front of the Met, wearing an evening gown, lots of gold jewelry, and a wide smile. Around her were many other reporters, none of whom was dressed quite as nicely. "I'm here at the opening of the new exhibit, *Vatican Treasures: A Journey Through Faith and Art*. Many of the artifacts have never before left the Vatican, or been seen by the public. And let me tell you, you can feel the electricity as the celebrity guests and donors arrive for this unprecedented event."

"Oh, get on with it already," Alaric growled at the television in frustration.

"This isn't what you wanted to see?" Meena asked.

"It will be on after this. Just wait."

"But *Vatican Treasures* isn't just about ancient relics, beautifully jeweled chalices, and priceless works by great artists like Michelangelo and Bernini," Genevieve assured her viewers. "It gives true believers a chance to connect to their faith up close. Earlier this afternoon, I got a chance to speak to Father Henrique Mauricio—"

"Oh no," Alaric said. He sank his head into his fists with a groan.

"—who's come all the way from the archdiocese of São Sebastio do Rio de Janeiro in Brazil to become the pastor of the newly renovated St. George's Cathedral . . ."

The shot shifted to Genevieve in an attractive sweater set, her hair down, her lips in an intelligent pout as she pointed her microphone into the face of an extremely good-looking, dark-haired priest.

Father Henrique's English was charmingly halting, his accent breathtakingly foreign.

"It's a very emotional thing. The artifacts in this exhibit speak to the heart, and reaffirm that which we already believe in. So by seeing them, our faith is supported. And that . . ." His eyes actually filled with tears on camera. A close-up of Genevieve's face showed that she, too, was visibly moved by Father Henrique's words. "How do you say it in English? Oh, it's . . . it's like a piece of the Vatican has been brought to us, here in New York City, like a gift. You can come here to see some of the greatest, most moving pieces in religious history. And they will, I promise you, restore your soul."

The shot shifted back to Genevieve, teary-eyed again, standing in her updo in front of the Met.

"Oh, Pat, I can't tell you how touched I was by those words of Father Henrique. He is so right. What an extraordinary, extraordinary man—"

"Extraordinary *ass!*" Alaric yelled at the screen. Jack Bauer barked enthusiastically, apparently in agreement.

"And he's just one of the many representatives from the archdiocese who will be here tonight to show support for this exhibit. And they're hoping many of our viewers will come experience this unique and, yes, moving show. Back to you, Pat."

"Thanks, Genevieve," Pat said. "Returning to a story we've been following for the past hour, that devastating house fire in Freewell, New Jersey—"

Meena gasped. Jonathan said, "Freewell? Isn't that where—"

"Yes," Alaric said. He turned up the volume. This was clearly the story he'd been waiting for.

"We have Dee Dee Chow, live on the scene in Freewell," Pat said. "Dee Dee, what can you tell us?"

The shot shifted, and Meena saw a female reporter standing on a familiar-looking road crowded with police cars, fire trucks, and rescue vehicles. Behind her sloped a lawn that at one time might have been green. Now it was charred black and littered with yellow caution tape.

"Pat," Dee Dee said, "witnesses say the fire started late this afternoon, when neighbors saw smoke billowing from beneath one of the garage doors and called 911."

A confusing view of the scene from a helicopter told Meena nothing.

"But despite firefighters' efforts, the inferno could not be contained and quickly spread throughout the house," Dee Dee went on.

The shot widened farther, and Meena saw evil-looking orange

flames shooting from every window of what had once been David Delmonico's New Jersey mansion.

"Abraham," she breathed. She hadn't meant to say the word out
loud. It just slipped out.

"Wait," Jonathan said. "Abraham *Holtzman*? Was he in that house?
What exactly were you guys doing in Freewell?"

Alaric's gaze never left the screen. He said nothing.

"Although it's too early in the investigation to speculate on a cause
for the blaze," Dee Dee continued, "officials say, due to the extreme
heat and rapidness with which it spread, there is some speculation that
an accelerant may have been employed."

Meena looked up into Alaric's impassive face. "How did you know
about this?" she asked. "Is the team all right? Did Abraham report in?"

"Shhh," he said impatiently.

"While firefighters have declared the scene still much too dangerous to enter in order to begin looking for human remains," the reporter
went on, "neighbors say that no one appeared to have been in the home
at the time the fire broke out . . . which may be the only piece of good
news so far for a family that appears to have lost everything. Reporting
live from Freewell, I'm—"

Alaric stood up and switched off the television.

"So . . ." Meena popped up as well. "We're going back to Freewell to
look for Abraham and the others, right?"

"We most certainly are not going to Freewell," Alaric said. "I'm
keeping you as far away as possible from Freewell . . . from all of New
Jersey, as a matter of fact. We're going to the Met, and then we're
coming straight back here."

"*What?*" Meena cried. "But Abraham—"

Alaric walked up to her until they stood just a few inches apart, apparently so he could look her in the eye. She restrained an urge to take
a step backward. She didn't want him to know how much his physical
proximity unnerved her. Instead, she raised her chin and stared right
back at him.

"I know you tried to warn me," he said, in a quiet voice, one that
was devoid of his usual self-confidence and swagger. "You didn't want

to leave him there, but I wouldn't listen. I was too stubborn. Abraham told me that, you know. He said that it's my worst fault. He said I think everyone should be like me. Including you. But it isn't true. I just always want to be right. I wish to God I'd been right this time. But I wasn't. Abraham is the closest thing I ever had to a father. But he's not here right now, and you are. I'm going to do everything within my power to make sure you stay alive. So no, we're not going to Freewell."

Meena gaped up at him, completely blown away by this speech. Alaric almost never admitted he'd been wrong, and just as rarely spoke of his feelings, except to complain that he was hungry, or hot, or unhappy about someone who was speaking too loudly on a cell phone in a restaurant.

She wasn't at all sure how to respond, especially since there was a look of almost boyish vulnerability on his face that made her long to put her arms around him and tell him everything was going to be all right.

But she knew that would not only be inappropriate—especially with her brother standing nearby, so awkwardly watching their entire exchange—it would be a lie. She'd known from the moment she'd seen Abraham disappearing around the corner of David's house that they were never going to see him again.

"This is all my fault," Meena said, her eyes filling with tears. "I should never have met David in the first place. If I hadn't, none of this—"

Alaric reached up to use a thumb to wipe away a single tear that had begun to roll down her cheek.

"You were just trying to do what you thought was right. You didn't know. How could you?"

"How could I *not*?" she asked, her voice breaking. "Knowing is what I do."

"Well," he said, "there's nothing either of us can do about it now, except our jobs."

She wasn't positive she could even do that anymore, though. Her head felt like the Magic 8 Ball someone had given her as a child, and which she'd shaken way too many times in an effort to get answers about herself, since she knew the answers about everyone else.

Reply hazy, try again.

"Alaric," she said, reaching out to take the large, callused hand that had just touched her face. "Listen to me. The reporter on the news said that no one seemed to be home at the time of the fire. So, that doesn't mean Abraham and the others aren't all right."

"Then why haven't they reported in?" Alaric asked. "You know how Abraham is. And Carolina was on the team, too. Abraham specifically requested her, because she's so good in the field."

Meena blanched. Carolina de Silva. Her only friend at work . . . besides Alaric, if she could consider him a friend. Carolina was regarded as one of the best guards on the force. If *she* hadn't reported in, whatever happened in Freewell could only have been catastrophic . . .

But when she probed at the part of her mind that told her whether or not people were living or dead and pictured Abraham or Carolina, the only answer she got in response was *Better not tell you now.*

But she wasn't sure if the words were what she desperately wanted to hear, or if Abraham and Carolina truly were in a place between life and death.

"And there's no sign of any of the team members' real-time GPS trackers on the computers back at headquarters either," Alaric said bitterly. "Either their cell phones melted in the heat of the fire, or . . ."

His voice trailed off. He didn't have to continue. Meena knew exactly what he was thinking.

Someone had disabled them.

Concentrate and ask again.

"It gets worse," Alaric said, digging his cell phone from his pocket with his free hand. "On my way over, I received this e-mail from headquarters: *'Due to continuing uncertainties regarding possible attacks by demonic entities, the Vatican has declared a worldwide state of emergency and an ongoing security threat to all personnel and their family members. Specifically, all nonessential travel to New Jersey is to be deferred until further notice.'*"

Jonathan, across the room whistled. "Jeez," he said. "Who knew New Jersey was such a hotbed for demonic activity?"

"It's not just New Jersey," Alaric said. He continued to read aloud. *"'Tonight's event at the museum is also considered to have a high potential for volatility.'"* He let out a bitter laugh. *"'All Alpha Level and above guards are to report to the museum's parking-garage entrance within the hour. All others are to report to headquarters.'"* Alaric dropped his cell back into his tuxedo pocket. "From there I suppose they'll be sent over the bridge to Freewell, where they'll be split into search parties to look for any sign of Holtzman and the rest of the extermination team."

"The museum?" Meena shook her head. "Why are they sending all Alpha Level guards to the *museum?*"

"Yeah," Jonathan said. "They're more worried about a bunch of rich donors and bishops and stuff than they are about their own *employees?*"

Alaric shrugged. "The Vatican doesn't declare a state of emergency every day. They've never done it before, in all the years I've worked for the Palatine. And I think it's highly unlikely they've done it tonight because some New Jersey dentist's wife has set fire to her house and is on the loose in the tristate area. I can guarantee you they're worried about a slightly bigger threat than Brianna Delmonico. I get the impression they're expecting a surprise celebrity guest at tonight's gala, for whom they felt the need to step up security."

"Really?" Jonathan asked, impressed. "Who? The mayor?"

"Not exactly," Alaric said, glancing at the crucifixes over the living room windows.

Meena gasped as the realization sank in.

"No," she said.

Chapter Seventeen

Meena could do nothing but scowl out of the window of the cab on their way to the Met. She couldn't help it.

She was just that angry.

And Alaric knew it.

"Cheer up," he said, from his side of the backseat. "The archbishop will be there tonight. You can put in a formal request to be transferred. Maybe to Ireland. You'll definitely never have to see me again if you transfer to Ireland. Too many leprechauns. I hate leprechauns. Greedy little bastards."

"It's not funny," she said to him, her rage bubbling over. "I can't *believe* you told them about my having seen Lucien last night."

"Meena." Alaric looked her straight in the eye. "I didn't tell them."

"Oh, right," she said. "All you did in the car on the way back from New Jersey was go on and on about your theory that Lucien Antonescu is the one killing all those tourists. Don't tell me that's not why they issued that state of emergency. Of course it is, Alaric."

At the apartment, when it had been revealed that the prince of darkness was back, Jonathan had cried, "Oh, great. This is just great. When were you going to tell *me*? Do I need to remind everyone that I once shot that guy? He's probably sitting around right now with all his minions trying to figure out how to get back at me. Oh my God. I need to go lie down." He'd then vanished with his SuperStaker into the bedroom.

"I told you in the car that Lucien *couldn't* be the one committing those murders," Meena raged to Alaric—although she kept her voice low enough that the taxi driver, behind the thick plastic screen separating the front from the backseat, couldn't overhear her. "And why would he, of all people, show up at tonight's event? Religious icons of any kind make vampires sick, so I highly doubt he's going to want to go see a bunch of treasures from the Vatican, let alone want to hang around a lot of church officials. This whole thing has gotten so out of hand. It's turned into some kind of witch hunt, like back in the sixteen-hundreds. You want to blame Lucien for everything wrong with the world, when the truth is—"

"I know. You already told me," Alaric interrupted. His own gaze wasn't exactly calm. "He's so weak and anemic and you're so worried about him, blah blah blah. But he wasn't too weak to rip the door off that Volvo, was he?"

Meena shook her head. "You don't get it," she said, leaning back in the seat and glaring at the traffic outside her window. "You just don't get it."

"I *get*," Alaric said, "that over fifty people have gone missing while visiting this city over the past few months—with ten of them having disappeared in the past two weeks alone—and there hasn't been one word about it in the media beyond a mention here and there of a family not having checked out of their hotel room after visiting Madame Tussauds wax museum or Ground Zero. Maybe their vanishing from the Big Apple without a trace is news back in Wisconsin, or wherever they're from, but here, because their bodies haven't shown up, no one cares, except possibly for my immediate supervisor, who started looking into it the minute I showed him the commonality between all their cases. But now he's gone missing, too, which frankly I find just a little too coincidental for comfort."

Meena turned to look at him, too startled to remember that she was angry with him. "What do you mean?" she asked.

"You know exactly what I mean," Alaric said. "My immediate supervisor is missing, and so is his team . . . and yet for some reason my superiors seem to think it's more important to assign all their best guards to a party at a museum tonight rather than to the area where my colleagues vanished. I didn't report your Lucien sighting to anyone yet because as far as I'm concerned, I don't *have* anyone to report it to.

Whoever's in charge now that Abraham is gone either has his priorities somewhat askew, or he knows something we don't."

Meena thought for a moment. "Well," she said finally, "if you didn't report it, then that alert the Vatican sent out can't have anything to do with Lucien."

"Maybe it doesn't," he said. "But just in case . . ." He stuck his hand into the pocket of his tuxedo jacket, and pulled from it a small flat box in a familiar shade of robin's-egg blue. "Here."

He tossed it into her lap. The word *Tiffany* was stamped in black lettering on top of the box.

"Alaric." Meena immediately felt herself turning red. "What *is* this?"

"Something I should have given you a long time ago," he said. "You certainly need it more than anyone else I know. It might have kept you from getting that most recent bite. Which I can still see, by the way. You didn't do a very good job with the concealer."

With this decidedly unromantic remark—if he'd even meant the moment to be romantic—Alaric shifted his attention beyond his passenger window, leaving Meena with nothing to do but open the box.

Inside lay a sleek, gleaming silver cross on a slim black leather choker.

"*Oh,*" she said, in a soft voice.

It was perfect . . . exactly what she would have chosen for herself, if she'd ever have allowed herself to make such an extravagant purchase.

"Do me a favor," he said, finally turning to look at her. "Put it on, and no matter what, *do not* take it off."

She did as he asked, her fingers trembling.

"Thank you," she said.

"Are you *crying?*" he asked, sounding shocked.

"No," she said, averting her face as she fumbled with the clasp.

"You are," he said accusingly. "What is *wrong* with you?"

"Nothing," she insisted. "It's just so . . ." She struggled to come up with the right word. "Perfect. No one's ever gotten me something so perfect before."

"Here," he said, clearly growing impatient with her inability to work the clasp. "Turn around." She did as he asked, lifting her hair. She felt his fingers on the sensitive skin on the back of her neck. "The vampire gave you a purse," he pointed out.

"It was a tote," she corrected him.

"You wanted the purse," he said. "I know you didn't want this." He finished fastening the clasp, and leaned back. "But you clearly need it."

"Thank you," she said again.

"Don't mention it," he replied. "Meena."

She looked at him. His gaze was very bright. Even if she'd wanted to, she could not have looked away.

"Yes?"

"I . . . bought a house in Antigua."

She widened her eyes. "Today?"

A look of irritation flashed across his face.

"No, not today," he said. "When would I have had time to buy a house in Antigua today?"

"I don't know," Meena said. She felt stupid. Especially because the information that he had bought a house in Antigua had made her feel very sad. She had never thought about it before, but of course Alaric's assignment in New York City was only temporary. Of course he would be moving away eventually. "I'm not sure what I'm supposed to say. Congratulations?"

"Don't congratulate me," he said, looking more annoyed than ever. "Do you know why I bought a house in Antigua?"

She shook her head, bewildered.

"Because Antigua is the only island in the Caribbean that suffers from frequent droughts," he said. "That's how close to the equator it is. The sun shines every day, all day. It rains sometimes, but not often. And do you know what they've never had in Antigua?"

She shook her head, still bewildered.

He pointed at the cross.

"Vampires," he said. "They don't like it there. Too much sun."

She smiled, realizing he was joking. Or, knowing him, possibly not.

"So," she said, indicating the cross. "Is this for me to remember you by? When will you be leaving?"

He turned back to the window with a scowl. "Can't wait to get rid of me, eh?" he said. "So you can be alone with the prince?"

"No," she said, struck to the heart. Why could she never find the right thing to say to him? "That's not what I meant. You know that's not what I meant."

"Don't worry," he'd said with what sounded almost like a snarl. "I won't be leaving with any unsettled business."

She did not like the sound of that.

"Alaric," she said. "Look at me."

He looked at her then. But only to say, "Let's try to keep it professional, shall we?"

Chapter Eighteen

"Meena Harper. What a delight it is to meet you."

Father Henrique Mauricio looked even better in person than he had on TV. His skin seemed to glow with good health, and his teeth were pearly white, but just ever so slightly crooked, proving they were still his.

Alaric did not consider himself an expert in the field, but in his opinion, *Vatican Treasures* had brought out some of New York City's biggest phonies, Henrique Mauricio among them.

Most of them were pretending to care about the art, when in reality they were getting drunk, showing off their newest designer clothes, and laughing nervously over what Meena Harper had said about how they were going to die.

To her credit, she was being a good sport about the fact that someone had leaked the information to the crowd about her "gift." If it had been Alaric, he'd have punched each person who'd come up and said, "Oh, do me next!" in the face.

Meena, instead, said in a calm voice, taking the person's hand, "If you have a ski trip planned, I'd cancel it," or "You have a long, long life ahead of you," or "I think you need to watch your cholesterol intake."

This usually resulted in a cry of "Oh my goodness, that's uncanny!" or a delighted titter, or "My doctor just told me that!"

It could not be easy, Alaric realized, being Meena Harper, especially as the whispers and stares began. There were other celebrities in the room . . . an aging rock star, a former mayor, an athlete who'd murdered his wife and been famously acquitted on a technicality, though he was clearly guilty.

But she was the only person there who could look into the future and tell them how they were going to die.

No wonder Padre Caliente was all over her.

Of course, being the biggest phony of them all—except, Alaric supposed, for Lucien Antonescu. But despite Alaric's suspicions, there was no sign whatsoever of *him*—Father Henrique lifted up Meena's hand to kiss it.

"I've heard so much about you," Mauricio was gushing with a smile. The smile was the same self-effacing one Alaric had seen him give Genevieve Fox on the news. "I'm glad we're finally getting to meet after all of this time."

"Well, it's very nice to meet you, too, Father," Meena said. "Are you enjoying New York?"

"Oh." Father Henrique looked heavenward. "More than I can say. Of course I miss my beloved Rio, but who could not love the Big Apple, no? As they say, it grabs the heart, and will not let go."

Alaric rolled his eyes, scouting the next tray of smoked salmon. It was basically the only protein they were serving, and he was starving. The problem was, so was everyone else, so every time the salmon came around, people descended on the trays like vultures.

"Oh," someone Alaric didn't recognize was saying, but whom Meena had advised to stay away from boats, "it's so true. That's why I've always loved New York. And that's why it's so wonderful that this show came to New York first."

Alaric had no idea what this person was talking about. He did not mind art. In fact, he liked paintings of swimming pools and the ocean. They reminded him of the beach house he'd purchased in Antigua, the one he'd told Meena about, and to which he hoped to retire . . . not soon, but eventually. He'd know when the time was right. He had enough money saved to live on without working, and sometimes—on days like today, for instance—he thought he might just pack it all in and catch the next plane for the Caribbean. He didn't want to end up like Abraham, for whom he was fairly certain his superiors weren't even bothering seriously to search. He'd seen the look in Meena's eyes.

There was nothing left of Abraham to look for.

Still, they could at least *act* like they cared, instead of standing around at this party drinking champagne like nothing had happened.

Getting dragged around to meet phony church officials and donors was bad enough—especially when Alaric had to pretend that he wasn't actually scanning the room at every moment for danger in the form of the biggest phony of all, Lucien Antonescu.

But now Meena was being urged by some overenthusiastic church publicist to tell Padre Caliente how he was going to die.

Unbelievable.

"Oh no," she protested gently, as she did with everyone. Alaric could tell that she was tired. It had, after all, been a long day. "He doesn't want to know that."

"I do, I do," the padre insisted. "I have heard of this gift of yours. And I am so eager to know what Heavenly Father has in store for me."

A meat locker somewhere, Alaric fervently hoped, into which the man would be locked and then mistaken for burger and served to a starving Boy Scout troop. Although that was too good a death for him.

"A long and healthy life," Meena replied, to Alaric's extreme disappointment.

Padre Caliente beamed as everyone around him uttered congratulations.

"Well," he said, "I cannot wait to share these good tidings with my new congregation."

Alaric could contain himself no longer.

"Speaking of your new congregation," he burst out, "done any exorcisms since you got here, Padre?"

Looking confused, the priest said, "I'm sorry, I do not understand."

Was he actually pretending he didn't remember that complete disaster in that slum in Rio five years earlier? He had to be kidding. Alaric had never seen a grown man run so fast.

"Exorcisms," Alaric repeated. "Expulsions of demonic spirits from individuals who happen to be possessed by them. Done any since you got here?"

"Uh, no." Father Henrique glanced uncertainly at Father Bernard, who happened to be the only person left standing nearby, with the exception of Sister Gertrude. "I'm sorry. Should I have? Are exorcisms very common in the city? I thought there had not been so much activity of that nature here lately—"

Father Bernard—a kindly man whom Alaric had seen stake two vampires at once with a wooden candelabrum at the battle at St. George's Cathedral—seemed to take pity on the younger priest.

"Quite uncommon of late, I would say. I'm not sure what Alaric is referring to."

Father Henrique's gaze sharpened on Alaric.

"Alaric," he said. "Not . . . Alaric Wulf? Why, I remember you!" He stuck out his hand. "How are you? It has been many years, old friend!"

Alaric glared at him. Old friend? If he'd been the padre, he wouldn't have been as quick to assume the relationship. And he'd have been apologizing, not glad-handing. Had the man really not recognized him?

Or was he still so embarrassed over his cowardly behavior, he'd pretended not to recognize him (the more likely scenario)?

"Yes," Alaric said mildly. "It has been a few years, hasn't it?"

"Who would have thought?" Padre Caliente said wonderingly. "All that time ago, in that horrible slum. And now here we are, at this wonderful party, with so many beautiful people, in New York City. How strange life is, yes?"

Alaric stared.

"Yes," he said again. "Life is strange." Strange that no one had ever given the padre the swift kick in the rear that he so rightly deserved.

"What you must have thought of me that night!" Henrique looked at Meena, Father Bernard, and Sister Gertrude and said, "Imagine me, a very young priest, with my first congregation. And I get a call that one of my parishioners is possessed—yes, really, possessed—by an evil spirit. I am terrified. I have heard of such things, of course, but only in movies. I have no idea it can be real."

"Oh," Father Bernard said, "it's real, all right. I remember one I had in Brooklyn Heights—"

"Let him finish, Father," Alaric said. He was interested in seeing how the younger priest was going to excuse his behavior.

"So I get to the house—a shack, really—and there is this sweet, angel-faced little girl. And she is hovering a foot off the bed, in this sort of . . . circle of light. But these voices that are coming out of her . . . I had never heard such voices in my life." Padre Caliente shuddered. "The things they were saying."

"What were the voices saying?" Meena asked, owl-eyed.

The priest looked at her. "Oh," he said, "you don't want to know, believe me."

"Curse words, probably," Father Bernard said knowledgeably.

Alaric knew what the girl had been saying was far worse than that, but kept this information to himself.

"Anyway," Father Henrique went on, "there is the girl's family, weeping, begging me to help. And there is this man." Father Henrique nodded toward Alaric. "And he was telling me to get out my holy water and cross, and to start praying, and to hurry. Hurry! But I was so terrified. I had never in my life seen anything so . . . so . . ."

Father Bernard clapped a hand on the younger priest's shoulder. "I know. Pure evil. The first time you see it, you either flee or freeze."

Or fight, Alaric thought. *Or am I the only one who thought of this?* Sister Gertrude, he knew, had a set of Berettas hidden beneath her habit, and never hesitated to use them.

But no one had given her a parish on the Upper East Side to run.

"Yes," Father Henrique said, shooting Father Bernard a grateful look. "I dropped everything, and . . . well, I am ashamed to say, I ran."

Sister Gertrude shook her head. "Oh, you poor thing," she said. "Did you really?"

"I did," the priest said. "I have tried to make up for it since, by fighting against the Lamir in that same district—"

"The Lamir," Father Bernard said, looking impressed. "I hear they're quite a handful. South American vampires aren't like the rest of the species, from what I understand. Very aggressive."

"Yes," Father Henrique said. "They are very different from their European cousins. Local legend says they are descendants of the *Noctilio leporinus,* or great fishing bats, of South America. They're known for catching their prey by skimming the surfaces of rivers or lakes with their claws, then devouring their flesh—not just their blood—after they've caught them."

"Horrible," Sister Gertrude said, with a shudder. "And I think you've more than redeemed yourself for whatever happened at that exorcism if you've taken out a few of those nasty creatures."

"A few," Father Bernard cried. "I heard he's taken out a hundred."

"Well," Padre Caliente said modestly, "I try. I could never forgive myself for leaving this man to deal with that nasty business all by himself." He stepped toward Alaric to grasp his hand. "Thank you, my good friend. I can finally tell you now. Thank you for saving that poor, helpless little soul."

"I didn't save her," Alaric said. He didn't attempt to disguise his bitterness. "She needed more help than I could give her. That's why I sent for the local priest. After you ran off, she died."

There was a short silence. Sister Gertrude crossed herself, and said, "Bless her," beneath her breath.

Meena, her dark eyes welling with tears, said, "That's so sad."

Alaric looked at her in alarm. "Don't start crying now," he said. What was the matter with her? She'd been crying on and off all night. He could have sworn she'd been crying in the cab, when he'd given her the necklace. "Here comes the archbishop. And he's got Genevieve Fox with him."

"Oh God," Meena said, and reached up to wipe her eyes, sending a black streak of mascara across both temples. Alaric stared at the smudges in disbelief.

The archbishop, who'd been making his way steadily across the room, finally stopped beside them. So did the camera crew that had been following him.

"Your Excellency," Fathers Bernard and Henrique said, genuflecting. Sister Gertrude did the same. Alaric stayed where he was.

The archbishop didn't appear to notice.

"Ah," he said, beaming at them. "I'm so delighted that you could make it." He clearly didn't have the slightest idea who they were, with the possible exception of Father Henrique, with whom Alaric had noticed him schmoozing, and Meena, who'd already informed him earlier that he'd live a long, healthy life. "Thank you for sharing in this very special evening."

"Your Excellency," Father Henrique said, springing to his feet, "may I present Alaric Wulf, a very good friend of mine?"

The archbishop eyed Alaric.

"Your name sounds familiar," he said. Then he seemed to remember why. "Ah, yes," he said.

But he clearly didn't dare say more, because of the cameras. The Palatine was, after all, a secret organization. Or perhaps what the archbishop had heard about Alaric wasn't particularly complimentary. Alaric's reputation for killing demons was exemplary.

The rest of his reputation wasn't quite so spotless.

"Bless you, my children," the archbishop said, and made the sign of the cross over them all.

As soon as he'd moved away, Sister Gertrude said, "Meena, my dear." She pointed at her eyes.

Meena opened her purse and removed a compact from inside it. As soon as she saw her reflection, she uttered a word that was highly improper to say around members of the clergy. Then, realizing what she'd said, she covered her mouth with her hand.

"I'm so sorry," she said, looking guilty.

"Oh, it's all right," Sister Gertrude said, smiling. "I've heard worse. I live in the Village, remember. I was about to go the ladies' myself. Shall we?"

"*Yes,*" Meena said, and allowed the older woman to lead the way.

That's when Alaric's mobile phone chirped. He pulled it out of his pocket and was astonished—and relieved—to see Holtzman's name and number flash onto his screen.

"Where have you been?" he demanded, after he'd lifted the phone to his ear. "Everyone thought you were dead."

All he heard on the end of the line was static. "Holtzman?" he asked. He looked up. The rest of the partygoers were enjoying their drinks and what few snacks they'd been able to snag. He didn't see a single fellow Palatine Guard anywhere in the room . . . which apparently got terrible reception. He strode toward the nearest door. "*Holtzman?* Are you there?"

As he shoved open the exit door, he heard another burst of static, then his boss's voice, saying, "Oh, thank God, someone's picked up. I can't seem to get through to anyone at headquarters. Where *is* everyone? But never mind, you're there. We've . . . disaster . . . "

"Holtzman." Alaric stood in the hallway outside the exhibition, the phone pressed to his ear. Between the static, the faint connection, and the frantic tone in his boss's voice, he could barely hear a word he was saying. "Where are you?"

More static. Then, " . . . Jersey. You were right. You were right about everything. We found the bodies. And it's worse than you could ever imag—" More static.

Alaric, thrilled as he was to have his boss tell him he'd been right about something, was more concerned about his well-being, and that of the rest of the team.

"Abraham, can you hear me? *Where* in New Jersey are you?" Alaric asked desperately. "We've got people there looking for you now. For some reason we can't pick up your GPS locators. Abraham? Are you—"

"Oh no," Holtzman said, coming in loud and clear all of a sudden. "Of course you can't. That would be on account of—"

And then the static grew so thick, it turned into a whine that seemed nearly to pierce Alaric's eardrum.

Then the line went dead.

"Abraham," Alaric cried into the phone. "Abraham?"

But it was no good. He was gone.

Alaric quickly dialed headquarters. Amazingly, though he let it ring ten times, no one picked up.

Unbelievable. He understood that everyone was out looking for his boss—or attending this function. But at the very least someone ought to have been manning the computers. What was happening to his workplace?

He hung up and redialed, this time the IT department in the main office in Rome. It was staffed round the clock, so even though day was just dawning there, he knew someone would pick up.

"What do you want, Wulf?" a woman's voice asked him crankily in Italian.

"The GPS location of Abraham Holtzman's cell phone in America," Alaric said.

"It's gone." He recognized the voice as belonging to Johanna, a brilliant computer tech who'd helped him on previous cases, sometimes against the wishes of her superiors. But she rarely left the office, which could make her moody at times. "The satellite can't find it. And you know all your cell phones are equipped with indestructible state-of-the-art ultrathin real-time GPS trackers with motion sensors that give ten-second updates on your locations that are accurate by up to seven inches. So if the satellite can't find Abraham, that can only mean one thing." Then, seeming to remember Abraham was not only Alaric's boss, but also his friend, she added, "Sorry, Wulf."

"The satellite is wrong," Alaric said, trying to keep his voice calm. There was no use taking out his frustrations on blameless Johanna. "Because Holtzman called me from his cell phone not one minute ago. The connection was terrible, but he said he's still in New Jersey—"

"*What?*" Johanna sounded much more awake. Also alarmed. And angry. "But that's not possible. The data I'm getting from the satellite is telling me there's no sign whatsoever of—"

"I don't care what the data you're getting from the satellite is telling you," Alaric interrupted. "I'm telling you I just got a call from Abraham. So find out where it came from, pinpoint a location for Holtzman and the rest of his team, then notify the search party in New Jersey of their whereabouts and get them out of there. Do you understand me?"

He could actually hear Johanna typing. "Absolutely. It may take me a few minutes, but—"

"Whatever it takes. And be sure to call me, too, as soon as you have any information whatsoever."

"Of course," Johanna said. "Alaric?"

"What?"

"What is *going on* over there?" she whispered. "Is it . . . you know. *Him?* The dark prince?"

"I'm not sure," he said. "But as soon as I find out, I'll let you know." Alaric hung up.

What had Holtzman meant, that they'd found the bodies? And that it was more horrible than Alaric could imagine?

Alaric could imagine quite a bit.

What he could *not* imagine was that the organization he worked for would ever have its priorities so misplaced that it would send all its most skilled employees to a cocktail party, while others were obviously still alive—and apparently in some danger—in the field . . .

And then failed to have anyone manning the desks at its local headquarters while the search for them was under way.

Fuming, he went back into the art gallery, scanning it for any sign of someone—anyone—in some position of power at the Palatine.

Instead, all he saw was Genevieve Fox coming back toward him, steered by Father Henrique. A photographer followed in their wake.

"Come," Father Henrique was saying. "Miss Genevieve, I want you to meet my old friend Alaric Wulf. He knew me from my very early days in Rio. And now he lives in New York City."

Jesus Christ, Alaric thought. *Not now.* But he could see no way to escape without seeming rude. Besides, there was no one else in the room whom he recognized, aside from the archbishop.

"Well, Alaric Wulf," Genevieve purred, snaking out a well-manicured hand. The gold bangles draping her wrist jangled. She smelled of expensive perfume. "How is it that we've never met before?"

"I don't know," Alaric said. Her fingers felt like tiny twigs. Only they were alive.

"And what do you do?" Genevieve asked.

"Security," Alaric said. He looked over one of her bare, bony shoulders and saw Sister Gertrude emerge from the ladies' room. She met his gaze, gave him a wink, and waved, indicating that Meena was still inside, and all right. So, that was fine. He would give her another few minutes to compose herself. She was hardly likely to be attacked by Lucien Antonescu—if he was anywhere around—in the ladies' room.

And Sister Gertrude was always fully armed, anyway.

"Security," Genevieve purred. "You know, I could use some security."

"Yes," Alaric said, turning his gaze back toward her appraisingly. "I'm sure you could."

Genevieve threw back her head and laughed. "You're naughty."

"No," Alaric said. "I am not. Not tonight." Naughty was the last thing he was feeling. Angry, maybe. Frustrated, definitely. Perhaps even vengeful.

But not naughty.

Genevieve stopped laughing.

"Well," she said, "aren't you a party pooper."

"I thought you were a serious reporter," he said. His mind had begun to work furiously. Television. Journalist. Missing people. "Not a party girl."

"I guess you'll never know," Genevieve said, with a wink. "Will you?" She looked at her photographer. "Come on, Manny. Let's get this over with."

Then she stepped between Alaric and Father Henrique, immediately assuming a model stance, putting on a dazzling smile for the camera, and sucking in her stomach. He didn't know why such a slender woman would feel it necessary to make her already flat stomach look even flatter.

But then, her job was to look good on television.

Where she reported the news.

"Say 'cheese,' boys," she said. "This one is going onto the website."

Flashes started going off. Alaric was blinded, but Genevieve and Father Henrique seemed unaffected, perhaps because they posed for photos so often.

"Please e-mail me one," Father Henrique said. "Alaric Wulf and I are old friends. I would very much like a picture to remember this night."

"Certainly," Genevieve said, releasing them both. "Manny, get the priest's info." She looked up at Alaric. "What about you? Would you very much like to remember this night?"

"I don't think so," he said.

She smiled and tucked her business card into the front pocket of his tuxedo. "Anything I can do to change your mind about that?"

He thought about Holtzman's phone call. He had never heard such panic before in his boss's voice, and they'd been in some pretty tight spots in the past.

You were right, Holtzman had said. *You were right about everything. And it's worse than you could ever imagine.*

"Actually," Alaric said to Genevieve. "I think maybe there is something you can do."

"Well," she said, with a smile. "Looks like we both might find something to remember about this night after all."

Chapter Nineteen

Meena rested her forehead against the side of the toilet stall. The metal felt cool against her skin. She no longer felt like crying.

But she didn't want to leave the stall. If she did, it would mean she'd have to go back out into that crowd of people, and she really didn't want to do that. She still couldn't figure out why she had been invited to this event, except as the Palatine's pet freak. Why would she be on the guest list to what she'd heard Genevieve Fox reporting as "the star-studded social event of the year"? She'd already shaken hands with one of Jonathan's favorite rock-and-roll stars, a former mayor of New York, and, of course, the wife-murdering athlete.

It didn't help that she'd just started crying in front of all of them. Not that they'd noticed.

Still, she wasn't eager to go back out there. She couldn't do any more readings. Not that that's what she'd been doing, really. Half the people who'd asked for them she'd lied to.

Someone tapped on the door to her stall.

"Meena?" It was Sister Gertrude. "Are you all right, dear?"

"Oh," Meena replied, "I'm fine."

It was probably wrong to be lying to a nun. But it was only a small lie.

"Oh, good," Sister Gertrude said. "I'm just going outside to wait, then."

"Okay," Meena said. "I'll be there in a minute."

"Take your time," Sister Gertrude said.

Meena heard the nun's shoes clicking on the marble floor. A few seconds later, there were no sounds at all in the bathroom. She was alone.

She sighed with relief, then reached up to feel the newest addition to her wardrobe. It had been hanging, heavy as an anvil, at her throat all night.

Let's try to keep it professional, shall we? Alaric had said in the cab.

She fingered the smooth outline of the cross, wondering why he'd given it to her in the first place, if he hated her so much.

He probably just didn't want to bother with the paperwork that he would inevitably have to fill out if she was killed while under his protection.

She was stupid, she realized, not to have thought of wearing a cross before. Although truthfully, it seemed a bit simplistic as far as self-defense techniques went.

But remembering the story Father Henrique had been telling of how he and Alaric had met, she wondered. Certainly Alaric seemed to believe that if the priest hadn't fled the way he had, the two of them might have been able to help that poor little girl.

Maybe there *was* power in ancient symbols, and the people who wielded them.

The necklace obviously couldn't hurt.

There was a tap on her stall door.

"Just a minute," Meena said. "I'll be right out—"

She couldn't stay in a bathroom stall forever, she realized. She had to face reality sometime.

She stood up and opened the door.

And found herself standing in front of Mary Lou Antonescu.

Chapter Twenty

M eena. How are you, hon?"

Mary Lou reached out to give her a friendly hug hello . . . then paused, eyeing the cross at her throat.

"Oh," she said, her smile fading slightly. "How . . . pretty."

"Mary Lou." Meena looked quickly up and down the bathroom. No one else appeared to be in any of the stalls.

But that didn't mean anything. Sister Gertrude could be back at any moment.

"Are you insane?" Meena whispered. "This place is crawling with Alpha Level Palatine Guards. If any of them recognizes you, they'll stake you."

"Oh, hon," Mary Lou said. "Are you talking about that nun who was in here with you a minute ago? Don't worry. I just gave her a little ol' mental push toward the kitchens. She'll be in there looking for more salmon for hours."

Meena stared at the tall, elegant blonde. She was wearing a dark brown evening gown in a filmy material that hung from a jeweled dog collar all the way down to her ankles, a deep red layer of lipstick, and a pair of sky-high Louboutins. She looked exactly the way Meena had always pictured the famous spy Mata Hari.

"Mary Lou," Meena said, exasperated and yet oddly touched. "What are you doing here?"

"I'm supposed to be giving you a message," Mary Lou said. She waved a heavily ringed hand. "It's from Lucien, as if you hadn't already guessed. You know, he's just crazy for you."

"I think I need to sit down," Meena said faintly.

"Oh." Mary Lou looked around. "Well, look at that, there's a couch over here. It's nice to know all that money Emil and I have been donating to this place over the years has gone to something worthwhile. How many paintings of suffering saints do they have to have in one museum, anyway? Here, come sit."

Meena sank onto the couch. It was vinyl covered and clearly meant for mothers with nursing babies, but she didn't care.

"Where is Lucien?" she asked Mary Lou. "He isn't *here,* is he? In the museum? Please say no."

"Of course he is." Mary Lou was standing, admiring her own reflection in the mirrors. Gone were the days when vampires couldn't see themselves in mirrors or on film. Now that the world had gone digital, vampires could be caught on film—as well as admiring themselves in mirrors that weren't silver-backed—just like everyone else. "He said he'd meet you in your favorite place. I have no idea what that means, and I didn't ask. I'm nosy, but not that nosy. I assumed it was a little secret between y'all."

Meena knew exactly where Lucien meant.

She hadn't visited the painting of Saint Joan since the last time she'd seen it—that night Lucien had claimed to have special privileges to the Met and slipped her inside after visiting hours.

Of course his only privileges had been the kind all vampires had everywhere they went . . . the kind they abused with their powers of mental telepathy and ability to transmogrify into mist and, in Lucien's case, fly.

Visiting the painting of Saint Joan was too painful for Meena now, even though it was still her favorite.

"Mary Lou," Meena said. "You have to tell him to leave. The Vatican has issued a worldwide security alert, and Alaric thinks it's about him, like somehow they knew he was coming There are guards everywhere, just waiting for him to show up. He's going to get caught." Her voice strained to continue. "He's going to get killed."

Mary Lou stopped doing her eyes and stared at Meena's reflection in the mirror.

"Hon," she said, "it's the *prince*. No one is going to catch him, let alone kill him. But I'd take that thing off your neck before you go meet him. Not that he has anything against believers. It's just that, as far as accessories go, it isn't doing much for you."

Meena reached up to touch the necklace Alaric had given her. The metal felt warm from her skin.

"Mary Lou," she said. Her eyes had filled with tears again. "I mean it. This is *crazy*. And Alaric is here guarding me, by the way. How am I supposed to walk out of this party and go meet Lucien on another floor of the museum without Alaric noticing I'm gone?"

"Oh, honey," Mary Lou said. "You think I wouldn't create a diversion? Give me some credit. I can be very distracting when I want to be."

"Lucien asked you to do that?" Meena shook her head. "That's just . . . Mary Lou, you could be killed. How could Lucien be so selfish?"

"Selfish?" Mary Lou seemed surprised. "I don't think he's being selfish. I told you, he's crazy about you. He wants to see you, and this is where you are. If asking me to help him do that is selfish, well, then maybe it is, but if you think about it, this whole thing is my fault in the first place, like I was telling him earlier. I mean, I was the one who introduced y'all—"

"But I think it's more than that," Meena interrupted. "More than him just being crazy about me. Mary Lou, I'm worried. I think there's something wrong with him. I tried to get him to talk about it last night, but he wouldn't."

"Oh." Mary Lou paused while dabbing some lip gloss onto her mouth. *"That."*

Meena stared at her. "You know what I mean? You know what I'm talking about?"

"Oh, I know *exactly* what you're talking about. But good luck trying to get him to open up about it. I was after them both all day about it—him *and* Emil. I mean, why is the prince of darkness living in a *cave*? That's all I wanted to know. But would either of them tell me? No way."

"A cave?" Meena was more than just perplexed. She was shocked. "Lucien is living in a *cave*?"

"You got that right. But will anyone tell me why? Lord, no. Men never want to talk, do they? Unless it's about themselves. Then it's talk, talk, talk, all day long. They can be such babies, can't they? They think everything is about them. You know what Lucien thinks is about him?"

Meena got up and went to the sink to stand beside her. "What?"

"This show," Mary Lou said. "Can you believe it? The entire show. Apparently, the Vatican put it together to lure him here so they could capture him."

Meena stared at Mary Lou's reflection in the mirror. "What are you talking about?"

"Oh, there's some old book out there that Emil says used to belong to Lucien's mother. And of course he *has* to have it back. For the life of me, I don't know why. I went and had a look at it. It's on a little display pedestal. You probably walked right past it. I did, too, at first. It's a tiny little thing. I told Emil, couldn't Lucien just buy himself a nice Gutenberg Bible, or something, if he wants one so badly—though why he would, I can't imagine—and not go to all this trouble? But no, it has to be *this* book, because it was his mom's, apparently. Well, you know how men are about their mothers. Don't even get me started about Emil's. Good thing she died before I was ever born. And it's even worse with Lucien's mother, you know, because she—"

"Killed herself," Meena murmured.

She suddenly felt as if someone had poured a very cold drink down her back, something that actually used to happen to her with some frequency when she was a teenager and had been an unpopular guest at parties thanks to her dire warnings on the hazards of drinking and driving . . . warnings that generally came true.

"Oh, I know, I heard," Mary Lou said. "Wasn't that just awful? Jumped out the palace window when she heard the Turks were invading. Well, you know, if I heard some Turks were invading, I'd jump out the window, too, because let me tell you, they did some not very nice things to lady prisoners back in those days. Emil's told me some stories . . . trust me, you do *not* want to know. Still, Lucien never quite got over his mother's death. And neither did his father, apparently. Emil said Lucien's mother was a princess, and a very special lady. People even said she was—"

"An angel," Meena finished for her, sitting back down again.

This was her fault. All of it.

Because if it was true—and it had to be—who had put in the request to the Biblioteca Apostolica Vaticana for the book, alerting them to its presence in their catalog in the first place?

She had.

Oh *God*.

And now Lucien was here to get his mother's book back.

But so was Alaric . . . as well as every Alpha Level guard in the Palatine.

"Well, yes!" Mary Lou looked pleased that Meena was so knowledgeable about the subject. "An angel! Though that can't *literally* be true, of course. Because first of all, there's no such thing as angels. And second of all, how could an *angel* be married to Dracula? Let alone give birth to his son. Still, she was supposed to have been just the nicest, sweetest thing. That's why Lucien's father, Vlad Tepes, went off his rocker when he found out she was dead, and became 'Vladimir the Impaler'—" Mary Lou made little quotation marks in the air. "And then eventually *that* wasn't enough either, so he traded his soul to the devil so he could live forever and become—ta-da—Dracula . . . "

Meena let her head sink into her hands. But still, Mary Lou's voice droned on.

" . . . and then he passed down the title to Lucien . . . though if you ask me, Lucien's never been very committed to the role. I think he would rather have had this book of hours. It was the only thing he had left of his mom, but I guess it fell into enemy hands after Poenari Castle was taken by the Turks. Lucien thought it was lost forever. But what do you know? It turned out the Vatican had it all these years. And now it's here in New York, and Lucien's just itching to get it back, in addition to you . . . Meena? Meena! Where did you go?"

Chapter Twenty-one

Meena had been too caught up in her own misery to absorb the show. To her, it had just looked like a blur.

Now she headed straight for the display pedestal Mary Lou had described.

She didn't want to believe it was the book she'd seen in her dreams . . . the one she had told Lucien—and everyone else who would listen—about.

It couldn't possibly be the one she'd requested from the Biblioteca Apostolica Vaticana, thinking the description—*Book of Hours, Romanian origin, midfifteenth-century*—sounded right, although the few illustrations pictured online only vaguely fit the images she'd seen from her dream.

Because if it were, that would mean . . .

She didn't want to think what that would mean. She just had to look for herself. She had to be sure, before she did—or said—anything rash.

The manuscript—quite a small one, just as Mary Lou had said—stood upright in a glass cube. One exquisitely illustrated page had been separated from the others, and was backlit so that it glowed with an almost otherworldly light.

Meena knew from her research that this was because actual gold had been melted down into liquid and laid in paper-thin sheets on the vellum—that's what the manuscript pages were made of—all around the beautifully drawn illustration, which was of a dark-haired young woman wearing a long, royal-blue gown, and holding a lamb in her arms.

Meena stared at the woman inside the gleaming layer of gold, which had also been decorated with whimsical drawings of butterflies and flowers, gorgeously colored with red, yellow, green, blue, and white. According to her research, these paints would have been made by mixing lead, mercuric sulfide, arsenic, and lapis lazuli to give them their vibrant and lasting tones.

It wasn't the image she'd seen in her dream, the one the woman and the little boy had been looking at. But there was definitely something about it that . . .

"Lovely, is it not?"

Meena jumped about a foot. Then she glanced across the glass cube and realized it was only Father Henrique. He, too, was admiring the manuscript.

"Er," she said. "Yes."

She looked around. The party was still going strong, even though it was getting late. She could see Alaric across the room, deep in conversation with the reporter from New York's own twenty-four-hour news channel, Genevieve Fox. It appeared that he hadn't yet noticed that Meena had come out of the ladies' room.

"I do not know as much as I should about these books," Father Henrique was saying modestly, "but I once read that it was common when they were commissioned—as this one was said to be, by the owner's betrothed—that the artist would place, somewhere in the work, a portrait of the bride. Since this book was said to belong to a beautiful princess, I would think this woman, here, was she."

He pointed at the illuminated picture of the girl holding the lamb.

"She has no halo, you see?" Father Henrique was saying. "So she is not the Virgin Mary, or a saint. And she is very attractive and richly dressed."

Meena glanced back at the woman in the illustration. Was this Lucien's mother?

The portrait she'd once seen of Lucien's father—in this very museum—hadn't looked a thing like Lucien.

But the closer she bent to examine the portrait of the young woman in the illuminated illustration, the more she thought she saw a likeness to the woman in her dream . . . and to Lucien. It wasn't just in the flowing black hair, the darkness of the features, or the litheness in the figure.

There was the gentleness to the eyes that she recognized, and a certain humor—and kindness—about the small mouth that she would not have mistaken anywhere.

She didn't think she was seeing it because she wanted to either. She *didn't* want to see it. Because if this was the book from her dream, the same one she'd requested from the catalog, the fact that the Vatican had put it on display like this, and not sent it to her, the way she'd asked, could only mean . . .

Well, exactly what Lucien—and even Alaric—had been suggesting:

That this show *had* been put together for a single purpose . . . to lure the prince of darkness from hiding so that the Palatine could capture him.

She had to let Alaric know about this. This was exactly what he'd been suspecting all along.

But she couldn't. Because she couldn't put Lucien in any more danger than he already was in.

Besides, Alaric seemed to be completely engrossed in his conversation with Genevieve Fox. Or rather, Genevieve was completely engrossed in her conversation with him. She had even removed something from her evening bag, and was—

Good God. It was her BlackBerry.

Genevieve Fox was putting Alaric Wulf's phone number into her BlackBerry.

Wulf. Fox. And they actually made an attractive couple. They were both so tall and blond.

Meena wondered why this realization caused her insides to give a convulsive twist.

She didn't have time to think about that, however. She had to go warn Lucien, and *without* Alaric noticing she'd left the room. Actually, she could put his conversation with Genevieve Fox to good use.

But first, she had to get rid of Father Henrique, who was still speaking.

"These little books were extremely popular in the fifteenth century," he was explaining, "and their contents were generally uniform. Excerpts from the Gospels, the hours of the cross, the seven penitential psalms, a calendar of the church feasts, and various devotionals. This one, however, is a bit unusual. It also has the astrological signs and the different phases of the moon."

"That's very interesting," she murmured.

Meena couldn't deny it. The longer she gazed at it, the more strongly she believed the woman in the picture was the woman from her dream . . . the woman who'd thrown herself into what was now known as Princess River rather than be taken captive by her husband's enemies. And so had driven Vlad Tepes mad with grief, and turned him into Vlad the Impaler.

This was the woman who'd created Dracula, and given birth to his son, Lucien.

And because Meena had drawn so much attention to her book of hours, *she* was the woman who—albeit inadvertently—would soon contribute to the capture, and ultimate demise of that son.

She had to go. She had to go warn Lucien to get out of the museum *as soon as possible* . . .

"Forgive me for saying so," Father Henrique said. He startled her by reaching out to touch her arm. His smile had vanished. He wore an expression of gentle concern. "But you seem unwell. May I get you something? A glass of wine, perhaps? Or some water?"

"I . . . I'm fine," Meena said. Was it her imagination, or had his English seemed to have improved since the last time she'd spoken to him? "I just remembered I have to go make a quick phone call. So if you'll excuse me—"

"I hope you don't mind me mentioning it," Father Henrique said. "But you seem like an unhappy person. And I don't blame you. I don't think I could be happy either, knowing how everyone around me is going to die."

"I try to help keep them from dying," Meena replied automatically. She had to get out of the room before Alaric finished his conversation with Genevieve Fox. "No one's future is certain. It depends on the choices they make. I like to think that with my help, maybe they can make better ones. I try to make things right. Now, if you'll just . . ."

Father Henrique nodded solemnly. "That is what devotionals like this were for." He indicated the book of hours. "To help the women who owned them make better choices, and stay upon the correct path. Back when this was made, there were very few books. Most people would go their entire lives never learning how to read, much less own or even see a book. There were so few enlightened people—like you and me—to help guide the uninformed, and show them the true way. It was so easy, even then, to slip into the darkness. Now it's even easier and"—he looked across the room at Genevieve Fox and sighed—"people look to women like her for their enlightenment. Well. What can we do but, as you say, keep trying?"

She stared at him. What did he know, she wondered, about slipping into the darkness? He'd run *away* from the darkness that night of the exorcism with Alaric. He'd admitted it himself. Maybe he was taking strides to fight it now.

But putting down Genevieve, who'd given him such a nice interview, didn't seem like the best way to go about doing that.

"Ready to go?" a deep voice asked.

Meena, startled, whipped around to see Alaric standing beside her. Where had he come from? The last time she'd looked, he'd been all the way across the room . . . and looking as if he were going to be there awhile.

"Uh . . . " Meena couldn't believe it. How was she going to get away now? "I'm not quite ready—"

She broke off. Mary Lou was striding toward them from across the room.

"What?" Alaric asked impatiently. He seemed annoyed, but whether it was with her, or with seeing that Father Henrique was standing right there, didn't really matter. Mary Lou was coming straight at them, a big smile on her ruby-red lips. "If you need to go back to the bathroom before we leave, just say so. I'll wait. You think I'm not used to it? You spend half your life in the bathroom."

"I—" Meena's eyes widened as Mary Lou reached out, grasped Alaric by both shoulders, then spun him around.

"Alaric," Mary Lou said happily. "Darling, there you are. I've missed you. It's been too long."

Then she kissed him, full on the mouth.

Chapter Twenty-two

Meena had long suspected Alaric of having a soft spot for Mary Lou Antonescu.

But she'd never known the real reason why until she saw the way Mary Lou kissed. The woman was like a Dyson vacuum cleaner. A hundred years from now, Meena doubted Mary Lou would have lost any of her sucking action.

The second Mary Lou released Alaric, the alert seemed to go out:
Vampire!

Meena wasn't certain who said it first. Definitely not Alaric. He looked stunned, but pleasantly so.

In fact, as Mary Lou pulled her face away from his, Alaric—who, Carolina had once told Meena, was famous among his colleagues for having ordered a field full of teenagers, enjoying an outdoor festival featuring their favorite horror-core bands, crop-dusted with holy water; it was pure luck, Carolina insisted, that the members of that band all turned out to have been vampires, and the worst the teenagers endured was a dousing—murmured, "Oh, hello. How have *you* been?"

Alaric was the only one in the room—besides Meena, Genevieve Fox, and the murderous athlete—who didn't pull out a weapon the minute the cry went up.

Vampire!

That's when Mary Lou did a back handspring, knocking over the pedestal containing Lucien's mother's book of hours. It spilled to the carpet without suffering any apparent harm. Mary Lou snatched it up and tucked it neatly into her pagoda bag.

Then, with a wink in Alaric's direction, she darted off toward where the caterers had been coming and going all night with the trays of salmon.

Most of the party guests and all of the museum's security guards took off after her, including Father Henrique and Alaric, the latter shouting at Meena, *"Don't move."* Then he disappeared.

So it ended up being quite easy for Meena to slip out the main door unseen, and walk down the museum's corridors until she found an elevator. She pressed the button, then, when the doors slid open, got inside.

She took the car to the floor where Mary Lou had said Lucien was waiting.

She didn't know what she was going to say to him when she saw him—except that he needed to leave. Forever this time. No amount of kissing on his part was going to change her mind. He needed to go his way, and she needed to go hers, and the two of them needed to stay apart forever, start over, make *different* choices . . . like Father Henrique had said the book of hours had offered its readers.

Maybe if she closed her eyes and prayed hard enough, when the elevator doors slid open, she would magically have the strength to make this happen. Why not? For a long time, she had not known there was such a thing as vampires and demons in the world. Why couldn't it turn out that there was such a thing as magic?

But when the elevator doors slid open, there was the gallery to the nineteenth-century wing, just as it always had been. There was the painting of Saint Joan that she knew so well, looking beatifically off into the distance in her peasant clothes, as saints whispered urgently into her ear of her important destiny.

And there was Lucien Antonescu, standing in front of the painting, waiting for her.

And a wave of desire for him slammed into her, so hard that it nearly knocked her off her feet.

"Meena," he said. His voice wasn't quite steady. His eyes, so dark, so luminous, were exactly like the eyes of the woman she'd seen in his mother's manuscript downstairs. "I knew you'd come."

He was wearing a charcoal-gray sweater in some kind of soft mate-

rial that clung to every curve of his muscular chest, the sleeves casually
pushed up so that she could see the smooth, bare skin of his forearms.

And he was looking at her with those dark eyes, and they were filled
with so much love. Love for her.

She closed her eyes. *No.*

There was no magic. And this wasn't a dream. This was real. There
was no way she could turn back the hours, or undo the damage their
relationship had done to so many others.

She could only do what she'd told Father Henrique she always did:
try to make it right.

But she couldn't do that if Lucien touched her. She knew that. If he
touched her, she'd fall apart, the way she always did.

She punched the down button, then shrank back against the far
wall of the elevator—it was imperative that she put as much distance
between her and Lucien Antonescu as she possibly could—and said, as
the doors were closing, "I'm sorry, Lucien. This was a mistake. It's a
trap. They're waiting for you. I have to go."

But he had other ideas. Moving so rapidly he was a blur, his arms
shot through the opening between the closing doors. A second later, his
large hands had wrapped around her upper arms, dragging her out of
the elevator and into the gallery . . .

. . . and to him, until she collided with the rock-hard muscle wall of
his chest.

Now she was the trapped one. She heard the elevators close behind
her, with a *ding.*

The sound might well have signaled the closing of what was left of
the rational world.

Lifting her head to throw an anguished glance up at him, she saw
that he was looking down at her with sheer agony on his face, those
dark eyes stormy with emotion, that mouth, every bit as sensitive as she
remembered it, grimly set.

"Meena," he said, grinding out the words, "what do you think you're
doing?"

"Lucien," she said, breathless as if she'd been running, "you've got to
listen to me. It isn't safe—"

But he didn't let her finish. His mouth started to come down to crush hers, and she knew, with a sense of inevitability that was as sickeningly disappointing as it was exciting, that the minute their lips met, she wouldn't be able to resist him. She didn't *want* to resist him. She was powerless in his embrace. She closed her eyes, letting her head drop back against his strong arm.

Except . . . as the seconds ticked by, his lips never touched hers. Instead . . .

Nothing.

When she opened her eyes to see what was happening, she saw that he was looking down at her curiously. Not at her mouth either, or into her eyes, but gazing at her neck.

She also saw—or thought she saw—a hint of red in the center of each one of those dark brown eyes of his.

"What's this?" he asked, running a finger along the black cord that held in place the silver cross Alaric had given her.

She was jolted back to reality as quickly as if someone had slapped her. What was she doing?

"Lucien," she said, dropping her arms from around his neck, where she'd instinctively wrapped them. "Y-you can't stay here. It's much too dangerous. They're already after Mary Lou. You've got to go—"

He still hadn't lifted his gaze from the cross. She couldn't be sure in the dim glow of the security lights along the floor of the gallery—the only light, besides the gleam from the display bulbs on the paintings . . .

. . . But she thought she could still see that red blaze there. Very faintly.

"Where did you get it?" he asked, pulling on the choker. He kept his finger well away from the silver cross. "All your jewelry was destroyed by my clan. That's an expensive piece. I've never seen you wear it before."

"Great," she said. "Now you've been spying on me?"

Lucien didn't smile.

"Not spying," he said. "Watching over you. I told you I would. How else do you think I saw the attack on you last night? And I've never seen you wear that bef—"

She put her hand over his mouth. She didn't want him talking about how well he knew her wardrobe, especially from observing her since they'd broken up.

And she *definitely* didn't want him asking about the necklace. This line of questioning was causing her heart to thump way too hard, and she was certain, since he was still holding her so closely, he would be able to feel it through the thin, clingy material of her dress.

"Focus on what's important here," she said. "Your mother's book, the one Mary Lou just stole?" She tried to keep her voice firm and steady. Except that she didn't feel firm. Or very steady. But she had to act that way. For both of them. "It's the one from my dreams, the one I tried to tell you about last night. It's the one I requested from the Vatican library a few months ago, Lucien. And that means something really creepy is going on . . . besides the normal, demon-variety creepy that always seems to be going on wherever you're concerned. First David got turned into a vampire, and now my boss, who went to go look for David's wife, is missing. And so are a bunch of other people. And yet there haven't been any vampire sightings reported here for months. And there are no bodies. Where are all the bodies?"

Lucien pulled her hand from his mouth . . . but kept an iron grip on her wrist.

"I have to be honest with you," he said, looking down into her face very intently. "I don't like that necklace very much. I would feel much more comfortable if you would take it off."

"Well, *I* have to be honest with *you*," she said, pulling her wrist from his grasp. "The only reason I'm wearing this necklace is because members of your species keep trying to bite me. So if you don't mind, I'm going to keep it on."

"*I'm* here," Lucien said. "So you won't need a necklace to protect you anymore."

His voice had assumed the thunderous tone it tended to take on whenever anyone disagreed with him.

And the red warning glow she'd thought she'd seen in his pupils was very much in evidence now.

"Lucien," Meena said, struggling to escape his embrace. "What's happening to you? Let go of me."

"*He* gave it to you, didn't he?" Lucien's grip only tightened on her. "*Alaric Wulf.*"

He said the name like it was a curse. His pupils were twin flames.

Meena's heart lurched. But now it was with fear for Alaric.

"No," she lied, still squirming in his arms. "Why would he give me a present? We're colleagues; we work together."

"Because he's in love with you," he said. "And you obviously have feelings for him, too, or you wouldn't be lying about it."

"I don't have feelings for him," she said. "I mean, we're friends, but—"

"You feel more for him than friendship," Lucien said. "You're afraid for him right now. I can feel your heart pounding—"

"Because you're holding me too tight," she said. "You're actually cutting off my circulation. I would really appreciate it if you would just let me go so we could discuss this like rational human beings."

He did let go of her then. But only so he could cup her face in his hands in a grip that wasn't any less restrictive than the one he'd had around her wrist.

"Meena." His voice was a rasp, completely unlike his own, it was so hoarse and uneven. "You still don't understand. I *can't* be rational. Not where you're concerned. And I'm not a human being. Not anymore."

"Lucien." She reached up to touch his cheek, struck with sudden pity for him. "Of course you are. At least a part of you still is. Don't you see? I don't really understand it, but I think that's what the dream I keep having is about, what I've been trying to tell you, that you still have a choice—"

"*No.*" His hands went to her shoulders. She could tell he was trying to restrain himself, but the effort was costing him. "I *don't.* That's what I've been trying to tell *you.* What I've become is *better* than human."

She dropped her hand from his face. "Lucien," she said, horrified. "You can't mean that."

"Why not?" he demanded. "What's so great about human beings? You said it yourself. Your own *employers*—who, I'd like to point out, are human beings—tricked and used you. Not just tonight, but last night, too."

She blinked at him in confusion. "How? What are you—?"

"You think it was a coincidence that it was someone like David, someone you'd never suspect, but not someone you saw every day, who was turned?" he demanded. "Of course not. But who would have access to that kind of information about you? Some random vampire clan? I don't think so."

"What . . . ?" She was shocked. "Are you saying you think the *Vatican*—"

"They didn't know that book had anything to do with me until you asked for it, Meena. Then they put it—and you—on display to lure me here so they could kill me. First they sent David to attack you, to make sure I came out of hiding. Then they used the book to bring me out into the open. I've known them for five hundred years, and nothing's changed in that time. Look what they were willing to do to their own employees, just to get at me. Look what they've done to *you*." He pulled her closer . . . always careful, however, to leave a distance between himself and the cross. "Leave them. Come away with me. Mary Lou has the book, and she and Emil should be waiting for me. All that's missing is you. We can go now. We'll never come back. You'll be safe with me."

"But . . ." She couldn't think. She felt physically exhausted . . . and mentally confused. Everything he'd said made sense . . .

Which only made it worse.

"But don't you see, Lucien?" she asked. "If what you say is true, then I *can't* leave. I've *got* to stay."

"*Why?*" He shook her with the force of his hold.

"Well, who else is going to try to stop them?" she asked him simply. Then she glanced behind him, at the painting she'd always loved.

His grip on her shoulders tightened.

"Learn something from her mistake," Lucien said menacingly. "Her employer sold her out to the enemy for ten thousand francs. Then she was executed as a traitor and a heretic to the Church. *By* the Church."

She shook her head. She didn't know what was happening to Lucien, or what he'd been going through since they'd been apart. Obviously it had to have been something horrible, since he certainly didn't seem happy. She knew he didn't mean what he was saying. He couldn't. That wasn't the person with whom she'd fallen in love . . .

. . . or the little boy she'd seen in her dream every night, whose life had been so filled with love and light. How could that boy have become someone filled with so much darkness . . . ?

"No," she said, shaking her head. "Don't you see, Lucien? If what you're saying about David is true, that's exactly the reason I *have* to stay, to try to keep it from happening again to someone else."

She laid a hand upon his face.

"And I don't believe you," she said, "when you say what you've become is better than human. I know you, and I know there's still a part of you—the best, most important part—that *is* human . . . if by human you mean good. And that's the part of you I love. Don't try to deny that part of you, Lucien. Because I think that might be the message of my dream. Denying that part of you could be what was making you so . . ."

"So what?" he demanded, his eyes glittering dangerously.

She swallowed. She'd wanted to say that she thought it could be what had been making him so sick the night before.

But he didn't seem sick at all now. So she must be wrong.

"Nothing. I really think you need to go now, Lucien. Protect yourself. Not me. I'm not the one they want. You are. Your staying here is what's putting me in danger. If you really loved me, and really wanted to protect me, you'd go. I'm not just saying that because I love you and want to keep you safe. I'm saying it because I know it's true. I know if you stay, it's not going to end well for anyone. *I know it.*"

Because she did. She knew it the way she'd known she and Alaric should never have left Abraham in Freewell. The way she'd known from the day she'd met him that David was going to die young. The way she'd known every time she'd ever looked at that painting of Joan of Arc that, much as she admired it, something equally bad was probably going to happen to her.

And now it was.

Because instead of releasing her, Lucien's arms tightened around her. His eyes flared a bright, deep vermilion.

Then he bent and scooped her into his arms.

"Lucien," she said, panicking. "Wait . . . What are you doing? No. Don't—"

She felt his feet begin to leave the floor, and she screamed, flinging her arms around his neck in terror as he headed directly for the skylight above their heads.

That's when the elevator doors opened with a *ding,* and Alaric Wulf came striding out into the gallery.

"Meena," he said, "I thought I told you not to move."

Then he pulled out the sword he kept strapped in a scabbard beneath the back of his tuxedo jacket.

Chapter Twenty-three

L ucien could simply have ignored the fact that Alaric Wulf was rushing at him with a sword. A few more feet, and he would have reached the skylight, which he intended to crash through—protecting Meena with his body, so she would not be harmed—to the roof.

But the sword was a taunt he could not resist, especially after the cross.

Meena had not admitted that Wulf had given the necklace to her. But Lucien didn't see who else could have. She certainly hadn't bought it for herself.

And the thick modern solidity of the gleaming metal cross fairly screamed that it had been chosen by a vampire hunter of Gaulish descent.

"Come down here," Wulf called to him, "and fight like a man. Or have you been depending on those demonic tricks of yours for so long, you've forgotten what the word *man* means?"

Lucien dropped back to the floor. It had been months since he'd last felt this strong. He wasn't sure whether it was due to Meena's proximity or to the Mannette. Maybe its waters were finally starting to have the kind of effect he'd been hoping for.

In any case, he felt invincible, like there wasn't anything—or anyone—on earth that could keep him from getting what he wanted. Not this time. Certainly not Alaric Wulf.

"I already spared your life once, Wulf," he said, in a warning tone. "Don't try me again."

Wulf raised his eyebrows. "Are you referring to the time you collapsed a building on top of me, then set it on fire? Because actually, it didn't seem like you were sparing me much of anything, considering the fact that I only survived because the tourniquet your girlfriend applied kept me from bleeding to death."

"Don't call me that," Meena said as she attempted to free herself from Lucien's embrace by pounding on his chest. But she might as well have been pounding on a wall.

"What?" Wulf asked. "Girlfriend? But you two seem to be getting along so well."

Lucien shrugged. "You're right," he said. "I should have killed you. I'm ready to rectify that now, though."

"Good. So why don't you release her so we can get busy?"

"I'm afraid that . . ." Lucien winced as Meena burned him with the necklace, although he didn't think she'd done it on purpose, or even realized it had happened. If she had, he was sure she'd have burned him more. He kept one arm anchored around her waist, regardless. "Much as I'd like to, I'm a bit preoccupied at the moment."

Wulf lowered the sword. "Seriously? Meena, are you listening? This is the man you've chosen to be with. He's using you as a human shield."

"No, he's not," Meena grunted. She elbowed Lucien in the throat, to no avail. "He knows if he lets me go, I'll run."

Lucien didn't comment on this remark, just looked at Wulf. "You understand that there's someone working from inside your organization who was willing to allow her to be killed, just to get at me," he said.

"What is he talking about?" Wulf asked Meena.

"It's true," Meena said. "The book that Mary Lou stole is the one from my dream. It belonged to Lucien's mother. Someone planted it in the show to try to lure Lucien here so he could be caught."

"Oh, well, good thing that didn't work," Wulf said sarcastically.

Lucien looked at him with distaste. Not having killed Alaric Wulf when he'd had the chance was quickly turning into his biggest regret. "Meena says there have been murders. I have not committed any. Someone else is doing this, and trying to make it look like it was me so that idiots like you would believe it."

"Oh yes," Wulf said, the sarcasm in his voice deepening. "You're a very innocent man. You certainly look like one right now. Most innocent men take hostages."

"They've already used her once to try to get to me," Lucien said, his rage quickening. "Has it ever occurred to you that now you're the one being used?"

Wulf raised his sword again. "I don't care," he said. "I only care about seeing you dead."

Lucien smiled to himself. Wulf had just made things very, very easy for him.

It was possible that Meena was right. Maybe there *was* a little bit of humanity remaining in him. And maybe it was that humanity that had made him spare Wulf's life the last time they'd met.

But it didn't matter. That little bit of humanity would soon be gone, if the Mannette did its work.

And so, in a minute, would Wulf.

And Meena couldn't even be angry with him for it, because Lucien could say he was only defending himself. Wulf had just threatened him.

"Fine," Lucien said. "If allowing you the chance to kill me will satisfy you, I'm happy to oblige." More than happy. Nothing would give him greater pleasure.

"*What?*"

Meena looked terrified. Lucien had loosened his hold so that he could defend himself against Wulf . . . so suddenly that she had stumbled, and fallen to her knees.

Now she'd climbed back to her feet and stood between the two men, two bright spots of color on her cheeks, her dark eyes seeming to blaze.

"No," she said. Her voice was shaking. "*No*. No one is killing anyone. Not anymore. We're going to figure this thing out together, without killing, like normal rational people."

Lucien almost smiled. She still didn't understand who he was now . . . what he'd become.

Neither did Wulf, or he would not have been so foolhardy as to ask for this fight.

"Meena," Alaric said, impatient. "Get out of the way."

"*No*," she said again. "The killing has got to stop. Do you hear me? It's wrong. *The killing has got to stop.*"

At that exact moment, the skylight burst above their heads.

Lucien realized right away what was happening, and was angry with himself for once again allowing a human weakness—jealousy of Wulf—to distract him. If he had simply ignored him, all of this might have been avoided.

Now men—all dressed in black—came soaring down from the gaping opening in the ceiling on rappelling wires. Shards of glass and metal crashed down, the fragments weaving in and around what looked like a great metallic spiderweb.

Lucien dove to protect Meena from the debris, but he wasn't quick enough. Other men, also dressed in black, some carrying crossbows, had appeared from the sides of the room, and pulled her quickly away. They had done the same thing to Alaric Wulf, who was nevertheless fighting them, and trying to cut through the bits of spiderweb that he could reach with his sword.

Alaric Wulf, clearly, had known nothing of the trap. If Lucien hadn't been so furious himself, he'd have laughed at the idea of Wulf cutting the massive metal web with his sword.

But he had more pressing concerns. The web had been shot directly at him, and covered him completely. And it was made of heavy links of silver, a substance that not only felt uncomfortable to his skin, but burned it with more than usual intensity, as well. It took him a moment to realize why.

Holy water. They had soaked the silver chain in holy water.

"Hold him," he could hear someone shouting. He thought the voice sounded familiar. "Hold him down!"

Before he had a chance to see if he could recognize the face belonging to the voice, something sharp struck his skin. He looked down and saw that it was a dart. A tranquilizer dart.

If it weren't for the searing pain from the silver and the holy water, he would have smiled a little. It was amusing that they thought they could sedate him with a tranquilizer dart.

He knew without a doubt that Alaric Wulf was not in charge of this operation. He would never have employed such a stupid weapon against a vampire. Especially the son of Dracula.

He thought about letting them take him, just so that he could see who was behind this ham-handed and amateurish attempt to capture him.

But then he heard a sound that made him forget everything else: Meena Harper's scream.

And he knew that he was needed elsewhere.

So he turned himself into mist and drifted up through the openings between the silver links, then toward the skylight and off into the night sky.

Chapter Twenty-four

The sight of Lucien floating away through the skylight threw the people holding Meena captive into a frenzy.

But it was a great relief to her, even angry as she was at Lucien for what he'd tried to do to her. It served the Palatine right that he'd gotten away. How could they have done something so stupid as try to throw a net over him, even one made of silver? This never would have happened if Abraham had still been in charge.

But when she whirled around to tell this to whoever it was who had cuffed her—whom she'd already kicked several times. Why was she being handcuffed?—she was shocked—more than shocked—to see that it was Father Henrique.

"So sorry," he said, apparently referring to the handcuffs. "I'll be happy to take these off just as soon as you tell us where he's gone."

He'd removed his white surplice. Beneath it he wore one of the sleek black uniforms all the rest of the unit were wearing, complete with a small gold emblem above the right breast of a knight on a horse, slaying a dragon—Saint George, the patron saint of the Palatine.

Meena was so overcome with rage, she replied by attempting to give Father Henrique another kick. But a female Palatine officer she'd never met before stopped her.

Father Henrique shook his head ruefully.

"You are hardly behaving like the professional I understood you to be, Miss Harper," he said. "But if that's how you choose to conduct yourself, so be it." He shrugged and waved his hand. The female officer began to shove Meena toward the elevator.

"Oh," Meena said, with a sneer to Father Henrique as she went past him, "and *you're* such a professional, I suppose. I thought you were transferred here to lead the parish of St. George's, but apparently it was because you're such an expert on the Lamir. Which Lucien *isn't*. Didn't you know he can turn into mist? Because everyone else here knew that."

To her surprise, just as the elevator doors were about to close, Father Henrique stepped into the car with her, gesturing for the female guard to step out. She did so. When the doors slid shut again, it was only Meena and Father Henrique in the elevator. She eyed him uneasily, wondering what she'd just gotten herself into.

"I do not think you understand the gravity of the situation, Meena," he said, hitting the down button. "It is vitally imperative that Lucien Antonescu be captured."

His English was a *lot* better now than it had been during his television interview with Genevieve Fox, as well as when he'd been talking to her and Father Bernard and Sister Gertrude . . . both of whom, Meena had noticed, were conspicuously absent from this operation.

"Do you think I don't know that?" Meena asked. "But I don't see how handcuffing *me* is helping the situation—"

Father Henrique leaned over her. He was quite a bit taller than she was.

"Don't pretend you haven't been consorting with him," he said. "You were seen with him last night. You've helped create this situation. From what I understand, you're the one who dreamed about it—the book—and put in the request for it. I imagine you even *told* him about it. And now he has it. You can't even begin to conceive of what you've done. You've basically unleashed in him powers he never even knew he had. Now he'll be unstoppable."

Meena, shaken, looked up at him. "I . . . I don't know what you're talking about. That wasn't in my dream. That wasn't what I dreamed about at *all*."

"I told you before," he said, "that it isn't an ordinary devotional. And now that it's fallen into his hands, there is no telling what he'll do. So if you know where he is, you had better tell us, or you will basically be responsible for undoing everything—everything—we've worked so hard to achieve."

The elevator doors slid open, and he took her arm.

"But of course," he said, guiding her out into the hallway and toward a back exit, where a number of other guards were waiting, "it's up to you."

It was at this point that she'd heard Alaric shout, "Don't tell that bastard anything, Meena!" before his voice was stifled by the slamming of a car door. They'd stuffed him into a waiting van, which immediately drove off. Another van was idling behind it . . . for Meena, as it turned out.

Meena's heart had begun to thump with fear. She had no idea what Father Henrique was talking about, or what was about to happen to her. This was the Palatine, after all, a *secret* unit of the Vatican. No one even knew it existed. They could do whatever they wanted to her, she realized, and not be held accountable.

Not that she really believed anything Lucien had been saying earlier, about how it had been her employer who'd sent David after her. That was absurd. The Palatine didn't keep vampires captive to infect innocent civilians, then turn them loose into the population just to lure their number one target out into the open . . .

Did they?

"S-sorry," Meena said, looking up at Father Henrique. "But I really don't know where Lucien is."

Actually, this wasn't entirely true. Mary Lou had said something about a cave. But she wasn't about to share that information. Not just because of what Alaric had shouted. But because in her heart, she didn't believe the priest was telling the truth.

Father Henrique's expression hardened.

"I see," he'd said. "May I give you a word of advice, Miss Harper? Choose your boyfriends with better care. Nothing good ever seems to end up happening to them. And I'd hate to have to say the same about Alaric Wulf someday."

Meena blinked. Had he really just made a threat against Alaric? She wasn't entirely sure since, a second later, he smiled at her, as charmingly as he'd smiled at Genevieve Fox on TV.

"I'll see you back at headquarters," he said.

Then he strolled off, leaving her to be hauled, openmouthed in shock, into the waiting van.

She was almost sure they were going to drive her straight to the river to shoot her, then shove her—along with Alaric—into the dark waters.

But of course they didn't. They took her straight to Palatine headquarters at St. Bernadette's, which ought to have been comforting, but wasn't. She didn't see the van into which they'd shoved Alaric, nor could she hear his voice in the hallway. After what Father Henrique had said about him, she had begun to get a very bad feeling. Whether or not Lucien was correct about there being some kind of conspiracy within the Palatine, there was obviously no love lost between Alaric and Father Henrique.

And now Father Henrique appeared to have been promoted to a position of some power. Not that she thought he'd abuse that power . . . but what had he meant about not wanting something bad to happen to Alaric? Had he meant that without Meena's help, something bad would happen to him? It must surely have been that. Because everyone had seen Lucien intending to do bad things to Alaric (but only because Alaric had been trying to help her).

Surely the priest hadn't meant that he himself intended to do bad things to Alaric. Because when Meena pictured Alaric in her head, she didn't get the feeling that he was in any danger . . . at least, not of the mortal kind. But she had no idea where he was. She herself was locked in the school's old nurse's office, clearly used in the past for isolating contagious children from the rest of the student population. There was absolutely no way out.

And—should anyone happen to be thinking of rescuing her—absolutely no way in either, save the door. And that was locked.

But evidently no one was thinking of rescuing her, since, as the hours crept by, the knob on the door never moved.

The building was, of course, as thoroughly demon-proofed as Meena's home, so Lucien couldn't have gotten in if he'd wanted to.

Which she had to admit was a bit of a relief, after the way he'd been acting during those last few minutes in the museum. Sorry as she'd felt for him when she'd seen the smoke rising from his skin as a result of its contact with the holy water, she still couldn't believe what he'd tried to do to her. He had been acting like someone she didn't even know. What had he been thinking, trying to kidnap her like that?

Meena had plenty of time to wonder. Left alone in the nurse's office for hours, she had nothing else to do. They'd removed her handcuffs, but taken her cell phone away. Eventually, she must have fallen into an exhausted, troubled sleep on the examination table, since the next thing she knew, she was being shaken awake.

"No!" she cried. "I don't know! I swear I don't know where he is!"

"That," Father Henrique said, drawing a chair close to the examination table, "is unfortunate. I was hoping you might have given our recent discussion some thought, and changed your mind."

Meena, blinking, shook her head.

"No," she said. "And you can't keep me here. I demand to be released. Where's Alaric?"

"Actually," Father Henrique said, "I have every right to keep you here. You are withholding valuable evidence we need in our pursuit of the most wanted criminal in the world . . . perhaps in the history of the world. But I'm not here to fight with you. I'm actually on your side, believe it or not."

Meena said, "I don't believe it. If you were on my side, you wouldn't have locked me in this room."

"It's for your own safety," Father Henrique said. "You do realize that Lucien Antonescu was going to try to turn you tonight, don't you?"

Meena glared at him. "He would never do that," she said. Although, actually, he had tried it before. But they'd discussed it, and agreed he wasn't to do so again. Had he changed his mind? She refused to believe it. And even if he had, how would Father Henrique know? "Not without my permission."

"That's exactly what I was trying to tell you," Father Henrique said. "He has the book now. Things are different. *He's* different. With that book in his possession, Lucien Antonescu will become invincible. Compared to his father . . . well, that would be like comparing a baby to a charging bull. That book will make him the most powerful being the world has ever known. Perhaps . . . *all*-powerful."

Meena stared at him. There was nothing evil about the book she'd seen in her dreams. There hadn't been anything evil about the book she'd seen in the museum either.

Although she'd definitely seen a change in Lucien.

That change, however, had come *before* he'd gotten his hands on the book.

"I don't understand what you're talking about," she said finally. "I thought Lucien already *was* all-powerful. Isn't that what *prince of darkness* means? How much more powerful—or evil—can he possibly get?"

Father Henrique shook his head. "I'm sure you've heard," he said, "of the horrors Lucien's father inflicted upon his own people. The tens of thousands of men, women, and children he had impaled, alive, for no other reason than to intimidate his enemies. *That* is what I am talking about."

Meena, already tired and confused, could not even begin to reconcile this image with the one she had in her head—and heart—of Lucien. It was not possible.

"If letting this book fall into Lucien's hands could cause this," Meena said, "then why on earth did the Vatican allow it out of Rome in the first place?"

Father Henrique's expression darkened.

"Not everyone believes as strongly as I do that such a little book could contain so much strength over the dark lord. Obviously they believe he wants it back, because it belonged to his mother, and they were willing to use it as bait to lure him out . . . but they never realized the ramifications of allowing it to fall into his hands. I know *you* believe, Meena. Because I can see it in your face. Otherwise you never would have dreamed of it. You know of its power over him . . . *you* believe. And you can stop what's about to happen . . . by just telling us where he is." Father Henrique looked sad. "Believe me, Meena, I know how painful it can be sometimes to do the right thing, as opposed to the easy thing. But I've learned over the years, the greater good is more important than our own selfish needs. And if you truly wish to help him, you'll tell me where he is."

Meena sighed.

"You're right," she said.

Father Henrique's face brightened. "I am?"

"About the book," she said. "I do believe it's more important than anyone else seems to believe. But you're wrong about Lucien. He's not evil."

Father Henrique's face fell. "Miss Harper—" he began.

"I have faith in him. Even if no one else does," Meena said. "He'll do the right thing. Now, where's Alaric?"

Father Henrique stared down at her with the angriest expression Meena had ever seen on the face of a man who had pledged his life to the service of others. It seemed to take him some time before he was able to calm himself down enough to say simply, "Good night, Miss Harper."

Then he walked from the room, locking the door behind him.

Even though she disliked him intensely, Meena found herself feeling a little sorry for Father Henrique. He had obviously been thrust into a position for which he was both ill-qualified and ill-suited. She wondered who'd recommended him for this promotion, and if whoever it was was going to get fired. They deserved to be.

Yet a little after dawn, the door opened, and Dr. Fiske, Alaric's therapist, came in, announcing with an apologetic smile that he'd been appointed temporary head of human resources in Abraham Holtzman's absence.

He hadn't come to torture or kill her, or even ask her where Lucien was. Instead, he only came to present her with a letter.

A letter of termination of employment.

Meena, not Father Henrique, was the one who was fired.

Dr. Fiske had her read the letter over carefully to make sure she understood it, and asked her to sign it to verify receipt.

Then he gave her back her purse and cell phone and said that a car was waiting to take her home.

Meena, dazed, hopped down from the examination table. This was worse than being tortured in a way, because it was so mundane after what she'd been expecting.

She was *fired*?

Dr. Fiske wasn't unkind. He was actually very understanding, and even sympathetic and friendly.

But Meena, he said, had broken just about every rule in the *Palatine Guard Human Resources Handbook,* many in the past forty-eight hours alone.

And so it was really very unlikely, given the magnitude, breadth, and scope of the damage her actions had caused—this line was used in the letter—that even if she appealed, she would be allowed to continue in the Vatican's employ.

So her services were no longer required.

When Meena asked where Alaric was, Dr. Fiske glanced at his watch and said, "I believe he's now on private transport back to Rome."

Of all the things Meena had been expecting to hear, nothing could have prepared her for this.

"*Rome?*" Her voice cracked in disbelief.

"Well," Dr. Fiske said, looking somewhat surprised by her reaction. "It wasn't the easiest administrative decision to make, of course. It was either a transfer or terminating his employment. And since he's obviously an extremely valuable asset to the organization, I opted to transfer him. It seemed to make the most sense."

Meena shook her head. What might have made sense to Dr. Fiske made no sense to her.

"And Alaric *agreed?* With Lucien Antonescu apparently in possession of some book that is going to make him the most powerful demon in the history of the world?"

For the first time, Dr. Fiske looked slightly uncomfortable. "Well, I don't know about all of that. I'm just in administration. But I'm told he was perfectly amenable to the—"

"You were *told?*" The alarm bells going off in Meena's head were so loud that she thought for a second they were the building's smoke detectors. "You haven't spoken to Alaric *yourself?*"

"Miss Harper," Dr. Fiske said. He peered at her from above the rims of his reading glasses. "We are, as you stated, in pursuit of the most powerful demon in the world. I have had to step into the shoes of a missing colleague, who, I would like to point out, did not leave his desk

in the most organized of conditions. But I have been Alaric Wulf's psy-
chotherapist for almost six months, and I think I am qualified to say
that Alaric's allowed his emotions to compromise his decision-making
abilities, and has been doing so for some time. Ever since he met you,
to be exact."

This did not in any way silence the alarm bells. "But I don't think
Alaric would—"

He laid a hand on her shoulder, and interrupted gently, "Even you
can't deny, Meena, that you and Alaric Wulf have developed a relationship that has become so unhealthily codependent, it has already caused
the deaths of several of our colleagues. It's for the best that you achieve
some distance and perspective. That's why Alaric agreed to the transfer,
and is on his way back to Rome, and you are being let go. Now please
don't ask me any more questions about Alaric, as I wouldn't like to vio-
late my obligation to maintain patient-doctor confidentiality—"

The words *caused the deaths of several of our colleagues* hit Meena hard.

Not because she believed she'd caused the deaths of Abraham and
Carolina, and the rest of the team that had been sent to Freewell. She
still didn't know where they were, or why they hadn't checked in. But
when she pictured their faces in her mind, she was quite sure that they
were alive.

Still, it was because of her that they had gone to Freewell. It was
because of her that they—and Brianna Delmonico—were missing.

David's death, on the other hand . . . well, that she *had* caused. It was
because of her that he'd been turned into a vampire.

She knew that, and was willing to accept it, as well as her dismissal
from the Palatine.

There was just one thing she wasn't willing to accept. Something
Dr. Fiske, apparently, did not know.

"There, there," Dr. Fiske said, seeing her expression, and apparently
misinterpreting it. "I know it seems like the end of the world at the
moment. But you'll feel better in a few days. The sun has come up now,
and it's safe for you to go. A car is waiting for you. Good-bye, Meena."

Feeling numb, she took the letter Dr. Fiske handed to her. Then she
walked out of the nurse's office and down the empty corridor until she

stood blinking in the early-morning sunlight on the steps of Palatine headquarters, near the fountain of Saint Bernadette kneeling before the footless Madonna, empty of water as it had always been.

Because it was only just after dawn, no one was around, except for the car that, just as Dr. Fiske had assured her, was waiting beyond the arches at the end of the courtyard. Meena stared at it, her eyes aching, her mouth dry.

What was it Alaric had said in the taxi on the way to the museum, when she'd asked when he'd be going to Antigua? Oh yes:

Don't worry. I won't be leaving with any unsettled business.

Meena knew there was no way that Alaric Wulf had boarded a private transport to Rome. Not willingly. Not without saying good-bye to her first. And not with Lucien Antonescu still at large.

Alaric simply had too much unsettled business in New York to have left for Rome.

Meena was certain that Dr. Fiske believed that he himself had not been lying. He'd truly believed what he'd been saying.

Which meant someone had been lying to Dr. Fiske.

As she stood on the steps to St. Bernadette's in the early light of dawn, having had so little sleep and with her emotions stretched so thin, the complexity of her situation finally began to sink in . . . as did the realization that she was alone in this now. Everything was up to her. She was going to have to figure it out on her own.

But it was all right. She could do it.

She hoped.

She slipped past the waiting Town Car—the driver inside was so engrossed in the morning paper he did not even look up—then walked back to her apartment.

Part 3

Sunday, September 19

Chapter Twenty-five

Jon glared at the three guys who had come into the Beanery and taken the table beneath the flat-screen TV that hung on the exposed brick wall in the corner.

They seemed to think they could buy the cheapest thing on the menu—Americanos, tall—then occupy a table for hours just because they'd brought their expensive laptops and popped them open.

They hadn't even paid for the Wi-Fi. He could see that they had broadband-access cards.

The least they could have done was order a muffin.

Also, he couldn't figure out what it was they were finding so fascinating on the television. The sound wasn't even on. It was tuned to the twenty-four-hour local news station, the way the owner—which happened to be the Catholic Church, or more specifically, the Shrine of St. Clare, although this was not public knowledge—insisted.

Jon would have liked to turn it to ESPN or even the financial news, but he'd tried this once, and Father Bernard—who'd happened to glance in the window on his way back to the church from the thrift shop next door—had nearly had a coronary.

It wasn't worth the risk. Jon needed this gig, even if it had only been given to him out of pity. Especially now, since he hadn't had a chance to show Alaric Wulf his SuperStaker.

Jon didn't know what had happened. Meena hadn't come home from the event she and Alaric had gone to until God knows when—Jon suspected it had been after dawn. When he'd glanced into her room shortly before leaving for work, he'd seen that she was asleep. She'd fallen into bed fully dressed.

And there'd been no sign of Alaric.

Weird. Maybe the thing with Lucien Antonescu had been a false alarm, or something.

Which meant he was going to have to do this by himself. And he knew how, too:

He was going to SuperStake one of the vamps sitting at the table in front of the TV.

It was going to be tricky, of course, because if the SuperStaker didn't work—if it only singed the vamp slightly, and didn't dust him—he'd have an extremely angry demon on his hands ... plus his two friends.

Still, Jon couldn't get Adam's words from the day before out of his head ... that he had to take that first step, and do *something*. Otherwise, he'd always have the same stupid problems—slight addiction to video games, lack of employment, depending on his sister for a place to live— and never the kind of problems he *wanted* to have ... the kind Adam had: a wife, a baby, a mortgage. These were normal problems for a guy his age. Proper problems. Jon would do *anything* for problems like that.

So today, he'd brought the gun to work. All he had to was find a vamp to shoot.

And now here he was, with three of them sitting in front of him. Problem solved.

Of course, it was possible these guys weren't vampires at all. Now that Jon thought about it, how had they even gotten into the café in the first place without getting burned up, since it was quite sunny outside?

They didn't look particularly vampy either, in their khakis and polos with the collars popped. They resembled guys like himself, if his luck had gone a different way ... guys with jobs in the investment community, who'd been given the morning off while their wives were at the Mommy-and-Me read-along at the independent bookstore down the street. As soon as the read-along was over, and their wives met them back here, they'd pack their laptops into their kids' expensive strollers and roll on down to the San Gennaro Festival, where they would eat a slice and a cannoli, then grab a cab back to the their doorman building in Tribeca, or wherever.

Oh, well. They hadn't left a tip. If they weren't vampires, the ultra-violet ray wouldn't hurt them. And if they were . . . *poof.*

He raised his gun. One small step for him, one giant step for vamp killers everywhere . . .

"Good morning, Jon."

Yalena stood on the other side of the counter, looking fresh-faced and gorgeous, as always.

"Uh . . . h-hi," he stammered, feeling himself turning red. He lowered the SuperStaker at once.

He hadn't even heard the door open. He was really losing his grip if the most beautiful girl in the world had just come walking into the shop, and he hadn't even noticed.

"I see you got stucked with the Sunday-morning shift, too," Yalena said, smiling in that amazing way she had, that made it seem as though the sun was shining inside.

"Stuck," Jon corrected her automatically. Not that he minded the way she sometimes mispronounced things. It was one her most adorable qualities. He hoped she never learned to speak English correctly. "And yeah, I did. How are you? Can I get you the usual? Cappuccino?"

"Oh yes, thanks, that would be great." Yalena hauled her gigantic bag onto the counter. "I'm good. 'Stuck.' I always forget this. What have you got there? A hair dryer? You bring this to work with you?"

Jon hastily shoved the SuperStaker into his apron pocket.

"No, no," he said. "Nothing. Just a little project I've been working on. For the, uh, Palatine."

The minute the word was out of his mouth, he regretted it.

"Oh." Yalena's entire face lit up. "You work for them now, too? Like your sister?"

Jon wished he had kept his mouth shut. What had come over him?

Now Yalena was going to think he was employed by the Palatine, when he wasn't. At least, not until he killed those guys over there, who, if he really thought about it, definitely weren't vampires at all. Vampires wouldn't pop their collars. Vampires wouldn't even wear polos. At least, he'd never seen one in a polo.

"Well, on the side," he said. "Sort of a secret project."

"Oh, secret project," Yalena said. "How exciting!" She was pulling out her wallet, but Jon waved her money aside.

"Come on, don't be crazy," he said. "You know it's on me. Or on the boss, really. You know. The big guy." He looked up, indicating heaven. "I don't think He'll mind."

"Oh, Jonathan," she said, laughing. He loved the way she said his name. No one else said it that way. Like it was special. "You are so sweet. When everything was so bad with me last spring when . . . well, when it was the bad time for me, you were the only one who could make me laugh again. I don't know what I would have done without you all these months." As he passed her the cappuccino, her hand met his, and she allowed the touch to linger. "I am so glad to know you."

"Oh," he said, his heart speeding up a little.

This was it, he thought. What Adam had been talking about . . . his chance to take the first step. Maybe he didn't need a SuperStaker after all. Yalena had said she didn't know what she'd have done without him. She thought he was sweet. He made her laugh. She was so glad to know him!

And her hand was still resting on his as they both held her drink.

His heart felt as if it were going to detonate inside his chest, it was so filled with joy . . . and nervousness.

Do it, he said to himself.

"I feel the same way about you, Yalena," he said. "You know, I was thinking maybe after our shifts, we could go to the San Gennaro Festival together, maybe grab a bite to—"

"Dude."

Pink Popped Collar had gotten up and come over to the counter. "Can you turn up the sound?" He pointed at the TV.

Jon had never in his life felt so much like murdering someone. Especially since at that moment Yalena took her drink and set it down on the counter, breaking the contact between them.

"Uh," Jon said. "No. That's why the closed captioning is on. The sound disturbs the customers, who come here to enjoy a quiet break."

Pink Popped Collar looked around the empty café. "*What* other customers? We're the only ones in here. And we want to hear this. It's a major breaking news story." He turned to his friends. "Am I right?"

One of his friends—his polo was lime green—looked up from his computer screen. "Dude, screw that guy. I just found the live feed on the channel's Web site."

"Ha. Suck it, barista," Pink Popped Collar said, and went back to his seat to turn up the sound on his laptop. From where Jon stood, he could hear only a tinny murmuring sound.

What assholes.

That's all Jon could think.

Oh, sure, vampires bit you on the neck and sucked out your life-blood. But at least they didn't completely humiliate you in front of the girl you loved. They just killed you.

"Okay, Jon," Yalena was saying. "Well, I—"

"Hey, you guys."

Suddenly Jon's sister Meena was standing at the counter beside Yalena, wearing dark sunglasses, an ancient T-shirt, and an even more ancient pair of jeans, topped off with a hooded sweatshirt tied around her waist. She had some sort of weird necklace on that Jon had never seen her wear before. It was unclear whether or not she'd witnessed the unpleasantness between Jon and his three customers, or if she had, whether it had registered. It hadn't seemed to register with Yalena, who'd turned to give Meena a delighted hug.

"Oh, hi, Meena!" she cried. "How are you?"

"Hi," Meena said, hugging Yalena back. "How have you been? You look great, as always."

"Oh, thank you," Yalena said. "You, too."

Yalena was obviously only saying this to be nice, because Meena did not look great. She looked like she'd just crawled out of bed, pulled on the first items of clothing she could find, and come over. It was possible she hadn't even showered, but Jon wasn't sure.

She had the dog with her. He wasn't supposed to allow people to bring their pets inside. There was a "No Pets" sign right on the door. Was everyone who came in here today—except Yalena, of course—just going to blatantly refuse to follow the rules?

"Uh, no, I don't look great, Yalena," Meena said with a laugh. "Thanks for being so sweet. I had a really bad night. Speaking of which, Jon, I was wondering if I could talk to you, in private? And could I get a large coffee, light, and one of those huge blueberry muffins?"

Jon wanted to say they were out of muffins so Meena would leave and he'd have a few more minutes alone with Yalena, but unfortunately there was a muffin sitting right under the glass case in front of her.

And he was pretty certain that after Yalena witnessed his humiliation by the Popped Collar Trio, he would never have another chance with her in a million years.

Plus, Meena had said she'd wanted to talk to him. In private.

Great. Now Yalena was going to leave.

It had never been fun having the You're Gonna Die Girl as a sister, but he'd thought he'd gotten used to it, and had always had a pretty good sense of humor about it.

Until now.

"Sure," he said, and bent to pull out the muffin, then fix Meena's coffee.

"Well, I have to be opening the shop anyway," Yalena said, smiling at them, "so I will see you. Thank you so much, again, Jonathan. And I would very much like to go to the San Gennaro Festival with you tonight. I will come here to meet you when I am done working. Bye bye!"

Jon, Meena's cup of coffee in his hand, murmured, "Bye," back to her, feeling like a man in a daze. He couldn't believe his good fortune.

Yes. Incredibly, she'd said yes.

Everything was going to be all right. Everything was going to be fine.

He watched in shock as she walked past the table where the Popped Collar Trio was sitting, then disappeared out the door.

It was happening. He'd taken that first step. And she'd said yes!

Over at the table in front of the TV, the three guys in polo shirts had started snickering the minute Yalena had left. Jon wasn't going to let them ruin his now joyous mood.

"Jon," Meena said. "Listen. I know you're good with computers. I was wondering if you could— "

Behind her, the snickering continued.

"Excuse me," Jon said, raising his voice as he thumped Meena's coffee onto the counter. It didn't slosh, because he'd put a lid on it.

"Jon," Meena warned, with a quick look in the direction of the three dumb-asses. She'd pushed her sunglasses back onto her head, and Jon saw that though she'd made up her eyes, they were swollen and red-rimmed. He didn't think it was from lack of sleep. "Let it go. I've got something more important we need to deal with right—"

"No," he said to her. "You know what, Meena? I've let it go long enough. I'm done letting it go." To the three douche bags, he called, "Hey, you guys. What's so funny?"

"You," Pink Popped Collar said, with a smirk.

"Really?" Jon felt the weight of the SuperStaker in his apron pocket. It—and the fact that Yalena had said yes—gave him confidence. "How so?"

"Jon," Meena said. "Seriously. Something bad has happened. Really bad. We don't have time to—"

"You think," Pink Popped Collar said, "*you* have a chance with *her?*" He tilted his head in the direction of the door. He meant Yalena.

Lime-Green Popped Collar looked thoughtful. "He might," he said, "if he makes a helluva a lot more later on today in tips than we gave him."

This caused his companions to laugh so hard, they were forced to clutch the tabletop in front of them to keep from falling over.

Jon glanced at Meena in disbelief. "Did you hear what they just said?" he asked her.

"Yeah," she said. Her eyes had gone to the flat-screen hanging above the guys' heads. "Can you turn up the sound?"

"They just implied that Yalena would only go out with me if I pay her to," Jon said, not sure she'd understood him. "Meaning they think Yalena is a *prostitute*."

"Jon," Meena said, her gaze still glued to the TV screen. "Seriously. You have no idea what is going on. Turn it up."

"In a minute," Jon said. "First I have to take care of something."

He pulled the SuperStaker out of his apron pocket, then came out from behind the counter, walked up to the table where the three assholes were sitting, and said, "What was that you just said about my girlfriend?"

"Uh," Pink Popped Collar said, looking up from his computer screen. "Is that a hair dryer?"

"It's not a hair dryer," Jon said. "Say hello to the SuperStaker. Now feel the burn."

He pulled the trigger. The blue-light-emitting diode with which he'd retrofitted it the night before—because he really felt his demonstration in front of Adam had not been impressive enough—turned on, and displayed a solid beam on Pink Popped Collar's chest.

But nothing happened to Pink Popped Collar, except that an annoyed look crossed his face.

"Dude," he said. "Stop being a pain in the ass, and go get me a refill, okay?" He held out his cup. "And I'm serious about your girlfriend, man. You do not want to take her to the San Gennaro Festival right now. There's some psychotic killer running around, offing all the tourists. Girl with an accent like that, you want to keep her inside till they catch the guy who's doing it. Although he'd probably be doing you a favor . . . she's clearly only after you for the green card anyway."

This inspired a new wave of guffaws from Pink Popped Collar's companions.

Jon lowered the SuperStaker and kicked their table over.

Chapter Twenty-six

Meena made sure the door to the café was locked, and the "Welcome! Come in" sign in the window was flipped to CLOSED.

She didn't think it was a particularly good idea for her brother to be waiting on customers in his condition.

She'd barely been able to convince the men whose table he'd kicked over not to call the police. She'd had to tell them that Jon was suffering from side effects of the allergy medication he was taking. One of the men whose laptop had suffered the most damage—it was only a little dent; it still ran perfectly fine—was threatening to contact the manager.

Meena almost wished they *had* been vampires. The whole thing would have been a lot simpler if she could have staked them.

Unfortunately, they weren't.

"They fired you," Jon said, from the couch onto which he'd sunk with the coffee Meena had poured him.

"That's right," Meena said. She sat down at a table, then pried the lid from her own coffee and took a sip. Of course it was only lukewarm now.

She didn't care, though. Jack Bauer took up a post beneath her chair, looking up at her with eager expectedness, hopeful for any crumb from the muffin she might drop, even though Meena had already fed him breakfast back at the apartment.

"And transferred Alaric," Jon said. "To *Rome*."

"That's what I was told," Meena said. The muffin was settling like a rock at the bottom of her stomach.

At least it was food. She needed food. She needed *normalcy*.

But that wasn't something she expected she'd be seeing much of for a long time.

"But I don't understand. You're the good guys," Jon said.

"Honestly, I don't think I know who the good guys are anymore." Meena reached into the back pocket of her jeans and pulled out a crumpled letter, then tossed it into Jon's lap.

"Wait," Jon said again, after he'd unfolded and read it. "This says it serves as a *final* warning that unless there is an immediate and sustained improvement in your work performance, your position will be terminated. But there was no first warning. And you said they terminated you anyway."

"I know," she said. Her eyes burned as she looked out the window, at all the happy, carefree people walking toward the street festival. She wondered how many people felt the way she did . . . like their lives were over, and they were basically walking dead people.

None of them, as far as she could tell. They were all smiling, excited about the adventure they were about to have.

Obviously, very few of them had seen Genevieve Fox's news report about the city's sudden spike in missing people . . . all tourists. And yet, Genevieve pointed out, for some reason alerts to the media about these people had not been issued. Was this because the mayor did not wish to disseminate to the public warnings about a vicious serial killer in their midst during a time when tourism to the city was at an all-time peak?

The mayor's office had already issued a statement assuring the public that there was no cause for alarm. There had been no change in the procedure for disseminating reports of missing persons to the press . . . merely a concern that the potential downside to such reporting was that the public might become "desensitized" over time. The mayor's office and police were aware of and actively working on each and every case Genevieve had mentioned.

This, however, did not exactly jibe with the interviews Genevieve's colleagues managed to snag with family members of the missing.

And though Alaric's name was never mentioned, "a source working closely with the NYPD" was said to have grave doubts that anyone there was taking these cases very seriously.

"And where does that leave ten-year-old Kaileigh Anderson," Genevieve looked into the screen and inquired, "who only wants to know why her nineteen-year-old brother, Jeff, didn't return to their home in Fairfield, Connecticut, after what was supposed to be a fun night out clubbing with friends in Manhattan last Saturday night?"

"Please," Kaileigh sobbed into the camera while she clutched a photo of a Goth-looking young man. "Someone find my brother."

"Jesus Christ, Meena," Jon said, turning down the volume on the TV as he skimmed her letter of termination. "What, exactly, is going on?"

"I don't know," she admitted. She lifted her purse onto her thighs. "That's why I need your help. I know how good you are with computers." From inside the roomy bag, where she already kept her wallet, hair product, antibacterial gel, and an assortment of makeup, notebooks, pens, wooden stakes, and vials of holy water, she pulled Jon's laptop. "I want you to hack into the Palatine's computer mainframe and find Alaric."

"*What?*" Jon looked shocked. "You just said they transferred him to Rome!"

"That's what someone *wants* me to believe," Meena said. "And I can see how they're going to try to justify it. All that stuff Genevieve Fox is saying on the news about the people gone missing? I saw Alaric talking to her last night. That's *his* theory—that there's something eating all these tourists, and there's a cover-up going on—"

Meena could barely get the words out. Last night a tiny part of her had thought Alaric had been hitting on Genevieve Fox, and vice versa.

Now that she'd seen the news story—and it was the lead story on *every* local channel; she'd made Jon check—she knew what they'd actually been discussing.

She fingered the necklace Alaric had given her, which she hadn't removed, even while showering, per his orders. She supposed that wherever he was, Alaric regretted giving it to her now. She would, if she'd been him.

She'd been an idiot.

"Wait," Jon said. "Why don't you think that's really where he is?"

She gave him a scornful look.

"Oh, right, Jon," Meena said. "Alaric just went back to Rome. Without saying good-bye to us. With Abraham still missing. With some kind of demented killer roaming loose in the city, killing all the tourists. With Lucien still evading capture. Because that sounds so like Alaric Wulf."

Jon nodded. "Okay. Yeah, you're right. Alaric isn't in Rome. But, Meena, even talented as I am—and I am incredibly talented—I cannot hack into the mainframe of a secret demon-hunting military force of the Vatican and—*what* is it you want me to do?"

"We all carry cell phones with GPS trackers," Meena said, holding up hers. "I've called his a dozen times, and it goes straight to voice mail. He hasn't returned any of my messages. They've changed all my passwords, so I can't log on to the system anymore, and when I call anyone at headquarters, either here in the city or in Rome, I can't get through. I think they're blocking me. Jon, I know Alaric hasn't left the city. He's here somewhere, and he's in trouble. I need you to find out where he really is so we can go rescue him." She pushed his laptop across the table. "You've got to help me."

"Oh, sure," Jon said sarcastically. "No problem. I'll get right on it." He leaned across the table to take the phone, not the laptop, then examined it. "Meena, this is an expensive piece of equipment. If they went to all the trouble of changing your passwords to keep you out of the computer system, why did they let you keep this phone?"

"Isn't it obvious?" she asked, with a shrug. "They're using it to track me."

"You?" He shook his head. "What for? Where do they think you're going to go?"

"It doesn't matter where I go," she said. "It's who they think is going to come to me."

Jon looked at her. "Oh my God. They're using you to find Lucien. They really *don't* care what happens to you, do they?"

"No," she said, plucking the phone from his fingers and dropping it into her half-full cup of coffee. "Are you going to help me or not?"

Jon's eyes widened. "But, Meena . . . do you realize what you're saying? Who you're going up against?"

"Do you have a better suggestion?" she asked.

"Uh," Jon said, "run?" He grabbed his laptop and stood up. "Let's go rent a car and get out of here. If we leave now and ignore any speed limits, we can make it to Georgia by nightfall."

"Jon," Meena said, "I'm pretty sure Lucien and the Palatine can still find us in Georgia. Besides, what about Alaric?"

"Oh." He looked crestfallen. "Yeah."

They both jumped at a sudden pounding on the glass door to the Beanery. Jack Bauer, who'd given up on any crumbs that might drop from Meena's muffin, leaped up from beneath her chair and began to bark.

"Jesus!" Jon cried, alarmed.

It turned out to be only the three men with the popped collars whose table Jon had kicked over.

Meena relaxed . . . until she saw that two New York City police officers were accompanying them. One of the police officers pointed at the door handle and shouted, "Open up. Now."

Meena looked at the police officers, and then at her brother.

"Is there a back exit to this place?" she asked.

"Uh," he said, "yeah. But it just leads to an alley. It's where all the shop fronts here put their garbage until trash day. It's pretty disgusting."

"Can you get to it from around the front?" she asked.

"No," he said. "Only through here. Wait . . . Are you seriously suggesting what I think you are? I mean, we can't just—"

"You can stay here if you want," she said, picking up her bag and Jack Bauer's leash. "I'm going to go look for Alaric."

Chapter Twenty-seven

Considering the direction in which her life had been heading lately, Meena shouldn't have been surprised when she walked out the back door of the Beanery and was attacked by a vampire.

Sure, it was broad daylight. But the alley received no sun whatsoever at that time of day, thanks to the buildings rising up on either side.

She'd only turned her back for a second to watch her brother lock up behind him.

It had been less than twelve hours since she'd been fired from the Palatine, and she'd already forgotten rule number one of demon fighting: never turn your back.

It was Jack Bauer who saved her life. He began growling and tugging on the end of his leash.

When Meena turned to see what was wrong with her dog, she noticed a flash of movement from the corner of her eye. It appeared to be coming from the direction of a Dumpster a few feet away.

She could never say later what made her duck . . . her gift, or simple instinct. But she did, letting out a warning scream to Jon.

And so Brianna Delmonico—who leaped for her, gaping jaw first—crashed against the back door of the Beanery, missing Meena, her intended target, entirely, but half flattening Jon with the force of her momentum.

"Jesus Christ," Jon cried, dropping his keys in surprise.

Brianna did not look as if she'd spent the past forty-eight hours attending Mommy-and-Me read-alongs at the local bookstore, or anything of that nature. She was wearing a velour tracksuit that might at one time have been pink, but was now stained bright red—at least down the front—with blood.

The blood did not appear to be her own. She lifted her head from the door and whipped it around to face Meena—completely ignoring Jon—letting out a hiss that revealed a set of blood-soaked fangs. Clearly dental hygiene was no longer a priority in the Delmonico household.

"Get out of here," Meena shouted to her brother from the pavement of the alley, to which she'd dropped. "Go!"

Jon didn't hesitate. He wriggled past Brianna and into the alley, fumbling in his apron pocket.

"Oh my God," Meena heard him saying a few seconds later. "Oh my God . . . I think I'm going to be sick."

Meena didn't have time for her brother's problems. She was busy dealing with Brianna, who'd lunged at her again.

And this time Meena couldn't duck, because she was already on the ground. She had nowhere to go. She grunted as the larger woman's body hit hers, momentarily knocking the breath out of her. Vampires were naturally strong, but in life, Brianna must have spent a lot of time working out, because her muscles were like rocks. Meena regretted the many nights she'd picked the Palatine's research library over the gym.

Fortunately, not content to be left out of the fight, Jack Bauer threw himself at Brianna Delmonico, viciously assaulting her ankles just above her Nikes.

Brianna let out a guttural sound, clearly in pain. But even Jack Bauer's sharp little fangs sinking into her flesh didn't distract her from trying to sink her own into Meena's.

"Jon," Meena cried, reaching up to wrap her hands around the throat of the woman with whom she'd shared a boyfriend. "A little help, please."

"Hold on—" she heard Jon say. Then he made a sound like he was retching.

Was he *throwing up?*

Then, just as those inch-long incisors were about to plunge into the same holes the woman's husband had made in Meena's neck, Brianna turned her face away with a look of absolute repulsion.

It wasn't until she saw the direction of Brianna's gaze that Meena realized why: Alaric's cross.

For a moment, the two of them lay there, Meena breathing hard, Brianna . . . well, Brianna not breathing at all, just hissing in anger and disgust.

That was all the time Jon needed to recover from whatever was wrong with him, reach out, grab a handful of Brianna's blond hair, then flip her off Meena and onto her back.

Before the vampire even knew what had hit her, Jon was standing over her, one foot pressed to her chest, and the SuperStaker pointed in her face.

Meena lay still on the alley floor, sucking in as much air as she could, grateful finally to have the weight of Brianna's body lifted from her. She gazed up at the thin slice of blue sky she could see between the tall buildings, across which a couple of fluffy white clouds slowly drifted.

The clouds looked exactly like the ones that had drifted across the sky outside the window of the castle in her dream about Lucien and his mother, so peaceful and serene. Meena wished she could lie there forever, enjoying the view.

Then Jack Bauer trotted up to her face, gave her cheek a little lick, and went quickly back to growl at Brianna some more.

"All right," Jon was saying to Brianna. "I saw what you did to that guy over there. If you think I'm going to let you do that to my sister—"

Brianna lunged at him, her jaw snapping. Jon squeezed the trigger on his hair dryer. A blue dot of light appeared on Brianna's head.

She instantly began screaming in pain and fell back to the ground, writhing and clutching her head. A trail of smoke wisped up from her burning hair.

"Jon!" Meena cried, gasping as she sat up.

"Holy crap," Jon said in a stunned voice, looking down at the Super-Staker. "It works. It actually works."

"Jon!" Meena cried again, this time because Brianna had lunged again. Only now she was going for the hand that held the SuperStaker.

Jon pressed the trigger once more, hitting Brianna in the chest with the blue dot. She began to writhe, then crab-walked until her back came up against the wall of the opposite building, not seeming to know what had hit her.

"Jon," Meena said, again, climbing to her feet, "what *is* that thing?"

"It's a gun that shoots UV rays," he said. "I invented it. Well, I made an adjustment to a gun of a similar design that the police are already using in crime-scene analysis—"

Noticing that Jon was distracted, Brianna tried to slink away. Jon was too fast for her, however. He trained the blue light on her throat, causing her to squeal and back up against the wall once more, looking back and forth frantically for some means of escape.

There was none. She was trapped.

"As you can see," Jon continued to Meena, "it's pretty effective."

Meena, impressed, said, "Ask her where all that blood down her shirt came from."

Meena still felt that Alaric, Abraham, and Carolina were all right . . . but the sight of all that blood was making her nervous. *This woman had hurt someone she knew.* She could feel it.

"If you've done anything to any of my friends," Meena warned Brianna, her insides clenching, "I'm going to have my brother set you on fire with this thing."

Brianna glared at Meena venomously. "I always hated you," she said. "I was glad when they sent me to kill you."

"Blast her," Meena said to her brother. "And make it quick. We don't have a whole lot of time. Those cops looked mad."

"I know where some of that blood came from," Jon said. "Go take a look behind that Dumpster."

Hesitantly, Meena walked toward the Dumpster to peer around it . . .

. . . and instantly understood why Jon had been retching earlier.

They'd found one of Alaric's missing tourists.

Or at least, what was left of him.

This one was missing a large chunk of his neck. It was clear now where the blood down Brianna's tracksuit had come from. Judging by the dead man's expression, which seemed startled, death had clearly come as a surprise . . . for which Meena supposed he could only be thankful. She remembered David's bite, and how she hadn't even known it was there until Lucien had pointed out that it was bleeding.

There had to be some kind of anesthetizing agent in their fangs. She wondered if the man had been on his way from sampling some of the food booths at the San Gennaro Festival. He'd probably just wanted to explore the neighborhood and digest his meal a little—his last, as it turned out—when Brianna attacked.

Meena thought she was going to be sick.

"What kind of vampire are you?" Jon was asking Brianna, threatening her with the SuperStaker. "You're supposed to drink people's blood, not chew big holes in them. You're getting this all wrong."

Meena turned away from the corpse, something stirring in the back of her mind. A vampire that ate its prey's flesh . . . where had she heard that before?

"Who sent you here?" Jon demanded of Brianna. "Who turned you?"

Brianna continued to snarl at him, almost as ferociously as Jack Bauer was snarling at her.

Backed into a corner as she was, however, there was nowhere she could go.

"Here," Meena said, kneeling beside her brother. "Let me try."

Jon thrust an arm out in front of her protectively. "Not too close," he warned, holding up the SuperStaker.

"It's all right," Meena said. Looking Brianna straight in the eye, she said, "Brianna, I'm sorry this happened to you. It's all my fault. I know that. And I'm so, so sorry."

Jon looked at her like she was nuts. "Sorry?" he cried. "For *what*? Her husband tried to kill you. And so did she. She *did* just kill that guy over there!"

"I know," Meena said. "But none of it would have happened if it weren't for me. And—"

"Oh, Jesus Christ," Jon interrupted. "*You* didn't start any of this. And anyway, she stole your boyfriend, remember?"

Meena glared at him. "She didn't steal him. He walked. And would you let me finish? Just because she's been turned into a vampire doesn't mean she's lost of all of her humanity. There could still be something left of the old Brianna in there, fighting to get out. I think that's what my dream is trying to tell me about Lucien." She looked down at Brianna. "It could be true of her, too."

Brianna looked straight back at her, bared her fangs, and hissed.

"Yeah," Jon said. "I've never seen Lucien do that. Except the time he tried to fry us all alive." He aimed the SuperStaker at Brianna's head. "Tell us who turned you, or I swear I will burn a hole the size of a quarter right through your scalp—"

Before he got a chance to follow through on his threat, however, the back door to the Shrine of St. Clare's thrift shop burst open, and Yalena stepped out.

"Jon?" she called, looking around. "Jon, are you out here? There are some police officers who—"

Then several things happened at once.

Yalena saw the dead body behind the Dumpster and screamed.

Jon saw Yalena, and was so distracted, he relaxed his grip on the SuperStaker.

And Brianna saw that Jon had relaxed his grip on the SuperStaker. She leaped onto Jon, sinking her fangs into his shoulder.

Chapter Twenty-eight

Alaric Wulf was not in Rome.

He had not been entirely sure where he was when he first lifted his head after regaining consciousness. But slowly he was getting his bearings. He had been in this room before, though only once, when he'd first toured the building.

What he could not figure out was why he was in this room now . . . and hanging by his wrists from a thick pipe in the middle of the ceiling. He had no way of telling how long he'd been there, since they had taken away all of his belongings, including his watch, his cell phone, his belt, his sword, his shoes, his socks, and, for some reason, his shirt, all of which it was presumably believed he could use as deadly weapons.

Alaric thought this was interesting, both because his feet—and his bare hands, if he could just get them loose—would more than suffice as deadly weapons.

Someone evidently had something to fear from him.

Someone was right.

Alaric didn't know why it was that he'd been struck over the head, then strung up in the boiler room of St. Bernadette's. He imagined no one at the Palatine was too happy with him for discussing the missing tourists with Genevieve Fox.

He'd expected a disciplinary letter, at most. Possibly probation. This seemed to be taking matters too far.

The last thing he could remember was being hauled from the van that had taken him from the Met. He had been understandably—in his opinion, anyway—upset at that turn of events. Where had that squadron of uniformed idiots, led by Henrique Mauricio, come from, anyway?

Had that net they'd tried to use to capture Lucien Antonescu just as Alaric had been about to slice his head been Caliente's idea? Probably. The whole thing had been handled ham-fistedly enough.

And Alaric had had every intention of saying so to whomever he could get to listen . . . though his first priority had been trying to make them aware of the phone call he'd received from Abraham. They needed to know that the team was alive, and in jeopardy. Someone needed to get in touch with Johanna and see how she was progressing with the satellite tracking, and then send a recon team to wherever Holtzman and the others were—

No sooner were the words out of his mouth than the blow had struck the back of his head. After that, there'd been only darkness. He'd woken up in this sorry state.

Apparently, he'd struck a nerve. Someone—and he had a fairly good idea who—didn't want him talking about the phone call he'd received from Holtzman. It was a call he apparently wasn't supposed to have received and might be why he was in his current position.

Interesting. But also aggravating.

Because how could he help Holtzman when he was in this position?

Gravity had long since pulled the blood from his hands and arms, and he'd lost all feeling in them. He was thirsty, and his head hurt where he'd been coldcocked.

He'd been strung up in such a manner before, of course, but never by his own employer . . . and he knew it was his employer who'd done it because the restraints around his wrists were the soft leather ones they used on recalcitrant humans who would not give up the location of their vampire lovers. They did not leave marks on the skin, no matter how much the prisoner struggled, but were incredibly secure, and impossible to break free from . . .

. . . unless, of course, one had worked with them as often as Alaric had, and knew their weaknesses.

He needed to get out of there, and as soon as possible. It wasn't only the situation with Holtzman and the rest of the team in New Jersey that was worrying him. He was worried about Meena, as well. He'd heard the way Caliente had been speaking to her outside the museum.

If they had Alaric hanging by his arms in a boiler room—and only because they mistrusted and disliked him—what were they doing to her in order to get her to reveal the whereabouts of Lucien Antonescu?

Alaric knew. He knew perfectly well. He also knew that he had to stop it, because last night in the museum, he'd looked in Antonescu's eyes and—despite Meena's assertions to the contrary—seen nothing there but demon.

It was possible, of course, that Meena was right, and at one time Lucien Antonescu hadn't been a complete monster.

Alaric didn't believe that was true anymore. Meena was only seeing what she wanted to see.

Alaric, meanwhile, was going to concentrate his efforts on saving the people worth saving—Meena, and the rest of his friends.

So he went to work.

Chapter Twenty-nine

Meena snatched up the gun as soon as Jon dropped it, which he did when Brianna's body weight hit him. Then she aimed, and pressed down on the trigger.

Not knowing how the gun worked, Meena had no idea what to expect. Certainly not what happened, which was that fire burst from the center of Brianna's chest. That's because Meena had kept holding down the trigger. Brianna immediately leaped up from Jon and screamed. Yalena, running down the steps from the back of the thrift shop toward Jon, also screamed. Jack Bauer barked madly.

Then Brianna darted away, down the alley and toward the low basement window of a building opposite the thrift shop. The window was broken, and had once been boarded up, but it was clear someone had kicked—or clawed—the board away.

Brianna dove back through the opening now, disappearing into the darkness, escaping from the harsh glare of the SuperStaker.

"Jon!" Yalena sank down onto the pavement beside Meena's brother. "Are you all right? Oh no!"

Meena turned away from the window through which Brianna had vanished and looked down. Jon was already sitting up, one hand pressed to his shoulder.

"I'm okay," he assured them. "I'm fine. Look, barely a scratch on me."

Jon had no idea, because he couldn't see himself. Blood had already begun to stain his white Beanery apron scarlet.

"Come on," he said, starting to get up. "Let's go. We can't let her get away."

"No, Jon," Yalena cried. She pulled him back to the ground. "You're hurt!"

"I'm fine," Jon kept saying. He obviously couldn't feel the pain of the wound because of the anesthetic in Brianna's fangs. "I'm good, really."

Meena remembered the hooded sweatshirt she'd tied around her waist. She pulled it off and handed it to Yalena.

"Here," she said. "Use this."

Yalena grabbed it and shoved the cotton material against Jon's wound, attempting to stop the bleeding.

It was right then that the two police officers stepped out the back door of the thrift shop. For a second or two they just stood there, staring, trying to take it all in.

Then Yalena looked up at them and screamed, "Call an ambulance!"

One of the officers snapped to attention, pulling out his radio and murmuring into it urgently. The second jumped down to help Yalena apply pressure to the wound.

"What happened?" he asked them. His gaze darted toward the corpse by the Dumpster, then back to Jon's wound. "What's that over there?"

"We just walked out and found him like that," Meena told him. She'd shoved the SuperStaker into her purse. "The killer, the one they've been talking about on the news. It has to be him. We must have interrupted him. So he attacked my brother. He *bit* him."

"Jesus, Mary, and Joseph," the police officer said, looking shaken. He reached for his own radio. "Did you see which way he went?"

"Yes," Meena said, nodding. "That way." She pointed in the opposite direction from the one in which Brianna had fled.

The officer began speaking rapidly into his radio. Meena looked across her brother's body at Yalena. The younger girl's eyes were wide and frightened.

"Listen to me, Yalena," Meena said, in a low, serious voice. "I want you to go with Jon to the hospital. Do *not* leave his side. If anyone asks you, you're family. Tell them you're his sister, whatever you have to do."

Yalena nodded. "I will."

"She's not my sister," Jon said, giggling. "That would be gross."

He was clearly becoming disoriented from blood loss.

"Shut up, Jon," Meena said. To Yalena, she said, "Call Sister Gertrude and Father Bernard. No one else. They're the only ones we can trust."

Yalena's eyes grew huge, but she nodded. "I just saw them both this morning. They were talking about how things seemed . . . strange last night at the museum."

"That's a good sign," Meena said. "Tell them I can't find Alaric."

"Tell Alaric about the SuperStaker," Jon said. "It's going to take vampire killing to a new level."

Meena laid a finger over Jon's lips. "Call Adam Weinberg, too," she said to Yalena, handing her Jack Bauer's leash. "That's Jon's friend. You'll find his number on Jon's phone. He'll come take Jack."

Yalena had looked frightened before.

Now she looked terrified.

"Wait," she said. "Jack? Jack Bauer? You're not taking him? But . . . you take him everywhere."

"Not where I'm going," Meena said. "It's too dangerous for him."

"Meena." Yalena reached out and grasped Meena's wrist just as she was getting up. "Where are you going?"

Meena looked toward the window through which Brianna had disappeared.

"To do my job," she said.

Chapter Thirty

Once, when Meena had been researching a story line she'd wanted to pitch to the producers of *Insatiable,* the soap opera she used to write for, she'd read that beneath New York City ran many underground caverns, tunnels, and subbasements built so far in the past that no one even remembered they were there. It was a wonder the entire place hadn't caved in years ago.

And considering that the city sat on top of an active fault line, the chances were it probably would, someday.

When she slipped through the window Brianna had used to make her getaway minutes before—the police officers had been distracted by the three men Jon had so aggravated in the café, who had come out into the alley through the thrift shop to see what was taking so long and had instantly become sickened at the sight of both his wounds and the dead man by the Dumpster—she realized she was in one of those subbasements. It seemed to stretch almost the entire block, interrupted only by metal support pillars and metal cages containing the belongings of some resident from above.

A perfect place for a vampire to nest, since the only sunlight was the occasional beam that spilled in from a mostly boarded-up window at street level.

Even though it was dark, it wasn't difficult to track the path Brianna had taken. The SuperStaker had singed her badly enough that she left behind a faintly burned odor.

Meena quickly lost her bearings, however, moving through the enormous, dark maze of subbasements. She could hear—and even feel—the subway rumbling close by, but she had no idea what street she was beneath, or even what building. Goose bumps had broken out on her flesh, but she couldn't do anything about it, because she'd left her sweatshirt with Jon.

Her heart thumping, she drew out the SuperStaker, beginning to question the sanity of what she was doing. What was she going to do if she found Brianna, interrogate her? Even if Brianna had the answers Meena was seeking about who had turned her and David and why, Meena was probably going to have to torture her to get them. And in the end, she was still going to have to kill her.

And Meena wasn't sure she could stomach torturing and then killing another Delmonico this weekend, even one as savage as Brianna.

This was *not* how she'd pictured things going when she'd signed on to work for the Palatine. She thought she'd be saving lives and making the world a better place. Instead, people she'd thought were her friends were proving to be her enemies, and the people she loved were either getting hurt or disappearing.

And nothing she did or said seemed to make a difference. It was almost the *opposite* of what the woman in her dream had been trying to assure her little boy. All of God's creatures may indeed have had the ability to choose between good and evil, but so far, Meena had encountered very few who were choosing to be good . . .

Sometimes she wished she could have had the normal, boring life her parents had always envisioned for her, like the lives of those people she could hear walking around up there, above her head, enjoying themselves at the street festival.

They didn't have prophetic dreams (that turned out not to be so prophetic, after all, apparently).

They didn't adopt dogs that turned out to be able to scent vampires.

They didn't get fired from their jobs (twice) because the guy they'd started dating turned out to be the prince of darkness.

They didn't have their apartments trashed, their friends and family terrorized, and their lives destroyed, and basically have to go into hiding because of their poor romantic choices.

Then again, they didn't have the ability to predict how everyone they met was going to die . . . which might actually have been a bit more useful of a skill if it had extended to herself.

Because as she crept around that particularly dark corner, she suddenly felt sure she was walking into some kind of a trap. She could almost sense someone's gaze on her . . . and with an intensity that was all too familiar.

Which could mean only one thing.

When she felt a sudden *whoosh* of air against her right side that was colder than any wind, she didn't even have to turn her head to look. She knew who it was.

"Lucien," she started to say. "Don't even—"

She ought to have looked.

The last thing she saw before something struck her hard, first in the chest, then in the head, when everything went dark, was Brianna Delmonico's bloodied face, rushing at her, fangs first.

Chapter Thirty-one

Meena wasn't sure which she found more disturbing: that she'd been hunting her ex-boyfriend's murderous wife with a hair dryer beneath the streets of Manhattan, or that when she opened her eyes after having been knocked unconscious by this person, she realized she'd been rescued by another one of her ex-boyfriends.

She thought it might actually be the latter.

"Lucien," she heard herself say in a voice that didn't sound at all like her own. "What happened?"

"It was my fault," he said, his dark gaze locked on her. "But you're safe now."

She tried to sit up, then fell back against something soft when a wave of pain hit her.

"Shhh," he said, pressing a cool cloth to her forehead. "You hit your head against the concrete when that woman attacked you. Don't worry, though. She shan't be troubling anyone again."

Meena didn't want to ask. She did manage to sit up this time without pain . . .

. . . but when she got a good look at her surroundings, she nearly lost consciousness again. Only this time it was from shock.

She could not believe it. She was in a cave. A *cave*.

With Lucien.

She'd thought secret subterranean hideouts of billionaires existed only in fiction. It appeared, however, that Lucien had created one of his own, right beneath the streets of downtown Manhattan, and furnished it the way only a five-hundred-year-old European vampire would. Everything was leather or antique, with the exception of Lucien himself, who was gazing down at her with concern as she lay stretched out on a couch that was both leather *and* antique . . . or at least had been artfully crafted to look that way.

If a butler had come in and offered her tea, she wouldn't have been surprised.

"What *is* this place?" she demanded, eyeing him suspiciously.

They had better still be in Manhattan—and she thought they were, because she could dimly hear, off in the distance, the grumble of the subway—or she was going to . . .

Panicking, she looked around for the SuperStaker.

She relaxed a little after seeing it sticking out of her purse, which sat next to the side of the couch, on a stone floor that sloped down toward an interior water feature . . . some kind of trickling brown stream.

"So suspicious," Lucien said with a grin, having noticed her frantic glance at her bag. Of course, he didn't know what the bag contained. He probably really did think the SuperStaker was a hair dryer.

"Honestly, Lucien, after what you tried to do to me last night, I think I have a right to be suspicious," Meena said in a tired voice.

He was sitting on top of a leather trunk beside the couch. He looked outrageously handsome, as always. Whatever burns he might have sustained from the incident the night before had already healed. One of his superpowers was the ability to heal instantaneously.

Meanwhile, her head was pounding so hard she could barely hear anything else . . . not the distant sound of the traffic from high above them, or the farther-off growling of the subway, or the trickling of water from the stream, or anything at all, really, except her own pulse.

"Meena," he said, in a tone that was half pleading, half penitent. "You know it was only because I lo—"

"*No,*" she said firmly. "There's no excuse. This isn't the 1400s, and I'm not some sultan's daughter you can just sweep up and ride off with into the sunset. You know better. How *could* you?"

He reached out as if to take her in his arms . . .

But before he could touch her, she had the SuperStaker out of her bag and in both hands, pointed at the center of his chest.

"Really," she said. Her hands might have been trembling, but her voice wasn't. "I mean it. *Don't.*"

He let his arms fall, his expression perplexed . . . but cautious.

"Meena," he said, "what is that?"

"It's called the SuperStaker," she said. "My brother invented it. Do you see this button?" She pointed to a red button on top of the gun.

"I do," he said, still looking perplexed . . . and also slightly amused, judging by the slightly upturned corners of his mouth.

"If it lights up," Meena informed him, "it means a UV ray is being shot wherever the person aims. And if the target happens to be a vampire, that means you're going to be in pain. A lot of it. I know, because I used it on Brianna. And she didn't like it. It burned a hole in her, as a matter of fact. That's how I was able to find her down here. I just followed the smell of burning vampire."

"Actually," Lucien said, his smile turning wry, "I think *she* found *you*. I'm not going to argue with you, however, since you're holding a gun on me. Do you really hate me that much, Meena, that you'd burn a hole through me?"

"I'm . . . concerned about you," she said. "You tried to *kidnap* me. You've basically shown that you can't be trusted. There's no telling what you'll try to do next. You aren't the person you were when I fell in love with you. You . . . you've changed."

He spread his hands wide, giving a very convincing imitation of an innocent man. "I still love you. In that way, I haven't changed. I'll admit that last night I might have exercised poor judgment. And the night before that, I obviously wasn't myself either. For that, I humbly beg your pardon. But I'm much better now, Meena. You've helped make that possible."

She eyed him doubtfully. "How did I do that? You don't listen to a word I say."

"I feel strong," he said, his dark eyes glowing in the firelight from the sconces along the wall. "Stronger than I've ever been in my life. I was depending on the Mannette to make the transformation for me, but I didn't realize it couldn't do that while there was still such a vital part of me missing. That part was you, Meena. Once you came back into my life, everything fell into place."

Meena stared at him, confused. "What transformation? What is the Mannette?"

"The Mannette is another name for the Minetta Stream," Lucien explained, nodding toward the water she could see trickling past the carpets on the ground. "The original inhabitants of this island thought it to be very powerful, but later settlers forced it underground . . . in a manner not dissimilar to the way our kind has always been forced into hiding—"

"I know what the Minetta Stream is," Meena said. She recalled having read something about it as part of the research she'd done on New York City's underground tunnels. "But what do you mean, *our* kind? Your kind likes to eat my kind."

"Meena." He reached up as if he were going to stroke her hair, but saw that she still had the SuperStaker trained on him and lowered his hand. "I meant those who are different. You know perfectly well that if you had been born in another century, you'd have been burned at the stake, or pressed under rocks until you suffocated, or drowned, for your ability to predict the future."

"Being a psychic," Meena said, "is not the same as being an immortal who can only survive on human blood." She glanced around the cave and gave a shiver. "You can put all the fancy furniture in here that you want, Lucien, but this place is never going to seem very homey. I can't believe you've been living here."

"It's near you," Lucien said, with another one of his heart-melting smiles. "And it's a sacred place." The smile faded. "Which makes it all the more insulting that you continue to point that thing at me. I could have done anything I wanted to you while you were unconscious, including turning you into one of my kind. But I did not. So why can't you trust me?"

Meena only narrowed her eyes in disbelief at this.

"You couldn't have turned me into one of your kind," she said. "To be turned into a vampire, a person has to be bitten three times, then drink a vampire's blood. You couldn't force me to drink your blood while I was *unconscious*. So you don't get points for that. And anyway," Meena added, "I have some things I need you to do for me. And since you aren't going to like doing them, I will probably have to shoot you a couple of times to motivate you."

"There's nothing in the world that would make me happier than doing something for you," Lucien said.

"Fine," she said, shrugging. "Find Alaric Wulf."

He raised his eyebrows, surprised . . . but he didn't look angry.

Since this was hardly the reaction she'd been expecting, she said, "Maybe you didn't hear me. I said I want you to—"

"Oh no," he said. "I heard you. And I quite understand. You want me to find Alaric Wulf."

"He isn't answering his cell phone," she said. "Which means something has to be wrong. He *always* picks up. They told me they sent him back to Rome, but you and I both know he'd never have allowed that to happen. I was on my way to his place to look for him when Brianna attacked me. I'm hoping he'll be there, but—"

"Oh," Lucien said knowingly. "He isn't."

Meena felt a chill run down her spine that had nothing to do with the temperature of the cave.

"What do you mean, he isn't?" she asked. "How would you know? Did you *go* there?"

"I didn't have to," Lucien said. "I know he isn't there. I'm looking for him, too."

Meena almost squeezed the trigger on the SuperStaker in surprise. This was why, she now realized, people shouldn't own guns—or at least, people like her. Because of their tendency accidentally to shoot them. She removed her finger from the trigger.

"*Why?*" she asked. "That net with the holy water wasn't his idea, Lucien. Nor was the opening last night. He had nothing to do with that. And he'd *never* have tried to lure you out into the open by turning my friends into vampires and setting them loose into society. So why on *earth* are you looking for Alaric?"

"Because I believe he has something of mine," Lucien said, his voice dropping to the same cool temperature as the cave. "Something I want very badly. So despite what you may think of my opinion of him, I actually hold his safety in the very highest regard. And so I've been searching for him all day. That's why I wasn't there for you when you needed me. Mary Lou and Emil are searching for him as well. Therefore you really needn't continue to hold that gun on me, Meena. I'm more than prepared to join forces with you to find him. In fact, I already have."

Meena shook her head. She felt so confused, and she was pretty sure it wasn't due to the blow she'd received to her skull. "But . . . what could Alaric possibly have of yours?"

"That's not actually important right now," Lucien said. He reached up and laid a hand on the barrel of the SuperStaker. "Though I'd like to point out something that is."

"What?" she asked.

"That you're currently attempting to use force to get me to do something," he said, in his deep, hypnotically soothing voice. "Which is exactly what I believe you strongly objected to my doing to you last night."

She blinked. He was right. She wasn't treating him any differently than he'd treated her the night before. She was actually treating him worse, because he'd done what he had out of desperation, loneliness, and, she presumed—because he kept insisting it was true—love.

She was acting out of . . . well, she wasn't even sure anymore.

"Oh, Lucien," she said, her shoulders sagging. "I'm so sorry."

"You should be," he said, and plucked the SuperStaker lightly out of her hands. She watched as he set it on the far side of the couch, out of her reach, unless she wanted to crawl across him to get it.

"You are many things, Meena," he went on, "but a hardened criminal isn't one of them. If there's something you'd like me to do for you, I'd suggest a different form of persuasion."

Then, before she knew what was happening, he'd wrapped his arms around her.

She would have liked to think it was her very recent head injury that caused her to do nothing to fight off this embrace. After all, she probably had a concussion. Without an X-ray or CAT scan, she'd never know for sure.

The truth was, the feeling of his hard chest as it pressed up against her, the reassuring strength of his arms as they tightened around her, even the scent of him . . . all of these brought familiar and welcome sensations. For a dizzying second or two, it was as if no time had gone by, and things were back to the way they should be, the way they'd been before . . . before all the damage had been done, none of the lies had been told, none of the terrible things had happened . . .

But that, of course, wasn't reality.

Reality was that people were dead. A lot of people.

Reality was the pain Lucien had put her—and her friends and family—through.

Reality was her realization that, just as his lips were about to touch hers, the smell of something burning was filling the air.

Chapter Thirty-two

Lucien pulled away with a blistering curse, then looked down at the triangle of skin framed by the open collar of his white shirt. Emblazoned on his flesh, like a brand, was the image of the cross Alaric had given her, and which still hung at her throat.

Meena gasped . . . but not as loudly as Lucien did.

"I thought I told you to take that damned thing off," he said furiously.

"It's saved my life," she murmured, still staring at his singed skin. It had saved her life several times, actually.

"I wasn't going to hurt you," he said. "You know I would never hurt you. Take it off."

"I don't want to," she said. "And previous experience indicates otherwise."

He threw her a stinging look. The burn on his chest was already starting to heal before her eyes.

The injury she'd just inflicted to his heart would not be as easily soothed.

"That's not fair," he said. "I want only what's best for you . . . to protect you. No one else seems to. You saw what happened today when I wasn't there—"

Her voice cracked in disbelief. "Lucien, I don't think you heard me before. My brother's in the hospital. I don't know where my boss or Alaric is. And I got *fired*. All because of you. And while you've been making yourself a snug little . . . *whatever this is* down here . . . vampires have apparently been running around the streets of Manhattan eating their victims whole—blood, skin, bones, and all—"

"That's impossible," Lucien said shortly. "Vampires don't eat flesh. Only zombies and werewolves do that."

"No, Lucien," she said, "it's not impossible. Because I saw it for myself. Brianna, the vampire you killed? She took a chunk out of my brother, and that was after snacking on some poor tourist she'd caught and dragged behind a Dumpster." She swung her legs from the couch. "And this new guy at the Palatine, Father Henrique Mauricio, the one who tried to catch you last night, told me about this species of vampires from South America . . . the Lamir. They're supposed to be descended from some kind of fishing bat that eats the flesh of its prey."

"The Lamir," Lucien muttered darkly, staring at the small stream that ran through the middle of his living room. "I know of them."

"You know of them?" Again Meena's voice cracked. "Lucien, you're supposed to be the prince of darkness, the son of Satan. Aren't you supposed to be a little more in tune with this stuff?"

"I am aware," Lucien said, in a cold voice, still staring down at the stream, "that in the past I haven't always shown the full commitment to my position that I should have. And for that, I have been made to suffer."

"What's that supposed to mean?" Although she didn't feel a hundred percent steady on them yet, Meena managed to climb to her feet and walk to Lucien's side. Up close, she noticed, the Minetta Stream had a stale odor, like something that had been bottled up for too long. She took a hasty step away from the murky brown water that was about to touch the tip of one of her sneakers. "How have you suffered? How have you not shown the full commitment that you ought to have?"

He swung his dark gaze upon her. "How do you think, Meena?" he asked, his tone bitterly sardonic. "How do you think I have suffered? Open your eyes. You ask why I would *choose* to live here? I didn't choose to . . . I *must*, if I hope to regain enough strength not to be destroyed by my enemies in my next battle with them. And how have I not shown my commitment? What kind of vampire bids his minions *not* to kill? What kind of dark prince does not know—or even care—the names of those who serve him . . . much less falls in love with a mortal who is convinced she was put on this earth to save it from the likes of him?"

"Lucien," Meena said anxiously, taking another step away from him . . . and the murky brown stream. She wished she could have moved toward him, to comfort him in some way. The raw anger in his voice—and the foul smell from the water—seemed to be warning her to keep her distance, however.

"You didn't know," Lucien said. He stared down into the brackish water, which—it was not Meena's imagination—had begun to rise. Just a fraction of an inch, but unmistakably. And it was definitely burbling with more vitality. "How could you? But that's who the prince of darkness is, Meena. That was the pact my father made . . . to become, in exchange for his soul, Lucifer's son on earth. And when the Palatine killed my father, that title was passed on to me. It's true I've had my struggles accepting it—especially after I met you."

He turned his head so that the full heat of his dark-eyed gaze fell upon her. Meena wanted to take another step backward, but she forced herself to stay where she was.

"But now I've begun to realize that I've had the solution to my problems all along," he said. The anger left his tone, and he even managed a smile . . . although not a very convincing one. "And that was simply to accept my fate, not fight it. Isn't that what they say on all of those television talk shows? Embrace what you are, and others will embrace you as well? Find what it is that you do well, then do it, and the rest will fall into place?"

Meena shook her head. She didn't like this. Any of it. It smelled about as badly as the stream.

"Lucien," she said. "No, that's not what they mean. Not when it comes to being good at doing evil. Does this have anything to do with why you wanted your mother's book so badly?"

Lucien glanced at her sharply. "What has my mother's book to do with any of this?" he asked, sounding stunned.

"Because Father Henrique says possessing your mother's book of hours will make you all-powerful."

Meena wasn't sure, considering everything Lucien had just been saying, that this was information she ought to be revealing to him.

On the other hand, her feelings about the book she'd seen in her dream were the opposite of Father Henrique's. She was sure that there was nothing terrible in it, and that the reason she'd been having the dream was that someone—or something—wanted to make sure she showed the book to Lucien. She desperately wanted to see what Lucien himself thought . . . and she wanted to see the book itself so she could confirm her beliefs.

"He says it isn't an ordinary devotional," Meena went on, "and your getting control of it will mean the end of the world."

Lucien looked surprised. "*Who* said this?"

"Father Henrique," she said. "The priest who tried to capture you with the net, and then had me fired. It didn't make any sense to me either. Because if something like that existed, the Vatican would never be stupid enough to let it out of Rome. Not if they knew what it was."

Lucien's dark eyebrows furrowed. "Of course not," he said. But his gaze suddenly looked far away. "You're perfectly correct."

Meena began to feel as if she'd only made matters worse. What *was* it about that book that was making everyone—except her—so nervous?

"So," she said, "it's *not* true, then, about your mother's book? He was just making it up to get me to tell him where you were?"

"Of course," Lucien said, glancing back toward her with another one of those smiles that didn't reach his eyes. "There's nothing like that inside it. How could there be? When my father had that book made for my mother, he was in love. He was happy. He was looking forward to what he thought was going to be many years of domestic bliss. He had no idea of what awaited him . . . or my mother . . . or me."

His gaze drifted away from her. Meena followed it and saw that he was looking at the stream again. She remembered having read that Minetta Lane was named for a stream that used to run through the center of Fifth Avenue, all the way down Spring Street. It had been covered up because of its tendency to flood local homes, sometimes even killing people. Once it had supposedly provided water for the fountain that had been turned off in the courtyard of St. Bernadette's School, because of a terrible accident nearly a century earlier. Apparently this brown trickle was all that was left of the stream.

It seemed strange to her that Lucien was so drawn to it. Something about that bothered her. *Mannette*. She was certain she'd heard—or read—that word before.

"Maybe," she said, trying to stick to the matter at hand, "we should just check the book. Because it's possible that after your mother's death, your father did something to it . . . altered it in some way, with an occult element. And that some members of the clergy—like Father Henrique—know about it, and others don't. And that's how it ended up in the show. The Catholic Church, I'm figuring out, is a bureaucracy like any other company." And unjustly fired people, like any other company, she thought but didn't add. "For every employee to be involved in every detail is sheer impossibility . . . So, where is it?"

Lucien appeared startled by the question. "Where is what?"

"Your mother's book," she said patiently. Although she wasn't feeling very patient anymore. More like frightened. The constant trickling sound of the water was making her want to scream.

"That," Lucien said, "is exactly what I'd like to know. And why I'd like to find your friend Alaric Wulf."

"Alaric?" Meena shook her head. A knot had suddenly formed between her shoulder blades. "Why would Alaric know where your book is? Mary Lou stole it. I saw her. Everyone chased after her."

"Yes," Lucien said, speaking very carefully. "Everyone did chase after Mary Lou. But only one person caught up to her and snatched her bag away before she managed to escape. The bag containing my mother's book of hours."

Meena stared at Lucien in growing horror. She remembered Mary Lou's bag. It had been shaped like a pagoda.

"You mean . . ." She could barely speak the words.

"Yes," he said. "Your *friend* . . . Alaric." He pronounced the word *friend* as if it were a curse.

"Alaric didn't have the bag when we were arrested," she said, thinking back to when she'd seen him by the vans.

"No," Lucien said. "He did not. Emil found his wife's bag later that night, when he returned to the museum thinking, by some miracle, it had been dropped in all the confusion. It had. It had been stuffed into a wastebasket in a men's bathroom. The bag was empty."

"But," Meena said, "that would mean Alaric had to have had the book on him. Or that he hid it at the museum somewhere—"

"Precisely," Lucien said. He looked so angry, his eyes were beginning to flare red. It might have been Meena's imagination, but the trickling of the stream had also begun to sound significantly louder. "Emil has been at the museum all day, looking for it. He's found nothing. And Mary Lou has been watching Palatine headquarters since last night. She says she saw them drag Alaric Wulf inside just after they brought you there. But so far, she's yet to see him come out."

Meena looked at him, her heart flying suddenly in her throat.

"Alaric's still in there," she said.

Chapter Thirty-three

Alaric didn't have to chew through the cuffs holding his wrists in place after all, which he'd feared he was going to have to do. He was able to undo the buckles with his teeth, although it took some time, and there was nothing at all dignified about the position in which he'd had to contort—and hold—his body to do so.

After dropping to the floor, he had to rest for a while in order to recover. He was bone-tired, dehydrated, hungry, and most of all, furious.

His employers were really slipping. What if they made it this easy for vampires or other demons to escape?

After he could feel his extremities again, he explored the boiler room. There wasn't much to find, though he did drink liberally from the faucet of the rusty-piped sink he'd discovered in one corner. Then he pondered how next to proceed.

He had no phone, no access to a phone, and no shoes, shirt, or belt. He had no weapon and knew that the door to the boiler was not only locked but probably guarded.

There weren't any windows or other form of egress from the room except a small locked door he found behind the industrial, freight car–sized boiler that said NO UNAUTHORIZED ENTRY.

He really had no other choice but to kick this open. Otherwise, he could wait, batlike, in the rafters, for someone to come through the main door, drop upon them, and hope, using the element of surprise, to take them out, then escape.

He was fairly certain they'd be expecting a move like this from him, though, and would be sure only to enter his holding area in large, well-armed groups.

Really, his best option seemed to be the "No Unauthorized Entry" door. Even if it led only to an electrical room, perhaps he could find a way to call Johanna by doing some rewiring of the internal phone system.

He kept his mind carefully blank about what he was going to do after that. As someone who had spent many years of his life in a state of uncertainty about where his next meal was coming from, Alaric had learned that it was usually better not to plan too far ahead. He would take it one step at a time.

First, he needed to leave the boiler room.

He kicked out the small, locked door.

Behind it he found another room, considerably smaller than the boiler room, and much better furnished for human habitation with industrial-grade carpeting, fluorescent lighting, a cot, and even a desk with a computer on it. At the desk sat a man Alaric instantly recognized.

"Oh," Abraham Holtzman said, seeming unsurprised to see him. "Hello. I couldn't get that panel open. I wondered why I hadn't heard from you. What on earth happened to your shirt?"

Chapter Thirty-four

"Freewell was a disaster," Holtzman explained. "David Delmonico's wife was in the house, you know. I've never seen anything like it. And you know I thought I'd seen nearly every form of evil under the sun. But when she came leaping out at us from the laundry room . . ." He shuddered. "It was terrible."

"Abraham." Although Alaric was happy to see that his boss and friend was alive and well, he was starting to regret having found him. His head was still throbbing, and Holtzman seemed to have a need to process what he'd been through.

Alaric did not. He needed only to concentrate on how he was going to get them all out of the building.

"Brianna Delmonico went for Carolina's throat," Holtzman said. "And she would have gotten to it, if Patrick hadn't been in the way. Patrick Chen, the tech, did you know him?" Holtzman asked. "Very reliable. He does excellent analysis work—used to, I mean."

"What do you mean, used to?" Alaric asked.

"That woman just"—Holtzman shook his head, his expression haunted by the memory—"*attacked* him. Blood and brain matter everywhere. Then—Alaric, I swear to you this is true—she *ate* it. Not just the blood. *All of it.*"

Alaric stared at his boss, feeling sickened. He hadn't known Patrick Chen.

But he felt as if nothing could surprise him anymore.

"Where is Carolina now?" Alaric asked. "And the others?"

"Oh," Holtzman said, tilting his head, "she's next door. Santiago and Morioka are down the hall. We've been put on administrative probation for ineffectively analyzing critical data—can you believe that? We can communicate via e-mail—" He nodded at the computer on the desk. "But they aren't allowing us any access to outside communications, pending their investigation into what went wrong in Freewell. Morioka thinks he can break through their firewall, but I have my doubts."

"Who's *they*?" Alaric demanded, pressing his face to the door.

"If you're listening for guards, you needn't waste your time," Holtzman assured him. "Trust me, they haven't even bothered to post any. They say we aren't prisoners. And yet the doors are locked. Spring-latch bolt. Key-code entry. Impossible to bypass." He shook his head. "Believe me, I've tried. They've changed all the pass codes—"

"We've been ineffectively analyzing the data, all right," Alaric assured him. He nodded at the computer on Holtzman's desk. "Does that thing let you go on the Internet?" .

Holtzman looked at his computer. "No. I just told you. It's only for interoffice communication—"

"What about Meena Harper?" Alaric asked. "Can you contact her?"

"Alaric," Holtzman said. "I just explained that they've set them so that we can only contact *one another,* so we can work together on our alleged defense. It's one of our employee—what are you doing?"

Alaric had begun to open the desk drawers, each one of which he pulled out and tipped over onto the floor.

"Oh, Alaric," Holtzman said with a sigh. "Now you're just making a mess. There's nothing you can use there to open the door. Even the hinges are on the other side."

"I might notice something you overlooked," Alaric said. "But go on. Did anyone *do* anything while Chen was being eaten?"

"Of *course,*" Holtzman said, horrified at the suggestion that they'd sat idle while a colleague was being consumed. "Carolina got out that blade of hers—the twelve-inch one. But before she could take a swing, the vampire just bolted. Straight through a plate-glass window. Of course, she grabbed a cashmere throw off the couch before she ran, so that offered her some protection from the daylight. And she didn't have to go far to reach shade. The back of the house sits along the western edge of the Pine Barrens."

Alaric raised his eyebrows. "The Barrens? Is that where you were when you called me?"

Holtzman nodded. "Yes. We gave chase, though we weren't exactly equipped for traipsing through heavily forested coastal plains. As you know, there are over a hundred thousand acres of pinelands there, and the trees can become quite dense . . . and the mobile-phone reception is, quite frankly, terrible. Hardly any cell towers. We tried calling for backup multiple times, and could neither get through nor get an answer, until I reached you. That was after . . ." Holtzman's face went a shade grayer beneath the fluorescent light. "After we found it, of course."

Alaric looked up from the pile of paper clips and Post-it notes he'd made on the floor. "Found what?" he asked.

Though, judging from Holtzman's expression, he wasn't sure he wanted to know.

"Its nest," Abraham said. "It was in the darkest part of the woods I've ever been. A sort of swampy area. I don't know if anyone—anyone human—had ever been there. Certainly not lately, anyway . . . not while they were alive. Brianna Delmonico led us right to it, as if she'd been guided there by some kind of homing beacon. You know I've always believed that there are places of great evil, just as there are places of great goodness. Well, this was one of those, Alaric. It was right beside the water. You could smell the stench of death and decay. And there it was, standing there by its nest, its wings folded, gnawing on something."

"There *what* was?" Alaric asked, feeling a chill. Although he already knew.

"The devil," Holtzman said simply. "He was exactly the way all those people who live around the Barrens have reported seeing him . . . bipedal, winged, horse-headed. He seemed quite surprised to see us. And disappointed that we weren't bearing gifts."

"Gifts?"

"Yes," Holtzman said. "It appeared that usually when he was visited, it was by someone carrying food. The nest was surrounded by bones. They were piled all around his nest."

"Bones?" Alaric repeated. He'd heard of some strange things in his years on the job. But never anything quite like this.

"Yes," Holtzman said. "Human bones. I believe we found your missing tourists, Alaric."

Alaric stared at him in shock. "*That's* how the remains are being disposed of? By giving them to the New Jersey Devil?"

"It appears so," Holtzman said. "Clever, if you think about it. One demon using another to cover up its crimes."

Diabolical was the word Alaric would have chosen, not *clever*. "So what did you do?" he asked.

Holtzman blinked in surprise at the question. "Well, we hit him with everything we had, of course," he said. "Holy water, stakes, blades. Carolina kicked him a few times in the head. Morioka had a Glock loaded with silver bullets. He shot him in the heart. That seemed to do the trick. Squawked a few times, but that was all. Then he turned to ash. Quite satisfying, as kills go."

"Nice," Alaric said admiringly.

"I thought so myself," Holtzman said. "Surprisingly, however, Father Henrique seemed less than pleased when he arrived—"

Alaric thought he must have spent so much time hanging by his arms that a blood clot had formed in them, traveled into his brain, and popped.

That's what it felt like, anyway, when Holtzman said the words *Father Henrique.*

"*What?*" he almost shouted.

"Yes," Holtzman said. "I found that curious, too, at first. And I knew you would react that way when I told you about it, because, of course, I assured you that he'd been assigned here only as a pastor, not as part of our unit. That, however, apparently is not the case. He's been given a position of unprecedented authority, from what I can gather—"

Alaric bit back a colorful stream of curse words so that Holtzman could finish.

"—with some new internal division I've never heard of," Holtzman said. "He and his team seemed quite distressed about the cryptid. He even accused us of excessive force. Apparently they'd have preferred to take it alive. And the helicopter scared off the vampire, who of course was still—"

"They came by *helicopter?*" Alaric could hardly believe what he was hearing.

"Oh yes," Holtzman said. "I was surprised by that, too. Quite a needless expense. It wasn't as if we were in mortal peril. I could have understood it if we'd been under attack, but we were not. Then Father Henrique began ordering his team to begin immediate disposal of the remains, the way they did at the house in Freewell, to cover up what had happened to Patrick, poor man. There was no possible way to explain so much carnage to the local authorities. And there are frequent forest fires in the Barrens. Considering the dryness this past summer, it wouldn't be at all surprising for one to start now, according to Father Henrique."

Alaric had finally heard enough.

"Did he not take into consideration that if those bodies are the tourists who've gone missing over the past few weeks," he asked, "DNA analysis needs to be done on them so they can be identified, and their families notified of their deaths? I understand that we need to keep the public ignorant of the truth of the existence of supernatural beings in order to avoid worldwide panic. But these were people's *family* members, Abraham."

Holtzman looked tired. He sank down onto the cot. It had been neatly made, with hospital corners. Abraham Holtzman had never married. He didn't think it would be fair to ask a partner to worry at home about him while he was out fighting demons. He'd devoted his entire life to the job.

And now this. He appeared haggard and pale in the fluorescent lights.

"Do you think we didn't mention that, Alaric?" he asked. "That's when things began to get a little . . . a little heated. We were all on edge. We'd spent nearly twelve hours in the Barrens, and lost a team member, and in a particularly gruesome manner. True, we killed the New Jersey Devil. But then Henrique shows up in this helicopter, the vampire gets away, and he announces he's torching the entire place. That's when Carolina . . . well, you know how she is. She had some words with Father Henrique—in their native tongue, so I'm not entirely certain what was said. Carolina believes Father Henrique might be trying to hide something from us. I don't think the words exchanged were pleasant."

"I'm sure they weren't," Alaric muttered. He knew Carolina de Silva. She was devoted to her job at the Palatine, and a consummate professional. She'd have seen through Padre Caliente's phoniness in a red-hot second. "What happened then?"

Holtzman looked uncomfortable. "Father Henrique said we could settle the matter here, during debriefing. But there was no debriefing. We were escorted from the helipad to these rooms, where I received an official reprimand for failing to supervise my staff properly, and we were all put on administrative probation by Dr. Fiske. I don't mind telling you, Alaric, I'm becoming concerned that Carolina might actually be right."

Alaric set his jaw, staring at the mess he'd made on the floor without really seeing it. He was relieved to have found Holtzman and the others, since he'd escaped in part to find them.

But their turning out to be locked up with him in the headquarters of their former employer was complicating things. Obviously, Alaric now had to think of a way to get all of them out. Otherwise, like the evidence left behind in Freewell and the Pine Barrens, they were going to be eliminated, neatly and efficiently. They knew too much to be allowed to live. There was only one reason he could think of that they hadn't been gotten rid of already . . . and that was the other person he needed to rescue, Meena Harper.

If anything bad were to happen to any of them, Meena would know.

Alaric had seen the look on Mauricio's face when the net had failed to hold Antonescu. It had been an expression of utter terror. Henrique Mauricio needed Lucien Antonescu dead—or locked up tight.

The key to finding Lucien, though, was Meena Harper. Mauricio might try to intimidate Meena, but he wouldn't dare do anything to risk really upsetting her . . . not yet. She was the queen bee, and Antonescu the honey. Mauricio might stir up the hive, but he wasn't ready to smash it.

Alaric, on the other hand, didn't have such reservations.

"You can communicate with Carolina and the others?" he asked his boss. Or former boss, he supposed.

"Yes, of course," Holtzman replied. "I already told you that."

Alaric smiled. "Then I want you to send them a message."

Holtzman looked surprised. But he got up and went to his keyboard.

"Fine," he said, beginning to type. "What's the message?"

"Tell them," Alaric said, "heads up."

Chapter Thirty-five

E mil joined Lucien at the table where he was sitting in the large front window of the pretentiously Euro-shabby café.

"Everything seems secure," Emil said.

"Excellent," Lucien said.

"Nasty day it turned out to be," Emil remarked.

"Isn't it?" Lucien agreed. He didn't look the least bit unhappy about it.

The same could not be said for all of the pedestrians streaming by from the now nearly empty San Gennaro Festival. Huddled beneath umbrellas hastily purchased from street vendors or delis, they were heading home, wet and thoroughly dispirited. The forecast had called for sunny skies, with only a 10 percent chance of precipitation.

Overhead, thunder rumbled ominously.

The forecast had clearly been wrong.

"This is chancing fate a bit, though, isn't it, my lord?" Emil nodded toward the building across the street. "All any of them have to do is step outside, and they could very easily see you sitting here. They do know what you look like."

Lucien stirred sugar into his coffee. The café used genuine cubes, which he found rather charming, but he knew others thought unhygienic, since the sugar cubes weren't sealed in individual packets.

"They know I'm coming," he said. "Surprise is not an element I'm going for in this battle."

Emil raised his eyebrows. "Like with your father in Targoviste?"

"Exactly like with my father in Targoviste," Lucien said. "Only I shan't be impaling anyone. At least"—he paused with his coffee cup halfway to his lips to signal the heavily tattooed waitress to bring another cup for his cousin—"not any members of my own royal court, and not merely to get the attention of my enemies. Sitting in a café across the street from them will do. For now, anyway."

Emil looked relieved. "That's good to know, sire," he said.

The waitress arrived, and set a cup in front of Emil. He thanked her politely—after admiring the tattooed sleeve of roses, complete with thorns, crawling up both her arms—then added cream and two lumps of sugar as she hurried to collect the bill from the customer at the next table, who was leaving. Outside, the sky only seemed to be growing darker, and everyone was anxious to get home before the storm got worse . . .

. . . and from the looks being darted in the direction of Lucien, the storm they were concerned about wasn't just the one gathering overhead.

"If I might ask, my lord," Emil said, after a sip, "when, exactly, *will* we be making our move?"

"Oh," Lucien said. "You'll know when the time is right. You always had a good head for that kind of thing."

"Well—" Emil began, then broke off in astonishment.

Because at that moment his wife appeared from the back of the café, her bright red lipstick newly reapplied and a black beret tugged down over her sleek bob. She'd evidently been in the ladies' room, where she'd changed into what she considered battle wear: a cheetah-patterned trench coat and black patent-leather stiletto boots.

"Hello, darling," she said, giving Emil a peck on the cheek as she slipped back into her chair. "Oh, yuck, you're all wet. Lucien, this rain is just too much. Can't you turn it off?"

"It suits my mood," Lucien said to Mary Lou. To Emil, he said, "You were saying?"

"B-but . . ." Emil looked dumbfounded. "What's *she* doing here?"

"Oh, don't be stupid, darling," Mary Lou said. "I've been here all day, scouting the territory. You know that. I just changed into something a little more conspicuous, so they'll remember me."

"But she can't be here *now*," Emil said to Lucien. "We're going *in*. It's too dangerous."

"For them, you mean." Mary Lou rested her chin in her hands and stared out the window, at the school across the street. "I know. I feel sorry for them, too. Poor lambs."

"I don't mean to sound completely fifteenth century," Emil complained. "But is a battle between the prince of darkness and the Palatine, on Palatine territory, really a place for a woman?"

"Well, the prince seems to think so, since he brought *her,*" Mary Lou said, pointing to Meena, who was standing by the bar, speaking urgently into the café's pay phone.

Emil's eyes widened. "What's *she* doing here?" he sputtered. He turned toward the prince with an astonished expression. "Begging your pardon, my lord, but she's one of *them*. And a *mortal*."

"Not for long," Lucien said, and calmly took a sip of coffee.

"Oh." Emil closed his mouth, then exchanged a nervous glance with his wife. Mary Lou looked tactfully down and away.

Lucien glanced out the window, pretending not to have noticed the couple's discomfort. They would, he knew, adjust to the new situation . . . as would Meena. True, she might be upset, at first, but she would soon come to see that his way was best. Especially when her only other option was death.

She'd been correct when she'd stated that only by biting her a third time, then forcing her to drink his own blood, could he make her one of his kind.

There was, however, another way. If she were to die, he had the power to bring her back to life as one of them. That was what his father had done to him, and what he, as prince of darkness, had the power to do to others.

She would be unhappy for a while, of course, as he had been. But she really only protested against being one of them because she had not yet experienced it. Humans were notoriously afraid of the unknown.

They were also fragile, and easily led. It was why they were such easy marks for charlatans who promised them all means of redemption, usually in exchange for their money.

This was why he had to save Meena . . . from herself. Because she was committed to a fool's errand that was only going to conclude in heartache and misery, where so many of her kind had ended before.

He'd tried to warn her—she'd spoken of the futility of her quest herself, by mentioning so often what had happened to Joan of Arc—but she wouldn't listen.

So he felt fully justified in what he was about to do.

The only possible glitch Lucien foresaw in his plan was that Meena had insisted on embarking on this mission to "save" Alaric.

But of course he had no intention whatsoever of "saving" Alaric.

The difficulty was going to be—once he'd gotten the book from Wulf—how to murder him without Meena seeing him do it.

Meena was going to have far more important things to worry about in the near future than Alaric, of course. But Lucien had faith that her generally sweet temper would cause her to forgive him for her own murder quickly enough.

A sudden downpour began to lash the wide glass pane, momentarily obscuring his view of the courtyard across street.

Emil tilted his head toward Meena. "Who is she talking to?" he wanted to know. *"Them?"*

"Of course not," Lucien said. "Her brother."

"Saying good-bye," Mary Lou said. "How sweet."

Emil looked uncomfortable. "Mary Lou," he said, "please. Use your head. How can she be saying good-bye? She doesn't know she's going anywhere."

Mary Lou frowned. "Oh, right. Well, I still think it's sweet. And *romantic,*" she added, with a smile in Lucien's direction.

"I don't," Emil said firmly. "As your closest—and, I feel I must add, *only*—adviser, my lord, I am stating right now that I do not like the odds in this fight. Alaric Wulf plays rough."

"Just the way I like it," Mary Lou purred.

Both Lucien and her husband shot her astonished looks.

"What do *you* know," Emil asked, "about how Alaric Wulf plays?"

"Nothing," Mary Lou said quickly. "Where is that waitress? I asked her for a latte ages ago . . ." She caught the waitress's eye, and waved.

The waitress—who seemed in a rush to see them leave—set a large latte down in front of Mary Lou. Mary Lou tossed her a dazzling smile. "Oh, thank you, aren't you the sweetest thing?"

"I'll bring your check whenever you're ready," the waitress said, darting a nervous glance at Lucien. Then she hurried away.

Outside, the sky had grown even darker, though the rain had fallen off. Lights had begun to come on in some of the windows in nearby buildings. The crowds had diminished. There was hardly anyone to be seen on the street. Even all the cabs seemed to have mysteriously disap-peared, as they always did when it rained.

It was right then that Meena, who'd finally finished her phone call, joined them, her eyes very bright. There were rosy spots of color on her high cheekbones.

"Sorry about that," she said to them. "Jon's on a lot of pain medi-cation, so it was sort of hard to have a conversation with him. They're keeping him overnight. But he's doing very well, considering." She glanced at Emil, and said, "Oh, hello. I haven't seen you since—well, it's been a long time." She kissed him on the cheek before she sat down in the empty chair between him and Lucien.

Emil looked flustered. "Hello," he said.

Meena, Lucien noticed, seemed nervous. But then, she believed they were about to storm her former place of work to rescue the man she—he was beginning to suspect—loved.

So it was only natural she'd be a bit jittery. She could not possibly suspect anything else. She had stated numerous times that she could only predict the deaths of others, not her own.

"I'm sorry, darling, but what exactly happened to your brother again?" Mary Lou asked. "Kitchen accident?"

"Meena believes he was attacked by a Lamir," Lucien said smoothly.

"Oh no," Mary Lou said. "Not *them*. We met some Lamir the last time we were in Rio, remember, Emil? Nasty things. Such kind, lovely people, too, the Brazilians. The human ones, I mean. How they got cursed with such terrible vampires, I will never understand. I didn't know they'd already gotten here. Too bad. New York is doomed."

"Why?" Meena asked, sounding alarmed.

"Well," Mary Lou said, "there were such enormous numbers of them back then—the Lamir, I mean—and no one was stopping them." She seemed to notice her husband's nervous glance at Lucien and added,

"You never allowed the Dracul to kill, sire, and you were careful about how large our population was allowed to grow. But the Lamir weren't your minions. Nobody seemed to be giving them any rules, and the Palatine had virtually no presence—"

"Father Henrique is from there and claims to have staked over a hundred of them," Meena said.

Mary Lou raised her eyebrows. "Well, it wasn't enough. I couldn't imagine, even back then, how they were going to be able to sustain themselves. They were killing off most of their food source before it had a chance to repopulate itself. Eventually something was going to have to give. So I'm not surprised they finally decided to move up here. I'm just shocked it took them this long. The Lamir are flesh-eaters, you know." She scrunched her face with distaste. "Disgusting habit."

Meena shook her head. "Brianna Delmonico was infected by a Lamir, then," she said. She looked at Lucien. "All those missing tourists were eaten by them . . . Alaric was right."

If Lucien heard the name *Alaric* one more time, he might have to lift up the table and toss it through the plate-glass window.

"They waited until we were gone to make the move," Emil remarked. "Which makes sense, I suppose. What doesn't is that they timed it to coincide with the priest's relocation to the city. If he has been slaying the Lamir at the rate he claims, why would they travel to the place where he is currently living? Wouldn't they fear him?"

"Not if he is the one who planned the trap for me last night," Lucien said. "Because he is obviously an inept fool who has never killed anyone."

"So." Meena blinked a few times. "You think he's been lying about killing all those Lamir? Because that's what Alaric thinks."

She reached up to finger the necklace that had burned Lucien nearly to the bone earlier that afternoon. Though she had never positively confirmed that Alaric Wulf had given it to her, every time she mentioned his name, she reached up to touch the silver talisman.

He ought, Lucien reflected, to have killed her when he'd had the chance, while she'd been unconscious that afternoon. Then he could have blamed her death on Brianna Delmonico, and played the noble gentleman by bringing her back to life.

He could also have ripped the necklace off before reviving her, then told her it must have been lost in the tunnels during her struggle. Stupidly, he'd been too consumed with rage at the vampire who'd dared to attack her to think of doing any of these things until after she'd awoken. Now she was not only still alive, she was still wearing it.

Sometimes he wondered if his transformation had really been complete after all.

That was when a thunderclap—but much, much louder—struck.

Only it wasn't a thunderclap, because it hadn't been preceded by any lightning.

And it was so loud it caused the entire building—and possibly every building on the entire block—to shake. Lucien seized Meena's hand, as well as the tabletop, to keep his coffee cup from tumbling off it.

"What was *that*?" she cried.

They had only to turn their heads for the answer. Thick white smoke had already begun to pour from the windows of St. Bernadette's that had been blown out by the force of the blast.

"What happened?" the waitress was crying as she picked up the phone to call 911. "What caused that?"

Lucien knew. Lucien knew exactly what had happened to cause that.

Two words, and two words only.

Alaric Wulf.

Chapter Thirty-six

Smoke.

Everyone knew the best way to eradicate any hostile infestation—bees, ants, termites, protesters, squatters, war criminals, flesh-eating vampires, or other unsavory types—was to provoke discomfort sufficient to drive them into the open, where they could then be dealt with properly.

The easiest way was to smoke them out. No one could stand the heat and fumes of smoke for long . . . unless of course they did not breathe oxygen.

Where there was smoke, there was usually fire. And Alaric had yet to see any creature, living or dead, stand firm against the threat of fire.

With a boiler as old and as poorly maintained as the one in the building the Palatine had chosen for their new Manhattan headquarters, it was actually quite easy to cause the kind of disruption Alaric hoped for, even in the middle of an unseasonably warm September, when the heat wasn't turned on. Hot water was being conducted into the structure. People were turning it on in the locker rooms for their showers, and in the washrooms to wash their hands, and in the commissary, for cooking and washing up.

And that meant all he had to do to cause the series of catastrophic events that led to the explosion that rocked Spring Street was to disconnect the feed water valve, then bypass the low-water cutoff. He'd made sure any emergency safety measures the machine itself might be programmed to take were avoided after shutting off the boiler's main release valve, then closing the return.

And despite wrapping one of the leather cuffs around it, he ended up injuring his foot (aggravating his old leg wound) quite badly while kicking off one of the valves, a measure to which he'd had to resort in the unlikely event anyone with some know-how both happened to be in the building on a Sunday and attempted to repair the damage Alaric had done.

His only concern was not to blow up himself, along with his friends, though he knew the boiler would give off plenty of warning before it erupted. The thing was as big as a UPS truck. It wasn't going to go out without a fight.

Twenty. Nineteen. Eighteen.

The boiler let out a series of groans that sounded like a yeti in heat. He was certain that they could be heard—and felt—all over the building.

He found a small chair in one corner of the room, pulled it to the center, then sat down in it, careful to keep the weight off his injured leg. He folded his hands behind his head and thought about what he'd like to have for breakfast, although he was sure it was probably closer to dinnertime by now.

Scrambled eggs. And bacon. Real bacon, not the turkey kind he generally only allowed himself.

Seventeen. Sixteen.

The boiler let out a sound like a pistol shot.

He heard the lock to the boiler room door being undone. Then it was flung open. Padre Caliente himself stepped onto the grated metal staircase that led down into the room in which Alaric was sitting.

The padre hadn't come alone, of course. He was much too cowardly for that. He was flanked by several men dressed in black whom Alaric recognized from the disastrous attempt to capture Antonescu the night before. They were holding crossbows—the exact same aluminum-stock crossbows (with fiber-optic sights) that Holtzman had assured him last month were too expensive (and unrealistic for urban usage) for the Manhattan unit's tight budget.

Mauricio was dressed in flowing priest's robes—white with green and gold trim. He looked especially handsome and trustworthy. Alaric wondered if he'd come straight from performing a Mass . . . or possibly from another television interview.

Padre Caliente looked down at Alaric the way the pope looked down at the faithful when they gathered outside the Vatican on Sunday morning.

"What," he said, in a tired-sounding voice, "did you do, Wulf?"

Alaric tried to look innocent. "Me? I didn't do anything," he said. "I'm sure it's nothing. But I'd start evacuating the building, just to be on the safe side. You can never be too sure about these old units."

"I see," Mauricio said, calling his bluff. "How fortuitous that this happened today, of all days. I guess Heavenly Father wanted to spare me the sin of having to order these men to split your brain in two with a hardwood arrow."

Alaric tipped back in his chair, keeping his injured foot balanced on his knee. Mauricio had evidently decided to drop the pretense. Even the accent was mostly gone.

"So why haven't you done it already?" Alaric asked.

Mauricio glared down at him. "One more word out of you," he said, "and I will."

"No, you won't," Alaric said. "And I know why. Why you didn't have the guts to kill Holtzman or any of his team back at the Barrens either. If you'd have touched a hair on any of our heads—if you'd even have *thought* about doing so—Meena Harper would have known. And she'd have brought *him* here. And that'd be your worst nightmare, wouldn't it? Because you're terrified of Lucien Antonescu."

Mauricio's gaze darted away from Alaric and toward the guards posted on either side of the balcony on which he stood.

But, just as Alaric had suspected, he didn't order them to shoot.

"That's the most farcical thing I've ever heard," Mauricio said with a sneer. "I want to find Lucien Antonescu more than anyone. That's why I ordered Meena Harper dismissed from the Palatine's employment. We've been tracking her via her cell phone ever since she left here. I'm hoping she'll lead us straight to him, and when she does, we'll do what *you* were never able to do in all the months you've been here. We'll destroy him."

"Really," Alaric said, raising a dubious eyebrow. "That's what I was trying to do when you interrupted me with your fancy nets and very tight uniforms and made such a huge disaster out of everything. But never mind that now. I'm not saying it's wrong to be frightened of the prince of darkness, because he *is* the dark lord. I'm just saying you don't need all the bells and whistles. A simple sword to the heart will do. So where is Meena now?"

Mauricio looked slightly uncomfortable. "Well," he said, "we seem to be having a bit of trouble with the satellite at the moment . . ."

"I see," Alaric said. "Not to give you too much bad news at once, but do you think there's a possibility she might have caught on to your plan and tossed her cell phone? And that she and Antonescu might be on their way here?"

Mauricio appeared more shaken by this news than he ought to have been for a man surrounded by armed guards. "Why on earth would they be doing that?"

"Well, for one thing," Alaric said, "I'm going to guess that Antonescu wants his book back. And they've probably figured out by now where I am. Meena's got that psychic thing." He shrugged. "*Her* satellite doesn't go out. At least, not unless it's being blocked by a hellmouth."

Mauricio looked startled, but still didn't quite catch Alaric's meaning. "So?" he asked. "I still don't see—"

"Well," Alaric said, "I do know where the book is, after all."

Mauricio was surprised. More than surprised. He was staggered. He reached out to wrap his hands around the balcony railing. Alaric saw his knuckles go white.

"Th-that cannot be," Mauricio stammered. "*Antonescu* has the book. He escaped with it last night. You were there. You saw him do it."

"He escaped last night," Alaric said. "But not with the book. I have it. And I hid it. Unless you let my friends go, though, I'm not going to tell you where it is. And," he added as the boiler let out another moan, "you really should think about evacuating the building. I've seen this type of thing before." He shook his head. "Not pretty. Chunks of mortar and charred flesh everywhere. It really won't look good in the press that you were in charge and just let us all burn."

Mauricio's gaze darted toward the boiler, which shuddered like an elephant in labor. Alaric saw the men standing around him exchange nervous glances.

Fifteen. Fourteen. Thirteen.

"If you're lying about the book," Mauricio warned him, "I *will* kill you, Meena Harper or not. Go on and get him," he said to two of the guards. To the others, he said, "Get the rest of them. And then find the building manager. Someone's got to be able to fix this thing."

"Excellent call," Alaric said, though of course he knew it was far too late for anyone to fix it.

He rose obligingly when the guards reached him, and didn't protest when they took him by either arm and steered him roughly toward the staircase. His leg was killing him, and he needed help getting up the stairs. Once they were in the hallway, it would be a different matter, of course. Then he was going to get his hands on one of those crossbows . . .

"It's been on its last legs for a while," Alaric remarked, about the boiler. "They ought to have replaced it a long time ago. But you've heard about the budgetary concerns, I'm sure."

Twelve. Eleven. Ten.

"I don't have time for this discussion," Mauricio complained. "The archbishop has been breathing down my neck all day about what happened last night. He's furious that Antonescu got away."

"I can imagine," Alaric said. He was halfway up the stairs. He could hear doors being opened in the hallway, and Carolina's aggravated, slightly accented voice asking, "Why? Why are we being evacuated? What's happening?" Alaric hoped that Holtzman had delivered his message. When the boiler blew, it would likely take out the wall behind it . . . the wall connected to the office where they'd locked Holtzman. And the wall behind that room, as well. "But he'll be glad that the book, at least, is safe."

"He won't care," Mauricio said. "He wouldn't listen to me about its significance in the first place. I tried to explain to him that the net wouldn't work either. But he saw that trick on some television show. That's the problem with these old men. They won't listen to anyone younger than they are. Once they get an idea in their heads about something, they always think they're right."

Alaric was up the stairs now. He'd had to lean heavily on the arms of the guards for support, but he'd made it.

Until he was sure Holtzman and the others were safely out of the building, he was going to behave as if he were on Mauricio's side.

Although the truth was, he wasn't certain whose side he was on anymore.

Nine. Eight. Seven.

"Absolutely," Alaric said. "And what do *they* know about anything? They've never been in the field. Most of them have never even seen a vampire in the flesh. If one of those bloodsuckers walked up to them and showed them his fangs, they'd probably bless him, and think he was cured."

Mauricio threw him an amused glance.

"Exactly," he said. "They're completely out of touch. It's high time for new management. A new guard."

"I completely agree," Alaric said. "Only how do we go about it?"

"I've been working on that," Mauricio said, "for some time, as a matter of fact. And the answer is, from the inside. It's really the only way."

"From the inside, eh?" Now that he was in the hallway, Alaric could see Holtzman being led away. Unfortunately, Holtzman also noticed him.

"Alaric?" Holtzman said, looking startled. "Father Henrique? What's happening? Anything I can do to help?"

Father Henrique waved reassuringly at Holtzman. "Everything's fine, Dr. Holtzman," he called. "Just the boiler acting up."

"The boiler?" Holtzman widened his eyes at Alaric. "Oh no—"

The door to the stairwell to the main floor closed, shutting off the sound of his voice.

Six. Five. Four.

The priest went on. "Once we're fully able to infiltrate from the inside, we won't have any more of these bothersome worries."

"Oh?" Alaric asked. He had glanced at the faces of the guards. He didn't recognize a single one. Who were they? Where had they come from? He thought he knew everyone in the Palatine. True, there were always new recruits, but the organization wasn't really that big.

"Like that disaster in the museum last night," Mauricio said.

Alaric's pulse had begun to drum. He wasn't sure if it was from lack of food, the pain in his leg, or the anticipation of what he knew was about to happen. It definitely wasn't from fear. His goal had been to smoke out the bad guys. Those flesh-eating vampires had to be around here somewhere.

So, he was certain, was Lucien Antonescu.

The problem was Meena. Why did her intuition only work on other people? Why was she forever showing up at *exactly* the wrong time, and in the most dangerous place for her to be?

"It was always very important that the dark prince didn't get his hands on that book," Mauricio said. "I tried to tell them that. The book has the intrinsic power of linking Lucien Antonescu with forces beyond his control—beyond the control of anyone."

"Then it was fairly stupid," Alaric said, dryly, "to put it on display in a museum in the city in which he currently abides."

"Again," Mauricio said, "not a decision I would have made had I been in charge. And a mistake I've been attempting to rectify ever since I heard about it."

"Have you?" Alaric asked. His throat was bone-dry, despite all the rusty water he'd drunk.

Mauricio had almost reached the door to the main stairwell.

"Once I explained the situation to a few key individuals, of course," he was saying, "I was given full rein to do whatever was needed in order to gain control."

"I've been meaning to ask you about that," Alaric said. "Because it seems to me like what you did to gain control was turn an ex-boyfriend of Meena Harper's into a vampire."

"Yes," Mauricio said, grinning at him. "That's precisely what I did. Only not just Meena Harper's ex-boyfriend."

It was only then that Alaric noticed Father Henrique's teeth. Or, more accurately, fangs.

Three. Two. One.

Boom.

Chapter Thirty-seven

Meena dashed up the steps and threw open the doors to what had once been St. Bernadette's Catholic Elementary School. A thick cloud of white smoke hit her in the face. She fell back, coughing.

"Meena." Lucien had come up behind her. He seized her by the shoulders and pulled her back down the steps. "Stop."

"No," she said, straining against his grip. "It's all right. I'm all right."

"You're not." He guided her back into the courtyard, toward the broken fountain, where the smoke wasn't as thick. "It's no good. You can't go in there. You can't breathe."

"But . . ." she said. Tears had already begun to stream down her face from the acrid smoke. She wiped them away with her wrist. "Alaric—"

Lucien's face tightened. He was as worried as she was, she could tell. But only, she knew, about the fate of his book.

"*We'll* go," Mary Lou said, reaching out to give Meena a reassuring hug. "We'll find him, honey, don't worry. Smoke doesn't affect us."

"But fire does," her husband reminded her, pointing at some windows along the building's basement level. The smoke that had begun billowing from them was blacker than it was elsewhere, a sure sign of flames.

"Oh," Mary Lou said, "*that* doesn't look good."

"What could be down there," Meena wondered, "that could have caused such a huge explosion?"

"I don't know," Mary Lou said. "The boiler, maybe?"

Oh God.

"The boiler," Meena repeated weakly. "It was ancient. This whole place is ancient. They closed it because it wasn't safe for children. Abraham said there wasn't any money in the budget to fix it up, but—"

She was starting to babble. Lucien put his arm around her, then walked with her until they stood beneath one of the archways and were out of the steady drizzle that had started up again.

"Meena." Lucien grasped her by both shoulders once more. "Look at me. I'm quite sure that boiler did not explode accidentally. Do you understand me? That explosion was no accident."

It took a full ten seconds for the meaning of what he was saying to sink in. Then, when it did, she turned around and dove once more for the doors.

This time Lucien didn't have to stop her from going inside the building. The doors themselves did, by bursting open. Through them began to pour a stream of people, none of whom seemed to notice the three vampires or the teary-eyed, frightened girl in the courtyard. They were too focused on escaping the burning building . . .

Meena stood at the bottom of the steps, anxiously hoping. The rain began to flatten her hair against her head and turn her faux-leather purse a darker brown as she waited. People streamed past her, and she scanned each one, searching for a familiar face she could ask about Alaric.

But she didn't recognize a single person.

"Who *are* these people?" she finally blurted out.

Lucien had come up beside her and wrapped his coat around her shoulders to ward off some of the rain. "What are you talking about?" he asked.

"I . . ." Meena glanced around.

Her gaze drifted back to the front doors of the building, which someone had now wedged open to let out the smoke and the rest of the people coming through them. The knot she'd been feeling in her shoulders was tighter than ever.

"I . . . don't know who these people are," she said to Lucien. "I've never seen them before in my life."

"My lord." Emil stepped up beside them. "If I may . . . this is probably not the wisest place to be standing, as you are the most wanted man in Palatine history, and this *is* their Manhattan headquarters . . ."

"I don't think that's going to be a problem," Mary Lou said. "Look."

Other people had rushed into the courtyard, local shop owners with bottles of water and umbrellas, and the few stragglers who still happened to be out on the street, despite the weather, all eager to help in any way they could. Meena could hear the sound of sirens off in the distance.

They didn't seem to be getting any closer.

"The streets are flooded," Meena overheard the waitress from the café shout to everyone. She had her cell phone clutched to her ear. She was evidently speaking to a 911 operator. "The emergency vehicles can't get through. Something about so much rain in such a short period of time . . . and some kind of underground stream. I don't know what she's talking about. I never heard of any underground stream."

Meena looked up at Lucien in consternation. "The Minetta," she said.

He just looked away.

But the victims of the explosion at St. Bernadette's didn't seem to care. They gathered in the courtyard in the pouring rain, not taking the umbrellas people were offering them, or even lifting a cell phone to call loved ones.

They just stood there . . . *waiting.*

"None of them is coughing," Mary Lou said tightly. "Not so much as a watering eye in the bunch."

Meena's heart gave a lurch. Mary Lou was right.

"I thought this school had been shut down," Meena overheard the deli owner from the café across the street mutter to his son, who'd helped him carry over a box full of umbrellas and water bottles.

"I heard a new Internet start-up bought the building," his son said. "Obviously. I mean, look at them."

It was true, Meena thought. Everyone who'd come out of the building was lean, wearing black, and looked exceptionally pale . . .

Oh God, she thought. What had happened? What had happened to the Palatine? Who had done this? *Where was Alaric?*

Then Meena heard a cough. Never in her life had she been more grateful for the sound. She spun around . . . then let out a joyful shriek.

"Carolina!"

A tall, dark-haired woman who'd just tumbled from the open doorway turned at the sound of her name ... then, seeing Meena racing toward her, held out her arms. The two women embraced.

"I thought you were dead," Meena exclaimed.

"No," Carolina said. "Just in New Jersey."

"What about Abraham?" Meena asked. "Where's Alaric? Is Alaric all right?"

"Abraham is fine," Carolina said. "He should be right behind me. Alaric, too."

A weight she never even knew had been there seemed to lift from Meena's heart. The pain between her shoulder blades vanished, as well.

"He's all right?" She felt almost giddy. "Alaric's all right? Where is he?"

Carolina glanced over her shoulder. "I don't know. They were both—oh, there's Abraham."

Abraham, looking far older than his actual age, appeared in the doorway, covered in soot and coughing with considerable force. Meena raced to his side. So did Carolina. The deli owner and his son rushed over to offer him water and an umbrella.

"What?" Abraham looked perplexed. "Oh my, yes, it's raining. Thank you. Oh, Meena, hello. Water? No, no, I don't need water, I'm fine."

The coughing fit into which he promptly sank belied this statement, and despite his protests, water was forced onto him. They helped him onto a nearby bench, where he was resting, trying to catch his breath, when his eyes widened at the sight of something standing beyond Meena's left shoulder. He lifted a trembling finger, his mouth opening.

"What the *hell*?" Carolina said, after she'd spun around to see what had startled him so badly. Then her face froze into a similar expression of fear. "Jesus Christ!"

"Quite the opposite," Lucien said drily.

Carolina groped automatically at her belt ... until she remembered she'd been relieved of her weapon. Then she groaned.

"Pardon me, sir," the deli owner said to Lucien. "But do you need an umbrella?"

"No, thank you," Lucien said.

"That man," Abraham managed to choke out, "is the devil on earth! He is Satan's messenger."

"If Lucien was here to kill you, don't you think he'd have done it already?" Meena leaned down to whisper to him. "We have way bigger problems than him right now, anyway. *All* of these people are vampires." She pointed at the men and women in black who were standing in the courtyard, seeming to be awaiting an order. "The Palatine has been completely infiltrated. Maybe more than just the Palatine. Maybe even the entire Church."

"That's . . . that's impossible," Abraham said.

Carolina pressed her lips together. "No, it isn't," she said. "It's what I've been trying to tell you all along, Abraham. Mauricio. He's the one!" Then she threw Meena a startled look. "Alaric! He's still in there. With Mauricio!"

Meena spun around. The doors to the building stood empty. The only thing coming out now was smoke.

Meena lifted her anxious gaze toward Lucien. "We've got to go in there," she said. "We've got to help him. He can't see. He can't breathe—"

"I'll go," Lucien said, and laid a kiss on Meena's forehead. "I'll take care of everything." He began striding toward the steps.

"I'm not sure that's the best idea," Abraham said.

"Oh, my dears . . ." Sister Gertrude appeared, one hand pressed to her chest as she tried to catch her breath while attempting to weave her way between the soaking-wet people standing around the courtyard. Father Bernard was hurrying behind her. "We came as quickly as we could. The streets are like rivers, so we had to wade to get here. But your brother said there might be trouble. And it looks as if he was right. Are we too late?"

Meena looked from them to Lucien as he climbed the steps to the building, an expression of grim determination on his face.

"I'll let you know," she said, and raced after him.

Chapter Thirty-eight

Alaric had known the explosion would plunge them into darkness. It would be impossible to see anything in all that smoke . . . at least for a human being.

So he'd memorized where each of the guards was standing.

Then, when the blast occurred, and everything went dark, he was able to reach out quickly and disarm them. After all, he'd been expecting it. They weren't.

Suddenly he had two aluminum-stock crossbows, and they had none. This was a vast improvement over the situation he'd been in mere seconds earlier.

Of course, he also had ears that were ringing from the trauma of the blast, lungs that were quickly filling with acrid-smelling smoke, and he couldn't see anything. The vampires with whom he was trapped in this hallway had none of these problems.

So, this was a definite minus.

On the plus side, he had a thorough knowledge of the layout of the building, even in the dark, because he'd spent so much time in it.

So as soon as he'd secured the crossbows, he performed a quick front shoulder roll (which kept him off his injured leg) through the door to the main stairwell, where he hoped the air might be a little clearer.

It was.

Unfortunately, the guards did not take kindly to having had their crossbows confiscated and followed him.

It didn't take long to dispatch them, although Alaric was bitten several times. This was unfortunate, but hard to avoid in conditions of such low visibility. He also lost several arrows. He'd been able to snag the quiver of one of the guards, however, by groping him in the dark. This was an unpleasant experience for both of them, but couldn't be helped.

What was even more unpleasant was hearing the door to the stairwell burst open and Henrique Mauricio shouting, "Wulf!" in a voice that sounded not unlike the one that had come from that little girl whose body had been taken over by a demonic spirit the night they'd met.

Alaric hastily loaded the crossbow, not an easy trick to perform with an unfamiliar weapon while crouched on the landing of a dark, smoky stairwell with an injured leg. Especially when he was distracted by the sound of sirens and the footsteps of people coming down the stairs, another flight up. Doors to the outside had been opened. The smoke, now that it had a place to go, was being sucked past him with even greater force.

"I know you're there, Wulf," Mauricio called up the stairwell. "You might as well give it up."

"Or maybe I should run away," Alaric said. "Like you did the night of exorcism in Vidigal."

Mauricio chuckled. "Not one of my finer moments, I'll admit," he said. "Baptisms, Communions, masses . . . those are easy enough to fake. But expel the dark beast from the soul of a child? How could I do that . . . especially when the dark beast is my master? You'd have spotted me as a fake in a second. I had no choice but to run."

"Wrong choice," Alaric said. "I spotted you as a fake anyway."

"I know. I should have killed you that night."

"I should have killed *you* that night."

"Clearly. But instead, here we are. You know, it doesn't have to be this way. There are advantages to being on my team. You could have a very pleasant life if you chose—"

"Please don't try to tell me about all the Vatican gold with which you intend to shower me," Alaric interrupted tiredly. "I'm already very well off financially, and you are behind the times. The Vatican has been operating at a deficit for years."

"That isn't quite what I mean," Mauricio said. "I meant that you're obviously in pain right now. I can hear it in your voice. You're tired, and I'm certain you're feeling weak because of the smoke in your lungs. Imagine a life where you'd never have to feel weakness or pain again. Imagine a life where you never feel the need to sleep, never grow a day older, *and* have superhuman strength. Think how useful those abilities would be in defeating your enemies."

"*You're* my enemy," Alaric pointed out.

"Am I?" Mauricio asked. "I took the liberty of peeking at your personnel file, Alaric, and I think I know who your real enemy is. And it isn't me, or any vampire. It's your father, isn't it, Alaric? The man who abandoned you as a baby? Wouldn't your becoming a vampire make the revenge I'm sure you must be planning to take on him someday just that much more glorious?"

"Why doesn't anyone get it?" Alaric asked, really frustrated now. "*I don't like vampires.*"

He stood up and fired. He couldn't even see where he was aiming, because of the smoke.

But he'd been listening closely to Mauricio's voice, and seen the red glow of the vampire's eyes. The crossbow was an automatic repeater, which shot multiple arrows one after the other. *One* of them, at least, must have hit true.

Then he saw a foot emerge from the smoke and land on the step closest to him. Instinctively, he backed up.

Especially when the shadowy figure that emerged proved to have been hit by *all* the arrows he'd shot . . . every single one of them, each projecting dead center from where Henrique Mauricio's heart should have been.

And yet he wasn't dead. He was still coming toward Alaric, a tiny smile playing on his lips.

"I will say one for thing for you, Wulf," Mauricio said. "You don't give up easily. I like that about you. That's what would make you such a winning asset to my team."

"How . . . ?" Alaric was stunned. "How is this possible? You should be dead. All of those arrows hit you in the heart."

"I know," Father Henrique said with a shrug. "There's only one thing that can kill me, however. And you haven't found it. Now, let's talk about where you put that book."

Chapter Thirty-nine

I'm not sure that's the best idea.

Abraham's words echoed through Meena's head. Even before she'd heard them, she'd known.

She couldn't trust Lucien. A part of her would always love him, but she knew she could never trust him . . . not with something that mattered to her as much as Alaric's life. Especially not now, with all Lucien's talk about the Mannette. There was something about that place that had made her feel the *opposite* of the way her dream about Lucien and his mother did.

And so she raced up the steps after him, despite everyone's cries to stop.

It didn't matter, though. First because, in her haste, she'd forgotten her purse, complete with stakes, holy water, and SuperStaker inside. She'd left it on the bench with Abraham.

And second because, before Lucien even had a chance to set foot inside the building, Alaric and Father Henrique appeared in the doorway, in as bizarre a manner as Meena had ever seen.

Alaric was shirtless as well as shoeless, with a crossbow strapped to his back. Another crossbow was in his arms. Father Henrique, in flowing priest's robes that had once been white, was grappling with him, trying to take this crossbow away. Like Abraham, they were both covered in soot and grime. Neither seemed to notice that they were standing in a doorway, being observed.

Meena froze, gasping. Not just because there were four arrows sticking out of Father Henrique's chest, but because the priest was snarling, and the fangs protruding from his jaw were clearly visible, even from a distance.

Meena was not the only one who was completely shocked to see that Father Henrique was a vampire whom not even wooden stakes to the heart would kill. She heard the deli owner's son drop his box of water bottles and umbrellas . . . and he did not even know the priest.

The sound of the box hitting the ground startled Alaric, who seemed to have reached the end of his endurance. He turned his head and looked shocked to see them all standing there . . . particularly Meena. For an agonizing second, their gazes locked.

And she read all the pain, heartache, and loneliness that he'd been going through for the past twenty-four hours, right there in those ice-blue eyes . . . but also the hope and joy he was experiencing, seeing her there now.

That was her mistake.

Because Alaric, bone-tired, allowed himself to be distracted by her gaze, and loosened his hold on the crossbow for a fraction of a second.

And Father Henrique snatched the weapon from his hands, spun around, seized Meena by the arm, then pointed the crossbow . . .

At Meena's head.

Stunned silence fell across the courtyard. Except for the hiss of the rain, not a single sound could be heard. Even the sirens in the distance had fallen still. All traffic in any nearby streets was blocked, and so the city was, for once, completely without noise.

Which might be why Lucien's voice, when he spoke, sounded as loud as a crack of thunder.

"Release her now," he said to Father Henrique, "or die."

Alaric, who'd fallen back against the door frame—he seemed no longer able to support his own weight—shook his head. He looked defeated, spent, and more bitter than Meena had ever seen him. Her heart twisted for him.

"He can't be killed," Alaric said to Lucien. "Believe me, I've already tried."

"Well," Sister Gertrude said, and whipped her twin set of Berettas from beneath her habit, "I haven't met a bloodsucker yet who hasn't turned to dust after meeting my pretty silver betties."

The vampires standing around her began to back away, snarling.

"Don't," Alaric warned Sister Gertrude. "You might hit Meena."

The nun looked offended. "I happened to have qualified as the most distinguished expert out of all the seniors at last year's finals."

"Bullets can't kill me," Father Henrique informed them all loudly. "Neither can stakes, immersion in holy water, sunlight, crosses, or fire. My lord"—this was directed to Lucien—"I know what this might look like, but I promise you I have no intention whatsoever of harming this girl . . . so long as you'll hear me out. Everything that I have done, I have done in service to you."

"I'm finding that a bit hard to believe," Lucien said, exchanging glances with Emil. "But release her, and we can discuss it."

"Gladly, sire," Father Henrique said. He made no move to loosen his hold on Meena, however. "I'm fully aware of how this must appear, but if you're thinking about that net and the holy water, I can assure you that *wasn't* me, my lord. That was the archbishops. They felt the Palatine wasn't doing enough to flush you out, and decided it was time to take matters into their own hands . . ."

Even from where she was standing, Meena could hear Abraham, wounded to the quick by this slight against his division, inhale sharply.

"When I learned of their scheme," Father Henrique went on, "of course I argued strenuously against it. The old men wouldn't listen. So I offered instead to step in and supervise, knowing I could help your lordship by making sure their methods were ineffective—"

"So you infected my ex-boyfriend and sent him after me to kill me?" Meena demanded incredulously. "That was one of the methods you made sure was *ineffective?*"

"That was another of the archbishops' suggestions," Father Henrique said defensively. "And though I had no choice but to follow through with it, I made certain his lordship *wasn't* captured. I am sorry that you were injured, Miss Harper. And that the wife of the gentleman in question was turned, and slipped from our grasp. That was all an unfortunate mistake—"

"*Mistake?*" Abraham seemed unable to keep silent a second longer. "Do you expect us to believe that the archbishops *mistakenly* permitted a vampire to be sent after Meena? Were the bodies we found in the Barrens put there by mistake *as well?*"

Father Henrique only smiled. "That's a matter you'll have to take up with your superiors," he said. "All I did was make sure their orders got followed, while at the same time doing nothing that might endanger my own superior . . ." He made a slight bow to Lucien.

"What bodies?" Meena murmured.

Alaric answered tiredly, "Of all the dead tourists. He took them out to the Pine Barrens. There's a hellmouth there. That's where Abraham and the others were . . . that's why you couldn't sense them. Hellmouths are dead zones. Nothing can exist there but evil."

Meena remembered Abraham describing hellmouths to her in the car the day before—what seemed like a thousand years ago.

"I don't ask for any sort of reward, my lord," Father Henrique was saying to Lucien. "I did nothing out of the ordinary . . . merely took advantage of the opportunity as it presented itself. If I've done well, it was only because of your inspiration. The best way to avoid defeat by the enemy is to infiltrate its ranks and then rise up through them, slowly replacing their troops with your own."

Meena, shivering, looked out across the courtyard at all the Palatine Guards she didn't recognize. They were staring up at Father Henrique with unblinking loyalty.

Lucien had been right all along: her own employer had been behind the attacks against her.

The demons she could forgive . . . sort of. They couldn't help it. But the humans who'd allowed this to happen, blindly promoting Father Henrique while he'd been a vampire all along? How could it have happened? How could it be that no one—except Alaric, who'd always hated him—had noticed?

Finally, Lucien spoke. His voice wasn't thunderous anymore.

"You've done well," he said to Father Henrique. "Just give me the girl, and I'll leave you to your . . . activities."

"*What?*" Meena could not believe what she'd just heard.

And she wasn't the only one. The ripple of indignation that went across the courtyard—from the humans, anyway—was unmistakable.

"Thank you, my lord," Father Henrique said, bowing again. He beamed with pleasure. "I knew you would approve, once you learned the truth."

"This," Carolina burst out, from where she stood next to Abraham, "is *bullshit*!"

Some of the vampires near her took a step closer, but Carolina had discovered the vials of holy water in Meena's purse and was holding them threateningly over her head. Sister Gertrude was brandishing her Berettas, while Abraham had found the SuperStaker and soon discovered what happened when the trigger was pressed. They were managing to keep a wide circle around them . . . but how long it would last after they ran out of ammunition was anyone's guess.

"Lucien," Meena said, anxiously scanning his face through the rain for some sign that he was bluffing. Lucien couldn't possibly intend to allow this . . . *thing* to get away with what he had done.

But as he leaned across the steps, holding his hand toward her, she didn't see the slightest indication on his face that Lucien hadn't meant a word he'd said to Father Henrique.

"Come, Meena," he said, with an impatient wave of his hand.

"But," she said as the rain fell between them, "he'll kill them. He'll kill them all."

Lucien's voice was hard. "Meena," he said, "they were willing to let you die. Are you going to give your life trying to save people like that? I don't think so. Let's go."

Meena glanced at Alaric. He had slid down the door frame, unable to remain standing anymore. He sat with his back against the doorway, clearly doing everything he could just to stay conscious. Still, he managed to summon the strength to lift his head and say, "Meena. Just go."

"You heard the man," Father Henrique said to her. His dark brown eyes gazed into hers with an expression that she couldn't read. It reminded her of the look she'd seen him wear during his TV interview with Genevieve Fox.

It took her a moment before she realized what the expression meant. It was triumph. He had won.

"He wants you to go," Father Henrique said, smiling.

"No," Meena said, shaking her head. "*No.*"

"Meena." Lucien's voice cracked like a whip. "Come to me. *Now.*"

She felt frozen where she stood. What did Father Henrique think he had won? And what had happened to Lucien that had turned him into the *opposite* of the man with whom she'd fallen in love? A man drawn to darkness instead of light, a man who lived beneath the streets in tunnels carved out by the waters of a forgotten stream?

And suddenly she remembered what had been bothering her about the Mannette . . . a snippet of information she'd read during her long-ago research:

When Dutch colonists settled in Manhattan during the 1620s, they learned from local Native Americans about a small brook the Lenape called Mannette. Translated, this meant "Devil's Water."

There were places, Abraham had told her, to which creatures of a malevolent nature were drawn, because they were thought to have direct links to the devil.

Meena turned toward Lucien, tears streaming down her face along with the rain.

"Is that what you were doing down by the Minetta Stream all this time, Lucien?" she asked, her voice catching. "Drawing the energy you needed from *your master* to do *this* to me . . . and my friends?"

As soon as she saw the furious look on his face, she knew that she was right. Her desperate hope that there was some other explanation for his behavior—anything other than what she suspected—was just that: desperate.

In a flash, he was up the steps, seizing her arm with fingers that sank deeply into her skin. He didn't care anymore that a crossbow was trained on her skull. Why should he care that he was causing her pain?

"Meena," he said, in a voice that was as brutal as his grip on her, "we're going. *It's over.*"

She knew precisely what he meant by those words. Not only was the conversation over, but so were her struggles to bring him back to her side . . . the side of humanity. The demon inside of him had won, and finally taken over. Lucien had *allowed* it to take over, had fed and nurtured it beside the waters of the Mannette. There was nothing she could do now to get through to him, because concepts like good and evil—and life and death—meant nothing to him anymore. It was all the same, as long as he had what he wanted.

More frightened than she had ever felt in her life, she looked down at Alaric, so beaten and exhausted that he seemed to have given up . . .

. . . except that in that moment, as Lucien pulled her away from Father Henrique, Alaric lifted his head. As their gazes met, an image burst into her mind with such startling clarity, it was as if Alaric had physically shoved it there.

"What about the book?" Meena heard herself blurting.

Father Henrique's hands, which had lowered the crossbow, suddenly swung it back up. Lucien's fingers tightened on Meena's arm.

"What book?" the priest asked, with unmistakable nervousness.

"The book," Meena said. "Lucien's book, the one his mother left him." She looked up at Lucien. "Didn't you want it back?"

Lucien's expression changed. Before, he'd looked furiously angry, and seemingly intent on a single purpose: getting Meena back.

Now his focus shifted slightly.

Overhead, thunder rumbled. Some of the non-Palatine humans who'd been standing in the courtyard turned around and tried to leave, but the Lamir swiftly blocked their paths.

"Of course." Father Henrique smiled weakly at Lucien. "I'm so sorry about that, my lord. That was another of the schemes they came up with to capture you. But I—"

"Didn't you tell me that we needed to keep the book from falling into Lucien's possession at all costs?" Meena asked innocently. "Because it would make him all-powerful?"

Father Henrique's eyes widened. "I did," he said. "But I said those things only to be convincing in the role I was playing as one of—"

"Where is the book?" Lucien snapped. The tension in his voice wasn't the only signal that he was getting impatient. The lightning and sudden increase in wind velocity said their piece, as well.

"Only Alaric Wulf knows," Father Henrique said quickly. "And he won't say. I believe he probably destroyed it."

Meena felt the ground tremble and looked around in confusion because she'd heard no explosion. It took her a moment to realize that it hadn't been the boiler again. It was the Mannette. Lucien was angry and getting more so, and his wrath could be felt beneath their feet. It had probably been detected for miles around, and misread by geologists as a minor earthquake instead of what it was . . . the rumbling of a hellmouth.

"Oh, good heavens," Sister Gertrude exclaimed, after she'd recovered from the shock of the trembler. "Alaric didn't destroy it. He gave it to me, last night at the museum. He ran into me while he was looking for Meena. He said to keep it with me at all times, and not to give it to anyone."

The vampires that were gathered around her stepped back after she drew from beneath her habit the small manuscript, in its hard, jeweled-encrusted cover.

Out of the display lights, and in the dark of the storm, it looked considerably less like a mystical religious object and more like a very old, very fragile book.

Nevertheless, when Lucien's gaze fell upon it, his entire face changed. The tension seemed to leave it, and the red glow Meena had gotten used to seeing in his eyes dimmed.

"Give it to me," he said, in a voice that was devoid of any thunder.

Sister Gertrude moved nervously through the crowd of vampires and up the steps, where she cast a long glance at Alaric, who'd apparently spent the last reserves of his energy throwing Meena the mental image of the book, since his head had dropped down to his chest. He appeared to be unconscious.

"I want you to know I've read it," Sister Gertrude said as she handed the book to Lucien. She could not seem to help the air of strong disapproval she radiated . . . disapproval not of the book, Meena knew, but of Lucien and Father Henrique. "I minored in Latin."

Lucien, after hesitating for a fraction of a second, reached out and took the book from her.

The moment his fingers touched the jeweled case, the rain stopped.

"It's a lovely book," Sister Gertrude said.

Lucien had already opened it, and had begun to turn the pages, gazing down at it with fascination.

Meena looked up. The clouds overhead were breaking apart.

"Oh," Sister Gertrude said, turning around on her way down the steps, "and you might want to pay particular attention to page seventy-four—"

That's when Father Henrique thrust Meena aside, aimed his crossbow directly at Sister Gertrude, and fired.

Chapter Forty

The shot would have been instantly fatal if it hadn't been for two things.

First, Carolina saw what Father Henrique was about to do and leaped at Sister Gertrude, knocking her out of the direct path of the four arrows that were set loose, one after the other, from the repeater. Instead of embedding themselves in Sister Gertrude's wide, generous heart, they hit her in the shoulder as Carolina tackled her.

And second, Meena rammed Father Henrique as hard as she could in the solar plexus with her elbow. The priest lost his balance, but didn't release his hold on Meena. Both of them went staggering down the steps, and the shot veered slightly wide.

"Sister!" Father Bernard bent beside the stricken nun's side. "Are you all right?"

"Don't touch them," Abraham warned as the son of the deli owner was about to do what anyone, instinctively, would. "She'll bleed out. We need an ambulance."

"No emergency vehicles can get through," Morioka reminded them.

"Do you see?" Meena spun around to demand hotly of Lucien. "There's something in that book he doesn't want you to see. She was trying to help you, and he shot her. *This* is why we can't simply walk away."

Emil, who'd raced over to pick up the crossbow Father Henrique had dropped when Meena struck him, seemed to agree.

"My lord," he said as he looked up at the priest, who was nearly a head taller than he was, "I beg your pardon, but I do feel as if there is something familiar about this . . . creature."

"No, no, you are mistaken," Father Henrique said quickly. "I thought the nun was going for her gun. I was only trying to defend his lordship."

"No," Lucien said. He was still flipping slowly—almost reverently—through the manuscript's pages. "Emil is right. Up close, you do look slightly familiar. How do I know you? Other than from last night at the Met."

"You don't," Father Henrique said, quickly. "I'm from South America. I've never even been in this part of the world before."

"I know it sounds unlikely," Emil said. "But something about him is reminding me of your father, my lord."

"Never," Father Henrique said, with a nervous laugh. "Though, of course, I thank you for the compliment—"

Lucien had stopped turning pages. He stared down at something. From where Meena was standing, she could see a brilliantly illuminated illustration of a familiar-looking man holding what appeared to be the earth in his arms. Above it was a depiction of heaven, complete with an angel. Below it, hell, and Lucifer.

There was some writing alongside the picture. The writing was in flowing script in a language Meena couldn't decipher, especially upside down.

But she already knew what it said, because she'd heard the writing read aloud so many times. It was the illustration from her dream . . . the one at which Lucien and his mother had been gazing on the seat by the window.

Lucien evidently recognized it as well . . . only his association with it was far different from Meena's. He lifted his head with a snap to stare at Father Henrique.

"It was *you*," Lucien said. His gaze was back to burning red-hot.

"What?" Father Henrique's eyes went wide with denial . . . and fear. "No, no, my lord. I don't know what you—"

"This is you." Lucien held up the book. With a clear view of the illustration for the first time—in her dream, she had only ever been able to get a glimpse of it—Meena could see that he was right. The figure in the illustration was Father Henrique. The resemblance was unmistakable: the dark curly hair, dark eyes, and strong, handsome chin. Even the flowing priest's robes were the same.

The only difference was that back then, Father Henrique had worn a tonsure, a sheared circle of hair in the center of his head.

"I remember," Lucien said, sounding much more like the man she'd fallen in love with than he had in the past few days. "I remember you now. You were the priest at Poenari Castle. Father Henric. You performed all the masses. You gave me my first Communion. You baptized me. *You taught me catechism lessons from this book.*"

Father Henric seemed to realize he'd been caught . . . and to decide it was wise to try a different tack.

"Why, yes," he said obsequiously. "Yes, my lord, I did. I'm so honored that you'd remember. I didn't think it was worth mentioning because it was so long ago, and you've risen to such great heights in the world since then, whereas I—"

"South America?" Lucien looked back down at the book. "What have you been doing all this time in South America?"

"Oh," Father Henric said, "same thing as always. Giving masses. First Communions. Teaching catechism. Baptisms . . ."

"How can you?" Emil asked, in wonder. "The holy water alone . . ."

Father Henric smiled. "When a priest invokes the dark side at the behest of a parishioner," he said, "as I did for your father, my lord, upon the death of your mother, he is taking an enormous risk. And things were very different in those days than they are now. I could have been excommunicated, or worse. It was only right that I be rewarded. Immortality was the least I deserved, but the dark prince himself chose to repay me with far more than that. After he bit me and made me one of his kind, I found that not only did I have the gift of everlasting life, but I seemed also to have a built-in immunity to all the things that kill most demons—light, stakes, crosses—"

To illustrate his point, the priest reached out and laid a hand over Meena's necklace. Then, a few seconds later, he lifted his hand and held it out.

His palm was unmarked.

"See?" He shrugged. "That was your father's gift to me, sire, for the favor I did him. And I wouldn't have taken that risk for any other parishioner. Your father was a very, very remarkable man—he loved your mother so much. She was such a special woman. And after she was gone, well, you know he changed. He became quite—"

"Mad," Lucien said curtly.

"*Concerned*," Henric corrected him. "For you and your brother, may he rest in peace. Your father wished that there was a way he could make sure all of you could live forever. The death of your mother was so painful to him that he didn't think he could bear the idea of having to cope with the loss of either of you. So he asked me to see if I could come up with a way to make all of you immortal. And so . . . " The priest shrugged. "I did. And you're welcome for it."

This time, there was no tremor from the Mannette. No thunder. No lightning. Lucien didn't respond to Father Henric's statement at all.

He merely opened his hands, allowing his mother's book—which he'd been holding so closely—to fall to the courtyard floor.

It landed in a puddle. Meena watched as the sooty water lapped at the golden pages.

And from that small gesture, she knew. It burst upon her with as much startling clarity as if Lucien's mother herself had come back to life and whispered it into her ear. She not only knew, but she understood—not only why Lucien had sought out the Mannette, but all the horror and pain Lucien must have gone through for the five centuries during which he'd watched his father torture and kill hundreds of thousands of people, unable to do a thing to stop him . . .

. . . because Lucien himself had been inflicted with the same unquenchable thirst for blood, and had killed—or been responsible for the killing of—just as many people.

Only unlike his father or half brother, he had never given up his soul. Not entirely. He couldn't.

Because it was a physical impossibility.

"Your father was most pleased by my gift, my lord," Father Henric was going on boastfully. "And I want you to know, I stood by him until the very end. When I fled from those Palatine fiends in London, right after they murdered him," he said, "I never stopped thinking of you, my lord. I traveled as far as I could to get away from them—the jungles of South America—where I discovered the Lamir. Right then, I began building an army with which to return to you and help avenge his death. I couldn't stand by, knowing you'd lost your beloved mother, and then your father, and then your half brother. You shouldn't have to be preyed upon like this, hunted like an animal. Something has to be done. That's why I'm here."

"He's lying."

A new voice rang out in the courtyard. Meena turned her head and was astonished to see Alaric not only standing but holding the crossbow that had been strapped around his back. He'd reloaded it, and now he had it trained on Henric, even though he knew perfectly well that the priest wasn't vulnerable to arrows. It must have been force of habit.

"He's not indestructible," Alaric said to Lucien. "He told me inside that there's one way to kill him."

"*He's* lying to you, my lord," Henric said quickly. "Don't you see? They all lie, because they don't understand the beauty of what we are."

"There's nothing beautiful about what you are," Meena said angrily. "What's so beautiful about that?" She pointed at Sister Gertrude, who lay on the ground surrounded by a ring of Lamir, hungrily sniffing the scent of her blood in the air. Only Abraham, clutching the SuperStaker, and Carolina, Morioka, Santiago, and Father Bernard were keeping them away, using the stakes and holy water they'd found in Meena's purse.

"This situation," Emil said nervously, "has become untenable, my lord."

"I'm going to have to agree," Mary Lou murmured.

Lucien looked from them to Henric. But he didn't seem to see any of them.

"Stay out of this," he said. "It doesn't concern you."

"Yes, it does," Meena said. "It concerns all of us." She stooped to lift the book of hours from the puddle.

It actually didn't appear to have been damaged that badly. She'd forgotten that the pages were made of vellum, which was chemically treated leather, and essentially waterproof. It was possible that, once it dried out, it might be all right. As all of them might be . . .

. . . if they lived.

"There's only one good thing Father Henric has ever done," Meena said. "And at the time, he had no idea what it could lead to. And as soon as he figured it out, he tried everything in his power to keep it hidden from you, Lucien, because it's the one thing that can destroy him. *That's* why he's here. Right, Father Henric?"

"Please tell me you're not going to listen to her, my lord, " Father Henric protested. "A *human? They're* the ones who've been trying to destroy us, and why? We can't help what we are. Why must we be hounded and persecuted and even starved, when we are only doing what nature intended?"

"Nature?" Meena asked, with a humorless laugh. "What was *natural* about what you did to Lucien—the spirits you invoked the night that you made his father into what he was? Didn't that go against the laws of *nature?*"

"His father was my prince," Father Henric shot back. "I did as he asked."

"Didn't you also serve a *higher prince?*" Meena demanded. "Shouldn't you have consulted *him* in the matter first?"

"I did," Henric said, with a triumphant look.

"Oh," Meena said, opening the book to the page 74, the one from her dream. "You mean this prince?" She pointed at the illustration of Lucifer.

Henric's grin faltered slightly. "Precisely."

"He's not a prince," Meena said. "As you know perfectly well, he's a fallen angel. And what was Lucien's mother?"

"A p-princess," Henric stammered. But there was terror in his eyes.

"No," Lucien said, shaking his head. "She was an angel."

Meena swung around to look at him. Tears glittered in her eyes as she gazed up into his, which had gone back to their normal deep brown.

"Yes, Lucien," she said, holding the book open in front of him. "*That's* why Henric was trying to keep this from you. Because he realized it was the one thing that might help you remember what your mother always taught you. You, of *all* people, really do have a choice. You can choose to be good . . . because you *are* part good. No matter how hard you try to be the devil's son, you've still got an angel for a mother."

She could see that he understood now. That he not only understood, but that the knowledge had always been there, just beneath the surface, like the Minetta Stream.

It had only needed to be released.

Lucien lifted his gaze from the golden pages of the book she was holding to look into her eyes.

"Meena," he said, in wonder.

She smiled back at him. "You're welcome," she replied.

Which was why she only dimly heard someone say, "Give me that," from behind her. Emil's warning shout was distant.

Then she was snatched roughly away from Lucien, and the crossbow Emil had been holding was being pressed to her chest by Father Henric.

She dropped Lucien's book back into the mud.

"Did you think it was that book that could destroy me?" Father Henric snarled at them "No. It's *him.* Only he can destroy me."

Meena's gaze met Lucien's. He seemed as confused as she was. Only the arrow-pointing side of a crossbow wasn't bruising the skin above his rib cage as it was hers, so she suspected he wasn't as frightened.

Or possibly he was. His eyes didn't have a speck of red in them. They'd gone as dark as night.

"Now you know," Father Henric said as he began to drag Meena toward the arches leading away from the courtyard. "So I suggest you keep a wide distance, my lord, or I will shoot this girl in the heart. Do you understand?"

"I think I do," Lucien said. "I think I understand everything now." His gaze never wavered from Meena's.

"Good," Henric said. "You won't be seeing me again."

"That," Lucien said in a calm voice, "I'm not so sure of. Wulf?"

Alaric was standing in the middle of the courtyard, his own crossbow raised and aimed at Father Henric's head, even though he already knew the weapon would have no effect. "What?"

"I know you've never liked me very much," Meena heard Lucien saying in a calm voice.

Alaric didn't even glance in Lucien's direction. "That's right," he replied.

"And you have no reason in the world to trust me."

"That is correct," Alaric said.

"But I know you care about Meena Harper," Lucien continued. "And you'd do anything for her."

"Also correct," Alaric said, still not looking away from Father Henric, whose gaze was darting nervously between the two men.

"In that case," Lucien said, "I think you know what I need you to do."

"As much as I would love to," Alaric said, still not taking his gaze off the priest, "it won't work. He's got her at point-blank range. I can't get the shot off quickly enough. He'll end up killing her anyway. And frankly, neither one of you bastards is worth that."

"Stop it," Father Henric screamed, jabbing the crossbow harder into Meena's chest. "Whatever you're talking about, stop it now!"

Talking wasn't necessary anymore, however. Meena knew what Lucien wanted Alaric to do . . . and what Alaric, miracle of miracles, was refusing to do.

She also realized what Father Henric had meant by Lucien being the only one who could destroy him. She knew what she was going to have to do.

She didn't want it to end like this. It shouldn't *have* to end like this.

But she also knew that this was the only way it *could* end, thanks to the choices made by a lot of other people . . . some of whom had died long before she'd been born.

Meena wondered if Joan of Arc had felt like this when they'd lit the stake to which, after faithfully serving her king and country, she'd been tied in punishment for heresy. Joan had done nothing but refuse to lie, and in the end, she'd gotten burned.

Literally.

Meena supposed Joan must have felt the way she herself was feeling at the instant when she lifted her foot and slammed her heel as hard as she could into Father Henric's shin, then felt him pull the crossbow's trigger in surprise.

Like it just wasn't fair.

Chapter Forty-one

Lucien didn't think. He wasn't even aware of moving. There was nothing to do after he saw what Meena had done except shoot forward with a kind of speed he'd never known he possessed, so fast that he was a blur to everyone watching.

Then he shoved Meena out of the way so that his body, instead of hers, took those four arrows in the heart.

He was surprised that it didn't hurt.

It was better, he thought, that it end this way. He'd realized it as soon as Meena had shown him the book—that book he remembered so well from the days when he'd been happy—and explained everything to him.

After that, the past had begun to make sense in a way it hadn't in . . . well, centuries. And when Meena had let herself get shot, he'd known exactly what he had to do.

Sacrificing his life for Meena's was nothing. His only wish was that they could have had more time together, so that he could apologize for the wrongs he'd done her.

Afterward, she rolled over, apparently unhurt, and peered down at him. Somehow, her hair had changed back to the original brown color it had been when he'd first met her. It was long, and was blowing in the slight breeze.

Overhead, the sky was blue, and filled with white, puffy clouds. This was wonderful, since he hadn't been able to lie beneath a blue sky in five hundred years. He took a deep breath. That was another thing he hadn't done in centuries. It felt wonderful.

"Lucien," she said, tears in her eyes, "I'm so, so sorry."

He didn't know why she was apologizing. *He* was the one who'd hurt her, so many times.

"*I'm* sorry," he said, and lifted a hand to smooth some of the flyaway wisps of dark hair from her cheek.

"You were the only thing that could kill him," Meena said. "But only by dying. That doesn't seem fair."

"Yes, it was," he assured her. "He was the creator of my father's evil, and the only thing that could extinguish that was good. He knew that . . . and so did you. I had to sacrifice my life in order for his to be destroyed. I didn't want you to be hurt, though. I might have wanted that at one time, but not anymore." Lucien looked up at her. She was so beautiful. He didn't know how they could be talking like this. He should be dust.

"I know," she said. "You made the right choice, Lucien. Thank you." She lowered her head to kiss him.

Birds were singing. It was perfect.

He was happy.

Chapter Forty-two

"Meena, *no!*"

Alaric didn't understand anything that was happening. Lucien Antonescu had asked him to shoot him, and Alaric had refused because there was too much of a risk of Meena being killed instead.

And then Meena had gone insane and deliberately tried to get herself shot anyway.

Although he tried to reach Mauricio in time to stop it, Alaric knew there was no point. Meena was already dead. As he'd tried to point out to Lucien Antonescu, no one—no one human, anyway—could survive the direct hit of four sharpened sticks to the chest, shot at point-blank range by an automatic crossbow.

Except that . . . Meena did. Because Lucien Antonescu got to her first.

And somehow he'd managed to insinuate *himself* between the arrows and Meena's body. Which was physically impossible, considering how quickly the shafts had been moving, and the distance from which Mauricio had shot them.

Dimly, Alaric became aware of Henric screaming, *"No!"*

That was because after the arrows entered Antonescu's body, there was a blinding bright white. It seemed to emanate from him, then quickly spread all around. It was like the video footage Alaric had seen of nuclear bombs exploding. The light just spread and spread.

Only this light didn't seem to harm anyone human . . . just demons. When it receded, there was nothing left of almost any of them, except little piles of dust.

In fact that's what Alaric—who'd already been in midair when he noticed Antonescu had also launched himself at Meena—landed in: the pile of dust where Antonescu should have been.

But instead, there was nothing there but Meena, who was crying.

Alaric couldn't understand any of it.

Especially why, in the next moment, the dried-out old fountain that—for all the months that Alaric had worked at St. Bernadette's, anyway—had never produced so much as a single drop of water, suddenly burst to life, spraying pure, crystal clear jets of water everywhere . . . almost like at the miracle of Lourdes.

Alaric didn't question any of these extraordinary events, however. Instead he wrapped his arms around Meena as the water from the fountain flowed over them, washing away the ashes, pulled her against him, and began to cry, too.

He didn't even care if anyone noticed.

Part 4

Saturday, October 2

Chapter Forty-three

They wanted to hire her back.

They were offering her twice her old salary, plus a bonus.

Meena said she needed time to think about it.

"What's to think about?" Jon asked her. He was on the couch in the living room, eating pizza. "We could get a bigger place. Two bathrooms. Something with a balcony. And a view."

"Are you chipping in on rent?" Meena asked.

"Now that I'm finally solvent," Jon said, "yes."

The newly restaffed Palatine—Abraham Holtzman had been made associate director, a promotion allowing him a range of administrative power that made him giddy—had been extremely impressed by the SuperStaker. They were taking on both Jon and Adam in the Manhattan unit's technical design department. Leisha was beginning to admit that there might actually be such a thing as demons after all. The family was visiting animal shelters to find a dog the baby liked as much as Jack Bauer, and which had Jack's same extraordinary gift, so that Leisha could feel secure about her husband's new profession.

"We could finally work together," Jon said to Meena, with his mouth full. "I think it would be *sweet*."

"Yeah," Meena said, leaning in the doorway to her bedroom. "I don't know. I think I need more time."

"Look." Jon laid down his slice of pizza and regarded her seriously. "You're still freaked out. I get it. I'm freaked out, too." He pointed to his shoulder, which was swathed in white bandages. "They won't even put stitches in this thing for fear of infection. Fortunately I have Yalena now to change my bandages for me." He got a dreamy look on his face. "She's on her way over."

"Okay," Meena said. She reached for Jack Bauer's leash. "I need to go for a walk. I'll talk to you later."

"It's all right," Jon assured her. "So long as it's really the bandage changing you're avoiding, and not, you know. Something else."

She bent down to attach the leash to Jack's shoulder harness . . . not an easy task, since the dog was dancing around, so excited about his walk, she could barely get him to hold still.

"What do you mean, something else?" she asked.

"Meena," Jon said. He closed the pizza box. "It's okay. I get that you're avoiding the topic. And no one's going to be sending you in for any psych evals since Dr. Fiske is on psych leave himself for turning out to be a vampire feedbag. But I don't have to be a shrink to be qualified to tell you it's all right. *He's gone.* You can move on now. You could even, I don't know, call Alaric. Nothing bad's going to happen."

Her gaze drifted toward the bedroom. "It's hard to believe he's *completely* gone."

Jon followed her gaze. "Okay. I'll admit, it's hard to believe he's *completely* gone. But think of it this way: You haven't lost a vampire lover. You've gained a guardian angel."

"Uh," Meena said, "thanks. That's very comforting. But I've never heard of a guardian angel who leaves a half-million-dollar painting stolen from the Metropolitan Museum of Art on his girlfriend's bedroom wall."

Jon shrugged. "It's your favorite painting. I think it was Lucien's way of letting you know he's all right. And thanks. And that you need to get back to work."

"Maybe," Meena said, her eyes flashing, "the reason I haven't told them whether or not I'm going back to work is because I'm really not sure I *want* to go back to work. And I don't like pushy big brothers—or so-called guardian angels—telling me what to do. Maybe I genuinely *want* out of the vampire-hunting racket."

Jon shrugged. "Alaric Wulf is saying the same thing. But I don't believe it."

"Yeah," she said. "Well, nobody strung you up from a pipe for twenty-four hours."

"You're right," Jon said. "You *do* need to go for a walk. And pick up some milk on your way home." He stretched back out on the couch. "We're out."

Meena glared at him, then took Jack and left.

It wasn't that she regretted, even for a second, what she'd done. She'd had to do it. There was no other way.

It was just that every time she closed her eyes, she saw Lucien's, gazing into hers in that second right before he'd disappeared.

There'd been no reproach or bitterness in his gaze. In fact, in that moment, she'd felt almost as if he understood what she'd done.

Why was it, then, that she couldn't make the decision about whether or not to go back to work for the Palatine?

Maybe *because* of that painting hanging in her bedroom.

She could not have been more shocked when she'd come home from that long day, Lucien's ashes still in her hair, and found it hanging on the wall.

She'd known instantly how it had gotten there.

Yes, Mary Lou and Emil could have done it. But she doubted it. They'd disappeared as soon as Lucien had . . . only not into ash. She'd seen them, soaking wet from the jets of the fountain at St. Bernadette's, slinking off down the street. They'd gone back to Singapore, or whatever city they next hoped to make their home. Apparently, there wasn't enough wickedness in their hearts for them to be destroyed along with the rest of the demons in the courtyard. Or maybe the water from the Minetta had, like Lucien, been cleansed of evil, and had washed away their sins, allowing them to survive.

But Meena still didn't feel a sense of closure about the incident. The police never discovered the real reason behind the disappearances of all those tourists, and a fire at the Pine Barrens destroyed both the hellmouth and any DNA evidence that might have helped them solve the mystery.

Maybe *that* was the real reason Meena hadn't agreed to return to her old job. It didn't seem right, somehow. Abraham and Carolina and the others were eager to get back to work in this new world . . . a world where demons were more human, like Dr. Fiske and all those archbishops Father Henric had duped, who'd been so nonchalant about turning David Delmonico into a vampire in order to catch Lucien, and ultimately destroying the lives of so many people.

Meena wasn't sure she could work for such people anymore. It was like Lucien's mother's book, which she'd retrieved from the mud, and given to Abraham for safekeeping. Dried out, it had cleaned up nicely.

But how could Meena look at its pages again without feeling that they'd been tarnished in some way? It was the same with the painting of Joan of Arc, hanging in her bedroom, and the Palatine. She still admired and even loved them both . . . but neither of them held the same allure for her as they had before.

She supposed she shouldn't have been surprised when she ended up in front of Alaric's apartment building. She'd barely seen him since the day of the explosion. She'd been told he'd reinjured his leg and was taking some time to recover.

Beyond that, she knew little else. She supposed Jon was right. She ought to have called him. He had tried to save her life.

But she, who knew so many things, didn't seem to know what to say to him.

Standing in front of his building—which was, of course, one of the more expensive ones in his neighborhood; Alaric was fond of his creature comforts—she decided that it didn't matter. At the very least, she could ask Alaric why he hadn't yet agreed to come back to the Palatine.

But after Alaric buzzed her in, and then the big metal door to his place opened—it was designed to slide like the door to a freight car—and she actually saw him, she immediately began to have second thoughts.

As always, he looked startlingly tall and muscular.

But because he was wearing a sport coat over his black T-shirt and jeans, and his blond hair was slightly tousled on top, as if he'd just showered, it looked to Meena as if he were on his way somewhere.

Her heart gave a flop inside her chest. *A date,* she thought. *He's going on a date.*

Let's just keep things professional. She was the one who'd said it first. Now she was paying for it.

"Oh," she said, "I'm sorry. I was just in the neighborhood. I—"

He held the door open as if her visit had been expected.

"You're just in time," he said. "The car to the airport is arriving in an hour."

"Airport?" She moved hesitantly past him into the loft, Jack Bauer trotting in behind her, his tail wagging happily and his ears perked. "Where are you going?"

"Antigua," Alaric said. He pulled the door closed. "My beach house. I told you about it."

"Oh," Meena said, her heart sinking further.

His beach house in Antigua. Of course. Less than two weeks had gone by since the two of them had discovered a plot to spread vampirism throughout the Catholic church, Lucien Antonescu was dead, and he was leaving on vacation to his beach house in Antigua.

What had she expected?

Alaric Wulf had kissed her once—although he'd been delirious with pain and didn't remember it—and she hadn't found the sensation at all unpleasant.

But she'd been having an intimate relationship with a vampire Alaric wanted to kill.

She didn't have that problem anymore, she realized.

Only now Alaric was leaving for Antigua. Probably with Genevieve Fox.

Well, at least she had a guardian angel who hung paintings from the Metropolitan Museum of Art on her wall. But it still didn't seem fair.

"If I'd known you were coming," Alaric said, from behind the granite-topped island that separated the living room from the kitchen, "I'd have gotten some wine. But I don't think I have anything here. Except water."

"Oh," she said, "that's all right."

Alaric's loft was beautiful, all toweringly high ceilings and windows with a view of the river, gleaming chrome appliances, polished wooden floors, and expensive—but not uncomfortable-looking—modern European furniture that looked like it came straight out of some luxury boutique hotel.

Meena, coming to stand in the middle of the living room area, was horrified to see that Jack Bauer had made himself at home, hopping right up onto one of the large, home-theater-style armchairs.

"Jack," she said, *"get down."*

"He's all right," Alaric said mildly. "Those are comfortable chairs." He handed Meena a glass of ice water. "So," he said, "where's your bag?"

Meena shook her head, confused. "What bag?"

"I don't care if all you want to take with you to Antigua is what you have on," he said, looking down at her cardigan, black dress, and flats. "But most women take more than a purse and a dog when they travel."

"Oh." She sank down onto the blue suede couch. She didn't think her legs could support her anymore. "So *I'm* the one going to Antigua with you?"

"Who else?" he asked. "I thought we discussed this. When I gave you that." He pointed at the necklace she was wearing.

"Alaric," Meena said. She wanted to laugh. Except for the part of her that wanted to cry. "We never discussed my going to Antigua with you."

He sat down on the couch beside her. "Well, then why are you here?" he asked. "And don't try to act like you didn't know that I'm leaving for Antigua in an hour."

"I *didn't* know," Meena insisted. "How would I know?"

"Because," he said, "you're psychic. How many times do I have to say it? You know everything."

She blinked at him. "I *don't* know everything," she said. Her eyes were filling with tears. "If I knew everything, would I have gotten into this mess in the first place? I certainly don't know why you assume I'm going to drop everything and fly off to Antigua with you. I don't even know what I'm doing here. I don't know why we haven't talked in two weeks. And the worst part is, if I *do* go to Antigua with you, I don't know if I'll ever want to come back. I'm pretty sure I'll want to stay there with you forever." She was crying so hard, she couldn't even see him. "And the fact that I just said that out loud is even scarier to me than vampires. I've made a terrible mistake in coming here. Good-bye."

She sprang to her feet, and would have fled from the apartment if she could have seen where she was going through her tears and he hadn't reached out and pulled her back down onto the couch, and into his arms.

He didn't kiss her the way he had that night at St. George's. Not at all. This was a different kind of kiss, a demanding kiss, a kiss that seemed to lay his soul bare in front of her, and yet, at the same time, claim her for his own.

She could feel the intense heat rising from his body, the fierce pounding of his heart against hers, and his breathing, which became every bit as shallow as hers after a while.

These were things she hadn't felt while being kissed in a long, long time. Exciting things. Especially when he lowered his head to kiss her again, this time on the throat. That's when she felt that her heart might burst from happiness.

"You *do* know," he whispered softly. "You know the answer to all those things. I *want* you to stay with me forever. You know I love you. And that's why you're flying off to Antigua with me. That's why you came here. You know all these things. Admit it."

She looked up into his blue eyes, the exact same color as a summer sky, or the Caribbean sea.

And she smiled. Because she realized he was right. She did know. She'd known all along, knew it even before his mouth came back down over hers, just to make sure she knew it good and well before they left for the airport.

author's Note

Overbite is a work of fiction, but many of the details in it are based on facts or historical events.

The Minetta Stream is an actual water feature of lower New York City, but few people know of its existence, other than that it still occasionally floods some basements in Greenwich Village. The name given to it by the island of Manhattan's original residents, the Lenape Indians, was *Mannette,* which translates to *Devil's Water.* The stream has been built over, and was diverted into several fountains, one of which stands in the lobby of the New York University dormitory in which I used to work at 33 Washington Square West. That fountain features a figure of Pan. It has been inoperable for decades.

You can read more about the Minetta Stream at http://www.nycgovparks.org/.

The Palatine Guard was an actual military unit of the Vatican, formed in 1850 to defend Rome against attack from foreign invaders. Today the Palatine Guard is listed in most encyclopedias and search engines as defunct.

Vlad the Impaler's first wife is said to have died by throwing herself from a window of Poenari Castle into what is now referred to as Raul Doamnei, or Princess's River, saying she preferred suicide to death at the hands of the invading Ottoman army.

This is the only known reference to Vlad Tepes's first marriage, besides the fact that his wife was rumored to have been extremely kind and beautiful, almost "angelic." It was after her death that Vlad the Impaler began his many atrocities, eventually becoming the titular inspiration for Bram Stoker's *Dracula.*

So many people helped me with this book in so many ways, I couldn't begin to name them all, but I am exceedingly grateful for their support. Particular thanks go to Beth Ader, Nancy Bender, Jennifer Brown, Barbara Cabot, Carrie Feron, Michele Jaffe, Laura Langlie, Ann Larson, Janey Lee, Rachel Vail, Tessa Woodward, and Benjamin Egnatz.

And, of course, a very special thanks to all my wonderful readers! I could not have done it without you.

Meg Cabot

Turn the page for a sneak peek at the new
Heather Wells Mystery novel,
Size 12 and Ready to Rock,

from

MEG CABOT

and

WILLIAM MORROW

It's summer break at New York College, but that doesn't mean assistant residence hall director Heather Wells can kick back and relax. The students may have gone home, but Fischer Hall is as busy as ever.

Only instead of college freshmen, Heather's got a dorm full of squealing thirteen- and fourteen-year-old girls—the first-ever Tania Trace Teen Rock Camp, hosted by pop sensation (newly married to heartthrob Jordan Cartwright, Heather's ex) Tania Trace.

But when the producer of the reality television show that's filming Tania's every move at the camp ends up dead, and it becomes clear Tania was the intended victim, Grant Cartwright, head of Cartwright Records, turns to his son, family black sheep and private investigator Cooper Cartwright, for help, desperate to keep his new daughter-in-law—and the company's highest earning star—alive.

Heather knows perfectly well she's supposed to leave the detecting to Cooper, her ex's big brother and her own brand-new fiancé. But with hysterical mini divas-in-training freaking out all around her—not to mention their mothers—how can she help but get involved? Especially when Tania Trace herself begins to confide in Heather, revealing a secret that may be a little more "real" than Cartwright Records ever bargained for.

If an added bonus to solving the crime herself happens to be that Heather can convince Cooper to bury the hatchet with his family and agree to a large wedding, and not the elopement he's been insisting on, so all of Heather's friends can come, then maybe putting her own life on the line to save Tania's just might turn out to be worth it. . . .

Size 12 and Ready to Rock

A Heather Wells Mystery

by

MEG CABOT

*I like candy, I'm a candy kind of girl
If you've got candy, wanna give this girl a whirl?
I like candy, I eat it all I can
If you've got candy, wanna be my candy man?*

Candy Man
Tania Trace
Cartwright Records
14 consecutive weeks in the Top Ten
Billboard Hot 100

I stared at my reflection in the full-length mirrors. Three of them, side-by-side, and each told me the same thing: This was a mistake. A seriously huge mistake.

"Oh," the saleswoman said, adjusting the shoulder strap of the floor-skimming, empire-waisted, pure white gown that I was trying on. "It's you. It's just so you."

It was so *not* me.

"I look like a cannoli," I said to my reflection.

"A what?" The saleswoman got busy straightening out the folds of the gown I'd found crumpled in the sales rack, marked down to seventy-five percent off. That was the only reason I'd decided to try it on.

Well, that and the fact that it was the only one in my size, which I'd been interested to see was a 12. The last time I'd been shopping, it had been a 14.

Either all the rampant love-making Cooper and I had been doing since he'd finally admitted his true feelings for me had caused me to drop a few pounds or the entire retail fashion industry in New York City had gone insane.

I figured it was most likely the latter, since I'd read somewhere that love-making only burned 200 calories an hour. I'd eaten about four times that much at breakfast today alone, when I'd tried out a new recipe I'd invented in the cafeteria of the building where I worked, the soon-to-be-world-famous peanut-butter-and-banana-pancake sandwich.

"A cannoli is an Italian dessert pastry," I explained to the saleswoman. "You know. From the movie *The Godfather*? 'Leave the gun, take the cannoli.' That's what I look like in this dress. A cannoli."

"What? No. You look beautiful," the saleswoman lied. Because that was her job. "You're having a beach wedding, right? Then this is perfect, simply perfect."

I'd explained to her, but apparently in not enough detail, about Cooper's desire for an elopement, which was to take place in October on the Cape, making this summery gown about as appropriate as a bikini in Anchorage.

Still, it was a wedding gown. And I was getting married. And the dress was seventy-five percent off, in my size. How could I not try it on?

Maybe it would look better with one of those cute glittery cardigans they had on all the mannequins.

No. What was I thinking? No one wore a cardigan with a wedding gown.

Maybe I was deluding myself. The whole reason we were eloping was because Cooper hated all that wedding stuff. I always thought I did, too.

So what was I doing, trying on wedding dresses?

"Let me find you some accessories," the saleswoman was saying, enthusiastically. "How do you feel about headbands? Maybe one with a bow!"

Really, what could I say? When you spend your lunch hour in a store that specializes in preppy clothes that—you realize, belatedly—really only look good on the stick-thin models they always show in the catalogs that are forever sliding through the mail slot of your house, you pretty much get what you deserve. Headbands? Sure. Bows? Why not.

Fortunately, my cell phone whooped. Beyoncé's "Girls Rule the World."

"Oh," I said, glancing at the caller ID. "That's work. Looks like I gotta get back. Maybe another time."

The saleswoman looked disappointed. That was her commission off two hundred whole bucks, down the drain. I felt kind of bad. Except that she'd been trying to talk me into buying a dress in which I looked like a walking roll of toilet paper.

"Oh," she said, smiling brightly. "Well, come back when you have more time. And maybe bring a friend. Or your mom. It's a big decision to make on your own."

I tried to keep my own smile in place. Probably most brides' mothers don't run off to Argentina with the entire contents of their daughter's bank account. I was just glad the saleswoman hadn't recognized me. The ponytail had probably helped. And the fact that I was so many years older—and so many pounds heavier—than I'd been on my last album cover.

"Sure," I said. "Thanks, I will." I thought, but didn't add out loud, *when your company starts making dresses for girls my size that don't make us look like we're frosting oozing out of a hard pastry shell.*

Safely back out on the street, a little breathless from my narrow escape, I called back Sarah, the graduate assistant who worked in my office and who always made me feel inadequate because I didn't even have a bachelor's degree, let alone a master's or a BMI within the normal range.

But I was attending night school and even occasionally the student fitness center, and was confident that I was going to catch up with her by around the year 2050 or so.

"What's up?" I asked. I was sure it couldn't be much, which was why I'd treated myself to the long lunch of wedding dress shopping in stores that were wildly inappropriate for my age and body shape. Fischer Hall, the dorm where we both worked, was shut down for the summer for badly needed painting and repairs. It was amazing how much damage seven hundred undergraduates—whose parents were paying fifty thousand dollars a year for them to attend such a fine institution of higher learning—could do to a building in a mere nine months. After check-out, we'd found one room in which the four male suitemates had built a "door to Narnia," a hole they'd cut into the back of a university-issued wardrobe, which, when entered, led to an extra room of their suite that they'd decorated with lava lamps and UV lights, where they'd assembled an actual marijuana grow-house, complete with posters of Prince Caspian and one very suspicious-looking mattress, upon which we very much doubted anyone had done any actual sleeping.

What was even more shocking was that the suitemates' parents had then had the nerve to refuse to pay the charges we'd billed them for the cost of repairing the hole in the wardrobe and fumigation of the mattress, even though we'd sent them photographic evidence of their sons' extracurricular activities.

Rich people! They were crazy.

Sarah sounded slightly hysterical, but then, that's how she sounded most of the time. Sarah had a hard time going with the flow.

"They're here," she whispered into the phone. "And I don't understand why you didn't tell us. They're not in the computer. No one sent over any check-in cards. And of course none of the rooms are ready, so I can't assign them. We don't even have a hall director, because who would apply to work here after what happened to Dr. Veatch? And the person who had the job before him was a murderer. Or was that the one before? I can't even remember anymore, I'm just so upset. Why didn't you *tell us*?"

"Wait? What?" I could barely hear her. I was standing on the corner of Fifth Avenue and 18th Street. A *Sex and the City* double-decker tour bus was going by, taking summer tourists to see all the places where Carrie Bradshaw and the girls had gone for Cosmos and cupcakes a decade earlier. "Why are you whispering?"

"Because some of the mothers are standing right in front of me," Sarah said, her whisper growing even more hysterical. "And they're really pissed. Haven't you ever seen *Dance Moms*? Well, these moms are about a thousand times meaner. One of them saw some of the rooms already because Pete is such a wuss, he let her in, and she went snooping around the halls. And guess which one she saw? The one with the door to Narnia. I mean, that's not even fit for human—"

"Sarah." I turned around and began walking rapidly back toward Washington Square Park, where Fischer Hall was located. In the past year that I'd worked there, that place had become my home planet. "You know we're closed for the summer. Why is Pete allowing *anyone* to enter the building? There must be some mistake. No one is supposed to be checking in at all—"

"They said they have *your* permission," Sarah said. She sounded as if she were about to cry. "There are forty-five kids standing out in the lobby right now. Well, they're not really standing. They're screaming into their cell phones, and some of them are doing back handsprings up and down the handicapped-accessible ramp even though I asked them to please stop, and a couple of them were trying to break the Coke machine, I'm pretty sure on purpose. And they're all girls. All sixteen and under. With their moms, because you know university policy is no one that young can stay in the halls unless they have parental supervision. . . ."

"*My* permission?" I was shocked. "Sarah, there's obviously been a mix-up. Maybe they got my name off the university website, or something. But I've never spoken to any group, much less said they could check in today—"

Sarah sounded a little calmer. "Really? Okay. I thought I was going crazy. Because I couldn't find a single shred of paperwork about it. I thought it might be the Joffrey Ballet summer camp—you remember how the housing department mentioned this spring that the Joffrey was contracting with various city colleges to house the attendees of their summer program?"

I quickened my pace. I remembered that staff meeting all too well . . . *and* how my blood had frozen with horror at the mere mention of the word *ballet*. I'd seen *Black Swan*. Who hadn't? It had basically put me off all forms of dance forever.

"Listen to me, Sarah," I said. "I told Dr. Jessup that over my dead body would any teenage ballerinas be swanning it up in Fischer Hall this summer. We had way too much drama this past semester to deal with a bunch of bunheads. The Fischer Hall staff deserves the summer off—"

I thought bitterly of how much Simon Hague, the power-hungry director of Wasser Hall, would enjoy being the focus of attention of a troupe of mini Natalie Portmans. Why couldn't they put the bunheads in there? There was no justice in the world.

To Sarah, I said, "I can clear all this up with a phone call—"

Unfortunately, Sarah was way ahead of me.

"Well, they aren't even from the Joffrey, anyway," she said, sniffling. "Heather . . . I really thought you knew and had just forgotten to do the paperwork or tell me, which I admit isn't like you, but since you and Cooper . . . well, you know. You've been a little preoccupied."

I took total umbrage at this, but didn't push it, since Sarah seemed so stressed. And I shouldn't have been wedding dress shopping on my lunch hour. Or at all.

"It's just that this group . . . they've got receipts from the bursar's office," Sarah went on. "And letters of welcome from the *president's office*. He gave them the personal go-ahead to come over today. So now they're here. And they're all saying President Allington told them *you* said it was okay. Apparently, the person running the camp is someone you know."

"Someone *I* know?" My phone had begun buzzing. Someone else was trying to get through. I glanced at it. Cooper. He was going to have to wait a minute, though. My so-called career had to come before my love life right now. "Sarah, I don't know anyone who needs last-minute summer housing for forty-five teenage girls in Manhattan."

"I think you do," Sarah whispered. "I'm looking at the brochure one of them dropped. What was the name of the label you used to record under when you were a singer?"

I'd worked up a bit of a sweat power walking my way back to the building. It was July, so it was hot in the city.

Still, I felt a sudden chill in my bones.

"Cartwright Records?" I asked, pausing for a *Don't Walk* signal.

"That's right," Sarah said. "I guess the camp was supposed to be in some ritzy place in the Poconos, but they moved it here for some reason. That's why the moms are so mad. We don't have all the amenities they were promised. Or actually *any* of the amenities they were promised."

"Sarah," I said. The signal had changed to *Walk*, but I felt frozen where I stood. "Who is running this camp?"

"You know I don't listen to popular music, Heather," Sarah said. She sounded a lot better now that she knew she hadn't missed some important piece of paperwork. "I'm really much more into alternative folk artists. Oh, God, here it is. She's the one with that horrible hit single, 'Candy Man'? You can't go anywhere without hearing it, it's everyone's ringtone now, even Sebastian had it for a while but I made him change it. Tania Trace. Wait. . . ." Sarah's tone changed. Now she sounded horrified. "Didn't Tania Trace marry your ex-boyfriend? Cooper's *brother*?"

Suddenly the peanut-butter-and-banana-pancake sandwich I'd had for breakfast felt as if it were about to come back up.

"Sarah," I said. "I'll be right there to see if we can figure this all out." Then I hung up and called Cooper back.

"Hi," I said, in a voice I hoped sounded upbeat. "I've got a little problem."

"Hi," he said. "I've been trying to reach you. And you've actually got a huge problem."

Ali Smith

MEG CABOT was born in Bloomington, Indiana. In addition to her adult contemporary fiction, she is the author of the bestselling young adult fiction series The Princess Diaries. She lives in Key West, Florida, with her husband.

www.megcabot.com

Meg Cabot

BOOKS BY MEG CABOT

"She is the master of her genre."
—*Publishers Weekly*

OVERBITE
ISBN 978-0-06-173511-0 (paperback)
INSATIABLE
ISBN 978-0-06-173508-0 (paperback)
RANSOM MY HEART
ISBN 978-0-06-170007-1 (paperback)
SHE WENT ALL THE WAY
ISBN 978-0-06-134024-6 (paperback)

QUEEN OF BABBLE SERIES

QUEEN OF BABBLE
ISBN 978-0-06-085199-6 (paperback)
QUEEN OF BABBLE IN THE BIG CITY
ISBN 978-0-06-085201-6 (paperback)
QUEEN OF BABBLE GETS HITCHED
ISBN 978-0-06-085203-0 (paperback)

HEATHER WELLS MYSTERIES

SIZE 12 IS NOT FAT
ISBN 978-0-06-052511-8 (paperback)
SIZE 14 IS NOT FAT EITHER
ISBN 978-0-06-052512-5 (paperback)
BIG BONED
ISBN 978-0-06-052513-2 (paperback)
SIZE 12 AND READY TO ROCK
ISBN 978-0-06-173478-6 (paperback)
COMING SUMMER 2012

THE BOY SERIES

THE BOY NEXT DOOR
ISBN 978-0-06-009619-9 (paperback)
BOY MEETS GIRL
ISBN 978-0-06-008545-2 (paperback)
EVERY BOY'S GOT ONE
ISBN 978-0-06-008546-9 (paperback)

**For a complete list of Meg Cabot's books, visit
www.MegCabot.com**

Available wherever books are sold, or call 1-800-331-3761 to order.